In Sheep's Skin

Scott Hale

In Sheep's Skin

First Edition: May 2020

www.scotthalebooks.com

ISBN-13: 978-1-7330966-3-8

BOOKS BY SCOTT HALE

The Bones of the Earth series

The Bones of the Earth (Book 1)

The Three Heretics (Book 2)

The Blood of Before (Book .1)

The Cults of the Worm (Book 3)

The Agony of After (Book .2)

The Eight Apostates (Book 4)

Novels

In Sheep's Skin

The Body Is a Cruel Mistress (Coming Soon)

PART I

In a forgotten field stands a forgotten tree, a sheet of skin slung over limbs; white moon in its red rivulets. When the wind blows here, coarse hairs are kicked up and carried off like seeds. It's a cold night, when all words spoken are written ghostly. Still, there are pockets of warmth. They stink of sweat and blood, and the acrid gasses of a starved stomach. The heat and reek run from the tree to the tree line, where the woods, shaken bare in Fall's clockwork stick-up, show a shadowy tableau: a ribbon of road, lunar-lit, and beyond, a diner just as forgotten as the field and tree, soon to be forgotten no more.

THURSDAY, OCTOBER 1ST, 2020

1

"I saw you, Peter, with your head between her legs!" Mary cried, pointing her French fry accusatorily at him from across the table. "What the hell am I supposed to think, huh?"

Not expecting her to have gone that far, Peter gave the diner the once over. The constipated trucker in the corner hadn't heard them, or at least hadn't the mind to care: in one hand, a ham sandwich smashed against mouth, in the other, a beat-up cellphone on full bright—the modern-day torch. Across the sticky linoleum ocean, the hooded shape kept his head down; the occasional shifting of the bright pink headphone cables running across him the only sign of life coming out of that polyester black hole. The chain-smoker walking the perimeter outside obviously hadn't heard anything, but with the way she kept twitching and staring at everyone through the windows, he couldn't be too sure. Peter was fairly certain the fourteen-year-old dad with the bags under his eyes (certainly not the first, nor the last bags he'd pack) hadn't heard anything: He and his bride-to-be were too busy staring at each other in a pentagram-crossed lovers kind of way, while their hell-spawn in his booster seat rapped his knuckles and cried.

If anyone had heard Mary, it'd been the waitress, Rita, but as far as Peter could tell, it'd gone in one ear and out the other. Rita was posted up by the counter, gathering dust like the relic she was. She'd been here a long time, that's what Mary had said. Always was here, Mary reminisced. Twenty-to-life, like a prisoner without parole—that was

Rita's sentence for the crime of carrying on when everyone else in her life had probably said behind a cloud of smoke, "Why bother?" If they were going to get anyone's attention, but especially Rita's, who probably only responded to "Put the money in the bag!"… He and Mary were going to have to kick it up a notch if this was going to work.

"Well, I think you ought to get your eyes checked, Mary," Peter said, emphasizing her name. "While the doctors are having a look, why don't you see if they can—" he twirled his fingers around, "—reconnect some wires in your skull. You've lost your damned mind, woman. I'm not…" He corrected his accent. "I ain't that kind of man!"

"A man you are not. This is true."

Peter went red, cooled himself off with a slurp of soda. She was good at this. Probably always had been. What else did he not know about her?

Mary leaned in, elbows thumping the table, and said, dramatically, "I thought you were the one, Baby. How could you? How… could you?"

"I still am," Peter said, taking the bait. "You know that I am." He made eye contact with Rita the waitress, but her glazed-over pupils were quick to deflect. "But I hate what we've become. This ain't us."

"It is, though, Peter. It is." Mary's jaw dropped, in preparation for words taking their time to spill out. Then, finally: "We've done terrible things to each other because we're terrible people. A terrible thing is how we found each other. What'd you expect?"

Peter knew this conversation could go one way or the other. Thus far, it'd been a failure, so he took the path oft-traveled and rumbled, "You… bitch."

Mary shot back in her seat so fast, the chain-smoker outside on patrol did a double-take. He'd caught her off-guard. With no follow up on his part, this signaled the end of things. But seconds later, Mary was back in the game, teeth clenched and fists balled, with enough ammunition to carry on this war of words for hours to come. Peter didn't know her as well he should've or would've liked, but if he did know one thing, it was that Mary was one hell of an actor. She could be anyone, anything. It made him wonder how she'd settled on Mary.

"You bitch? You bitch. It always comes to that, doesn't it?" she said, voicing growing louder. "Now you sound like my father!"

Peter turned red as the fourteen-year-old dad turned around and gave him a sympathetic glance that said, "I feel you, brother." It wasn't what he needed right now, and it rang a little too true in the midst of all these theatrics.

Mary, face caught between a smile and a snarl, took a deep breath and said, "I don't—"

Rita the waitress stood beside their table, as if she'd teleported there. She gave her legs a scratch through her stretched-out leggings. "Together or separate?" She ripped a check off her pad of paper. "Who's paying?"

Peter stared at Mary. Mary stared at Peter. Then: Scene. They broke out laughing, totally forgetting for a moment poor Rita and all the tedious shit she had to take care of before closing the place up for the night. After a few seconds, she'd had enough and dropped the check on the table.

Peter snatched it up, while Mary cried after her, "Wait, no, I'm sorry. We're sorry! We're not laughing at you…"

Rita the waitress dug a wedgie out of her ass as she headed back towards the kitchen. The constipated trucker saw this and watched her pass, likely contemplating the meaning of the gesture and if it was meant to be directed towards him. A few seconds went by. He came to his senses, and then to his stubby feet, and looking at Peter as if to say, "Did you see that, brother?" he waddled into the men's restroom.

Peter went hard at his soda. Chewing on the straw, he said, "That was awful."

"Yeah," Mary said, grinning. "Oh my god, that was terrible."

"I know you said you didn't want to make stuff up, but…"

"Oh, we're going to bullshit this one, for sure." Mary forked the remnants of her burger. "We have to."

The project they were trying to accomplish here at Mare's Diner was one that'd been assigned to them by Intro to Psychology professor Ms. Selene. As she tied up her silver hair, a grin on her face, Ms. Selene had prefaced the project by telling them they weren't to do anything illegal or immoral, but most of their peers afterwards agreed Ms. Selene, tenured and tired of the same old, same old, was probably hoping for some sweet, sweet deviancy from the student body.

"Why else would you get into the field of mental health if not to hear about the freaky stuff?" she'd announced on the first day of class, the vest she was wearing at the time not all that far removed from a straitjacket.

After her warning, which sounded to most ears like a dare, she told them their project was to violate a social norm. To go against an unspoken rule in their community and observe the reactions of those around them, which they would report on later.

"I'm sorry, Pete," Mary said, with a mouthful of meat.

Waving her off, he said, "Don't be."

Peter and Mary had been sitting next to each other the entire semester. Neither one had chosen to sit next to the other; in fact, they'd both entered the room on the first day of class and had both sat down beside each other at the same time. It was as if they'd been assigned those seats long ago, and finally seeing them, something primal awoke within and drew them to them, to each other. Peter had felt it. He was pretty sure Mary had felt it, too. Up until this moment, though, they were simply acquaintances; tolerable semi-strangers who only interacted with one another for one hour each week. It wasn't that Peter had a crush on Mary or anything. It was something else. And it couldn't have been any more evident that day in class when the project had been assigned. At the same time, they'd turned to one another as everyone else was pairing off and suggested the same idea: to pose as a couple in public, arguing about their relationship problems.

He hadn't been able to put his finger on what brought them together, but as this night drew to its close, he found he almost had it in his grasp. It was there. He knew it was there. Familiar, yet foreign, like an alien organism in an inflatable pool.

Peter ran his hand through his hair, and it came back clammy. "So, uh, this place used to be the place, huh?"

Mary went dead-eyed.

"Hey, I'm not trying to give you a hard time."

"Yeah, yeah." She smiled, tugged on her earlobe. "Yeah, Dad and I used to come here a lot when I was little. I swear…" Mary turned around, took in Mare's Diner in a way she hadn't before. "It's crazy how much things change. You think things are one way…"

"Everything stays the same. Just you that changes."

"Exactly." She zeroed in on the hooded figure. "Like that dude? Dude's probably been here since I was eight. Place was probably always this lame."

Peter shrugged. "You know how it is. Things are a bigger deal when you're little. I…we're… we're going to be fine. I have complete faith in our ability to completely BS the paper."

"Oh, I know. It's just…"

"You were looking forward to coming back here."

She twisted up her mouth, put her dark, shoulder-length hair into a bun.

"I get it. I totally get it. I used to go this nature center with my mom back home." Peter leaned in over the table, a big grin on his face. "Shit was magical, let me tell you."

Ravenous in her intrigue, Mary mimicked Peter's excitement and said, "Tell me."

"I went back there with an ex a year ago. Now that I think about it, that might've been the mistake, but… Anyway, wasn't the same. Felt smaller. Felt emptier. I don't know. It's a weird thing."

"I got this theory," Mary said, "that screwed up people are drawn to Psychology classes."

"That's probably a fact at this point. Crazy people working with crazy people, trying to find some normalcy in at all."

Mary finished off her burger. "I like that. I never knew my mom."

Peter hesitated for a second, but only for a second. "I never knew my dad."

"I don't hear from Dad anymore," Mary said.

"Uh, yeah, I don't hear from my mom too much, either," Peter said, cocking his head.

Mary pointed her finger back and forth between them: "That's weird. Us, I mean. That's really…"

"It's weird."

"Or it's super common."

Peter threw his hands up in the air. "Who knows?"

"There's got to be someone out there who knows," Mary said, folding her napkin—human-shaped origami.

Bells at the front door. It whined as it opened, as it seemed to always do. A wayward woman came through. Nothing she wore would've rung up as anything but triple digits at check-out. With hair that screamed, "Let me see your manager," she hurried to the bar at the center of the diner and seemed ready to ask just that. Rita, Pavlov's lost pup, must've felt the tolling in her teeth, because she came sprinting from the back of the building, cigarette smoke still fuming from her mouth, and met the woman head-on.

"I'm so sorry, miss," the wayward woman said, sweetly. "I'm lost." She waved her phone. "Died on me a mile back." She laughed at herself. "I hate to bother you, but could you give me some directions?"

Rita smiled. Who knows how long it'd been since she'd been treated so nicely? "Honey, of course. Where you trying to get to?"

"Bitter Springs."

Not missing a beat, Rita: "Really?"

"Yeah, I know it." The wayward woman squeezed her designer purse. "Got to be in court there tomorrow morning with the ex."

"What'd he do?"

"What didn't he do?"

"I don't got a lot in this life," Rita said, "but I do got some time." Rita pressed her palm to the wayward woman's back and guided her to one of the booths at the back. "Promise you, you'll always get to a place quicker with a lighter load."

Peter watched the two women settle into the booth, and felt like a complete asshole, because in a way, he'd been one to the both of them. For messing with Rita. For judging the woman. It spoke to the uneasy feeling he'd had about the Intro to Psychology course. It got him thinking about things he hadn't thought about before; observing things he'd otherwise been blind to. Self-reflection was one thing, but he found himself sizing people up, tagging and bagging them. Ms. Selene had told the class they'd have diagnosed just about every mental illness in themselves and their friends and families by the time the semester was over, and she wasn't wrong. She told him not to worry, but he did. About himself. And right now? About Mary, too.

Looking away, Peter quickly looked back, looked beyond. Past the women, past the bar, to the hooded man, whose head, swallowed by darkness, had been down and was now slightly up. He was staring at Peter. Or was he staring at the women? Or nothing at all. He couldn't tell. It didn't make sense, but he couldn't see the man's eyes, so deeply set was his head in the hood. All that was there were two hungry glints of light; unbroken, because apparently, he never blinked.

"What's wrong?" Mary scooted across her seat until she was blocking his view. "You alright?" She turned around. The hooded man put his head back down. "What?"

"Oh, nothing." Peter smiled, grabbed the check. "I got this."

Mary's hand shot out to snatch it from him, but she caught herself and plunged it into her purse beside her, instead. "You sure?" She started rummaging for her wallet, but Peter could tell she was just turning things over until he told her exactly what she wanted to hear.

"Yes," he said, laughing.

She stopped rummaging, flashed him her wallet, which was thin and well-worn, and buried it deep.

The bill came out to fifteen dollars and some change. Peter took out a crisp, linty twenty from his pocket, slapped it down. He carried a credit and debit card like most every other human being on this continent, but there was always this nagging voice in the back of his mind, worrying at it like a termite. What if they didn't work? What if someone stole his identity? Sometimes, he felt as if he were phasing between the man he was and the man he would be in forty years' time. A glimpse of his future self to come—anxious, overcautious, and at the same time, out of control.

"Was it that guy? Did he do something?" Mary asked.

Self-reflection had sweated up his brow. He gave it the once over and said, "Huh?"

She tilted her head at the hooded man, who'd gone back to playing possum.

"Oh, yeah." He whispered, "Guy was staring right at us."

"Well…" Mary chewed on her lip," … we were acting kind of like idiots."

"Ha, yeah, that's true. You're right."

Through their window, Mary tracked the chain-smoker outside, who held her burner phone so close to her teeth, she might as well have been chewing on it.

"Maybe that's the point of the project," she said.

The chain-smoker mouthed "please" over and over again in between whatever she was saying. She didn't seem to begging. It was a filler word, filling in for "like" and "um."

"There's social norms, and then there's personal norms, and if you do one or the other, or both, long enough, it's… normal."

Peter nodded, said, "You did get pretty into it."

"Come on, you didn't?"

"A little," he said, but that was a lie. He was always aware of who he was, who he was trying to be. It was annoying.

"If you write the introduction and conclusion, I'll make up the rest," Mary said, zipping up her hoodie. "I know it's October, but damn—" she shivered, "it's cold."

There it was again, the voice in the back of his head, gnawing away. What if she overdid it? What if the professor found out they made it all up? This was his second year. He'd gotten straight As so far. A B wasn't bad, but if it was avoidable...

The wayward woman thanked Rita the waitress, got up from the bar, and exited the diner. Before the doors could shut, they were flung back open. The bells rang in the bitter wind that'd barged in, dried leaves like rats scurrying over the worn-down floor mat. The door cracked back, bounced off the empty gumball machine that'd unwisely been put beside it. Rita, cussing up a storm, hurried across the diner and wrestled the door from the elements. Before she shut it, though, she stopped. Her body went stiff. She stared into the darkness, as if she'd seen something there. Turning around as if to confirm with her patrons, she then suddenly seemed to remember the people she'd been serving this night, shut the door, and went back to the back, to hassle the cook some more.

"That sounds good..." Peter said. "But how about this? We give it one last try. I'll stomp out of here, go outside, rev up my bike, and peel out of the parking lot."

Mary, sounding somewhat unconvinced: "Okay."

"Then I'll come back a minute or two later. I'll just go down the road. Maybe someone will say something to you." Catching himself, Peter added, "If you feel... comfortable..."

Mary cocked her head. "Coming here was my idea. I don't need a knight in shining armor, just a sword." She took a knife out of her purse, put it back. "But, yeah, sure. Why not? I know you're not big on the lying thing."

"It's..."

"Fine, it's fine." Mary laughed and nudged his leg under the table with her toe. "I'm a bad influence. You know I cheat off you in class sometimes, right?"

He didn't know for sure, but he'd had his suspicions.

"Hey, listen to this, though. Why don't I speed off?"

"In your hatchback?"

Mary glared at him.

"What?"

"Shut up." She got to her feet, glare becoming a grin. "Don't hate on my hatchback."

Peter stood, put his jacket on. His phone started to buzz in his pocket. His heart went into overdrive. Some cheesy, 80s power ballad switched on in his brain. It always did when he got a text from her. Katie. He didn't need to check his phone to know it was her, because he knew it was her. She always sent one, and then a few seconds later, two more. And there they were, one after the other, on time, like clockwork. It was her signature move. Her way of announcing her arrival, and scrambling his senses until she signed off for the night. He had it bad for Katie. It was terminal.

"Get the fuck out of here!" Mary belted.

Literally wiping the smile off his face, Peter quickly caught on, said, "Gladly!" And then, for good measure: "Bitch!"

Peter didn't bother taking a survey of the diner. With Katie blowing up his phone, one anxiety had been replaced by another. This situation was a ticking time bomb. If he got his wires crossed, he'd blow it for sure. He was so close, so damn close to asking her out. He just needed to bank a couple more good conversations; get her out one last time; get her laughing like she'd been when he'd met her and her friends at the bar last weekend. The kind of laugh that cuts through the noise, etching two people out from their surroundings, leaving only them and the unspoken thing between them.

Peter didn't realize he'd left Mare's Diner until he was standing outside it, in the sign's neon glow. He hurried to his motorcycle, jumped on, and put the key in the ignition. He smelled smoke, but the chain-smoker was nowhere to be found. Giving the key a twist, the engine rumbled to life. He revved it up a few times, like an asshole, as he'd promised he would, and then took off, making sure to go slowly past the front of the diner, so everyone could see him. The instant he saw Mary through the glass, he peeled out of the parking lot.

For a man who worried about almost everything, the irony wasn't lost on him as he sped off down the pale country road, on a motorcycle, without a helmet, a few justifications away from whipping out his phone to see what Katie had texted him. His mother was the same way. She was a very careful woman. She always had her ducks in a row, except for when she didn't. Those things didn't last long; didn't often come back in one piece.

The October air burned his face with its frigid caress. He suffered it gladly. It was the shock to his senses he needed right now, before he pulled his bike over and lost them.

Deep in thought, he drove towards the full moon in the distance, until his form was lost amongst its changing light.

2

Not much surprised Mary in this life. At the ripe old age of twenty, she felt confident to claim she'd seen more than most. People usually didn't believe her when she said that, which meant she had to prove herself. She didn't like doing that. She'd done that enough for her dad. So, when challenged by some bro so far up his ass he had the shit-eating grin to prove it, she usually just came back with a heavy-hitter, like, "I found my mom dead when I was ten." Which was true.

But this restroom, though? It was like an oasis in the middle of the ashtray desert that was Mare's Diner. Rita the waitress was clearly the only employee here other than the cook, and at some point, she must've made the restroom her own personal project, because it was spotless. Ugly, as to be expected, but spotless. The floor's tiles were so immaculately scrubbed and buffed, you might as well have been walking on a mirror. The walls were impeccable; no water stains or spitballs or greasy, human-shaped blotches from fighting, fucking, or some combination of the two. It was the one public restroom you could probably wash your baby in the sink and feel like a (gutter) queen. And the stalls? They were painted a soft, blemish-free pink and stocked with jumbo-sized, extra soft, three-ply toilet paper that, to Mary's two-ply, dollar store eyes, might as well have been manna from heaven. The toilet seat sparkled. The bowl? Might as well have been brand new. The water inside it? Mountain spring. Pulling her pants and underwear down, she didn't even bother doing a once over to make sure the seat was clean. Rita wasn't just a waitress. She was a goddamn scientist.

Needless to say, though it needed to be said, often by Mary her-self, she was kind of superficial. She couldn't afford to actually be superficial, but in mind and spirit? One hundred percent. Dad would say she only acted that way to get back at him, but that wasn't true. If she wanted to get back at him, she'd find whatever hole he was living in now and call the police, citing some made-up disturbance. By the time they would have flushed him out, he'd be five felonies deep. It wasn't like that, though. As the sweet, but kind of boring, Peter had said, "Everything stays the same. Just you that changes." No, wait, she'd said that.

Mary usually was quick to pee, blasting it out hard enough as if she were a rocket trying to take flight. Not tonight, though. Tonight had been nice. Tonight had been different. Tonight didn't have to end just yet. She was always rushing through things, eager to get absolutely nowhere. Peter was sweet, but kind of boring, sure, but that didn't sound so bad right now. He'd been a steady, decent human being for the whole semester so far, which, in her opinion, was rarer than one might think. At some point, they'd exchanged numbers, but neither of them had texted each other. He was always texting someone named Katie, and she, well, she didn't text very much. She liked talking to people face to face. That always seemed to work more in her favor.

Mary gave herself a quick wipe, leaned forward on her knees. The window at the back of the restroom rattled, like the wind was trying to jimmy the lock. It'd been a howler of an October so far. Literally. The wind was constant, and it was so bad, it was like something was howling, day and night. At this point, it was more or less background noise to Mary. She'd given up trying to go outside without a hat. It was that, or look as if she was walking around with a rats' nest on top of her head. The beasts were bad enough in her apartment building. The last thing she wanted was to give them another reason to move in.

Listening for Peter's motorcycle, she heard the door open, instead. The door shut. Feet shuffled in. Stopped. Mary got up, pulled her pants up. She considered stealing one of the toilet paper rolls, but instead said, "Rita, this bathroom is… the best."

No response.

If that wasn't Rita standing in here, it was probably the chain-smoker, or some new customer. Mary tried to catch a peek of them through the gap between the door and the stall via the mirror opposite her, but no luck. It was pretty dim in here, and they were just out of view. This was probably one of those moments her friends would talk about, when they were alone or with some guy or girl and things didn't feel like they were going right. The whole butterfly-in-your-stomach thing. Phantom nausea. Mary never really experienced that.

She knew when she was supposed to, but she didn't, and as they say, knowing is half the battle. She lost every time.

Mary stepped out of the stall, purse swinging, and came to a hard stop. Men weren't supposed to be in women's restrooms. But here one stood. The hooded man dressed all in black, with the bright pink headphones feeding like arteries into his darkened face. His hands looked as if they were melting. They ran with blood.

Too hopped-up on adrenaline to scream, Mary hurled her purse instead. The man lunged, bashing it away with a bloody fist. Now, backpedaling, Mary did scream. It was short-lived. His arms shot out like shadows, longer than they should've been. He grabbed her by the throat with gloved hands and squeezed her into silence. She drove her fists down onto his arm, but his grip kept. She could feel the blood he'd brought warming on her collarbones. Choking, Mary flailed, grabbing at his arms, at his headphones. They popped out of his ears, dropped to the ground—church choir voices fading as they fell.

With his other hand, he grabbed her by the belt loop and brought her in close, a generic, vampiric embrace. She spit into his somehow still voided face and rasped, "Let… me… go."

And then he did.

Mary stumbled backwards, gasping for air. She held her neck where he'd constricted it, trying to rub out the pain with pain of her own doing.

The hooded man slipped his wet hands into his pockets, and both came back holding something. In his right, a pistol; in his left, a knife, with a fresh tendon caught on the hilt. He shook it off, and he growled, "Your choice."

She looked at the gun. That was for if she tried to run. She looked at the knife. That was for good behavior, and the night to come. The only choice she had was when she wanted to die. Mary tried to swallow her pride, but her throat was too swollen for that. Instead, she stared at the knife, seeing her short-lived life flash in that cold, uncaring steel.

"Good girl," the man said.

Simultaneously sweating and shivering, Mary moved towards him. She looked at her purse, realized her phone was inside, and wished she hadn't thrown it. The hooded man closed in on her every time she tried to make space between them. She had a thought. And then, a cut. It'd happened like that, so fast. He must've seen it in her eyes. The urge to run. He'd sliced the back of her leg. Not deep, but deep enough that her mind conjured meat when she touched the wound. The pain was sharp, and sobering.

He put the gun to her spine and rubbed the barrel against her bones. She shivered into it. Her left leg almost gave out. He was going to march her out of here like this? There would be witnesses. Rita, the trucker, the chain-smoker; whoever else might've come in. Peter, too, if he was back yet. He was stupid, and crazy. Mary told herself she could do this, and then she opened the door.

I can't do this.

The trucker lay dead at her feet, in a puddle of dirty blood that'd spread across the back hall. His face had been carved up. One eye gouged out, the other, turned to mush and packing up the cavity. His mouth was split from his left cheek down to his throat, which hadn't been so much as slit as it'd been sawed. His muscles twinkled under the fluorescents, like stars; outer space, turned inwards.

The killer urged her on. She went on. Coming out of the hall, all the color left her face, and all that howling wind she'd blocked out came back, full blast, boxing her ears, maddening her brain.

Everyone in Mare's Diner was dead. He'd killed them all. The chain-smoker had been stuffed into a mop bucket, the mop shoved so hard down her throat, the handle pressed against the inside of her stomach. Another customer had come in at some point, and now he lay face-first in a pool of blood at the bar, hand still gripping a menu. The cook, never seen but often heard, was on the ground. He looked as if he'd managed to crawl away. He wasn't crawling anymore, though. His chef-whites were now stained red, and his back, shredded, as if the killer had used his knife to dig through him.

Rita the waitress hadn't made it, either. She was sitting where Mary and Peter had been sitting, a rag in her hand. She'd been clearing the table off. A braid of intestines sat on her lap. Her stomach grinned and fumed. As the killer pushed Mary past her, she looked into Rita's eyes. She didn't know what she hoped to see in them, but in them, she saw nothing but harsh fluorescence.

The killer cocked the gun. Mary jumped, squeezed her eyes shut. Cringing, nearly whimpering, she made it to the front door and pushed it open. The wind did the rest, pulling it back and holding it for her. The world outside the diner was crazed. Howling and darkness; and the pointed silhouettes of the woods, like inquisitor's hoods. The buzzing neon sign baptized her in its dampening glow, while the moon, fuller and closer than before, offered no light, nor reprieve. No quarter. For her, it would be night forever. And the moon and the dark company it kept would hide what'd happened here, just long enough for him to get away with it.

The killer pushed Mary into the parking lot towards the beat-up green van parked over by the dumpster. Mary remembered remarking to Peter that a pedophile probably drove it.

Mary turned to…

The killer swiped at the back of her leg, cutting exactly in the same spot where he'd cut her before. She screamed, fell forward, and then screamed, "Help! Help! Peter!"

But Peter wasn't here. He wasn't anywhere. There was no one but her and him, and the howling wind and the voyeur glowing on high.

The killer stowed his knife, grabbed a handful of Mary's hair, and wrenched her towards the van. He threw her against the side, over and over, bruising her arms and body until, thinking she was weak enough, he opened the door and tossed her inside.

3

Peter pulled into the shadows on the side of the road, parked his motorcycle, and turned it off. The harsh wind kicked up, wailed warnings in his ears. The temperature must've dropped another four or five degrees, putting this night at a solid forty. He was grateful for the heat coming off his bike. It wasn't enough, though. Not as he exposed his hand and dug into his pocket and took out his phone. Someone was calling. Katie… was calling. He got off his bike and wandered towards the tree line. The night had lost five degrees, but he'd just gained fifteen. When it comes to crushes, it's always shorts weather.

He answered his phone, said, "H-Hey," and then: "Ow, what the…?" A low-hanging branch from above had gotten snagged on his hair. He broke it off with a mild tantrum his younger self would've approved of. There was noise on the line, but Katie wasn't.

It was getting colder again. He stared at his bike, remembered Mary. What time was it? Nine? When did he leave? Five minutes ago? He shook his head, for more reasons than one, because it was his head that often got him into trouble. It was always taking things too far, always distracting him with possibilities past and future, but never present. He'd been thinking of Katie, and if he hadn't stopped, he would've been clear across the county line in no time.

He marched back to his motorcycle. Holding out hope, he didn't hang up. She was somewhere, probably with someone, and she'd accidentally called him. The last text he'd gotten from her had been a *What's up?* Now, he wasn't so sure it'd been meant for him.

He fired up the motorcycle, closed his eyes when he ended the call. He turned the phone on vibrate, then silent, then vibrate; and slid it into his pocket. Walking the bike back to the road, he gave it a few revs. No cars coming from either side. There were no streetlights. Only the full moon looming over this part of the countryside, like a sadistic asteroid more content to inspire fear than it was to deliver the killing blow. Looking up at it, Peter felt as if he could touch it. He tried. His fingers were drawn to it, magnetized, electrified, by its lunar currents. It was out of reach, but not as much as he might've thought.

Peter tore down the moon-burned road. The speed limit was forty-five. He did fifty-five, a small concession for making Mary wait so long. His eyes darted back and forth between the sides of the road and the rear views, making sure he wasn't about get stuck in some cop's speed trap.

The woods through which the road cut narrowed, closing in on him as he headed towards the bend that unwound around the back of Mare's Diner. He tried not to pay them any mind, but they were alluring in a way.

Headlights spilled across the bend ahead. Peter rode the brakes. A green van skidded around the bend. As it drew nearer, Peter realized it was the same van he and Mary had seen at the diner. He'd always wondered who drove it, so in that brief moment when they passed one another, he looked through the driver's side window. It was too dark to make out who was inside, but he did notice an arm moving, as if they were waving to Peter.

"Okay," he mumbled under his breath, smiling. He threw up his hand as the van rumbled by and waved to return to the gesture.

Something shot out in front of him from the woods. Peter panicked, quickly grabbed the handlebars with both hands. He braked and swerved. Smoke and the smell of burnt rubber flooded his nostrils. Peeling out, he brought the motorcycle around to the opposite side of the road, so that he was facing the way he'd come. The van's rear lights were like two fading blood drops as it disappeared into the moon.

Peter tensed up. Pain shot through his muscles before dispersing like hot water around his neck. His heart was beating so fast, it might as well have not been beating at all. Shaking, damn near hyperventilating, he started walking his motorcycle back around to face what he'd almost hit.

He stopped. Because he heard panting. Because he heard growling. Because he heard heavy drops of saliva smacking the near-miss-warm pavement. And the clicking, the grinding, the scraping of nails.

Peter looked in his mirror.

A nightmare looked back.

One of matted, white fur and a mouthful of teeth. Eyes without pupils, and clawed hands as large as Peter's head. Its body was lean, muscular; milk dripped from its deflated tits. In shadows, it might've passed for human. But it wasn't in the shadows, and it wasn't human. It was seven feet tall, with the face of a dog, and a tongue that dripped blood and spit as it lolled over its black lips. At first, Peter thought there were exposed veins and arteries running up and down its body, but he realized they were markings. Human-shaped markings. As if, below this canine costume, the human within was trying to push through.

It was a werewolf.

Peter screamed and gunned it down the road, away from Mare's Diner. Thirty, forty, fifty miles per hour. Snarling, the beast gave chase. Even over the struggling engine, he could hear it howling and thundering after him. He glanced in the mirror. The werewolf was keeping pace, merely inches away from the tailpipe. Peter pushed the motorcycle harder, driving head-on into the moon. He bit his lip until it bled. He was squeezing the handlebars so hard, his hands were going numb. He stopped breathing. He forgot to breathe. He couldn't stop looking at it. The ravenous nightmare.

Again, the woods narrowed around him. He was riding the shoulder, wheel skipping between pavement and grass. Snarling. Growling. Howling. The motorcycle jerked to the left. It'd clipped the back end with its hand. Snot-nosed, about to cry, Peter went to swing the bike to the other side…

But the werewolf was already there, running alongside him. Mouth wide, each tooth in its mouth like a sharpened headstone, it leapt and snapped at Peter.

"Ah!" Peter yanked the motorcycle to the right. An embankment came up. He hit it, bounced off the ground. He'd been going sixty. The woods weren't about to have that. In a terrifying blur, tree after tree was thrown at him. He ducked, dodged, weaved. The ground swelled and sank. His wheels bounced off rocks, throwing him off his chaotic course. Branches and bushes whipped at his arms, at his face. Fresh cuts opened up on his forehead and dripped blood into his eyes. He struggled to hold on, but he had to. He couldn't hear the werewolf anymore, but he could feel it, in his gut and in his bones. If he survived this, that's where it'd be, for now and all eternity.

Peter barreled through a bush. He narrowly missed one tree, and then another. Ahead, a gap in the woods, a clearing covered in mist. He smiled, got a surge of relief. And then, he was flying.

The wheel had hit a hole in the ground. Peter was flung from the seat. Screaming, flailing his scored limbs, he flew into the clearing. His body broke the mist, and then it broke the ground. He smashed into the ruddy soil, right shoulder first, dislocating it. Momentum being a mother fucker, it spun him end over end, head first. His cheek got caught on a fossilized rock, got gashed. He slammed to a stop, smashing his hand under his hip.

His vision was blurry. He was groggy. The mist closed around him, and for a moment, he thought it might've poured out of his skull, he felt so out of it. He drew his knees to his chest. Face blood-splattered and grass-stained, he lay there, trying to look into the woods, trying to see if the beast were still after him.

He heard howling, but he couldn't tell if it was the wind or the werewolf. Or his brains leaking from his ear holes.

Peter looked forward, neck pain be damned. In the mist, shapes. Small shapes. Roots, and rooted shapes. Pumpkins. They were pumpkins. He dragged himself forward and found he'd landed on the edge of an overgrown pumpkin patch. Still going strong on the dregs of adrenaline, he cussed and winced his way to his feet.

The ground was covered in pumpkins. They glowed under the moon like orange beacons of hope. He followed them through the mist, mindful of their vines. His shuffling feet picked up speed when he heard a crashing behind him. He passed a lone tree with what looked like wet laundry hanging from it. But why was it so red?

If he had half a mind, he might've investigated, but he didn't have half a mind. He had a tenth at best. The portion meant for pure survival.

Further on, where the mist parted, there was the makings of a two-story house.

And in the driveway…

Peter smiled as best as he could without tearing his cheek any more.

And in the driveway, a green van.

4

Mary woke to darkness. It was itchy, and hot. Her eyes adjusted. Her mind managed. She smelled the blackness before her. It smelled of metal and leather, with a pubic sweat lacquer. She furrowed her brow. The darkness constricted. She wasn't blind. She wasn't in a dark room, or at least as far as she could tell. She'd been blindfolded with a belt. The same one the killer had been wearing when he'd abducted her. She knew, because beyond that masculine musk, there was Mare's Diner imprinted in the material. Coffee and cigarettes and fatty oils.

She jerked her arms, but they didn't go anywhere. She was bound to a chair. An old one, she figured, from the way it creaked when she moved. Other women might've been more subtle in their attempts to escape, but Mary wasn't like other women. Once she saw weakness in something, she sought it out immediately. Clenching her teeth, squeezing her eyes shut, she spazzed out. She thrashed so hard it hurt. The chair skidded and screeched across wet, gravelly ground. It hopped into the air, crashed down. She lost her balance, toppled over, face first. A drainpipe pressed against her lips. Black basement mush got caught like corn on her teeth. She spit, cussed, spit; and death-rolled the chair with her. It creaked and cracked and splintered, but despite the abuse, it held.

Mary kept going until a shelf checked her. She heard glass rattling, and then shattering, as heavy jars rained down around her. Shards exploded against her cheek and pricked her arms and sides. Inching towards the debris, she pawed for something sharp and serious. She gave blood and no small amount of suffering. But when her fingers had matching slits, she settled on a jagged piece. She went to work on her wrist binding, using the same hand, awkwardly bending it backwards as she sawed away at what felt like leather, too. The glass chewed up her palm as she hacked. When she missed the belt, it slit her wrists in a way they hadn't been slit since five years back.

She wasn't getting anywhere. Hearing footsteps, she realized she wasn't going anywhere, either. She sawed harder, cutting away leather and flesh in equal measures. The killer was near. She could track his movement through the floorboards above. Each step, a shriek, like a coffin lid being pried open. And why not? Some would say she'd been dead for a while. He'd come calling to unearth her. God, she felt so alive right now. And as soon as he saw it, he'd take it away.

Stairs gave away the killer's approach. He was coming into the basement. Not slowly or quickly, but regularly, calmly. Mary, screaming, dug as hard as she could into her bindings, but the glass broke and the leather wouldn't give.

"Good for you," the killer said, his voice startling her. He was still clear across the room, and yet he might as well have been whispering in her ear.

Mary didn't bother responding. Instead, she sank into the field of darkness before her; and on darker arms, she was lifted up. The killer pulled her from the ground, chair and all, and righted her. She was blinded, but her mind's eye could see. In it, a premonition of glinting steel; and seconds later, she felt it: a blade dragging across the belt wrapped around her head. He pricked the places where her eyes would've been if not for the belt. Phantom pains needled her corneas.

"Stay with me," he said.

The killer undid the bindings around her sweat-soaked wrists. With a knife to her neck, he issued his silent order for her to take care of the rest. Mary bent over in the chair, undid the belts around her ankles. On shaking legs, she stood. The first step she took, she stumbled, her ankle twisting, going under her. She caught herself, backed into the knife. It broke the skin, and she bled down to her clavicle.

She walked forward. The killer grabbed the back of her neck as if she were an animal and guided her. Her toes hit steps. Carefully, she went up them. They were uneven, and sticky. There was no back to them. The gaps between the steps might as well have been massive fissures. One false move, and she'd been falling for good, forever.

Mary's nose smashed into a door. The killer pushed her into it, opening it with her face. Out of the basement, elsewhere, he turned her left and urged her deeper into the house. She knew it was a house, because it smelled like a house—the lingering smoke of a snuffed candle; the sweet humidity from a dryer—and it sounded like a house—the hum of the refrigerator, the ticking of a clock; wind chimes. As she went, she kneed a chair or a couch, hit her shin against a coffee table. He wound her through somewhere spacious—a living room, maybe—and then had her going up another set of stairs. As she did, from outside, she heard a motorcycle in the distance. Also, howling. She thought of Peter, but not for long. What were the chances? It wasn't a rhetorical question. She really wanted to know.

Going up the stairs, the knife making superficial cuts to her neck with every step she took, Mary wondered what she had done to deserve this. She wasn't being a victim. She was being logical. Somewhere, at some point in her life, a chain of events had started that led her to this moment. Where had she gone wrong? How could she make this right? Peter. There was something about Peter. There had to be. It was easier that way, when it wasn't her. Ms. Selene, their Psychology professor, had said something to the effect of, "People who experience traumatic events in their life are at a higher risk of experience negative events in their life, as if they have a 'sign over their heads' telling everyone." Mary had a sense for these things. Wounded things. They'd come together. And maybe they shouldn't have. This was what had happened.

Mary stopped, went forward as she ducked. Holding onto the stairs, she kicked her leg backwards. Her foot slammed into the killer's gut. His fingers grasped for her shirt, but didn't catch. He gasped, flew backwards. She heard him tumbling down the staircase, until he hit the first floor and rolled hard into what must've been a wall.

Hands somehow as steady as a surgeon's, Mary reached for the belt, undid it, and yanked it off her head. Her eyes gasped for light like lungs would air. A tide of sweat broke over her brow. She wiped it away as she spun around. The killer lay like a black-cloaked doll at the end of the staircase, limbs twisted, face facing the other way. He wasn't moving. But he was breathing.

Mary held the belt in her hand like a whip. Her surroundings dissolved. She saw nothing, was aware of nothing, but the man who meant to kill her, lying in her way. He wasn't dead. Maybe he was playing opossum, waiting for her to step around him. Then, he'd grab her by the ankle; then he'd shove her down; and do what he felt needed to be done; to her, and to all women like her.

Caution wasn't going to her anywhere. Hesitation didn't work for deer. It wasn't going to work for her. She started down the steps.

The killer drew his pistol and, without looking, fired it directly at her.

The bullet whizzed past her knee, burrowing into the wall. She jumped, stumbled backwards. Whipping around, she hurried up the steps as a second shot exploded behind her, lighting up the stairwell. The second floor coughed up fabric and debris as the bullet hit the carpet there. Mary reached the next story, grabbed the corner, and flung herself around it. She went careening into the opposite wall, but kept going.

The hall ahead was long and filled with moonlight coming through window where it dead-ended. She passed door after door, but it was the one at the end which somehow made the most sense. The most obvious choice. She'd always had a skewed sense of survival. It was less about saving herself, and more about convincing herself she'd tried.

Mary opened the last door on the left and hurried in, paying no mind as to what was on the other side. Instead, she pressed herself against the door, shutting it slowly as she stared through the gap, watching for the killer coming with Death in the moonlight. She shut the door before she got a glimpse, and left it shut. Her heart gave a mighty thump. And then she turned around, and it damn near leapt from her chest.

A young woman, Mary's age, lay dead on the ground surrounded by candles. She'd been stripped naked and her arms and legs splayed. Her skin was pink and glistening, as if she'd recently been washed. She'd been shaved; tiny drops of blood and fields of irritated flesh along her legs, crotch, and forearms gave away the killer's impatience. Her hair, combed out, pooling around her like a puddle of paint—a combination of natural brunette, bottle blonde, and wound red from her bleeding scalp. Her eyes were open; in them, the moon, from the skylight above. At first, from the way she was laid out, and the way she'd been done-up, she looked like a sacrifice. An offering to the moon, as if her body were meant to be a meal, to keep it full and fat forever. But then, drawing closer, looking closer, she realized the corpse wasn't a sacrifice, but a blank canvas. A lifeless doll, the closest the human form could get to putty to be molded once more in presumptuous hands.

On the edge of the candlelight, there was an outfit laid out just as the woman had been. Except they weren't clothes from this decade. Acid-washed jeans. Rainbow socks. An oversized, green windbreaker with purple chevrons. To Mary, the nostalgia was nauseating. She recognized all these things, in one way or another. And in an instant, she hated what a second before she'd unironically loved.

Mary heard movement downstairs. And howling. She couldn't go out the way she came. The only way was up. Twelve feet of up over the dead girl to reach the skylight. Searching the shadows, she found junk. Dressers, cabinets, tables and chairs; a loveseat that hadn't seen much love since the same 90's the killer had just desecrated. Mary could make this work. She had to make this work.

She found a large table, shoved a few waterlogged boxes off. When they hit the floor, they split, spilling their vinyl record-shaped guts. Mary dragged the table to the corpse. The woman was in the way. Thinking she wouldn't want to go out like this, Mary bit her lip and steeled her stomach and rolled the body out of the light, into the dark. Let her get dirty. Let the rats have at her. Whatever the killer intended, she wasn't about to let him see it through, whether she made it out of here or not.

There was a human-shaped stain where the corpse had been; bathwater that smelled strongly of cheap soap. Mary pulled the table over the spot. She ran into the shadows, grabbed chairs, then boxes and crates. She piled them atop one another, climbing as she went. It wobbled and wavered, but it held. Mary scurried up and down it, like a rat in a sinking ship building a bridge to a distant shore.

Keep your head above the water. That's what Dad used to always say. Even if the fish chewed you to your bones from the neck down, always keep your head above water. No one has to know you struggled. They wouldn't care, anyway.

5

Peter hobbled like a hunchback from the pumpkin patch. A carpet of fog rolled out before him, as if to announce his pained arrival. His dislocated shoulder might as well have been broken, and his mangled fingers, so numb and swollen they couldn't have been a few hours out from a swift amputation. He wheezed when he breathed; and when he breathed, he smelled and tasted blood and wet fur. His mind was a mess, shaken, like how the kids on his old block used to shake the jars full of fireflies they'd caught. You can only take so much before all the lights go out. And his anxiety right now? It surely wasn't paying the bill.

The two-story house looked dead in a way, haunted in another. There was a coldness about it, like it'd stood here a very long time and seen all manner of things. The paint, faded from who-knows-what to white, was peeling. It almost looked scorched. The house hadn't been on fire as far as he could tell, but that didn't mean its owners or whoever lived here hadn't raised a little hell on the inside all the same. He was dragging himself from one bad situation to another—his senses, wrecked as they were, sensed that. He didn't have a choice, though.

Peter started towards the front of the house, but he heard the sound of something sharp slipping out a side door. Grunting, he hurried up the wraparound porch. The side door stood open. He exhaled, relieved; pushed the door open. Moonlight took the lead and made the dark give up its secrets. A laundry room waited on the other side. The washer was idling, waiting for whoever lived here to take out its load. The dryer still had a sphere of warmth around it. There was a clothes hamper further along, sideways. Peter crossed over.

Noises went off in the woods, like firecrackers. The werewolf was in there, watching him. He couldn't see it, but he could feel it; feel it pacing, tearing off tree limbs in place of his own, biding its time, waiting. Did it know this place? Did it know who lived here? Had it planned a dinner for one, and now, seeing as there might be guests, did it have to make changes to the itinerary? This thing was smart, Peter realized, closing the side door, locking it. A chill ran through his body. Any stronger, it would've brought him to his knees.

He crept through the laundry room. He shoved his hand into his pocket, looking for his phone that wasn't there. He'd lost it in the crash. Of course, he had. Coming up on the door ahead, he considered calling out, but something stopped him. His anxiety, really. It welled up his throat and sat in it, like a fist. He'd come here for help.

Why was his mind so determined he'd find something else, instead?

Peter nudged the door open. He stepped into a hall that let out to a kitchen. That's when it hit him: what he'd seen, what he'd been through. He stumbled forward and fell on the marble island. Its cold indifference spoke to just how alone he felt right now and how alone he knew he'd be hours from now. When the police arrived. When the ambulances came wailing through. When the local news got wind. They'd ask him what had happened. They'd ask him what he'd seen. Whether he told them the truth or a lie, he'd still be alone. He'd get no closure either way. Peter and the Wolf. The headline wrote itself, published or not.

He thought of Mary.

Someone fired a gun from inside the house.

Peter sprung up like the resurrected dead. The sound was deafening. He'd seen the muzzle flash go off ahead, spilling from around the bend. Seconds passed. Another shot boomed. He waited for wailing, thinking the werewolf might've just taken two in trying to attack the house. He didn't get wailing. He got feet pounding upstairs. Then came howling.

He hurried through the kitchen, leaving behind a small pool of blood on the island. He had to get to the van driver. The guy with the gun. Even if he was a pedophile like Mary had joked, surely they could find some common ground in their need to survive the night. He limped into a long hall, stopped at the staircase leading from it to the second floor. His nose twitched, the smoke from the gunshot still slithering through the air. Glancing at the steps, he saw a bullet hole staring back at him and wondered why the van driver fired into the house rather than outside it. Peter's heart sank. He became acutely aware of his dim and desolate surroundings. The werewolf was in the house, wasn't it?

Peter hobbled a few inches forward. A jingle jangled his nerves. A set of keys was caught under his toe. Bending down, spinning as he did so nothing could sneak up on him, he swiped the keys. He snapped back up. A loud crash came from upstairs; not long after, pattering on the roof; and then, a shower of shingles, scraping down the side of the house.

A blood vessel burst in Peter's eye. His dislocated shoulder dropped, as if some connective tissue had finally given way. He lurched forward, his knee having gone out the same way it always used to when he tried too hard in Gym. More shingles fell outside the house. A window exploded. Was that in the laundry room? He heard floorboards giving out. And a scream, unnatural, inhuman. He and the house were falling apart.

Keys in hand, guilt in his pocket, Peter forced himself deeper into the house, moving through a living room that smelled faintly of Mary. He didn't have time to think of her, so he left it at that. The living room fed into another hall, and there, yes there, wreathed in moonlight and standing ajar, the front door. Again, he smelled Mary, and pumpkins, and blood.

Peter ran outside, limbs as shredded as his clothes. Wielding the key like a knife, he hobbled towards the van but never quite made it. A few feet away, he stopped. There was something behind him. No matter how hard he tried, the only way to go forward was to go backwards. His anxiety had given him a long leash, and now, it had reached its limit. Like all starved beasts, it needed to feed from time to time.

He turned, and stumbled back into the front of the van. Mary was scrambling across the roof, nearing the edge and gutters. Across her eyes and wrists, red bands, not unlike war paint. And she might as well have been a berserker in the way she moved with a kind of careless violence that destroyed everything she touched, sending shingles and wood and metal fixtures flying.

"M-Mary?!" he cried.

Behind her, a dark figure emerged, holding a blade of moonlight in its hand.

Mary reached the edge of the roof, did a double-take…

Peter started towards the house.

…and she dropped off the roof.

Shock stopped him.

Mary hit the front lawn hard. Dirt and grass and bits of dead leaves exploded around her, as if her body had been a bomb. She didn't scream, but she was screaming. Her mouth was agape, and her eyes, slits. It was like she was dry-retching out her pain. No sounds came out but for the howling wind. It spoke for her. It spoke for them all.

Peter ran to Mary. "What are you…?"

She waved him off, grabbed the keys out of his hand, and got to her feet. She fell into him. He fell into her. Their bodies, battered, broken, and beaten, became supports for one another. Their free hands found the other's and held on tightly, the blood streaming down their arms mixed in their palms, forming a pact to suffer in tandem forever.

Peter told her, "It's going to be okay," as they made it to the van.

Mary started to smile as she slipped the key into the door, and then she glanced over her shoulder back towards the house and became dread itself.

The killer was still on the roof.

And the werewolf had joined him.

Two predators occupying the same hunting ground.

Any other night they might've fought, but tonight... Tonight there was enough to go around.

6

All it took was one glimpse for Mary to turn Scottish and cry, "Is that a cunting werewolf?!"

The beast bounded down the rooftop, paying the killer no mind. Mary swung the van door open, got inside. She started it up and had it in reverse as poor Peter, hobbled like the orphan he resembled, tried to climb into the passenger seat.

"Get..." Impatient, with half a mind to leave him behind, she grabbed him by his shirt and yanked him into the van. "Come on."

The windshield shattered. A mass of bloody, ashen fur swelled like a throbbing tumor on the dash. The werewolf had thrown itself at them. Dazed, but not dead, it started to move. Claws caught on the hood, screeching as they cut into the metal.

Mary kicked the gas pedal into the floor. The van spun out, and then it took off down the driveway. Mary jerked the steering wheel left, swinging it around to face the road. The werewolf slipped off the hood. It took a swipe at Peter's face before it fell. She thought it had missed him, but staring at him, seconds later, she saw five thin red lines bleeding out on his head, like he'd been branded.

Mary didn't know why she looked back. Of all the things Dad had taught her, it was never to look back. The past was a mirror, and everyone's a narcissist. But she did look back. In the rear view, at the house. The killer was gone. Wait, no, there was someone. There were people coming out the front door, a little boy and his father. The boy's hands were bound behind his back, and one leather strap still wrapped around his leg. His hair was spiked-up with gore-turned-product. His father was worse off. He wasn't keeping up. His kneecap was busted, moving around behind the skin, so that it looked like gelatin. The arm of a wooden chair hung off his wrist like a handcuff would a sprung prisoner's. Bare chested, the pot-bellied father was drenched in blood and seething cuts, from where it looked as if the killer had tried to sharpen his knife on the old man's bones.

She looked at Peter, but Peter wasn't looking at her. He'd looked back, too. He'd seen what she'd seen. Then he did look at her. One of them had to make the decision.

Howling. Impact. The werewolf threw itself against the driver's side of the van. Whatever decision Mary might've made became the only one she could've made. She floored it onto the country road. The werewolf kept pace, swiping at the tires to puncture them. Before the darkness swallowed the estate, she glanced back, but the father and son were already gone.

Peter mopped the blood off his face with the bottom of his shirt. He put his seatbelt on.

"What the fuck?" Mary cried, pushing the van past fifty.

The werewolf, bested or just winded, stopped giving chase. It took one last swipe at the van, ripping the brake light out, and paced there in the middle of the road. It's ashen fur dripped sweat and soil as its chest heaved. The beast let loose a howl different from the others. It wasn't anger or hunger that greased it's wanting pipes, but sorrow. It's wailing joined the wind's until the two were indistinguishable from the other. As its voice faded, so, too, did its body. The full moon seemed to be pulling away, its light receding. And when it passed where the werewolf paced, it took it, too; and the creature vanished into the night.

Mary didn't think too hard on what she'd just seen. Instead, she drove as fast as she could, barely making it around the bends in the road. Peter just sat there silently, bleeding all over himself while he held onto his seat belt strap with his one good hand. The moon was behind them now, but she could see it in his eyes. She wondered what he saw in her eyes. A naked woman on the floor? The killer? She knew what she saw. A little boy and his father, choking on exhaust fumes as their one chance hightailed it out on the low-road.

With most of the windshield gone, it wasn't long until whatever fire self-preservation had built inside them was snuffed out and the air had them shivering, seizure-like. Peter cranked the heat. They both leaned in towards the vent to suck up what little sputtered out.

"Mary…"

"I don't know," she said.

Before either of them realized it, they were back at Mare's Diner. Mary hit the brakes and they stopped just outside the parking lot. The restaurant was dead the last time she saw it, but now, it couldn't have been more alive. The place was swarming with police officers. Two news vans were parked near the dumpsters, the reporters by them bending like contortionists to see over the barrier the police had put in place. Mary had lost track of time. Maybe it wasn't as late as she thought it was, but still, she was surprised to see so many people idling on the road, clogging up the place. She smelled cigarettes and vitriol coming off the crowd. Someone had come into their territory and killed their own.

Mary let the engine run. With Peter, she stared off into the crime scene, mesmerized by the blue and red lights of the cruisers.

"What just happened?" he whispered, prodding his broken fingers.

"He killed everyone in there, except for me. Was… that a werewolf?"

He shrugged his shoulder and winced. "I guess."

Mary steadied her breathing. Her head hurt. Her mouth was so dry it was seconds away from catching fire. She looked around the van for something to drink. There was nothing, though. Except for the splotches of blood in the back from where the killer had thrown her in, it'd been scrubbed clean.

Peter fidgeted with the glove box. It popped open. Nothing was inside except for a photograph. A family. She didn't recognize the wife but the husband, son, and daughter? She did recognize them. Mary sat up. She'd figured this was the killer's van. But it was theirs. He'd been tracking them. Maybe even living amongst them. Her blood sugar spiked. She felt sick.

"They're coming," Peter said.

The reporters had spotted them. The police weren't far behind. They did look suspicious sitting here in the dark, their vehicle torn to shit, like it'd got into a fight with the world's largest can opener.

Mary settled into the seat. Her face itched from where the belt had been wrapped around it, but she wasn't going to scratch it. She was going to wait it out. She could look like anything to these people. No sudden movements.

Peter started to unbuckle, but she made a noise and he stopped. He stared at her like she was crazy, and she was, but he didn't know why. He let out a customary, "Help!" and got out of the van. The reporters went stiff. The police officers issued orders and drew their guns. Mary knew this scene all too well. Who the hell had given god the rights to remake her life?

PART II

MONDAY, OCTOBER 26ᵀᴴ, 2020

Peter popped some pills, and seconds later, Mary did the same. They were like two old folks at an old folks' home, taking their meds before they turned in for the night. Except they weren't at an old folks' home. They were in his living room, sitting on his futon, passing the time with a bottle of wine. And they weren't turning in for the night. They seldom slept since the incident, but they certainly wouldn't be counting sheep this week. Not with the full moon coming up on Friday.

"How was work?" Mary asked, head in hand, elbow propped up against the side of the futon.

Peter shrugged and took a swig of the red stuff. "You?"

Mary cringed in response. Not at his question, but at the light coming through his living room window. Peter groaned, got up. He lived in a run-down apartment building wedged between the Main Drag and the wasteland that'd become the city of Talbot. Amongst the sepulchral cityscape, there lay pockets of life. Bright lights and loud voices, and cars that didn't backfire when they high-tailed it through yellow lights. Here was one such place, with both sides of the six-lane street packed with just about any business one could wish for. You could get groceries at one end and a new wardrobe and top-of-the-line TV at the other; and if you happened to get robbed or stabbed, or set on fire, there was a police station, emergency room, and fire department in between.

All this convenience came at a cost, though. For those like Peter who'd been fortunate enough to secure a spot next to one of the few veins of Talbot's that hadn't collapsed, they had to trade their nights for neon. Peter's apartment was across from the local movie theater, Midian. The sign was massive, the lettering a deep, soft red that, when the blinds and blackout curtains weren't pulled shut, turned his apartment into a scene from an Italian horror movie. His bedroom wasn't any better off, either. The window in there caught the color from Midian and, also, the lush green swell that bloomed from the tattoo parlor's storefront below. He couldn't complain, though he would every other day about it. He'd take this nightmarish combination that called to mind a rotted Christmas card to the dismal dustpan that'd been the neighborhood he'd grown up in fifteen minutes from here.

"Much better," Mary said, as he closed the blinds and curtains, and kept them there with the heavy books on the windowsill. "I don't know how you put up with that. I'd go insane."

Peter stared at the television. They were watching the nature channel. "It's relaxing, kind of. Like white noise. You get used to it."

With a mouthful of wine, Mary swallowed to the contrary.

It'd been three and a half weeks since the attack. This drunken, pill-infused ritual of theirs had developed shortly after the police had finished questioning both of them. Thinking back, which was dangerous in and of itself, Peter had a hard time remembering what had been said and done between the time the police escorted them to the ambulance, to that morning last week when Detective Sono told them they had no further questions. There were even moments he'd forgotten about the werewolf and the killer completely. But his chewed-up fingers and battered body were quick to jog his memory.

Being that they were the sole survivors of the ordeal, they were also suspects. Mary told her tale of murder and kidnapping as it'd happened, and there was little disputing it. The van was registered to Vernal and Celeste Melancon, father and mother of Reginald and Nathalie Melancon. It'd been their house at 1981 Colony Road to which the killer had brought her. All signs pointed to the killer having entered the house over the weekend, as none of the family members had been seen at their jobs and school, or heard from by friends and family. According to the coroner's report, Nathalie had been dead a few days prior to when Mary found her. Vernal and Reginald on the other hand… Peter might as well have taken a punch to the gut when the detective told him… they'd been killed minutes after he and Mary had driven off. The police still hadn't located Celeste, but her bedroom was so soaked in her own blood, it was unlikely she was still alive.

When it was Peter's turn to tell his story, anxiety and common sense had eaten away at it like a plague of locusts. It didn't make sense without the werewolf, but without the werewolf, that was the only way he could make sense. Instead, he invented; a wolf, or bear; some large creature that'd driven him off the road and eventually onto the Melancons' property. Detective Sono said he didn't believe in coincidences. Peter agreed, but he hadn't liked what the man was implying. With that single sentence, Peter's vision narrowed, because all he saw from then on out were prison bars. And the other side of them? A career in business, a wife and a kid; a nice house in a nice neighborhood, with neighbors that were just as fun to talk shit about as they were to see every Sunday for the Big Game. A quiet life, an easy life, given a death sentence.

They both were in therapy, but this right here, with cheap wine and a pharmaceutical spread, was the only kind of therapy that worked for him right now. Peter had sworn he'd never do this to himself. He'd seen too many loved ones in the "Old Country"—that's what they called his neighborhood—die, in every way, to addiction. He wasn't addicted, though. He could stop anytime. It was a simple fact: He'd seen something that wasn't supposed to exist. How else was he supposed to cope besides getting torn up?

"Ever heard of liminal space?" Mary asked.

Peter settled in beside her. He propped his feet up on the coffee table. "Nope."

"Sharon…" she always called her therapist by her first name, "…said it today. It's, uh, like…" She clinked her teeth against the rim of her wine glass. "I can't remember now."

Peter nodded at their phones, which they both put on the coffee table. Surrendering them was part of the ritual.

"Eh, I don't care enough to look it up."

Peter nodded, grabbed a pillow, and held it, as a wolf on the TV slipped behind a massive snowdrift. He wasn't triggered, not in the way his therapist, Bruce, probably thought he would be. He was curious. His trauma didn't push him away from the truth. It drew him towards it. It was his anxiety that acted as the buffer, the membrane that filtered out the bad ideas. Somehow, it didn't see abusing drugs and alcohol as a bad idea, so at this moment, maybe it wasn't.

"We got an A on our project," Peter said.

Mary laughed.

"Did you even turn it in?"

"No, did you?"

"Nope."

"I bet you Ms. Selene is chomping at the bit to get us in and talk about what happened."

"For sure." Mary thought on this for a moment. "Maybe." And again: "How was work?"

Peter worked thirty hours at a Franklin's, a furniture story. He'd been back at the grind for about a week. How was work? "It was work. Think my boss is getting tired of taking it easy on me. Said I have to start pulling my sales up. You?"

"Cathartic," Mary said. She worked at Mid-City Meat and Deli, as a butcher. She hadn't gotten the job until after the incident. Before then, she never really said where she worked, and Peter never really cared enough to ask. "They're hiring. Apply. Come sublimate with me."

Peter rolled his eyes, took a drink. "If I wanted to channel my bullshit into something 'positive,' then shouldn't I work at an animal shelter or something?"

"I don't know. Depends on what you want to do to that… werewolf." She quickly downed her nighttime meds, one of which was an anti-psychotic and something else she'd been on for a while. "Werewolf… Jesus, I still don't know what to make of it all."

"Have you heard from Detective Sono lately?"

She shook her head. "No leads."

Peter stared at Mary. Her freckles were darker, more prominent, almost like they'd been pushed together. That's what it was about her. She'd been exposed to something, like a chemical spill, and now she was different because of it. Her hair, usually braided, was now unkempt. Her clothes, generally a T-shirt for a band he'd never heard of and some jeans, had been replaced with what she wore to work—a logo-less shirt and black slacks. There was dirt under her nails, often crust in the corners of her eyes and mouth. She smelled like cold meat. He knew she showered and wore fresh clothes, but it didn't seem to matter. She wasn't changed, but changing; and neither he nor her could say when it would end.

He wasn't any different, though. Looking at her might as well have been the same as looking into a mirror. It was a joke for someone with a belly full of wine and anti-anxieties to think of the word recovery; and he certainly wasn't expecting to be better so soon after everything that'd happened. What was weird was how he could see it, in her, and in himself. His whole body felt raw. His hair, oilier. Dog breath. He was eating tantamount to garbage, and yet he seemed leaner, not in a bodybuilder kind of way, but more of a scrappy, alley-dweller kind of way. Weren't these things supposed to not be visible to the naked eye? Didn't it take a close friend to tell you weren't the same person? That you needed to get your shit together? Can you still be completely self-aware and still spiral?

That damn Introduction to Psychology class had him taking a microscope to everything, and now, he'd turned it on himself. Maybe it didn't need to be a microscope. They were good for understanding things. Maybe what he needed was a piece of glass and a high-powered light. That way, he'd get the gist, and he'd get to burn it away, too.

Peter resituated himself on the futon and set his wine glass down on the table. Turning to Mary, holding his pillow as if he were about to tell a scary story at a sleepover, he said, "We can't keep doing this."

Mary squinted at him as she finished off her glass.

"Sitting here, I mean. Doing nothing." He grabbed his glass and finished it, too. "That fucking fucker is still out there. You said you've been getting weird vibes around your place. Like someone is watching and... Full moon's Friday! That was a cunting werewolf."

"Heh," Mary said, going to refill her glass before stopping herself.

"I mean I don't know how werewolves work. But... you..."

"He's not going to let me get away," Mary said.

"We just don't know."

"I know it's not helpful when someone says chill..."

"Yeah, it might just be me over-thinking things. But you haven't been?"

The stack of books on the windowsill toppled over. The curtains drew back, and the damping red light poured through, shading them Technicolor. All the differences he'd seen in her were gone to the pulverizing glow of neon. She was smoothed over, uncomplicated.

More of the way when he'd first met her, that first day of class.

"I have. I didn't want to say anything. I didn't know you felt the same way. He killed all those people, except for me; and he took me back to that house. My boss at the butcher shop? I've been having him show me how to stab a person, where to stab them; practicing on the meat. He's ex-military. I've been trying to do the whole be cool, be normal, use your coping skills, talk to your fucking Sharon thing… But if you're down, I'm down. I didn't think you would be, but I yeah, yes. I want to do something."

Peter smiled and filled her glass to the brim. "I have no idea where to start, but getting to the bottom of this bottle seems a good place."

Giving him the thumbs-up, she said, "Shit, I forgot to bring something to change into."

Peter got up, went to his room. Mary had been crashing on his futon every night since two nights after the attack. It was part of their ritual. It just kind of happened. He grabbed a pile of shirts, pants, and underwear—things she'd shed during her overnights. Bumping the desk next to the pile, his computer monitor snapped to life. On the screen: a browser with about fifty tabs open, most of which had to do with werewolves. He quickly turned off the monitor and headed back into the living room.

"Did you really wash them?" Mary asked as he handed them to her.

"Well, yeah."

"Thanks." She pressed a shirt to her face and breathed the fabric softener in. "Smells pretty. Everything you have smells pretty."

Peter fell into his well-worn groove on the futon. "That's what happens when you live only with your mom most of your life, I guess."

"Same, but not for the girly stuff." Mary chewed on her lip, eating the skin that came off. "Middle stage."

"Huh?"

She made circles with her finger. "The liminal space… thing. That thing I was talking about, that Sharon was talking about."

"Oh."

"Yeah, it means… It's like an in-between something and a something. What did she say? 'Disorientation that occurs in a middle stage of a rite of passage.'"

"Huh, alright," Peter said, confused. "Why was she talking about that?"

"I guess because the way I've been feeling after everything. Thinking that, maybe, there's more to this coming up. Just don't know when. I don't know. I can't begin to make heads or tails of Sharon."

Peter nodded, pretended to agree with Mary that he thought Sharon the therapist was an idiot. He didn't do much talking after that. He didn't need to. Without even realizing it, Mary had said it all.

TUESDAY, OCTOBER 27ᵀᴴ, 2020

1

Drunks make simultaneously the worst, and best, plans. Last night, Mary and Peter had been gung-ho to get down to brass tacks and take back control of their lives. When they woke six hours later at seven in the morning to the maddening chimes of his alarm, their motivations might as well have been tossed to the toilet they kept taking turns puking in. Peter had made a good point, though she didn't tell him that, about how it might make things worse if they dug too deep. His idea was for the two of them to spend the night at his apartment and invite some of their friends over for what would amount to a total pity party. Mary wasn't sure how many times she could hear, "Are you okay?" and "I'm so, so sorry," before she'd start wishing the killer had been her plus one. But whatever. His building was practically abandoned. She could crank the music until she was numb. A tried-and-true coping skill. Sharon would be proud.

It was the next day, and closing time at Mid-City Meat and Deli. Bossman was in the back, emptying the register and whatever else it was he did and said she'd have to do once she was out of training. Out of her white coat, Mary stood at the sink, scouring her hands with hot water. She was thinking of the Melancons. She'd been thinking about them all day. On her break, she found their social media pages. They'd been set to private, though. The police had asked if her if she had ever met the family before. She'd told them no. Now, she

40

wasn't so sure. She had a feeling she might've once, but she couldn't tell if it was because she really had, or if her mind wanted her to think she had, so that it could make sense about why the killer had chosen her of all people.

She dried off her hands, turned around, and gazed upon meat. Dad had been in meat, too. Jesus, at this rate, her life was going to turn into one big Freudian joke. But she'd known that for a while now. Ms. Selene and her Intro to Psychology hadn't opened her eyes to anything they hadn't already seen ten years ago. She doubted he'd be proud of her practicing in a similar trade. These things came dead to them. He preferred to visit death upon the living himself. He'd called himself a survivalist, but at the end of the day, he was just a pussy.

Bossman from the back of the shop: "Go home! You work too hard. It makes me nervous."

Mary leaned back on her heels, to catch a glimpse of the big butcher with a heart as big as his ham-sized hands. "Why's that?"

"Because you'll realize you're too good for this place," he said, with a belly laugh.

"No training today?"

He shook his head, his fat neck glistening like the scales on a constricting snake.

"See you Monday, then."

"Come in late," the Bossman said, while she went to the front of the shop. "You try too hard. You spoil me."

Mary didn't try that hard. The Bossman's standards were just so low, you'd have to tunnel past if you wanted to do the limbo under them. Stepping out onto the sidewalk, she was thinking about the Melancons again. The family name was French, but what little she could gather from her Internet searches was that they were from Louisiana. A Creole clan that'd migrated clear across the country. No family, she'd overheard the Detective say. They'd been here a long time, if the public records were right; in that house for about twenty years. That's how old Mary was. Shit. Had they eaten at Mare's Diner when Dad used to take her there? Had they sat across from one another? Locked eyes once?

Mary headed to her car on the street. She'd forgotten to feed the meter, but the meter maid never missed a meal herself, so she was a good block away. Mary knew it was sad to structure her days by the flaws of others, but it worked. She unlocked the door, got in. Putting the key in the ignition, she took a look at the street. She hadn't seen someone, but someone had seen her. A well-dressed man waiting at the crosswalk. He quickly turned away from her and went around the corner. *He could've been looking for anyone,* she thought, taking her foot off the brake pedal. But that's not how these things work, not after having gone through what she had. Everyone was looking at her at all times. She was already selfish. Being a victim just justified it. A trade-off to be sure.

She gave chase as much as everyone-just-got-off-work-traffic would let her. By the time she made it to the corner, the well-dressed man had multiplied: The bank had just purged itself of several of them. She leered at them, and went on her way.

Mary was headed to Peter's when she decided to take a detour. For the husk of a city that it was, Talbot's parks were surprisingly well-maintained; and that's where she usually found herself on days like today, when she needed to think, to be left alone. It made sense, she thought, pulling into the parking lot of Star's Gate—a cult name if she'd ever heard one. Talbot had its chance with the land. Now, nature was taking it back. And it seemed to be doing so with a vengeance. The bathroom could've been a piece out of a hedge garden; the tennis courts, a caged jungle. The woods were thicker than she remembered. You couldn't see the skeleton of the upper-class neighborhood that'd carved them up fifteen years back anymore. The park was overgrown, but elegant in its wildness.

She got out of the car, winter coat zipped up to her chin, scarf wrapped around her neck. She pulled a beanie over her head, past her ears. The howling wind always amped up in the evenings, and it seemed much worse since that night. Whenever she heard it, it took her back. Back to the van, where she'd been bound and blinded, hearing nothing but the blood in her ears and the tires thrumming on the road. That's all that night was: a series of sensations. Despite social media's insistence, you couldn't build a case out of sensations. She needed facts. Cold, hard, fleshy facts, with enough DNA all over the place you could have a judge and talk show host trade places and still get a conviction.

Mary made herself aware of her surroundings—a mom and daughter by the swing set, two tween boys trying to impress some teen girl on home base—and settled in at the nearest picnic table. She pulled out her phone. Common courtesy would have her calling Peter. She opened up the notepad app, instead, and typed in what she remembered about the killer. She'd done it before for the police, but this was different, because she was doing it for herself this time.

Five-foot-eight (she was five-seven). One hundred and ninety pounds of mostly muscle (Dad weighed about that). Thick forearms. Large hands. Breath smelled like mint. Low tone of voice, slow manner of speaking—both intentional but not that intentional. He had an accent. She'd heard it clipping through. A real subtle Southern inflection. He hadn't said much, but what he did say, at Mare's Diner and the Melancons'... it'd been encouraging. Sadistic, of course, in that cocky, serial killer kind of way, but still.

Are you serious right now? You want that fucker's approval?

Mary sighed, rolled her eyes at herself. It read like a list of ingredients to a ritual. Give it to a witch and a teeny-bopper and the results might be more alike than you'd imagine. But she wasn't trying to summon the perfect man. He was already here. She just needed to follow the smoke trails coming from whatever hellish vent he'd crawled out of.

What would Dad do?

God, there was a question she hadn't asked herself in a long time. Thinking it now made her shiver in ways this wailing wind never could. A few weeks before Ms. Selene had them acting like asses at Mare's Diner for an A, they'd been going over operant conditioning – behavior modification by way of reinforcement or punishment. What always stood out to her about the theory was the idea of extinction; that is, getting someone to stop doing something by no longer reinforcing the behavior. When the question *What would Dad do?* went the way of the dinosaurs, that's exactly what'd happened. She kept asking, and he stopped having answers.

But Ms. Selene warned that extinction didn't always last forever. It could have a resurgence. Spontaneous recovery. Here it was, unearthed and fresher than she'd expected, to haunt her all over again.

What would Dad do?

Mary started to rock without realizing it. She pressed her fists to her mouth and teethed them. Dad would call a meeting at Goetia, and all his Demons would come. They'd get out their knives and wives, and guns, too. They'd come in from the country with charm and swagger, to turn up rocks and put the squeeze on what lay under. They wouldn't always get their man, but they'd always get to use their hands.

She stared at her cellphone. She didn't have a clan of outcasts, just casual acquaintances. But she did remember, by heart (because that's where Dad said Goetia had put them), the Demons' true names. Those that weren't dead or in prison were still local. They could certainly put a hurt on someone better than Peter or herself could. They'd kill the killer, but in the end, she'd still be in danger, wouldn't she? That life had gone extinct. There was no saying that, if she brought it back, she or it would survive.

What would Dad do?

He'd say everything was connected, everything had meaning. His paranoia could keep a dying star on life support for eons to come. But when he was right, he was right—a dangerous conclusion to share aloud. And this time, he was right. Because just now, she realized she knew the name Melancon.

It was the name of the guy Dad used to write on the Wall of Goetia. Right beneath a picture of her mother. Before she went out for a six-pack and never came back. She was still waiting in line, Dad would tell her when she was little. And maybe that was true. But the line to the register and the gates of heaven were two different things. Or so she thought.

2

Pop culture was going to be the death of Peter. If there was any truth out there about werewolves and lycanthropy, he'd never know it. The creatures had become normalized, idolized; immortalized by books and movies. It was a foregone conclusion that werewolves were weak to silver. If you suggested werewolves came out on any other night but one featuring a full moon, you might as well say the sky isn't blue while you're at it. Maybe these things were true. But what if they weren't? What did that leave him with? Theories from bad fan fiction and sites with backgrounds of tiled gifs? In some ways, he envied Mary. At least her killer was human. You could use just about anything to kill a human, if you put your mind to it. But shit, maybe werewolves were the same way. What if they weren't, though? He didn't even know if the beast would come back for him on Saturday.

What if it did, though? What if it was out there, right now, tracking him in human form? Would the person even wait until Saturday? Has there ever been a serial killer werewolf? He wasn't ready. He'd never been so unready in his life.

Peter had called in sick to work today. It was 5:00 PM now, and for the last eight hours his thoughts had been locked in a pessimistic loop. In some ways, the loop was a ring. His anxiety had a death grip on it, because it was saving the ring, waiting for that special mental illness to slip it on and seal a marriage of madness that no therapist could separate. He'd read too much, which had made him think too much, which had made him feel even more powerless than before. Knowledge was a weapon. He'd never realized it was a double-edged sword.

He leaned back in his chair and grabbed his crotch through his sweatpants. He'd needed to piss for the last hour. About to get up, he leaned forward instead. His eyes ached from staring at the monitor all day, but, hand on the mouse and scrolling down, here was something new. Something he hadn't read. A page about lycanthropy on some janky site called *Black Occult Macabre*.

In Sheep's Skin:
The Beasts Without, and Within
By Connor Prendergast

For as much as been written over the centuries about werewolves, little is actually known about them. Like serial killers and shock rockers, their induction into the hall of public awareness has blinded us. They've lost their bite. What should inspire fear simply doesn't inspire at all. The monsters have been manufactured and mass-produced. The truth of their nature has been forgotten.

"That's what I'm saying," Peter said, rapping his fist upon the table. "That's exactly what I'm saying!"

Werewolves were a dying breed; a species on the brink of extinction. But for the last eighty years, they have found sanctuary in the simulacrum of Hollywood horrors paraded across the silver screen. A conspiracy theorist would suggest there is a cabal of lycanthropes responsible for decades of misinformation, but the truth of the matter is far less interesting. The beasts got lucky, and on the brink of oblivion, where they should've died, they evolved instead. Lycanthropy is a disease, both mental and physical, facilitated by parasitism. There is a relationship—

Peter, groaning, and about to piss himself, sprung out of his chair and hurried to the bathroom. He felt like a deflating balloon as he emptied his bladder. Standing there, cold feet on the clammy tile – the best he could get to the proverbial splash of water to the face – he tried to readjust his expectations. He'd read a lot of well-written, pseudo-scientific mumbo jumbo today. Just because this Connor guy was validating his nervous concerns didn't mean either of them were right. That was something he'd learned long ago. Something he had to remind himself of often.

The stream of urine turned into a trickle. He gave himself a squeeze and a few shakes, flushed. On his way back to his desk, his cellphone started to ring. He'd left it on his bed, face down. He grabbed it, answered it without looking to see who was calling. It was after five after all. Who would it be if not Mary letting him know she was on her way over?

Anyone. It could've been anyone. But it wasn't Mary.

It was Mom.

"Petey," she said, breathlessly.

He pressed his lips together, like a child would, as if to say, "I'll never tell."

"I heard about what happened. I'm sorry I didn't call sooner. I lost the phone that had your number in it."

"I'm… I'm fine."

Peter had been in his apartment seconds ago, but now, he was somewhere else. A locked room with no lights. And his mother's voice was the key.

"I wish you had called me, Petey."

In the mother-darkness, he smelled fried foods and hairspray. Lavender. Cigarettes.

"I'm your mother. I worry. I… I'm sorry." She laughed. "Let me rein myself in." Dramatic exhale. "Petey?"

"…Yeah?"

"Talk to me."

He squeezed his eyes shut. The mother-darkness lifted. He was back in his room. Not his room, but his old room. His childhood's. There were lines of dust where things used to be. She said she'd replace them. He'd told her she wouldn't have to if she didn't keep selling them. It was obvious. Why was it so hard for her to get?

"Uh, god, I don't know where to start," Peter said.

"Who was that girl?"

"Girl?"

"I saw her..."

"Girl I go to school with. Mary." He opened his eyes, reached inside himself for the dying embers of courage his mother's call had otherwise snuffed out. "Mom, it's too much—"

"I get it. I understand. I do. I do understand. Hey..."

He felt a phantom finger lift his chin.

"... It's okay. I'm just so glad you answered. I didn't think you would. Hurts my heart knowing that. It really does, Petey. But you answered."

The mother-darkness began to clear. His apartment phased back into view, starting with his peripheries. Like it'd been hiding. Waiting for her presence to be lifted.

"I'm back in town, you know?"

He swallowed hard. "Yeah?"

"Been back for a bit."

"I thought you couldn't..."

"You know your mom. Always putting my nose where it doesn't belong. The word 'no' never sat right with me, did it?"

"No."

She laughed, probably thinking he was being cute. "I have a loose end to tie up. Then I'll lay low for a bit. Then... we'll see!"

"See?" The room grew darker again. "See what?"

"See about... us! Being a family again! Getting the pack back together."

Don't say pack, he thought, and then, thinking further: *Fuck no. Fuck you, Mom. No, no, no.*

"It's going to be good."

"I..."

"Petey, it's going to be good. We both need this. I don't think how we left things between us... I don't think that was very fair some of those things you…" The sweetness had left her voice, or it'd never been there all along. Rot is misleading like that. "If I had done those things to my mother, she would've knocked my freaking head off."

"You did."

She scoffed. "You're lucky I didn't do worse." The phone beeped. She'd probably pressed a button from holding it too tightly. "Let's not do this. I don't want to do this with you. I have to go, Petey. I love you."

Peter didn't say it back. Instead, he ended the call and dropped onto his bed. Every muscle in his body hurt. Quickly, he turned off his phone, so she couldn't call him back. She would, too, to get the last word in. Even if it wasn't a word at all, but the sound of her breathing. "I brought you into this world, and I'll take you out of it," she used to say, and she seemed to apply the same phrase to every thing she did in life, in one way or another. She had to control every-thing, even if it meant letting something else control her. The moon was always full in her mind.

He'd lost his taste for lycanthropy. He got up, got dressed; left his apartment. The hall greeted him with hazy light coming through the smudged windows, and that unplaceable smell most semi-abandoned buildings like these seem to have drifting through them. Old carpet, moldering wood. Samples from centuries past. And something… else. It was something else that always got to him. Old soul extract, the kind aging hippies liked to go on about.

Peter's head was buzzing. His mouth tasted sweet, further fitting the imagery, as if to spite him. He wondered. He wasn't going any-where in particular. He passed abandoned apartment after abandoned apartment. Only he and three others lived here. One on this floor—Ms. Panina, who didn't speak a lick of English—and two others—Vanslow and Hearn—on the first and second floor respectively. He couldn't remember the last time he'd seen them.

After staring at moons all day, Peter decided he needed to see the sun. He passed the main stairwell, found the one tucked away by Ms. Panina's door. They used to keep it locked when he first moved in. Not anymore. Not wanting to alert Ms. Panina, he pulled the door open quietly, slipped into the shadows beyond, and made his way to the heavens.

The stairwell let out to the roof. The sun blinded him as he stepped onto it. The graveled ground crunched beneath his feet while he rubbed sight back into his eyes. Talbot came into view. He was facing south. He knew he was facing south because it was the only direction from this vantage point he could see across the city. It was here, in front of him, the buildings had been sliced apart, slid aside, leaving a spillway for wayward details to come through. Beyond, the Old Country, his old neighborhood, with its smashed homes and dried-out yards, and streets with potholes that swallowed tires whole; and its people, gypsy junkies forever chasing the alchemical properties of bullshittery.

No matter how hard he tried, he could never escape it. The world seemed to bend over backwards to make sure he never forgot where he came from. At first, he'd taken it as a reminder to be humble. But lately, and especially now, he took it as a threat. A peripheral promise. The Old Country was like a gang. Once you were in, you could never really get out.

And he certainly wasn't out anymore. Not now that Mom had called.

Her voice hadn't broken him, but he was dented. He felt hollow, like a black hole had opened up inside his stomach. The last time he had spoken to his mother had been about two years ago. She'd called him from a public library two states over. He'd had the house to himself that last week. His bags had been packed. He was going to move out. He'd just been waiting for her to come home, to see him off. "I'll be there tomorrow," she'd said. "Don't go anywhere," she'd pleaded. He'd given her another three days, and then, for the first time in his life, he didn't let her get her way.

Mom had only been there half his life, anyway, which was fitting, because he only had half a mother. The other half of her he didn't know. That woman was hard, and hard to love. She lived by night, played dead like an opossum during the day. She came and went like the tide. Her pull, just the same, always strongest before high and low. "Come out with me," she'd tell him, reeking of perfume and cigarette smoke, as he lay on the ground, trying to practice cursive. "Lay with your mother. Don't go," she'd mewl from the couch, as he tried to slip past her, so he didn't miss football practice.

She had a mental illness, you see. The kind that turned the inside of the medicine cabinet bright orange. A mood disorder. Bipolar, probably... definitely, after having learned what he'd learned in Intro to Psych. Normalcy was a social construct, his professor had told them, and he'd experienced that first-hand. Mom always kept him on a short leash. It wasn't until high school that he started spending more time at friends' houses and seeing what a "normal" family looked like. Even then, he had his doubts and his excuses. But he knew now. Now, he knew.

Peter went to the edge of the roof, sat, and threw his leg over the ledge. A jolt of anxiety coursed through his body, kick-started his puttering heart. He needed it. Maybe it'd been genetic. Mom had a touch of it, too, in her own manic kind of way. But for him, it was a coping mechanism. It kept his senses sharp. With Mom, anything could've happened at any time. He'd had a choice back then. To not care, or care too much. He chose to care too much. Or at least he'd told himself he had chosen. Maybe she'd done this to him. With her disappearing acts and broken promises. And the times they had to move, had to leave in the middle of the night. And all the men, some he'd known for months, others a half an hour, who'd come and gone in his life, always taking a piece of it, never giving it back. He would've never made it if he hadn't cared. He'd still be in the Old Country, somewhere between the corner store and an odd job, making ends meet, while at the same time never figuring out how to keep them together.

The wind began to howl. Night was coming. It'd be here soon. He started to shiver and brought his legs in. In the sky, the faint outline of the moon. And below, the traffic was thinning, the people dispersing. The tide going out, as everyone was going home. They'd be back soon, he thought. And would Mom be with them? Jesus, in some annoyingly subconscious way, was that what he'd been afraid of? Her? The drama-vulture. He should've known she would've found out about the attack. If the werewolf wasn't hunting him, she definitely was.

Peter hurried off the roof and headed back into his apartment. Picking up his phone to text Mary, he found she'd beat him to it. She'd sent him a picture of a dagger. *It's made out of silver,* she'd written. He smiled, told her to buy it. She said she already had.

Two birds, one stone, he thought morbidly. And then, just to be sure, he doubled-down on an order of wolfsbane.

Just to be sure.

<h1 style="text-align:center">WEDNESDAY, OCTOBER 28TH, 2020</h1>

1

Mary and Peter filed awkwardly into *Anthony's,* a snazzy Italian restaurant tucked away on Talbot's Main Drag. They'd both overdressed for the occasion, and their movements were so unnatural, they might as well have been alien visitors from a distant planet. As they moved through the place, Mary forced eye-contact with everyone she passed, and smiled when they shrank in their booths. She felt like a feral dog, making junkyards out of where she roamed. It felt good. Until it didn't. When her eyes left theirs, but theirs stayed, burning through her. Undoing her.

"Can you sit us next to the nearest exit?" Peter asked as the busser attempted to seat them at a table in the center of the dining room.

This was clearly the brace-faced busser's first job. Smiling, and overly-willing to please, she stammered out a lisped, "Shure!" and wedged them in a shadowy corner next to the emergency exit and bathrooms.

"Good call," Mary said, as they settled in.

Peter rubbed the back of his neck. His hand came away sweaty.

"You alright?"

"Yeah."

"It's a little… on the nose."

"Exposure therapy."

Mary picked at her napkin. "Your apartment was getting pretty ripe."

Peter shrugged, said, "Yeah. It'll be nice to have some food to wash the beer down with."

"Exactly."

Silence like a coroner's sheet fell over them. She knew what this was. They'd got along well enough in class, shared a moment of life-changing trauma, and now, with nothing but a handful of dust from what used to be, they were trying to put things back the way they were. Problem was, neither of them had factored into the other's equation before all of this. Whether they liked it or not, they were bound together. Violence was funny like that.

Their waiter, Shelly, materialized out of nowhere. "Have you two dined at *Anthony's* before?"

Peter did a double-take at Shelly. At first, Mary thought he'd recognized her, but it was simpler than that: He thought she was a babe. And she was, with her perfect skin and perfect hair, and that where-do-you-summer low-key vibe she had about her. Good for him. His chances weren't great, but at least that part of him still worked. Mary's, on the other hand, was on life support.

"Ye-no," Peter stammered.

"Well, we appreciate you coming in tonight. Our goal for this evening is to give you an authentic…"

Mary checked out until she heard Peter say, "Water," and she asked for the same.

Shelly smiled, spun around, and faded into the dim cacophony of phony laughs and clinking silverware.

Peter tugged on his dinner jacket and started to chuckle.

"What?"

"Eh, nothing." He paused, clicked his tongue against his teeth. "Ever since the parking lot, I've been trying to come up with some small talk."

"Same." That was a lie.

"The other day, at work, Brad…"

Mary arched an eyebrow.

"Fuck it. My wolfsbane should be here tomorrow. Next day shipping."

Mary leaned in, whispered, "I bought a gun."

Peter recoiled. He looked more impressed than concerned. "What?"

"I got a guy," she said, which was true. Ever since she took a trip down memory lane yesterday at Star's Gate, she'd been thinking about nothing but Goetia and everyone who used to call that hellhole home. Her guy used to be one of their suppliers. Called himself Guy, because: "Think about it! It's funny as shit!" These days, he spent most of his time peddling benzos to high-schoolers. But Guy was your guy, and if you buttered him up enough, he went along with just about anything. Besides, she was a daughter of Goetia. Who was he to refuse?

"You got a guy? Where do people get these 'guys'? I want a guy."

"You can have him. Seriously. What do you need a guy for, anyway?"

"Nothing." Peter laughed. "I just want to say I've got one. Holy shit, though, really? So, if you get caught…?"

"Take a deep breath, Nervous Nancy. I'd rather get caught then get caught dead."

"Fair enough. Do you have it on you?"

Mary gave her purse beside her a pat. "Holster's on its way. Next day shipping."

Peter laughed, but she wasn't joking.

Shelly materialized beside them with two sweating glasses of ice water. "Do you need some more time to look at the menu?"

They did, but they had a conversation to get back to, which didn't include Shelly or anyone else in this world, so they went with something safe and ordered steak. Peter's, medium. Mary's, medium-rare. Shelly made a face at that. Mentally, Mary deducted two dollars from her tip. She could almost hear Dad's voice, saying *Hit 'em where it hurts.*

"Your guy the guy who you got my knife from?" Peter asked, eying the emergency exit sign.

"No, I bought that off some metallurgist's shop on the Internet a few weeks back. It's pure silver, though."

"Oh, wow. Thanks, Mary."

"It's pure silver, though. Dude said if you're planning to hunt werewolves, it probably will break like the first time you hit it. Said that after I bought it. Ass."

Peter cringed. "Guess I didn't think about that."

"Really, who does?"

"Shit. I wonder if it's really got to be pure." Peter took a long drink of water. "Shit."

Mary gave his shins a kick under the table. "I'll get us some silver bullets. Cover all our bases. What're you supposed to with the wolfs-bane?"

"Shove it up its ass," Peter said, laughing way too hard at himself. "Yeah, something like that."

"We'll figure it out."

"If it comes to that."

Mary nodded, said, "Yeah, if it comes to that."

"Have you seen him?" Peter whispered.

Mary shook her head. She hadn't. Not definitely. There'd been moments. When she left for work in the morning, when she came home in the evening. Those heart-pounding seconds when she puts her key in the door, and wonders if, after she turns it, she'll find it unlocked. Those dreadful minutes when she finally goes inside and stands on the threshold, bathed in the colors of dusk, trying to read the shadows for signs like a fortune teller might her seemingly short-ening lifeline. No, she hadn't seen the killer. But he'd been with her. He was with her now. Somewhere behind all the chewing and slurp-ing and idle chatter, whispering. It was crazy. She was crazy. How many times could a person lose their mind until they realized they had no right to have one to begin with? That was a good question for Sharon. Therapists got all hot and bothered over shit like that.

"Same. The... werewolf I mean."

"I know."

"At least, I don't think. I don't know. I catch people looking at me all the time. I can't tell if they really know who I am or what."

"Could be the sweatpants and stained white tank."

Peter laughed: "That was one day! And I was just going down the street to the store to get some milk."

"I'm not judging!" Mary said. "I hate this. I still feel like we're waiting for something to happen."

"I'm used to it, but..." Peter sighed. "I can't have this on my shoulders forever. It's too heavy."

It might as well have been Mary's hands on his shoulders, pushing him down. Sometime during the aftermath, when they were both shivering side-by-side in the back of the ambulance, she'd considered this was merely the beginning of things to come. It scared her. Scared her in the way getting out of Goetia had scared her. So, she turned to Peter and seeded his soft mind with this simple statement: "It might come looking for you." He'd never been the same after that. The soil of his psyche was rich with paranoia. He was rooted.

Mary didn't have the heart to tell him otherwise. It was too late for that. If she'd said something earlier, he might've drifted away from her, as anyone would when paired up with a ticking time bomb. She could count on one hand the fun facts she knew about Peter, and yet, it was always his hand she saw when she inevitably exploded, picking up her pieces.

"That's why we're going to do something," she said.

"The party? I—"

A glass shattered.

"—I…" He laughed it off, but his face had gone emergency exit red. "What's the point? We go through all this and they don't show…"

"Then you buy yourself another month."

"Sure, but if they do… Then what're our friends? Meat shields?"

"No. No, no. Strength in numbers, man."

"I don't want anyone else getting hurt because of us."

It came out quickly, and sharply: "What about all those other people who get hurt because we didn't do anything?"

Peter laughed. His mouth twisted. Were they about to fight? "Seriously? That's what the cops are for!"

"They're hunting my problem. Not yours. Unless you're ready to go change your statement."

Peter stared at her. She was losing him to sense and survival instincts. He didn't know the way of Goetia. The way of dick-swinging men who thought they'd get to heaven by way of demonhood. Righteous republicans that smelled like chewing tobacco, and were marked by bubblegum lip gloss on their necks. He was from the Old Country, where you gave and you gave and got only what someone else thought you deserved. To get him to give, she had to, too.

"I'm connected to all this somehow," she said, the words dislodging from her throat. "I remembered something."

He took the bait with an exasperated, "What?"

"My dad used to talk about the Melancons all the time when I was little. I tried to forget a lot about my dad, but that I do remember. He, um… I'm pretty sure he thought my mom might've run off with one of them."

"Holy shit, Mary."

"I was really little. I don't remember when exactly."

"Holy shit."

"I don't know which Melancon…"

"Did you tell the detective?"

She winced, annoyed that he'd cut her off.

"Do you still talk to your mom?"

"She's dead, Peter."

He dropped the bait and sat back, face sweating like his glass of water.

Mom's murder was as clear as mud. Mary didn't have the full picture, just fragments. A memory book comprised of freeze-frames.

Dusky sky, gossamer-like; the sun and moon coming through in equal measures.

Vultures.

A bloody knee.

An acoustic guitar clanging out open notes at jarring intervals.

Then a cave, steepled; yawning wetly.

And her small hands, shadow-branded, as she stepped into that old, old church.

What came next was harder to imagine. Less visual, more auditory. The crunching of dried things beneath her feet. The slow but steady drip of condensation. When she'd entered the cave, she was swallowed; and like live prey pressed against stomach lining, everything she'd left behind became muffled. The cave broke her down. She'd been digested ever since.

There was always darkness, but never enough to lose her way in that place. At some point, she found a woman, and the woman had been Mom ever since. She'd been stripped naked and laid out on a slab of stone. Her body wept.

Shelly the waitress returned, plates along her arm. She gave Peter his, and Mary hers.

"How's it looking?"

Mary jabbed her steak till it bled. "The way it should."

Peter smiled and asked dryly, "Can I get a refill?"

Shelly vanished, and returned seconds later with a pitcher of water. As she poured it, her eyes darted back and forth between him and Mary. This would be the last time they'd see her, Mary knew. Shelly was a smart girl. She understood the value of self-preservation, and she didn't need signs to know that, from here on out, she'd be trespassing. Mary was about to open her world to Peter at fucking

Anthony's of all places. Like all things with a compromised immune system, you had to be careful about who or what you invited in.

Shelly said, "I'll be around if you need me," and, leaving the pitcher, went to serve a family of four.

"Up until a few years ago..." Mary stopped and stared at Peter. This was tacky, yet somehow, doing it here made it easier, because it was tacky. It was like when the doctor distracts you before jabbing the needle in. "Up until a few years ago..." She sighed. "I belonged to a place called Goetia."

Peter chewed on his lip. He scooted down the booth, closer to the wall, as if that'd make the world around them smaller, more personal. She did the same.

"Goetia?" he asked.

"It was like a commune. No, actually, it wasn't."

"Okay."

"Well..." A vein bulged in the side of Mary's head. Already, she was at odds with her old programming. "When I was six, Dad and some of his buddies got together for one of their hunting trips and... I can't do this."

Peter raised his eyebrow: "Oh, okay."

"I mean, not here."

Mary huffed and stared at her steak. It was bleeding before her, not all that different from the hunk of meat on Peter's plate. Revelations shouldn't be easy to swallow. They shouldn't be cheap meals shared under cheap lighting, where others might hear. They needed to be told in the dark, amongst desolation; as close as one could get to a deprivation chamber. If she was going to reveal herself to him, it needed to be on her terms, and she hadn't known what they were until just now. Because until just now, her terms had been vague, and her methods, brash and brutish. That way, when she inevitably scared someone off, she could blame them by saying they were too timid, too sensitive. Peter was different. She wanted him to know. She wanted him to stay. And if she was right about him, he probably felt the same way.

"Let's get out of here." Mary's hand shot up and flagged down Shelly. "Get some to-go boxes, and some beers on the way."

Peter nodded and threw the napkin from his lap onto the table. "Yeah, sure. Where are we going?"

Mary shrugged, asked for two boxes and the check, and said, "I'll know it when we see it."

"Driving separately?"

Bless your heart, she thought. *We might get through this yet.*

2

Peter tailed Mary for twenty minutes on his motorcycle after they'd the left restaurant. They were still in Talbot, but beyond the city proper. She was taking him to one of those wastelands you so often see off the side of highways. Those No-Woman's lands where construction companies went to die. Places where it seemed like anything could happen, but so often, nothing did.

Peter often wondered about these places in passing. Now that he was visiting one, he was thinking less of it and more of the person who was taking him there. Mary was connected to the killer in some way? She'd been part of a commune (cult) that was probably connected to the killer in some way, too? And now she was taking him to nowhere in the middle of nowhere to do… what? *Anything,* his mind responded with. She could do anything. She could be anyone.

There were no streetlights on this road. None that worked, at least. They'd gotten off the highway and onto a dusty corridor flanked on both sides by distant lights from better places. It was like they were moving through a hidden hallway, one that ran behind everything. They could see everything. No one could see them.

Peter started to pump the brakes. In his periphery, he'd noticed a turn-off, a way out. He breathed hard into the high collar of his leather jacket. There'd been no orange cones or warning signs that the road was out, or that'd it dead-end. There'd be no reason that, when he got back home, he couldn't change his phone number, or move apartments. There'd be no reason he'd have to face this oncoming train, when like any other well-adjusted individual, he could just hop the tracks.

But he wasn't well-adjusted, was he? He was the prototypical business major with a bad side. To Mary, he could do anything, and he could be anyone. If she wasn't taking him out here to kill him, then she was taking him out here to take him in. How many humans standing hand-in-hand would it take to stop a speeding train?

Peter laid off the brakes and kept going, to where Mary and the moon waited.

As Peter and Mary lay on the hood of her car, cracking open beers, he couldn't help but think that, somehow, this place reflected the surface of the moon. It certainly looked the part. The wasteland glowed lunar. The ground was pockmarked. From the recent rain, reflective, so that it seemed to mirror the lonely satellite above. You didn't need a space shuttle to get to the moon, Peter thought, sucking foam off the can; under the right circumstances, it'd come to you. Every month, with teeth and claws.

"I'm sorry for the theatrics," Mary said, not breaking contact with the constellations. "It got kind of real there for a second."

"It's fine, I get it. Is there something special about this place?" He laughed when he asked this.

"Nope, which is what makes it so special."

Peter held the beer with both hands over his belly. Staring at the moon, he said, "Ready when you are."

"When I was six, Dad and his buddies went hunting. They'd always go up to the forest outside Ansbach. You know where that is?"

Peter hummed, as if he might, but he didn't. He did that a lot.

"It's about forty minutes north of Mare's Diner, give or take. We lived about fifteen miles from Mare's. When they started letting me go hunting with them, we'd stop at Mare's for dinner, or a shake or something. Dad's treat."

"You hunted a lot, I take it?"

"Everywhere, and everything." Mary exhaled slowly. "I didn't go with them, though, this time I'm talking about. It was just Dad and the Boys. Me and Mom stayed home.

"The forest outside Ansbach is easy to get turned around in. It's dense, and dark, and you can't really hear or see anything once you're a half mile deep. They'd been up there a few times before, and last time, Dad had seen something on the way out. A place. Not a building. A place. That's what he'd kept calling it. But the Boys were tired, and they had some fresh kills, and it'd started to rain, so he didn't bother checking it out.

"The next time they went, Dad made sure they found that place again. He'd told me later it was way deeper than he thought. Like years after that, he thought maybe the place he'd found hadn't been the place he'd seen. Like they'd missed it, and he'd gone too far, and found something else, instead. Does that make any sense?"

Peter took a drink of his beer. "Yeah, I get what you're saying."

Mary laughed into her can. The sound echoed outwards across the wasteland. "You know, I've never told this to anyone?"

Peter shook his head. "Sounds like Sharon's going to be a little jealous."

"Sharon." Mary snorted. "Anyway, yeah, so Dad and his buddies found this place in the forest. It was an old, abandoned fort. Totally overgrown. A lot of it had collapsed. Dad said it'd been built during some war, but I don't think we ever found out which. They were supposed to be out there hunting, right?"

"Yeah," Peter said, noticing the excitement rising in Mary's voice.

"They stayed in that fort the whole weekend. Never needed to leave it, because the animals came to them. Well, that's what Dad said, at least. He said deer or rabbits would wander in and lay down, and let them kill them." Mary finished off her can, crushed it, and dropped it on the ground. "Oh boy, stay with me, Peter, okay?"

He turned his head to face her.

She kept her eyes on the heavens. "Dad said the animals wanted them to have them. Dad said them being there, in that place, was a convergence of ley lines. Like it was meant to be. My dad was fucking crazy, if you haven't already guessed."

Liminal space, Peter thought, but kept to himself.

"After that, Dad became obsessed with the place. His buddies, too, but mostly him. I think they were only excited about it because he was. Turned out no one owned that land. And there was an old road that ran near the fort. Still was a hike, even with it. He went back a few more times, too. Said the same thing happened every time. Brought seeds one weekend to plant in the fort, where the ceiling had been blown out. Next weekend? A bunch of ripe tomatoes were waiting for him in that same spot."

"What? Really?" Peter got up on his elbows. "You went, right?"

The wind kicked up something fierce and blew through the wasteland, howling like a banshee. Loose rocks and litter skipped across the ground, in and out of the shadows; the eternal chimes of these manmade craters. Mary, shivering, rolled off the side of the car, got something out of the backseat, and came back with a blanket, which she threw over the both of them as she lay back down on the hood. Her story was going to be told, hypothermia be damned.

"Mom played along at first. Then she got annoyed with him. And then, after he started stocking up on 'survival gear,' she finally agreed to go out there. I went with her, too.

"All I remember about that day is standing in the fort next to that spot I told you about with the tomatoes. Except Dad had all kinds of things growing there. Lettuce. Celery. Pumpkins. Things totally out of season. Mom and Dad were in another room, one Dad said I wasn't old enough to go in."

"The hell?"

"Right? But, yeah, I was standing there, and Mom was laughing and crying, and she had her arms around Dad's neck, and she kept saying, 'Thank you, thank you, thank you.'

"We moved to the fort like six months later. Me and Mom and Dad, and five other families. They got it fixed up. Made it livable. I… ha! I lived in a goddamn commune in the forest outside Ansbach for ten goddamn years, Peter. Bet you didn't see that coming when I sat down next to you in *Intro to Psych.*"

Peter didn't know what to say, so instead, he pulled the blanket tighter and inched up the hood, so that he was laying against the windshield. He opened another a beer and drank for a while. She did the same.

"I'm not going to lie, things were great for a while," Mary said. "It was fun. The other families had kids. We just did whatever we wanted. There was always food. Everyone was so nice. Mom and Dad didn't fight like they used to. And I do remember animals coming into the fort and just laying down. They weren't scared of us. It totally was like it was meant to be.

"But I got older. I had to go to school. Dad did fight with Mom on that for a while, until, I guess, they decided truancy charges weren't worth it. I wasn't allowed to have friends over. I wasn't allowed to tell people where I lived. I'd always go in with bumps and bruises and bug bites, and you know the teachers thought I was being abused. It got really annoying. People started talking. Kids started teasing me. Someone found out. Rumors spread I was dirt poor and living in the woods. All of a sudden I had 'supports' at school I was supposed to go to, and they tried to send me home with canned food and shit. I remember one of my math teachers stopping Dad after school one day, and Dad was so mad, I swear I thought he was going to punch my teacher's head off. It was bad. He was screaming and shoving his finger into my teacher's chest, and I remember he just kept saying, 'You don't tell me what to do. You have no right. Not like I do.'

"More families joined us. We shared everything. Dad and a few of the original guys started calling the place Goetia. It was written somewhere in the fort, he'd said, in that room he never let me go in. That's where they met, him and the other 'founders.'"

Peter asked, "Did you ever figure out what was going on? With the animals and the plants? It sounds too good to be true."

"Once they named it Goetia, it was like it was official," Mary said, "and one point we were up to like twelve families, with a few more who'd come by every week. Dad and the 'founders' started making rules, and going out a lot. He started calling his gang his Demons. It got really bad, Peter. It wasn't a cult at first. I don't know if it ever really turned into one. But Dad and the others in charge worshiped themselves, basically. They'd make contracts with people. Politicians. They'd go do things others wouldn't. Intimidate, and steal, and destroy property, and beat the shit out of people; and I think... I know... they killed."

"Jesus Christ," Peter whispered.

"Whew, blah. Fuck." Mary sat up, hopped off the car, and walked around in circles. "Oh, goddamn."

Peter got down from the car, the blanket wrapped around him. "What?"

"I just..." She put both her hands against her head. "Whew, goddamn. I feel nauseous, but in a good way. All that needed to come out. And that's not even the half of it. Not even a quarter." Mary continued to blow air in relief. "Goddamn."

Peter could tell her story was far from over, but what he couldn't tell was if she had it in her to continue on. Or, if in order for her to do so, he'd have to make an equal trade of terrible secrets. Mary didn't strike him as the giving type.

"Goetia's connected to the Melancons somehow?" he asked.

Mary nodded, said, "Yeah, maybe."

"Maybe one of the families that lived there?"

She shrugged. "I don't know. It wasn't as close-knit as the years went on."

Peter could sense she was putting her guard back up. She was getting impatient, edgy. But they were a part of something, and now, possibly a part of something more. So, he went for it: "When did your mom die?"

Hesitating to answer, she said, "When I was ten."

"When'd you get out of Goetia?"

"Eighteen…"

He took a step closer towards her. "What happened in between?"

Mary's mouth opened, but no words came out. She scrutinized him. And then she turned her back on him. Grabbing another beer, she sucked it down and slung it, half-finished, across the wasteland. It sailed through the shadows, before bouncing off an excavator that'd been parked beside a hole someone had started and likely would never finish digging. The hole swallowed the can. It sounded as if it were hitting other cans on the way down.

Peter felt guilty. He gave Mary the blanket as a peace offering. She took it, her mouth twisting into a smile. He thought about telling her about his Mom—who she was, what she'd done; why he'd had to get away from her. But he didn't. He kept all that to himself. Because in that moment, a dangerous thought entered his mind: What if all of this was Mary's fault?

Mary had a party to plan, and a killer to kill. Why did the former seem so much harder than the latter?

Her apartment was a wreck, too, and that seemed an impossible task in and of itself. Between spending time at work and Peter's, and whatever else she did during those odd hours she still couldn't quite recall, she hadn't given it the attention it needed, and really, deserved. The place was nice, vintage in a way, with high ceilings and tiled walls, original wood molding and flooring, and long windows with aquamarine-colored shutters. An old woman by the name of Laura-Louise used to live here. She'd had the place since it'd been constructed just shy of a century ago. Laura-Louise had been a prominent figurehead in the women's rights movement from the 1950s to the late 1990s. These walls were used to seeing history, not bags of trash and the undersides of feasting flies.

It was cold in here. She'd left a window open in the kitchen. Finding it, she shut it, and then she sat against the counter, knocking over the pile of mail that'd been multiplying there for the last year. Junk mail. Everything was junk mail these days.

The last decent thing Dad had done for her before she got out of Goetia was give her access to a trust fund he'd set up the same day she'd been brought kicking and screaming at 3:00 AM into this world. That was how she'd been able to afford this apartment. That was how she'd been able to pay for college without student loans. That was how she'd been able to change her name and shed the skin of the life she'd lived.

Mary got out a glass, filled it with water, and drank half before dumping the rest in the sink. She knelt down and grabbed some household cleaners from the cabinet underneath. Most of them were empty. She didn't have paper towels. Just a sad looking rag and a stack of napkins she'd stolen from various restaurants. She combined the cleaners into a concoction that made her nose runny. Pocketing the napkins, she picked a place – the kitchen table – and went to work.

Last night felt good. She still felt good because of it. Even with the chemicals she was spraying into the air, she could breathe in a way she hadn't in forever. It was a post-sex kind of high. She had her doubts that it'd been as good for Peter as it'd been for her, though. Not that this was all that surprising. Most of her partners, in one way or another, always accused her of being a selfish lover. Mary often agreed to disagree. She wasn't selfish. She was particular. The conditions had to be right for her to give herself to another. Last night, they'd been right.

When she was finished with the kitchen table, the clump of napkins in her hand came away like a bunch of used tampons. Old food, and stains, and the top layer of red paint seemed to be coming off. She wondered if, elsewhere in the apartment, she'd encounter the same problem: the surfaces giving way.

Mary opened up one of the many garbage bags in the kitchen and threw the napkins in. The smell of rotting food hit her hard. It was a struggle getting the bag closed again. There was about a month's worth of trash in the place. Maybe more.

Going to the furthest window, the one with the fire escape mounted beside it, she opened it up and stepped outside. The steel grating moaned underneath her weight. Leaning over the railing, she saw that, yes, the dumpster was still there, and still open. It'd been that way for the last two weeks.

Mary dragged garbage bag after garbage bag across the kitchen, out onto the fire escape, and then flung them over the railing, to the dumpster below. Most of them met their mark. Those that didn't, didn't. The smell was awful, strength-sapping. To distract herself, she thought about last night. What she told Peter. What she hadn't.

He was clever. Maybe not smart. But clever. He'd caught on to the fact that Mom's death hadn't been the thing to drive her from Goetia. She'd spent eight more years there after that. Mary wondered what he'd made of that, what kind of scenarios he'd come up with on his lonely ride home. Regardless, he had to think differently of her now. And it had been that exact reason in the past she'd never told anyone about her childhood. This time was different. This time, she felt as if it gave her the upper-hand. Whether it was over Peter, the killer, or the both of them, she wasn't sure. Her not-so-distant past was part of this, though. It was the splinter in her mind she'd been hoping to pass. It wasn't going anywhere. She knew that now. Either she would tear it free and wield it like the weapon it was, the way it'd been wielded against her by everyone she'd known and who knew; or the killer would take her by the chin and hammer it in for good—the final nail in her coffin; naivety masquerading as normalcy.

Next time I see him, I'll tell him the rest, she said to herself, tossing the last garbage bag over the railing. It missed the dumpster completely, exploding as it hit the ground into a bright red display of fetid decomposition. *I'll tell him about the drugs. The rituals.* She laughed at that. Rituals. A bunch of grown ass men swinging dick and making things up as they went. *Their wives ate it up, though. Guess I did, too.*

Mary closed the window and was about to wash her hands when someone started pounding on her front door. She stopped in her tracks. She wasn't expecting deliveries. She never had guests. Mary got her gun.

"Who is it?" she cried, coming into the living room.

No answer. Her visitor kept pounding. The deadbolt rattled. The chain lock danced.

"Hey! Asshole!" Mary trained the pistol on the door with perfect trigger discipline. Not everything taught to her in Goetia had soured. "Did you...?"

"Mary? I didn't hear you. It's Detective Sono."

She hadn't heard his voice in a while, but his was the kind of voice you didn't need to hear more than once to remember. It was raspy and high-pitched; he always sounded as if he'd just finished smoking a carton, after running a marathon.

Mary checked the peephole. There he was, Detective Sono, in blue slacks, a white shirt, and a leather jacket, a manila folder tucked under his arm. He was growing his hair out. He'd been bald last time she'd seen him. Now he was somewhere north of a #1. Or he'd stopped caring about his appearance. She hoped that was the case. He was going to want to come in.

Quickly stashing the pistol in a vase with fake flowers, she said, "Hang on," and then: "Detective," as she pulled open the door.

Detective Sono's nose twitched. He gave her the up-down. He wasn't a subtle man, or a sensitive man. She'd appreciated that about him. Now, she had a feeling she was going to regret it.

"Something new?" she asked.

"Yes. Let's sit."

Mary semi-blocked the doorway with her body. "It's disgusting in here. I just now started getting myself together. It's been a hard couple of weeks."

"You've been going to your therapist."

It was a statement, not a question.

"There are other resources we can tap into for you."

Mary went sideways. "That might be a good idea. Yeah, sure, come in."

Mary headed him off. He shut the door behind him. She sat on the couch, sprawled out across it like a self-absorbed desert queen, so that he'd have no choice but to sit on the nearest chair. The whole thing looked absolutely ridiculous, as if she were auditioning for some mid '90s romantic comedy. She dabbed her head on the sleeve of her shirt. Being coy always made her sweat. It didn't come naturally to her.

Detective Sono slapped the manila folder down on the coffee table. "How's Peter?"

Bobbing her eyebrows: "You following us around?"

"My men were. To make sure you weren't being followed. I told you we'd do that."

Had he? That night and morning after the incident… All she could remember from it was stale coffee and fluorescent lights, and pens writing scratchily.

"We're doing the best we can," she said.

Detective Sono stared at her for a moment. It wasn't pity in those bloodshot eyes of his but suspicion. "Do you know Ambrose Dickson?"

That was an easy no. Name like that you wouldn't soon forget it. "No, I…"

"Goes by Guy."

Shit.

"Also liked to be called Purveyor."

Shit. Her guy, Guy, used to go by that when Goetia was still up and running. He said it 'fit the mood, man'.

Detective Sono carefully opened the manila folder so she couldn't see what else was in there and removed a glossy 11x16 with Guy's gap-toothed grille placed front and center. If there'd been any doubt of his identity, the tattoo of Goetia's symbol on the side of his neck would easily clear things up. God, she hadn't seen it in a while; and seeing it now, it awoke something in her. It put a fire in her belly, and filled her nose with spices and vapors. The interlocked circles, and the scratchy line work linking them, gave her an acute sense of vertigo. For a moment, she felt as if she might fall into the photo. "Fall into the flesh," as Dad used to say it. "Fall into the flesh, and meet the demon within."

"Look familiar, Mary?" He gave her a second, and then: "You met him earlier in the week outside a known trap house in the Old Country."

That's decent of you. Springing the traps right before my eyes, just so I don't walk into them. Next level detective work right there.

"I bought weed off him," she said, not wanting him to take her gun.

Detective Sono chewed on his lip. "How'd you know him?"

"I mean, when you're in the Old Country, you can't take five steps without bumping into a drug dealer."

"Guy's dead, Mary."

So this is what passed for foreplay in the Sono household? The fire in Mary's gut went out; the bomb he dropped smothering it in the ashes of its aftermath.

"We found him a day later, in a shed behind that trap house. He'd been stripped naked. Someone had stirred his guts into soup with a butcher knife. That tattoo?" He tapped Guy's neck on the photo. "Removed."

"Fuck me," Mary said, finally sitting up right.

Detective Sono opened the manila folder. There was another photograph of Goetia's symbol. A forest. Holy shit, the old fort. And then… ghosts.

Mary didn't hide her surprise well. She might've, if it hadn't been for last night, but she'd let her guard down, opened her world up. She hadn't become immune to Goetia like she thought she had, only ignorant of it.

She called them ghosts, the people in the photographs, because that's what they used to call the members of Goetia who'd fallen into the flesh. "Ghosts of their former selves," Dad had told her, because at the time, she didn't understand the rhetoric. There were five ghosts here. Most she recognized, one she didn't. Lucy, David, Randy, and Sofia.

The one she couldn't place was the one Detective Sono had his thumb on. "Celeste." He stared at her, waiting for to make the connection. "Celeste Melancon."

"What?" Mary stared at the photograph so intensely that she almost burned a hole through it. "What?" She'd searched up Celeste Melancon on social media. That woman didn't look like her, until it did. "W-What is this?"

"Do you know this symbol?" he asked, referring to the brand of Goetia.

Quickly, she said, "No."

Detective Sono slumped and sighed. There was disappointment in the darkness under his eyes. She didn't need to lie to him; in fact, she shouldn't have. He was only trying to help her. But that was the thing about Goetia. It was Theirs, and the more you shared it, the less it was Yours. It hadn't been perfect. She'd left it for a reason. But, like riding a bike, once you learn about it, nothing short of a full-blown lobotomy could make you forget it. Dad always called Goetia "a place" and it was, not only on Earth, but in the fibers of your being.

Got to work to earn your paycheck, she thought, defiantly.

"Goetia—it was a commune not far from here a few years back," he said. "These five here belonged to it, along with Guy, as far as I can tell. They're all dead. We barely made the connection between the cases. They'd happened over the last two years, and not all of them in this state. In each murder, the victims had been stripped naked, cleaned, gutted with a knife, and had the symbol of Goetia removed. Crime scenes were always messy, with the families being murdered as well. But I think it's clear now the killer, or killers, had a target in mind with each of these cases.

"The Ansbach Sheriff was working the area back when Goetia was up and running. I've been working closely with him to nail down the other members."

Mary asked, "Do you think it's a revenge thing?"

"That's a lot of grudges." Detective Sono shook his head. "No, I think someone is working their way down the line." He eyed her neck and said plainly, "Mary."

He knew. She knew he knew. He was doing his damndest not to plant the seed of suggestion in case he was wrong. But he wasn't. He knew he wasn't.

"You changed your name when you turned eighteen," he said, closing the folder. "That's about when Goetia shut down. I'm guessing that's about the time you left, too. I know you've been keeping this from me, but I'm not mad at you."

Not mad at me? Is he patronizing me?

"It was another life, and up until a month ago, you'd left it behind."

What is this? You sound like Sharon.

"It was a small community. A lot of its members are already dead. So far, no one's talking. But if you were there…"

Here it comes.

"… you could help a lot of other people, especially yourself and Peter, if you tell…"

"Honestly, I don't remember much," Mary said. "I think I blocked most of it out." She picked up the folder, flipped through it to add to the act. "I'm sorry. If I remember anything…"

This was the part in the cheap, overly color-corrected police procedurals where the investigator would stand up and thank her for her time. Detective Sono glared at her. He wasn't budging. He'd exhausted what little patience and kindness he'd built up in his reserves over the years. That wasn't her fault, though. He should've known better to waste it on someone like her.

"Your dad was one of the ringleaders."

There weren't any "ringleaders" in Goetia. That's not how it worked, asshole.

"Most of his Demons…"

You know more… You think… I'm a suspect now.

"… Beth, Johnny, Solomon… are locked up in Alkali. Marilyn's been off the grid for years. Leon's got a warrant out for his arrest for solicitation. I know what happened to your mother. I visited her grave to be sure."

Mary's cheek twitched, thought: *Should've brought a shovel to be sure.* She'd started rolling up the folder in her hand. She'd seen a movie where someone tried to jam a rolled-up newspaper down someone's throat. She thought about that now.

"I don't know where Dad is," she said, her chest shaking as she spoke. "The last time I saw him was in my rear-view mirror."

In the rear-view mirror, as she drove away, his shape sinisterly dark against fire and smoke. She'd had his blood on her hands. He'd had hers on his. They'd just finished slaughtering sheep who'd come so willingly.

"I figured he died," she added. "He was an idiot. A survivalist nut who didn't know the first thing about surviving. He thought he could live 'outside the system,'" she scoffed.

"Why would you think he's dead?"

Mary crossed her arms. "He was an idiot. A lot of people didn't like him. No, I don't remember who. He's dead, because he never came looking for me."

"You changed your name, but not your locale," Detective Sono said. "Hiding in plain sight is still just that."

She'd had enough. Mary stood, smiling a fake smile, and said, "Before you leave here, let's just be clear: You're insinuating my dad is the killer."

Detective Sono stared up at her, his green eyes flecked with reptilian calculations. "No, unless you've got reason to think your dad would want to kill you."

"No, he wouldn't," she said, and that was the truest thing she'd said today.

"If he's not dead, then whoever is doing this could be looking for him next." Detective Sono made it towards the door. "Is that reason enough to 'remember'?"

"I'm still alive."

"And I'll be watching closely to keep it that way, Mary," he said, heading out. "I hate to say it, but you're not out of the woods yet."

Cute phrasing. She went to the door, started to close it.

"There's a full moon this Saturday. The others were killed on a full moon as well, Guy excluded. What are your plans with Peter this weekend?"

"We're going to throw a small get-together at his place."

"That's good. That's smart."

"Want to come?"

Detective Sono ran his hands through his stubble. "You know I'll be there in one form or another. Mary?"

She'd almost had the door shut. "What, Detective?"

"Where's your dog?"

Mary cocked her head and laughed. "It's around here some-where," she said, and then she shut the door.

FRIDAY, OCTOBER 30TH, 2020

Peter was in charge of the invitations, because according to Mary, she had no friends, except for those that came in glass bottles. That was fine with him. The more he learned about her, the more he worried about the people whom she might associate herself with. Sure, he wasn't any better, having been born of the Old Country. But that was one thing. Her thing was something else.

He hadn't slept well since the wasteland. His stomach had been in knots. Every time he tried to untie it with a bit of logic and reason, a slow drip of anxiety, like acid, always managed to eat away his efforts. One part of him was grateful to have a better understanding of what'd led up to the events at Mare's Diner, but the other part? The other part didn't appreciate having the 't's crossed and the 'i's dotted, because all of it alluded to something greater, grander. That was the thing about anxiety, he'd come to realize, that it was never satisfied. Every answer was met with another question, and every question, unreasonable answers.

Peter strolled down one of the massive, shipping lane-like aisles of Canto's, a superstore on the edge of the Old Country. Stocked with every want and need a red-blooded human could hope for, it wasn't uncommon to hear about people living in the store, moving from aisle to aisle to avoid detection. They'd pretend to shop during the day, and sleep by night in one of the lesser frequented departments, like Outdoor Decorations or Cycling. Good for them.

Mom used to work at Canto's, back when it was just a "store."

She'd come home with a weekly paycheck that barely made ends meet, and a purse full of toys she'd pilfered from the Kids department for Peter. "Manager doesn't believe in raises," she'd say, as she gave him the latest and greatest action figure. "He'll get a write-off. It's a win-win for everyone." The manager had gotten a write off. Mom, too—written right off the payroll into unemployment.

The superstore was dead. You'd have to put your ear to the ground to hear the weak pulse of the people milling about. It was nine in the morning, but still, that wasn't the way things used to be. Peter had made a conscious effort to come here, because Mom's voice and Mary's story had given him a kind of nostalgia that memory alone wouldn't cure. It was so easy to assume that, because things had been bad back in his day, things would be bad in the days to come. Truth be told, he missed these people, his people. They were flawed, but who wasn't? For all their unpredictable ways, they were all that more predictable because of them; and in that, he'd found some comfort. There weren't any Marys running the streets, with communes and killers riding their coattails. Or werewolves bounding through the alleys and backyards, in service to their mistress, the moon. But maybe there were. Not as far as he knew, though.

Damn. "These people?" He didn't want to refer to them as "these people." It was that same separation of class and trash that'd led to a place like the Old Country in the first place. He got it. That was the way humans made sense of things.

What the hell's wrong with me? He felt like a missionary touring some third-world country, gawking at it as if behind glass at a zoo. But whose life was he visiting? His, or what he'd thought Mary's had been? And why the hell was he comparing them? *I'm such a dick.*

Peter swept through Entertainment, checking out the newest releases, and after passing through the gutted Back to School section, stopped at his final destination: Sports and Outdoors. In less than a minute, you could fill your cart with a video game, some crayons, and a handgun. Canto's was never known for its tasteful layouts. When in the Old Country…

Out of his comfort zone, and not seeing a store associate behind the counter where the ammunition was kept, Peter camped out in Camping and started sending out text invitations for the get-together tomorrow. It took a few minutes. He didn't have any close friends, only casual acquaintances. A lot of buddies he'd get drinks with after work or class. He knew them by the memes they sent, and the plans they planned with their better friends and significant others. He did laugh with them a lot. They did quote old comedies a lot.

Then there was Mary. In a way, there had always been Mary. She hadn't so much inserted herself into his life, as she had filled the Mary-shaped hole that'd been there for as long as he could remember. He didn't have a crush on her. He didn't love her. He didn't know what he thought about her; and because she was more a question than an answer, he wanted to be rid of her.

Fucking Intro to Psych, he said to himself, sending out the last text to his bro, Chad Bradley. *Stop. Analyzing. Things.*

"Sir, can I help you?"

Peter snapped out of it and slipped his phone into his pocket. A store associate by the name of John was standing at the counter, a paper cup of coffee steaming in his grip.

Peter smiled and, trying to sound nonchalant, said, "I need some silver bullets."

"You got an ID on you?"

He approached the counter and handed over his driver's license.

"Alright, Peter. What kind of bullets?"

He smiled sheepishly.

"Is it a pistol?"

"… Yes?"

"You want to double-check and let me know? You might not know it, but ammunition isn't cheap. Twenty bucks a pop for a silver bullet."

Peter cringed. This was his first stop of a few to go. And he was fairly sure he didn't have a paycheck coming next week. If he made it to next week.

John leaned over the counter. Voice dropping to a thick whisper, he said, "You going werewolf hunting?"

Peter grinned.

"You hunting that werewolf?"

"Which… one…" Peter leaned in and matched this retired trucker's timbre. "Which one we talking about here, John?"

"The Beast of Stubbe Street."

Peter nodded and, choked up, said, "Yeah, yep. That's it."

Stubbe Street. One mile of ranch-style homes along a serpentine swell. He knew it well. Because he used to live there.

John the store associate gave Peter a discount on account of him being a fellow cryptohunter. He got six bullets, and then bailed before committing to John's grill-out this weekend.

Next up: Maiden, Mother, and Crone—a Wicca haunt.

Peter pulled into the unfinished parking lot, sweating bullets (if only they were silver, and also, real). The Beast of Stubbe Street. This was it. Exactly what he'd been looking for. A connection. Nothing was random. Everything had meaning. Someone was to blame.

Stubbe Street. The name carried itself like a curse, heavy and foreboding. He could see it well: pale asphalt pitted with potholes; uneven sidewalks held together by weeds; front yards, yellowed and parched, with dead grass lying flatly, like crop circles, from the cheap plastic pools left to stagnate there all summer. He could smell it, too: the cloying scent from the always-lit, cheap, convenience store cigars; rubber; and food, fast, fried, or otherwise, drifting from open windows and screen doors.

That was Stubbe Street during the day, though. Night was different. Night was shadows and streetlight-amber, and movement. It was simultaneously the eye and the storm itself. In each house and apartment building, chaos and order. Everywhere was a landmark. It was like a suburb turned inside out. Everyone knew everything about everyone. You had to. You couldn't afford not to.

Peter killed the engine and got out of the car. He stood in the shadow of Maiden, Mother, and Crone. He was just as out of place in front of it as it was between those storefronts that surrounded it. To its left: Good and Lubed, an auto store. To its right: Dragon Paradise, a nail salon He couldn't believe Good and Lubed was still open, actually. The owners had been on the news a few months back. They'd been busted for human trafficking. How was that for checking your assumptions?

Stepping into Maiden, Mother, and Crone was like stepping into the past. It was dark, and the air was heavy with incense that smelled like burning and made him want to nap. From the floors, the walls, to the shelves themselves, everything was fashioned from either recovered wood or stone. Also, plants. There were too many to count. They formed corridors. It wasn't long until he felt as if he were moving through a hut that'd been partially overtaken by a forest. It was like he'd stumbled into another realm, a small pocket of space separate from Talbot, from the Old Country. It was the Old, Old Country. When beasts outnumbered man. And you could still see all the stars in the sky.

"Hello," a woman said softly, coming from around the bend.

She was older, with white hair held up in braids. She wore a black shirt with a pentagram on the front, and faded jeans that sagged lopsidedly around her hips. On her feet, sneakers. On her hands and wrists, enough rings and bracelets an Old World jewel thief could have a field day with.

"My name's Parker. This is your first time here, isn't it?"

Peter smiled. "Yeah. What gave me away?"

"You're not a regular. Everyone who isn't a regular usually looks lost when they come in."

"It's great, but it is a little overwhelming."

"It shouldn't be. That's a shame, isn't it? That the natural way of things inspires discomfort." Parker gestured for him to follow, and he followed.

Peter didn't know what he was looking at, but he did his best. The store's inventory came at him in waves. Statues, of goddesses and fairies and demonic entities. Plants and roots, some fresh, others dried out, in handmade baskets. Then came stones and minerals, in every shape and color; some clouded, others metallic; all nestled safely in their respective places, placards above each describing their purposes. Books, too; so many books; some were new, others covered in dust; with thick covers and thick pages, and spines that spoke of spells and conjurations, women's rights, nature, and how to (truly) live. He saw clothing – dresses, pants, scarves, gloves, head wraps, and more – with price tags that made him do a double-take. And then, in passing as they passed, a darker corner, candlelit and filled with incense, where an altar had been placed, and things, like amulets, were suspended above it, winking out magical temptations.

Parker led them back to the check-out, which bothered him. The tablet and her cell phone beside it dispelled, for a moment, the illusion he was elsewhere. Time travel was the anxious' only true coping skill.

Taking out a deck of tarot cards and shuffling them, she said, "Care for a reading?"

He shook his head. "No, uh, no thank you. I..." He laughed at himself.

Parker put down the deck, picked up a bottle of soda, and took a swig. "You can say it. Take solace in knowing that of anywhere in this city, you can say it here."

"Were…" He corrected himself to sound more in-the-know. "Lycanthropes. Lycanthropy."

Parker's freckles came together on her face as she squinted at him. "I know you."

"I was on the news…"

"That's it. Mm. That's it." She set the soda down, and sat. "Come."

He went around the desk and sat in the seat next to her.

She took his hands and held them. "The murders at that diner."

"Oh, no." Peter pulled his hands away. "No, no. I'm not a werewolf. That wasn't me."

"I know." Parker took his hands again and ran her fingers over the lines in his palms. "I knew there was something more to all of that."

"Yeah, there was… is. A werewolf. I didn't really tell the police that part."

"They wouldn't know what to do even if you did."

It felt good to talk to someone else about this who wasn't Mary. He leaned into Parker and said, "I think it's the Beast of Stubbe Street. What do I do?"

"Lycanthropy is parasitism, biological, psychological, and social. When humans were hunters and gatherers, we were the invasive species, the parasites. We skinned and sustained ourselves on beasts, but in some animals, and in this case, wolves, there developed a defense mechanism. We depended upon them, and they developed a way to become dependent upon us. Exposure to wolf hide triggered a bond, a growth. Lycanthropy. Some humans became as wolves and hunted humans on behalf of wolves, to kill where they could not. The transformations were limited, so that the human thralls to the wolves would return to their normal selves, and thus make themselves more useful over a longer period of time. If they stayed werewolves forever, they would quickly be killed. The most effective parasite is the one that goes unnoticed."

Fuck, Peter thought, *that makes so much sense.*

"It's different these days, though. Humans don't live the way they used to. They don't need to, except in certain parts of the world. But the parasites are still out there. Either through exposure, or in some cases, genetics. Lycanthropy is more psychiatric in nature now, but I believe there are still those who undergo the full transformation. The thing is, Peter, that werewolves, like wolves, have their dens, their territories."

"So, there're two werewolves then? Stubbe Street is a long way from Mare's Diner."

"Possibly." Parker squeezed his hands. "Or it's not about geography anymore for them, the werewolves. The territory is within. Within the ones they hunt."

He shivered. "Like a name on a list. Okay, but if that's the case, then what happens if it kills everyone it needs to?"

"An animal attacks when it feels threatened," Parker said. "It'll feel safe again, I think."

"But I haven't done anything to anyone!"

Parker laid Peter's hands on his knees. "Threats are threats, whether they're real or perceived."

"Fuck." He started to rock back and forth, and picked up speed, as if to match the beating of his throbbing heart. "Fuck, what do I do?"

Parker leaned back, pulled out a joint, lit it, and passed it to him. "Smoke that, and then we'll see."

SATURDAY, OCTOBER 31ST, 2020

1

There was something sad about parties, Mary thought, while she stared at the bottom of her red solo cup, the meaning of life likely somewhere in that swill. The idea of cramming a bunch of people together and forcing them at alcohol-point to get along didn't make much sense to her. Sure, she could play the part. She'd always been able to play the part. That'd been part of being a daughter of Goetia and maintaining that "blessed" place. But the small talk? The bad jokes? The body odor and halitosis? It was all one mating ritual, either to fuck, or fuck someone over. In the end, they were all wolves in sheep's skin.

This party of theirs, though? It was especially sad, and it wasn't a party. It was like when well-meaning, out-of-the-loop parents throw a birthday bash for their special little girl, inviting everyone from their class, only to have no one show, except for the odd family member— the disheveled uncle who gifts gift cards and the aunt with the greasy top knot, who pays out with checks and hard candy. Nobody showed up that was supposed to have. Not a single one of Peter's so-called friends, which meant he either had far fewer friends than he'd boasted, or he, and by association, her, were contagious. You see, people were supposed to come running at the first whiff of tragedy. But they weren't tragic, were they? They were traumatic. The traumatized weren't fun, or romantic. They were work. Only the truly dedicated came running to people like Mary and Peter. And trust, they had their ears to the ground.

All wasn't lost. Like any party, you could always count on the uninvited to fill out the ranks. Peter's neighbors had filed in one after the other, as if the cracking open of a cold beer had sounded throughout the apartment building like a dinner bell.

First, Ms. Panina, the only other occupant on his floor. She was foreign. Mary couldn't place the accent because the woman didn't talk enough to give her a chance to. She was thirty, or sixty. From the front, she looked as if she'd been cut from leather. But from the back, with those high-schooler hand-me-downs, it was anyone's guess. She'd brought her own beer, though, so she had that going for her.

The others, Vanslow and Hearn, lived on the first and second floor. Now they were on the floor, literally, mopping up a mess they'd made when Hearn had backed into the table and knocked a half-full cup and a bowl of snacks onto the ground. The two must've been close. They looked close enough to be brothers, what with their jet-black hair and matching moustaches, and swishing tracksuits. They bickered like brothers, too.

"Got to watch where you're going," Vanslow said, on paper towel duty.

Hearn, with a fistful of pretzels and chips, said, "Don't start on me, V. I just want to have a nice night with our new friends."

Coming in from the kitchen with a garbage bag, Peter said, "Guys, it's fine. Really." He flashed an awkward smile at Mary.

She shrugged one shoulder and turned to face the window that overlooked the Main Drag. Across the way, weekend warriors were lined up around the block to get into the theater, Midian. Tonight, the marquee read: *The Beasts of Backwater* and *Death is Silver and Sharp*. A spaghetti western and a giallo slasher. It was crazy how similar their titles always were to bad heavy metal lyrics.

Pressing her forehead to glass, she looked straight down. Somewhere on this street was Detective Sono, keeping watch. After his visit the other day, she simultaneously liked him a little less and a little more than she had before. Where the line was drawn, and when, she couldn't say.

The window started to rattle. Ms. Panina had turned on some music with enough bass to shake the building to its foundations.

Where are you?

She searched the city for the killer. Her Killer. This was their night, after all. Sure, if he had any sense, he'd wait until tomorrow, break the pattern. But addictions can't wait, and neither can ritual. The moon was full. And with a room full of people, though not as many as she'd expected, the challenge was set. He'd come for her, because he had to. She was next on his list, maybe even the last. The last of Goetia. There was something oddly empowering about being on the brink of extinction. It hadn't always been Mary's plan to use the others for bait, but like most times in her life, it always seemed to work out that way all the same.

2

Esther Panina knew a bitch when she saw one. Tonight, Mary was that bitch.

Slowly sipping on her cheap, local beer, Esther turned on some jams, got comfortable on the couch, and watched Ms. Mary Quite Contrary from out the corner of her eye. She was Peter's girl. But she wasn't Peter's woman.

Today was Esther's birthday. At the stroke of midnight, she would officially be thirty-nine. When Peter had come to her door a few hours ago, she thought for a second someone had remembered. "Ms. Panina," he'd said, "I need a favor." He was throwing a party. None of the guests were going to show. She didn't ask for explanations. The poor boy had been through enough as it was. When he'd handed her a twenty as a bribe, she handed it back. "Go get me a six pack of something cheap." She would've spent the money on beer, anyway; and she didn't go out at night.

This Mary was trouble, though. She was dark. That's how Grandpa used to describe people like her. "They got dark," he'd say, as if it were something you could touch or see. He'd wag his finger (even now, she could still hear him chewing on pumpkin seeds) and say, "They got dark. Leave them be, leave them be. They got it. You'll get it, too."

Esther watched Vanslow and Hearn crawl around on the floor like a bunch of bugs. She'd lived in this building for six years. They'd been here for the last two. They were strange, but harmless. Gay, too. They lived in separate apartments. Esther's Grandpa and Grandma used to sleep in separate beds, but separate apartments? Well, if Grandpa and Grandma could have afforded it, they would have probably done the same

Peter came by, looking busy. "Doing okay?" he asked.

"Doing great!" she shouted over a rumbling bassline.

Peter nodded. Some sweat leapt off his brow. He hurried over to Mary. They looked out the window together, as if they were expecting someone.

Esther got up. Just being around Mary made her uneasy, so it was no wonder Peter looked so stressed. All that dark. Like a black hole.

She made her way into the kitchen. There wasn't much to it, but she didn't expect anything less from a man. White plates and bowls. One oven mitt. No magnets on the refrigerator. A little plant by the windowsill, overwatered.

If only she could be so barebones, she thought. Most of her walls were covered in picture frames of family members, angels, and Jesus Christ. Once you put things like that up, it's hard to take them down. It was disrespectful.

Esther was a snoop. She knew it, and she was proud of it. Drinking while she did so, she went through Peter's cabinets, pantry, refrigerator (depressingly empty, as she expected), and even his garbage. There wasn't too much in there. No way was Peter usually this clean. This last month, she could smell him when he came from work in the hallway. No way was he usually this clean. But maybe he was. Smelled pretty in here. That wasn't Mary's doing, she was sure of that.

"Ms. Panina?" Peter said behind her.

Caught, but certainly not embarrassed, Esther stopped rooting through the garbage.

"Did you drop something?"

Esther crushed her beer can and slipped it into the garbage.

"I'm sorry," he said. "I know this is really lame. Mary and me just wanted to do something to take our minds off things. Thanks for coming…"

The doorbell rang.

Peter turned white as wool. Around the corner, Esther caught sight of Mary. She looked the same, and also, fierce.

"B-Be right back," Peter said, patting himself down, looking for something he must have forgotten.

Esther stayed in the kitchen. Before answering the door, Peter and Mary disappeared into his room for a second. They looked even more suspicious. Like bank robbers

Esther shifted herself to get a better view of the door. When Peter opened it, she wanted to see if it was the woman who kept showing up outside his apartment at night. The tall one with the long hair and long nails. The one that smelled like dog.

3

Peter had his silver knife in one pocket, and Parker's potion in the other. Mary was strapped, her gun loaded with silver bullets. Someone was knocking at the front door. He had a peep hole, but it was too clouded over to see through. He gave Mary a nod. She gave him one back.

And then, heart beating louder than the music, he opened the door.

No killers.

Just Katie. His crush. Wearing cheap plastic cat ears.

Almost fainting, he stammered, "K-Katie? H-Hey, what… what's up? What're you doing here?"

"You're having a party, right?" she asked, smiling hard, as she tucked a strand of her long, blonde hair behind her ear. "Thanks for not inviting me." She mouthed *Gosh* and playfully punched his arm. "I brought some friends. Is that okay?"

She had, hadn't she? He hadn't even seen them there, standing behind her. Such a thing happens, though, when you stare too long at the sun. But there they were, coupled: Beth and Brian; Cindy and Stu. He'd met them once or twice. They were unremarkable in every regard. The kind of people who only talk about where they work and their plans six months from now. And you know what? That's exactly what Peter needed right now. Something basic, defanged and declawed. If he was going to die tonight, let it be death by boredom.

Peter invited them in. Mary stepped aside, and then drifted down the hall, as if to be away from them. At first, she seemed annoyed, but after a moment, doing what appeared to be some mental math, she returned.

"Katie?" she said. "*The* Katie?"

Katie smiled at Mary, but she didn't seem impressed with what she'd seen so far. Peter knew the look. She'd come expecting a good time, not the wake of a good time. He had to think quick to keep her here.

"That's me," Katie said, her skin turning red from the heat. She'd come out of the cold with no coat. A seasoned partier.

"Can I get you a-anything?" Peter said.

Mary pressed on. "Peter told me all kinds of good things about you."

Beth, Brian, Cindy, and Stu broke around Peter, their sights fixed on the snack bowls sandwiched between Vanslow and Hearn.

"Ah, Peter," Katie said, rolling her eyes. And then to Mary: "Who are you?"

Mary smiled at Katie, vacantly.

Peter said, "Hang on." He killed the music, and grabbing a cold one to calm his nerves, spoke to the room. "Alright, everybody…"

The murmuring died down. Katie's friends, with fistfuls of pretzels and potato chips, did their best to muffle their chewing. Ms. Panina came out of the kitchen, a dishrag in hand. It was soapy and wet.

"As people are coming in, we're going to take this thing out of here. The building's more or less empty, and there's a lot more on the way. The, uh, roof's—" he opened his beer; foam hissed over his fidgeting fingers, "—cold, but it's pretty decent. Good… good view and…"

Katie called from the cringing audience, "Where's your costume?"

And Mary told her, "He's wearing it."

Peter smiled, took a drink, quickly turned the music back on, and hated himself for having forgotten it was Halloween.

4

Vanslow couldn't stop staring at the crack of Hearn's ass. It excited him as much as it irritated him. Hearn was bent over—God, when wasn't he? —picking up the fragments of a picture frame that big ass of his had bumped into during this impromptu exodus. Two years was a long time, especially when you lived in the same building, yet slept in separate beds, in separate apartments. It was supposed to have been a break. Now, he wasn't so sure. It felt more like punishment disguised as atonement. That was Hearn, though, wasn't it? Always the first to the cross, nails in one hand, hammer in the other, a frown or a smile upon his face, depending upon where you knelt to deal the first blow.

Grabbing his hoodie off the couch, Vanslow followed the others out of Peter's apartment. Hearn was up ahead, sandwiched between the newcomers and the one called Mary. He was fairly certain that hadn't been her name back in junior high. He couldn't recall it now, but all the same, he recognized her. He'd literally bumped into her in the stairwell three weeks back, and she'd rattled, yes, rattled, like a pharmacy during an earthquake. It'd taken him a minute, but he was good with faces. Hers had been the one with the dirt on her cheeks. They used to make fun of her for that. "You guys don't have bathtubs in Crazy Town?" some of his friends would yell at her. Always from a distance, though. She'd been a twig, but her fists were rockhard. She got into so many fights back then, that when she stopped showing up to class, most just assumed she'd been expelled.

"I'm inviting some people, okay?" Katie announced to Peter from the head of the line as they shambled down the dim hallway.

Peter glanced back at Mary. Vanslow couldn't see her face, but he could tell she was nodding. This was Peter's show, but she was the one pulling all the strings.

Vanslow tried to move past Katie's friends to get to Hearn, but they were too busy taking pictures of themselves, the flashes from their cameras going off one after the other. It called to mind red carpet rollouts. Everyone was a celebrity these days.

"Honey?" Hearn said, planting himself, letting the millennials break over him.

Ever the dutiful servant, Vanslow caught up with him, and then kept pace as Hearn kept going after the rest of the group.

"What?" Vanslow asked.

"It's going to be so cold up there."

"We don't have to go up."

"I want to, though."

Vanslow must've sighed or rolled his eyes, or made some microscopic muscle movement, because the next thing he knew, Hearn was pissed.

"What?" Vanslow said, defensively. "What did I do now?"

Hearn huffed. "Just go back if you're not having a good time."

"I'm fine. This is fine. What are you…? Are you even having a good time?"

"I'm trying!" Hearn showed his hands, which were covered in tiny cuts from where he'd picked up the glass off the floor.

Vanlsow took his hands in his. Doing so, his face went hot, and he got hard. It was fucking ridiculous. He'd gone so deep into celibacy these last two years, he should've just joined the priesthood and gotten paid for his pain. He didn't even jerk off. He was saving himself in every way. Except from him.

"I'll get your jacket," Vanslow said as Hearn pulled his wounds away.

Hearn said, "Thanks," gave him his keys, and went up the stairs that led to the roof.

Vanslow made his way down the stairs to the second floor. The building shifted and wailed as he went, the howling wind coming through all the cracks and crevices. The lights flickered on and off. Appropriate for Halloween, but annoying any other night. Their absent landlord hadn't shown her face around here in years. Maintenance wasn't much better. They came at odd hours, though more frequently this last month. New guy, always listening to music with those bubblegum pink headphones of his. Despite his best efforts, nothing seemed to take. The lights barely worked, the whole place smelled like an animal shelter, and all the empty apartments had busted locks, which meant they kept finding places wide open. None of this surprised Vanslow all that much, though. Whatever the building had, it was terminal.

It got darker the closer he came to Hearn's apartment. But for the moonlight coming through the window at the end of the hall, he had nothing to work with but his sense of smell. Hearn had it bad for cheap air fresheners, especially apple cinnamon. When they were together, anytime Vanslow smelled something similar, his heart would beat faster and he'd smile. Now, it just made him sad.

He found the door, put the key in. Before he unlocked it, he considered making a quick trip to the hardware store to make a copy. But when the door opened on its own, apparently already unlocked, he shoved the thought aside.

"Huh," he said, pushing the door open to more darkness. "And you bitched at me for forgetting to put the garage door down."

Vanslow went in to the apartment, pawed the wall for the light switch, and flipped it. A light came on. Not from above but in front of him. A flashlight, shining directly in his eyes.

"Jesus Christ!" he shouted, blinded. "What…"

Vanslow's words ran with his blood from the sudden slit in his throat. He pressed his hands against it to stop the bleeding. The flashlight drew nearer until he saw nothing but white, hot light. He told himself this was heaven, and he was dead. Then came the knife to tell him otherwise.

5

Mary couldn't wait for the day that she could tell someone she didn't like another woman and not be called a jealous bitch for it. Katie was an idiot. Any idiot, including Katie, could see that. But she was a useful idiot with a lot of friends. They were already on their way, and some were here now, calling up to the roof from the street. A whole host of low-effort costumes mostly comprised of sexualized animals and cartoon characters (there were more scantily-clad men than women this year, so how's that for progress?), and Internet memes as old as this decaying building made flesh. The party was filling out. It wouldn't look so suspiciously sad. Now, there was a challenge. Now, the killer would have to try.

The other thing she appreciated about Katie was her effect on Peter. It was sedative. As Mary sat not far from Hearn on the edge of the roof, nursing her red solo cup, she could see him letting go, giving in. He'd been wound so tight since the first day they'd met—and even more so lately—that it'd been a miracle he'd had any blood flowing through him at all. He was all blood now, though. It was good. Good for him. He needed that, deserved that. Mary couldn't give him that. She took the wind out of everyone's sail. It was mutiny all the way down when it came to her.

Despite her best efforts to drink the cold away, Mary couldn't stop shivering. It wasn't even the cold that was getting to her, though it was certainly part of it (tomorrow, she and whoever else survived the night would surely pay their stupidity toll with snot and phlegm). No, this was more like adrenaline. Her body was ready. She wouldn't be caught off-guard again in the bathroom of some shitty diner. Trauma had its perks. This was one of them. She was sharp, sharper than she'd ever been. Let one of these basic fuck boys try to lay a hand on her. See how deep she cuts.

"Hey."

Mary craned her neck to find a strange man standing behind her. It wasn't her killer, though she imagined this one saw himself as a killer. A lady killer, to be exact, with broad shoulders and a broad chest, and a chin like only cartoon characters have. His dark hair was slicked back. She could smell him from here. He smelled like a bad idea all the smart girls would say they came up with themselves when their mascara started to run.

Mary tipped her cup at him. Her arms were as red as it, under the baptizing neon of theater Midian. This got her thinking of Goetia. The moment she almost fell through flesh. A knife in her hands, her father's clasped around them, guiding them. There'd been a guy, not all that different from this guy. They'd stripped him, cleaned him, and bound him to a rock in the woods. It was the first time she'd seen a man naked. She was twelve at the time, and in a cult. All things considered, an impressive feat.

"I'm Chad," he said, pointing to himself, as if he saw her sex as some foreigner from some strand land. "Chad Bradley."

Mary sucked her lips into her mouth to stop from laughing. She nodded, said, "Me, Mary."

"Cool," Chad said, and then he was off, merging into the wave of Katie's friends that'd just spilled out of the stairwell.

Mary watched him become one with the morons. She thought about him a little longer than she might've otherwise, and got up. It wasn't a good idea to be sitting on the edge of the roof like that. Not when she might die tonight.

6

"I won't be home until late," Detective Sono said to his wife over the phone, as he sat in his car in an alley off the Main Drag, watching Peter's apartment.

"First, you miss trick or treating with us." Nancy groaned. "Now, you're going to miss out on candy, too."

Candy was codeword for sex. His daughter, Elise, must've been nearby. It wasn't the best codeword, on account of him having diabetes and all. But it was Halloween. Stuffing the cauldron was a bit too on the nose, even for them.

"I'll take your silence as your apology," Nancy said.

"It's just a preamble of the penance to come."

Nancy was an English teacher. She liked it when he sounded fancy. And he just liked the sound of her voice, and when he could get some of it on these long shifts. It was the light he needed to keep the shadow of crime from getting him for good.

"I love you," she said.

He told her loved her, too, and hung up. He set his cellphone on the passenger seat and tried to get comfortable. It was no use, though, and honestly, better this way. This wasn't the kind of case a cop should get comfortable with. There were too many unanswered questions, too many loose ends. There was always a center to every illicit activity. A precipitating event to which all corpses and misdeeds were connected. Whether it was a theft, prostitution, or gang-related, it was all connected to a pivotal moment.

In his early years, Sono might've said Mary's killer was her center. And for the Brass, that, and a conviction, would've been enough. Now, he knew better. It wasn't the killer that was killing her, but Goetia and all it stood for. The place had, so far, over 20 victims to its name, which included former members and their families, as well as those that'd been killed at Mare's Diner. That number didn't even account for those that'd been killed by the founders while Goetia had been a thriving community of miscreants.

He'd been to the fort in the woods outside Ansbach. Was up there just the other day. He approached it the same way he imagined he would a decommissioned nuclear reactor: carefully, cautiously, and utterly convinced that, despite all the signs that suggested otherwise, there was still something deadly inside. Some walls were crumbling, others caved-in. Most of the fort had been closed off by thick roots and weeds, and the death-heavy spiderwebs built between them. Sono hadn't visited but a few rooms of the place. He had a family, and also, no backup. While he never found anything cultish, he did feel in the palms of his hand and the soles of his feet, a hum coming from the place. Goetia was dead, but it wasn't buried.

Sono killed the engine and got out of the car. Having the heat on high was making his skin itch. The cold took care of that quickly. He pulled his hat over his ears, so as to quiet the wind and its shrieking secrets. Standing there, looking like a cop, he drew the attention of the costumed Weekend Warriors roaming the Main Drag. He didn't know their names yet, but he would tomorrow, or the day after, when they came to him bloodied or violated, or on ice.

He caught sight of Mary on Peter's rooftop. Others were up there with her, and more coming in by the carload below. The party was working out. If Goetia was Mary's center, then what was Peter's? Peter's, he couldn't place. The "animal attack" they'd reported had been a curiosity that he and his supervisor had otherwise been forgotten. As far as he could tell from the students and professors he'd taken statements from, neither Peter or Mary had been particularly close prior to everything that'd happened. And they didn't seem particularly close now, either. They reminded him of his daughter and when they'd been trying to teach her how to swim. She'd had all the moves down. She'd known exactly what to do. But every time they took her out to the deep end, she wouldn't let them go. Of the two, Mary seemed the most likely to drown, and in her own time, likely take Peter down with her. She was grooming him for the undertow.

The Ansbach Sheriff said he knew Mary from back in the day. He hadn't been able to recall her real name. No one could. And it begged the question if she had ever changed it at all, or just given the impression she had. But still, the Sheriff knew her, and this is what he'd said about her:

"Goetia, huh? Guess it was only a matter of time until that place started to stink again. Her? Yeah, I knew her. I was highway patrol, then. She was, oh, fourteen or fifteen? Maybe thirteen? All that dirt and the clothes she was wearing aged her about ten years. I was on my way home one night when I came across her walking down the road, barefoot and blood up to her elbows. I asked her what'd happened. She said she'd fell. Emphasized 'fell,' like it meant something, which you and I both know now that it did. I told her to get in the cruiser with me, and she did, and I called it in. We didn't get but five miles before another cruiser came along and stopped me.

"I was new. Brand new. Still-kept-in-shape-and-thought-I-could-do-some-good-new. The officer in the other car said he'd take the girl back to Ansbach. I mean he was a real officer. I don't recall his name anymore, but he wasn't fake. I didn't get fooled or nothing like that. He took her from me.

"I rose through the ranks pretty quickly after that. Still saw that girl, your Mary, around, too. At school, going back to the woods. Something wasn't right, but she seemed okay, so I kept my mouth shut and didn't dig. You know, there's never been any formal investigation into Goetia until now?

"Yeah, well, we all turned a blind eye to that place. I couldn't tell you why. But I can tell you this, because this I know. This is factual:

They found a boy a month later not all that far from where Mary might've been walking when I stopped her. He was naked, down on his haunches, staring out over the local reservoir. The way they'd positioned his body, looked as if he'd been howling at the moon."

7

For the first time in his life, Peter let loose the reins. The party had spiraled out of control. Katie's friends and the friends of these friends were scattered throughout the building, from the roof to the basement, likely engaging in every illegal behavior short of murder (and even then, that was a matter of time, wasn't it?). There was no keeping track of everyone. If the landlord were ever to rise out of retirement from her tropics-induced coma, there'd surely be hell to pay for all the damages done.

He was drunk. Not just on alcohol, but on Katie. She wasn't anything like Mary. Katie could be described with basic adjectives. She was funny. She was cute. She was good. She was happy. She was more than that, he knew that; and he hoped to know more of just that before the night was over. He hoped she'd tell him in secret, maybe in his arms, or by her lips pressed to his. He was being simple and shallow, but that's exactly what he needed right now. Mary was his memento mori, a constant, complicated reminder that, one day, he would die.

"Earth to Peter," Katie said, shouldering him.

He snapped out of it and smiled.

"Where'd you go?"

Peter rubbed his wind-chaffed face. "I'm good. You good?"

Katie laughed: "Yeah."

They were sitting on the far end of the roof in two rusted lawn chairs he'd found propped up against the air conditioner units. Sitting there, staring out at Talbot and the shadowy stretch of the Old Country beyond, Peter felt like an old man having finally come home from a long day at work. Except his shift had been thirty-something days. And his duty? Not dying.

He stretched his legs and sipped his beer, and forgot, for the time being, the cocktail of highly potent poisonous flowers and powders packaged and packed into his pocket. Someone had turned the music up. Probably wouldn't take long before the cops showed. That was fine. The more, the merrier.

"So, what happened to you?"

Peter glanced over his shoulder, but Mary wasn't there. His stomach lurched, and yet, he was relieved.

Katie had caught on to this. "Why do you keep looking back at her? You guys together?"

"No, no. Not like that."

"Like what?"

He didn't know why, but at that moment, he thought of the phrase Mary had taught him: Liminal space.

"I saw it on the news, and you know how word spreads around Campus," she went on.

Liminal space. The place between what was and what's next.

"Then you were gone. Somehow, I deleted your number."

Is this what was next? Or were they still transitioning?

"I was really scared for you. You don't have to tell me if you don't want to tell me."

What were they becoming?

"I'm here, though, Peter, if you want to talk."

She took his hand. Hers was warm, warmer than it had any right to be on Halloween night.

"I do." He palmed her hand over his, as if he were some old grandmother comforting a grandchild. "I'd really like to get to know you, though."

"Oh," Katie said, making a face. "There's nothing to know about me. I'm as basic as they come."

"I don't think so."

"Trust me, you will."

The sound of something breaking. Peter jumped halfway out of his seat, heart racing. A group of shit-faced superheroes had ripped the door to the roof off the hinges. He didn't know how or why, and he didn't care. As long as there was flesh, not fur.

"God, sorry," Katie said, and then, yelling at the scrambling superheroes: "You're going to pay for that assholes! Come on, Brian!"

Peter sat down, laughing out his anxiety, and urged her on with a smirk.

"I shouldn't have invited so many people. Assholes. Seriously? God. Anyway, yeah, me. I'm boring. Really. I'm really boring. I go to school. I got to work."

"Where do you work?"

"… Chuckleclucks."

"In the m-mall?" It was getting harder to form his words.

"Yeah, the chicken place. Such a stupid name."

"I… like it." And now he was slurring his words. He stared at his beer, and then lodged it between his legs. Enough for now.

"That's it. Work and school, and then every other night and weekends, I'm with some of these idiots—" she twirled her hand in the air, "—drinking." She tipped her head back. He'd seen her take a pill earlier. Seemed like it was getting to her. "I don't really have any close friends."

"Same."

"What about Mary?"

Shit. He'd blurted that out pretty quickly. "Uh, yeah." He focused on the shadowy Old Country ahead. "But I know what you mean."

"I'm just really basic."

"You keep… keep saying that."

"I am, Peter. I'm so boring. My life is so… boring."

Sounds good, he thought. He asked, "Does it have to be?"

She stared at him as if she were deciphering him. "I like it this way."

"What's wrong then?"

This time, it was Katie who was looking over her shoulder, looking for her very own Mary.

"What?" Peter persisted.

She turned back to face him. "Hey, some of us were going to go camping next week. Josh, that one over there—" she pointed to the redneck with the red neck hocking tobacco chew over the side of the building, "—got a new truck. He wants to get it all muddied up. It's stupid, but…"

"Sounds fun, not stupid," Peter said, feeling warm all over.

"There's a place outside Ansbach we go to a lot. In the forest."

Ansbach. Mary's Ansbach. The fort in the forest outside Ansbach. How could something that was nothing now seem to be a part of everything? Was the world always this small, or was it just closing in? The anxiety in his gut bubbled like tar. He was sinking.

There were probably thirty or so people on the roof at this moment. A self-appointed DJ had taken over music duties, having swapped out Peter's playlist for his own. The songs were all bass.

They shook the building, so that when it moved, it sounded as if it were growling. The moon seemed closer than before, too. Close enough to touch, if he stood up and walked off the edge. At the rate it was pressing in, though, he wouldn't have to. The moon was coming to him.

Peter got close to Katie and whispered into her warm ear, "You got a mom and a dad?"

"Uh, yeah," she said awkwardly. She didn't think too much on it, though, apparently. "I saw them yesterday."

"What are they like?" *Fuck, I'm drunk.*

"Like, are they normal?"

"Yes."

"They are painfully normal. They're more basic than I am."

Peter rubbed his eyes. For once, he welcomed the biting wind. He'd gone numb all over, body and mind. He was on the threshold of drunken stupidity. That fleeting moment where he was simultaneously self-aware and had no fucks to give.

"You keep saying that. You're basic. They're basic." He stopped, knowing he should stop himself. But he kept going: "Why do you keep doing that? Because I was… involved in a crime scene?"

Katie looked as if she might cry.

"I'm not like a celebrity. I'm not like… reveling in it." He stared at theater Midian's neon lights, like an insect contemplating assisted suicide. "You don't have to one-up me or something. I don't expect…" he burped, "… some high-stakes… shit."

"I'm sorry, Peter. I'm sorry." She turned her chair, took his hands again, and held them against her knees. "I just didn't want to make you mad, or freak you out. I'm not good with this stuff."

"You're fine," he said, daring to run his thumb over her knuckles. "I'm being a jerk, and I'm drunk."

"Me, too," she said, laughing nervously.

"You're fine."

"Hey, uh, why'd you ask me about my mom and dad?"

Because I'm looking for someone that's not Mary, and not me.

Peter didn't answer her. He stood up, went to the edge of the roof, and planted his palms on the waist-high brickwork there. He searched for signs of the Beast of Stubbe Street, but there was nothing. It was all bright lights and pumpkins, and spider webs and eerie signs hung up in storefronts; and costumed drunks, and costumed kids, and old timers nursing steaming brews out of paper cups. It wasn't that the world had moved on, because the world was always moving on. It was him and Mary that'd stood their ground.

Katie came up behind him, put her chin upon his shoulder, and said, "Do you want to go somewhere quieter?"

Peter didn't turn around. He stared at the moon, instead, remembering something his mother had told him about it when he was little in relation to his anxiety.

"I understand the way you feel, Petey," she'd said, as they lay in the backyard on top of his plastic tent that'd collapsed thirty minutes earlier. It wasn't that they'd put it together wrong. They'd bought it on clearance. Someone'd returned it. "See that up there? The moon? It's like that. You can always can count on it. Sometimes it waits for the sun to go down. Sometimes it doesn't. But it's always there, Petey."

He hadn't liked her explanation for his constant worrying. Anytime she'd ever tried making things better, she always ended up making them a little bit worse. Usually, he'd keep that opinion to himself, but on that night, he was lying on the remnants of the tent he'd been looking forward to for weeks to sleeping in. The bugs had been eating him up, and one of the white, plastic tent poles had been digging into his side. That night, his mother's trailer trash philosophical musings hadn't cut it for him.

So, crossing his arms, he'd muttered, "Bullshit," and winced, waiting for her to pop him in the lip.

She didn't. She kept talking. "I know it's frustrating, Petey, but you can't always count on things in life. Even if it's bad, if you can count on it, and that's better than nothing. You know where you stand. You know who you are and what's coming to you."

Most people did pep-talks centered around the sun. Not Mom, though. The sun was her moon. She lived by night. In darkness, she was flawless.

Katie kissed his neck twice and whispered, "Peter."

He extended his hand to the moon, felt the surface of it against his fingertips; and just when, for the first time in his life, it was his to have and hold and make of it what he would, he turned away and went with Katie to do something unexpected.

8

Curtis had to get the lay of the land. There was too much action going on in this building to just stop on the stoop of the first floor stairs with the potheads perched there. This shit was crazy, though. An apartment building in the heart of the Main Drag, and it was all their own. As he moved through the halls, he couldn't believe something like this hadn't happened sooner. The place wasn't packed, but damn if this wasn't the place to be. Most of the apartments were empty, and a lot of them with a little... finesse... unlocked. Curtis had dreamed of such a place ever since eighth grade, where man and woman could get away, get high, and get it on. Yeah, yeah, there were places like this already. But those were shitholes. Not here, though. Here was potential. He could see it. He could feel it. Only on the streets could you get such an entrepreneurial spirit. At least, that's what he told himself, and anyone who'd listen.

"Hey, man," Dicky said, coming out of a cloud of smoke as Curtis climbed the stairs.

Curtis gave him a fist-bump and kept going. He knew everyone. Everyone knew him. The only people he didn't know were the ones who'd thrown the party. He had to meet them. This shit was crazy.

The second floor smelled of weed and meth. The lights were out. People were roaming the halls, the flashlights on their cameras on full-blast. He did the same. Every few steps he took, he almost bumped into or stepped on someone. He couldn't hear the lyrics of whatever song was playing, just the beat, throttling the walls. Shit was primal.

Fist bumps and hugs gave way to half-hearted nods: He had a lot of ground to cover. Holding his cellphone like a torch, he pushed past sweating bodies and kicked aside half-filled beer bottles. Groups of college kids asked if he was holding. Groups of high school kids tried to avoid eye contact. Some Old Country crews were here, too, hunting these weak-willed white kids. Curtis didn't say anything to them. It wasn't worth it. He knew their type. He'd scuffled with them plenty of times back in the day at the back of the library. They'd fight for anything. They had to.

Apple cinnamon. Curtis stopped in his tracks and breathed in. The apartment next to him smelled like apple cinnamon. Must've been one of the occupied ones. He took another deep breath, leaned across the dark threshold, said, "Sorry for the noise and all," and shut the door.

Curtis checked every door to every apartment he passed. Most of them were locked, but the few that weren't opened up to some furries taking a rip off a bong, a few kids dressed up like serial killers getting stupid over a Ouija board, and a gym rat gangbang.

"Hey, yo, Curtis."

He backed out of the last apartment as two blondes started doing lines off each other's asses.

"Ha, yeah? Who...?" He shined his light ahead and found Arjun headed towards him. "Oh, hey man, what's good?"

"This place, brother." Arjun lit up two cigarettes and gave one to Curtis. "People been here all of two hours and already acting like a bunch of wild animals."

"Halloween's Christmas for the crazies," Curtis said, taking a drag. "Hey, who started this thing?"

Arjun fell against the wall. "I don't know. Got the invite from Katie. Uh..." He checked his phone. "Some dude named Peter?"

Curtis shook his head, cigarette in his mouth, getting ash on the ground.

"Oh, shit. You know what?"

"What?"

The building rattled. Outside, police cruisers sped by, their wailing sirens disappearing behind the bass. For a brief moment, there was growling, and screaming, but Curtis didn't pay either much mind. Place like this, on a night like this, it was the things you couldn't hear you had to worry about.

Arjun got on his phone. "Yeah."

"Spit it out, man."

"This Peter guy. Katie said he's the guy who was one of the survivors from that Diner that got brutalized."

Curtis cocked his head. "No shit?"

"No shit."

"You lay eyes on him yet?"

Arjun finished off his cigarette, dropped it, and crushed it under his heel. "No, I mean... It's whatever."

Curtis knew a Peter, from the Old Country when he'd been eight or nine. Lived a few doors down from him. Peter used to stay with him and his uncle when his mom would go out for the weekends.

Good kid. They used to stay up all night watching scary movies and eating snacks out of Uncle's pony keg. Damn, he hadn't thought about him in a minute. Come to think of it, he'd seen Peter's mom a week ago. Shit, yeah, that'd been her. At the dog park in Star's Gate. She looked bad. Strung out. If he'd put two and two together earlier, he would've got something. Said something.

"I'd like to meet him," Curtis said. "Thank him, you know, for the hospitality."

Arjun shrugged, said, "Be my guest," and disappeared into the strobing dark.

Curtis was still thinking about Peter when he rounded a bend that dead-ended at an office, the door of which was open. He heard panting and moaning, and wetness. *Spade's a spade,* he thought, *and I'm looking to get laid.* He laughed at himself. Good line. He'd use it for later. Might make a few people laugh. Or he could throw it in a poem. People liked his self-deprecating shit.

He put his fist to the door, each knock pushing it open little by little. The first thing that hit him was the smell. It made him reel. Made his mouth salivate in an ashamed kind of way. The air was heavy, meaty, and hot. He smelled roadkill, and piss-sweetened shit. Metal, too. The same way your hands smelled after turning over coins while waiting in line at the store. Sweat and metal. Strain.

Curtis was smart, but at two hundred and thirty-three pounds and with a bad knee from too much cardio, he was not quick. The moment he tried to run was the moment it grabbed him. A clawed hand shot out of the dark and palmed his head. Each claw sank into his skull. Two were driven into his forehead. One twisted into his left eye, turning it to jelly. Another stabbed through his right ear canal. The last claw pierced the bottom of his jaw, going through his mouth and tongue before hooking onto his bottom row of teeth.

The werewolf reeled him into the office. As if he weighed nothing at all, the beast, while still holding on, flung him across the room with a flick of its wrist. The two claws in Curtis' forehead slipped out, taking bone fragments with them. The claw in his eye jerked free his optic nerve. His ear canal gushed gouts of blood when the claw was dislodged from it. The claw hooked onto his teeth held strong, so that, midair, his jaw was torn off, tongue along with it.

Curtis hit a wall, and fell into light. The office, or this part of the office, must've been on a different breaker. He crumpled over himself. Massive amounts of blood poured out of his gaping mouth. He couldn't breathe, because he was swallowing a lot of it, thinking that if he could just get some of it back inside himself, he might make it.

Before Curtis died, he saw something at the corner of his eye: a pile of mangled bodies, their costumes bulging from where their innards had spilled out and gotten caught behind the material. It'd made him feel somewhat better that he hadn't been the only idiot to fall into the creature's trap.

9

Mary pressed her mouth hard against Chad Bradley's. She shoved his hand down her pants, because he hadn't already. His fingers went limp, so she reached into his boxers to find things were no better down there. She held the whole of him in her fist. For a second, she considered he might be a grower, not a shower. But this sad story had been canceled before it'd even gotten started.

She let him go, got off him, and got out of Peter's bed. She turned on the lights to see him squirm. Instead, Chad lay there, pants around his ankles, baffled.

"What?" he said, sitting up. "What's wrong? You okay?"

"Not feeling it."

He pulled up his pants, said, "Oh, okay. Yeah. No problem. Did I do something?"

He hadn't. That was the problem. Even if he had fought her, that would've been something. She could usually work with that.

"You want to…" he stood, "… get back out there?"

Mary scrutinized him, looking for a way to call his bluff in this whole nice guy act. There didn't seem to be one, though. He'd been patient and understanding with her, and in a couple of seconds, he'd probably ask if her she just wanted to sit here and talk, instead.

"You know, we could just chill in here and talk, if you want."

She hated being right all the time. Of all the men in the world, who would've thought one named Chad Bradley wouldn't be a total chode? Perhaps there was still hope for this world.

"No, that's alright," she said.

She backed into Peter's computer desk. The mouse jumped, and the monitor snapped awake. On his screen: a webpage about lycanthropes.

Chad saw this and said, "Research for a Halloween costume?"

Mary grinned. "Something like that."

She'd been thinking of Goetia all night, but seeing Chad on the bed like that, naïve and vulnerable, really got her thinking about Dad.

Memories overtook her, tricking her nerves to relive past sensations. Smoke filled her nose. Insects fluttered past her eyes and ears. In her hands, wool. At her feet, fire. Her father lay before her, naked and splayed, among seven dead sheep. He was hyperventilating. The hole in his chest she'd put there, bleeding. The one he'd given to her on her side, the same. He'd fallen too deeply into the flesh, deeper than her. He'd never hurt her until that moment, when the bloodlust in the Giving Room had overtaken him. There'd been few left in Goetia at that point, but those that'd seen this had lost their faith because of it.

He'd become more than a Demon, and with his becoming came an appetite for all things he'd created, of not only his flesh, but the hides of others of whom he'd embraced, sheltered, fed, and loved; for if he were to find himself again, he'd have to fall through them all, and in doing so, be restored and reborn; and realized anew, enlightened, empowered, and elevated.

Peter's front door swung open from a mighty shove. Mary snapped out of her memory. She ran to the dresser, grabbed her gun she'd stowed there from behind the pile of clothes—

"Whoa, whoa," Chad said, scurrying backwards over and off the bed.

—and leaned out of his room, peering around the doorway. The door stood open. Either nothing had come through, or they were already in the apartment. She turned the safety off. Maintained trigger discipline just the way Dad told her to. And, holding everything in, waited.

You could count the seconds by the streams of sweat pouring down her brow. Her face was a clock. Soon, the killing hour.

She heard rummaging. Most of it was lost amongst the music coming from the hall, but it was there. Someone was inside the apartment, on the other side of the wall. Mary made her move...

... when Hearn stumbled into view, two bags of chips like life preservers pressed to his tits. All the pockets in his pants were filled with beers. And on top of his head, one of Peter's bright green, dollar store snack bowls.

Mary sucked in too much air. Quickly, she lowered her gun and held it behind her back.

Hearn stopped. He hadn't seen her, but he still had enough of his senses to know he'd been caught. Slowly, he turned.

From Chad: "What's… what's going on?"

Mary side-eyed him a *Shut the fuck up.*

"Oh," Hearn chirped.

"Restocking?" Mary said.

Hearn nodded, then shook his head. "No, I'm being bad."

"Tell me about it."

"I'm going—" he hiccupped, "—home." He scrunched up his face and struggled to stay balanced. "I sent Vanslow to get my hood-ie. He's been gone forever." Pausing, he seemed to be thinking on what he'd say next. "Screw it, right? Screw it. It's Halloween." Hearn took three steps towards her and stopped. It was the best he could do. "I gave him my key. I wanted him to wait for… me. First time. First time he's gotten it without—" another hiccup, "—having to be told. Hey?"

"Yeah?" Mary said, smiling.

Hearn wiggled his body, as if to gesture to all the things he'd decided to steal.

"Go for it."

"It's just… haven't been to the grocery store. Want us to have a n-nice night."

"I won't tell Peter."

"Really?" he asked.

"Really."

Hearn winked at her. "Who're you again?"

"Peter's sister."

Hearn nodded his head, mouthed *Cool,* and went on his way.

Mary turned back into Peter's room, every muscle in her body tented and tensed. She could feel him looking through her, at the gun she'd stowed.

Good for him, she thought. *Chad Bradley learned object permanence.*

"Mary…" He stood up, his hands out in that I-don't-want-any-trouble kind of way. "Uh, what's the gun for?"

Like all villainesses, Mary couldn't resist a soapbox. She started to say, "You know that thing that happened at—" when the music stopped. Her ears had gone numb to anything but repetitive beats and rappers rapping out nonsensical triplets. Sounds she'd taken for granted on a day-to-day basis came back to her, clearer than ever. She could hear the buzzing of lightbulbs; the whirling fan in Peter's computer; the creaking of the floorboards as she shifted her weight from one leg to the other. She could hear cars driving by; the wind buffeting the building, as if it'd been built at the top of some great summit; and voices, inside and out, not unlike insects.

She could hear herself breathing. She could hear her heart beating. Things she'd taken for granted.

Neither she nor Chad dared to speak and break this spell they'd fallen under. To Mary, it seemed as if something bad would happen to them if they did. Instead, they stared at one another, waiting for something to happen.

The voices dropped, inside and out. Like water to wine, they went from words to whispers. The air became electric. She could hear shoes snapping as they shuffled across the sticky floor. The walls thudded as bodies were pressed against them. Someone called out from the stairwell that led up to the roof, "Hey, what happened to the music?"

The power in Peter's apartment went out. Mary was never one to abandon ship. She hurried into the living room, maneuvering around furniture with ease. Her eyes had never had much trouble in the dark. She crept towards the front door, which Hearn had left open. There were still people in the hall. She had to stay silent. She couldn't let her presence be known; otherwise, they'd scatter. She needed her herd to hide within.

When Mary stepped into the doorway, everyone was looking at her. Even the five dead that lay gutted near the stairwell, bathed in moonlight. They were on their backs, but their heads had been tilted back, so that their lifeless eyes and gaping mouths greeted her. Between the corpses, blood flowed, traveling with the building's natural slope towards her. At first, to Mary, the symbolism couldn't have been any more obvious: this was a literal arrow indicating that she, a daughter of Goetia, was the one the killer had come for. But when blood pooled around her feet, and its color was lost to the dark about her, she didn't see an arrow but a gutter. She was his.

There he was. She hadn't seen him before, but there he was: in the shadows, on the staircase; not a silhouette but a sliver.

Screaming swelled from the floors below. Lumbering and growling echoed up the stairwell.

The killer leaned into the sounds of the massacre and listened for a moment.

A girl with pony-tails took a step back…

The killer fired a bullet straight through the side of her mouth, scattering her teeth to the ground like grim auspices.

And then he kept firing. At all of them.

10

Samantha told everyone else in the empty apartment, "Be quiet, be quiet. I hear something," and staggered towards the window.

The power went out.

Ally squealed, mostly just to get a rise out of Q, her new boy-friend. Stetson was too high to give a shit. He'd taken so much acid that even the dark had color.

Samantha braced herself against the windowsill. Her stomach grumbled. Hot pains pressed against her sides, as if steam was being released from her organs. She wasn't drunk. She wished she was, but she wasn't. She was sick. Her idiot friends had dragged her here after Katie sent out one of her infamous mass texts. They told her a little fresh air would do her some good, but you know what else would do her some good? A bullet to the head. Despite her body's best efforts, it hadn't managed to shit her brains out yet, so, yeah. A bullet to the head. That'd do it.

She opened the window. The wind blew in wailing, like it was throwing a fit for having been left out. Her temperature plummeted. She thought of a thermometer dropping to zero, and the image couldn't have been more satisfying.

Putting her elbows to the sill, she leaned into the night. The Main Drag was busy, but not as bad as last Halloween. There were fewer groups. More spaces between them. It was because of all the stuff in the news. The killings. The disappearances. The drugs. From where she stood, you could see where it'd literally taken a chunk out of Tal-bot. Two more years. Just two more years, and she'd graduate with her Bachelor's in Chemistry and be on her way to somewhere that didn't sound like it was dying when the wind blew through.

A rain drop hit the back of her neck. It was warm but welcome.

Ally cried, "Sam! What. Are. You. Doing?"

Without turning around, she shushed her with a wave of her hand. Across the street, something was happening. Some guy was running out of an alleyway, screaming into a cellphone. Was he waving at her? Another rain drop hit her neck. She wiped it away. He was waving at her. Pointing at her. Shouting at her. She cocked her head, put her hand to her ear to show she couldn't hear him.

"Uh, Sam?" Stetson said.

"Huh?" she asked, never taking her eyes off the man trying to get her attention.

He coughed. "Uh… You're bleeding."

Sam glanced back at him.

"Your neck."

Ally and Q were looking at her, too, confused.

She wiped herself. Her hand came back bloodied. Outside, she could hear the man screaming, "Above you!"

Samantha saw everything at once. Black pavement. Neon road. The man who'd been screaming, a gun in his hand. Claws. Her screaming friends. Fur.

Right before her neck broke and her head was twisted off her shoulders, she saw teeth. They flashed red, white, and blue, and thundered, like fireworks.

11

Peter made it about halfway down the staircase from the roof when Katie took his hand, pressed herself against the wall, and gently pulled him to her. At that moment, the music went out. With her eyes closed, she whispered, "Kiss me." He did. Sloppily, at first. He was inebriated. It'd been awhile. He needed to get his bearings. She helped him, aligning her lips with his, steering his want with the tip of her tongue. He found himself, and her hips. She was shivering. He was, too.

They came apart for air. Katie's face was flushed. She was smiling. Hooking her fingers around the belt loops of his pants, she gave him a tug. He took the hint with an intravenous hit of sobriety.

Her fingers flittered around the edge of his pockets, teasing him as they turned inward, until they inadvertently hit what he kept inside them. Parker's own concoction, courtesy of Maiden, Mother, and Crone's backroom. It probably wasn't what Katie thought it was. Unless she thought it was two vials of liquid wolfsbane and what amounted to an herb-infused smoke bomb. Then it was exactly that.

Peter took her hand and led her down the staircase. He knew what he wanted to do, but it wasn't what he had to do. He had to regroup with Mary. He had to confirm what he'd realized somewhere between his first drink and last drink, which was that they may have overreacted. That things were not nearly as bad as they thought they might be. That this Saturday morning cartoon shitshow of a set-up had been in vain. That for everything that suggested otherwise, they were, like everyone else here—Katie withstanding, of course—not that important.

When they reached the third floor, a gun went off. Deafening noise. A flash of light. Katie screamed. He screamed, too. Air got caught in his throat. He got ahead of her. In doing so, he noticed they weren't alone. The lights were out, but his eyes had adjusted. Several people were held up in front of his apartment. They weren't moving, let alone breathing. They were standing over the body of a girl on the floor. Her face had caved-in. It looked like a rotted pumpkin, with an ember for a candle burning inside.

Bullet after bullet ripped through the hall. Each muzzle flash growing brighter and brighter as the killer neared the bend. The partiers scattered, some into his apartment, others towards him. Nobody got far. With each body came a grisly fireworks display. A chain reaction of bone fragments and arterial spray, all going off one after the other, dousing the walls in hot, human sludge.

Two shoved past Peter and Katie, and in their wake: Mary.

"It's him!" she cried, running over the corpses, blood coming off her in streamers.

He cringed, half-expecting to see her gunned down. But the killer had stopped shooting.

"Come on!" Katie screamed in his ear, filling it with spit.

She grabbed him by the wrist and tried to run with him. He didn't know why he did it, but he did it. He didn't move. He planted himself and held out his free hand, waiting for Mary to take it.

Katie's arm jerked. She stumbled, let go. She looked back at Peter, her eyes wide, her mouth agape. He'd betrayed her. She'd thought of him, and he'd thought of *Her.*

When Mary grabbed Peter's hand, Katie's heart broke. Her chest opened like a flower and wept her red regret. Light swallowed her.

Smoke enveloped her. She was gone.

Mary screamed, "Forget her!"

Peter let Mary take the lead. If he got a bullet to the back, so be it. One life wasn't worth the lives of others.

As they hurried up the stairs to the roof, though, the bullet never came. In Mary's shadow, he was safe. It was those who fell outside it who weren't. Those they knew. Those they used. Those who'd never their read gravestones in the surface of the moon.

12

Detective Sono hurried up the steps to the apartment building, gun drawn. He could feel the eyes of the girl whose head the beast had twisted off watching him from the alley. It'd crawled down the side of the building from the second floor into a window on the first. He should've shot at it, but he didn't. He'd frozen, because what he'd seen couldn't have been.

Gunfire boomed from the third floor. The building lit-up like a haunted house mid-séance. He'd already called in back-up for an active shooter. He could hear them now. They weren't but ten seconds away. But in a country where you could stockpile ammunition with about as much ease as you could snacks, ten seconds was a long time. He'd asked for around-the-clock surveillance, and the higher-ups told him he was it. He should've been in the building. He'd been too much of a chickenshit to go into the building.

Not anymore, though. Sono made it to the front door, pulled it open. As he did so, three police cruisers rolled up and disgorged Talbot's finest onto the sidewalk. He shouted orders he couldn't remember saying, let alone thinking. Officers got into formation. They, Sono included, turned their flashlights on all at once. And all at once, their stomachs turned.

It was a slaughterhouse. In the fifteen seconds it'd taken Sono to call for backup and run from his car to the building, the beast, the killer, or both, had eviscerated every living thing on the first floor. There were no floors, walls, or ceilings. Only freestanding doors absorbed by gore. This part of the building didn't resemble a hall so much as a constipated bowel packed tightly with severed limbs and spools of flesh. It might've borne some semblance to the beast's intestines, had the beast eaten the meals it'd so sloppily prepared. It didn't seem as if the beast had eaten anyone, though. Its goal had been one thing and one thing alone: complete annihilation.

Some of Talbot's finest started vomiting. Sono, in a blood-fueled, blood rage daze, didn't bother reminding them to not taint the crime scene. The gunshots stopped for a moment, and then a single one broke the sulfur-scented silence. He heard screaming. Not from outside but above. There were still people alive on the roof.

Someone asked him what they should do.

He wanted to tell them to leave, to go home to their loved ones, and hold them in the way all the loved ones of those they now stepped over couldn't without the help of a body bag. He didn't tell them that, though. He didn't tell them anything at all.

13

Mary dislocated Peter's shoulder when she'd wrenched him by the hand into the stairwell. He didn't scream, or seem to notice. They bounded up the stairs together, two to three at a time. Every inch of her throbbed. Her blood felt as if it were trying to break free, to get on with the spilling inevitably to come. She wouldn't let it, though. Her blood was hers. It was the truth of her.

Ahead, night sky and polluted stars. She ran as hard as she could, dragging Peter behind her like a doll that had lost its stuffing.

"Come on!" she cried, pulling on his bad arm. Pain was always the best motivator. "We're almost..."

The defeating chill of providence crept up Mary's spine. For all her effort in getting them to the roof, now that she was there, it took everything she had to stop her from going back to where she'd come from.

The werewolf was here. When it moved, the moon moved with it. The creature's fur was heavy and wet, hanging from its limbs like moss. Gore-clogged cowlicks ran the length of its torso and sides. Its claws were like a seamstress' needle, hair and tendons wound tightly around them. Pacing, it left not paw prints but blood trails. When it settled its snarling gaze upon Peter, milk began to leak from its teats.

She hadn't even seen the dead at first. But they were there, throats torn out, guts torn open; raked with neon.

Police sirens whined from below. Waves of blue and red lapped against the side of the building. She could hear the officers making their way through the floors below. They were too late.

The werewolf lunged. Fetid debris was coughed into the air from its dust-off. Mary threw Peter off her, expecting him to be its target. But it wasn't. It was her.

14

Peter's feet went out from under him as he went sideways across the roof. He yelled, "What're you doing?!" before he tripped and fell over a corpse. "Mary!" he belted, palms slipping in bloody puddles. But she didn't respond. He couldn't see her. The werewolf dwarfed her. God knows what it was doing to her.

Out of the stairwell, the killer came. Gone was his gun. In its place, a shining knife. But for his face, he was dressed all in black. Over his head, he wore a white stocking, its tone and texture indistinguishable from the moon's.

Mary had saved Peter. He'd never been saved before in his life by anyone but himself.

He hesitated.

She screamed.

15

The werewolf bashed the side of Mary's head with an open paw. Blood that'd seeped into its fur got in her eyes. She saw red, and then stars.

Again, it came at her, pulling at her ankle, dropping her to her ass. A corpse cushioned her fall. The beast got down on all fours. Rabid with rage, it loomed over her, pouring drool into her screaming mouth, as if it meant to drown her. She threw out her hands, grabbed it by its oozing teats, and tried to push it off her. It wouldn't budge. It wouldn't abate. She'd never met anything she couldn't destroy.

The werewolf clamped its jaws down on the side of her neck. Teeth broke skin. It started gnawing. Its mouth smelled like earth and raw meat. She punched it, kicked it; drove her nails into its hide and dug at it. The creature didn't care. It'd suffered worse things than her.

Neck locked in its vice-like jaws, Mary held onto the corpse beneath her as the werewolf started flinging her around like a chew toy.

16

The killer walked over Peter, his gloved hands cracking as he tightened his grip on the knife. He glanced over his shoulder at the werewolf ravaging Mary and said, "The Giving Room gives."

Peter drove his foot straight into the killer's crotch. Not phased, he took Peter's leg and twisted it, forcing Peter onto his stomach. He tried to roll over, but the killer was quick. He was on him a second later, one knee in Peter's back.

"Who… what…" Peter stammered.

The killer said, "We don't choose our guardian angels."

Peter struggled. The killer drove his knee harder into his back. What he didn't see was Peter slipping his hand into his pocket.

"You should know. She was yours."

The killer grabbed Peter's hair, pulled his head back, and put the knife to his neck.

17

Mary grabbed the werewolf by its jaws, arched her back, and kicked her legs into its chest. She went opposite to the way it'd been pulling. Its teeth tore out a chunk of her neck, but she was free.

Scrambling, and losing consciousness, she reached behind her, took out her gun, and fired a silver bullet straight into the beast's heart.

18

The gunshot surprised the killer. The knife slipped, slicing open Peter's neck at an angle. He coughed, and he bucked, throwing the killer off his back.

Shaking, and about to bleed out, he took the vials of liquid wolfsbane out of his pocket, popped the stoppers, and doused the killer's mask in the killing flower.

19

Mary dragged herself across the roof towards Peter. Feverish, and vomiting from the pain, she noticed at the corner of her eye the werewolf's body transforming. Hair fell from its shortening limbs. Flesh, loose at first, was pulled tight. Claws retracted into fingernails.

"I need to see him, Peter," she said, crawling to the killer. "Let me see him!"

20

Peter ripped the white stocking off the killer's head. Using one arm, because his other hand was pressed to his neck, he shuffled past Mary to the werewolf.

Except it wasn't a werewolf anymore.

It was a woman. Naked. Mid-forties. Puncture marks on the bottom of her toes and up the inside of her forearm.

He crawled a little closer.

The police were at the bottom of the stairwell now, calling out, giving ultimatums.

He ignored them. Drew closer. And then, as if Death had cut every vein and artery in his body, he stopped.

He knew this woman.

This woman with dark blonde hair and bright blue eyes. With the uneven eyebrow from the scar running through. With the little moon tattooed behind her ear.

"Mom," he rasped, tears flooding his eyes.

She didn't answer. She didn't have answers for him.

Mary had killed her.

21

Mom? It hurt too much for Mary to do a double-take, but was that what Peter had just said? It didn't matter. She didn't care. He was here. Her killer was here. She'd been his. Now, he was hers.

Using the last of her strength, she heaved herself on top of a corpse and looked down upon him.

She knew this man.

This man with his black hair and green eyes. With the cleft chin he used to tap when he was deep in thought. With the symbol of Goetia tattooed onto the side of his head.

Dad convulsed, spitting up chunks of food. His breathing was shallow. His eyes, bloodshot. He was holding his stomach, writhing as he shit himself.

His face was covered in wolfsbane. Contact alone was enough to put a person down, but Mary had to do something. She pressed her palms to his cheeks and held him that way. If she took some of his death, then maybe he'd be spared long enough from his. He could give her some answers.

But her dad was death, all the way through. He didn't have any answers for her.

He died at her touch.

But it was Peter who had killed him.

PART III

SATURDAY, NOVEMBER 7TH, 2020

1

Mary woke up in the Seclusion Room. An antipsychotic nightcap had put her down for the count after she came to the conclusion that, due to her wounds from the werewolf, she only had three weeks or so left before her first of many transformations to come. She'd made the mistake of telling the staff this revelation. When they responded with clinical indifference, she'd pounced. Because she wasn't one to half-ass things, and also, because she hadn't been sleeping well, she played out the scene with homicidal threats and copious amounts of drool. Next thing she knew, she was restrained, and getting an injection, and on her way to snoring like a baby.

All part of the plan, she told herself, trying to get comfortable on her mattress on the floor. Things were always part of the plan, after the fact. She planned things on a subconscious level.

Mary had been in the hospital for a week, and on the psychiatric unit a day. At this point, she remembered most of what'd happened. Detective Sono and an amorphous mass of police officers had barged onto the roof, every one of them blood-touched in some way. It'd taken them a solid five minutes to pry both her and Peter off their respective parents. First Responders caught them somewhere in the carnage on the second floor and patched them up as best as they could, and sent them away on stretchers to the meat wagons below. During that time, after all that handling, Mary hadn't mentioned the wolfsbane all over her hands.

At the hospital, surgeons patched her up. Her neck hadn't been as

115

bad as it looked or felt, but she'd have what would equate to the world's worst hickey (if the hickey had come from a cannibal) from then on out. She'd been on constant observation while awake after the operation. Detective Sono and others like him visited often for statements and information.

Two nights ago, she'd apparently lost her mind. This she only knew from what she'd overheard from the doctors and their Bachelors-in-Psychology-I-like-to-help-people peons. They'd said she'd got out of bed at midnight, got naked, and laid on the floor until the night nurse came in to check on her. That's when Mary supposedly jumped to her feet, started growling, and screamed over and over again, "Fall into the flesh!"

Mary didn't doubt the details, but doing something so psychotic in front of others wasn't like her. It wasn't about to happen again, either, she'd decided, noticing the Seclusion Room door was ajar and staff were sitting outside it. From here on out, she'd be on her best behavior. As long as she could stop thinking about Dad.

2

Peter had been in a psychiatric hospital once before in his life. For anxiety and depression, and suicidal ideation. He'd been thirteen. Mom had been gone all weekend. There'd been no food in the house. The bed bugs had come back. A storm had spread and stayed. The power had gone out. The basement had flooded. The only person he could talk to was that kid Curtis who he hadn't thought about until just now, and he'd been out of town, at the beach. Peter, completely overwhelmed, with nothing to look forward to and no one to lie to him and tell him everything was going to be okay, called 911, gave his name, age, and address, said he had a plan to cut his throat, and went outside and waited in the rain.

Now, he was back, albeit in a different hospital, but again of his own accord. After the surgery on his neck, which wasn't as bad as it looked or felt, hospital staff asked him if he had any thoughts of harming himself or others. The doctor had ordered self-imposed mutism while he recovered, so abiding by his attending, he wrote on a dry-erase board with a dry-erase marker *Yes*. Being that he was one of two survivors from a high-profile case, and also having murdered in self-defense another human being, a simple yes had been enough to see him admitted to the psych unit for stabilization.

He wasn't actually suicidal, or depressed, or even anxious. He wasn't anything. And that's what surprised him. On that night, he'd finally left the in-between. He'd become something else. Just what it was, he couldn't yet say.

"It was an animal, I guess," Peter told his social worker, Marnie. She'd showed up a few minutes ago after Group let out. He'd met her yesterday, briefly, when he'd been admitted. She was young, new, and twitched every time something loud happened. There in his room now. Him on the edge of his bed. Her, in a chair, her back to the door.

"That must have been terrifying."

Out of everywhere, the hospital was probably the perfect place to tell them about the werewolf. Also, probably the worst.

"How are you sleeping?"

Peter shrugged. He stared at his roommate's bed. It was tidy. He was gone. Good for him.

"Have you had thoughts of wanting to hurt yourself or others?"

"No," he said. "That woman on the roof was my mom."

"I read that…"

Mary's dad made it sound like Mom was his guardian angel. Did they actually know each other, though? Or was it just coincidence that they both wanted to kill their children at the same place, at the same time, twice? What the hell is going…

"Have you experienced hearing things that weren't your own thoughts, Peter?"

I'm not responding to internal stimuli, Marnie, he thought, sarcastically. "No, just thinking, and still waking up."

"I hear, you, Peter. They get you guys up early here. How's your anxiety and depression?"

"Good. Better. Medication's helping a lot, I think." Also, he was no longer being hunted by a werewolf or, in a way, by a serial killer. No reason to give pharmaceuticals all the credit. There was something else going on inside his head, though. An engagement. An appointment. A commitment he'd written in a daze on a calendar, the date and purpose he couldn't yet recall. This wasn't over. Something was coming.

SUNDAY, NOVEMBER 8ᵀᴴ, 2020

1

Mary couldn't stop thinking about Peter. He was on the opposite end of the floor, in the men's unit – a few locked doors and well-meaning security officers between them. He was the only person she could talk to about what'd happened. Really talk about. Not dance around the details until she was dizzy and lying about the lies she'd lied about.

It was sometime after lunch. She could smell the cheap meat they'd fed her on her own breath. It pissed her off. She was sitting at a table in the milieu, coloring with crayons. She'd requested this. She needed to act her age.

Mary had always thought Dad might've survived that night. She'd stabbed him and left him for dead, to give back to the Giving Room. He'd taken things too far. He'd tried to kill her. The thing about it, though, was that she'd convinced herself he wanted her to do it. To kill him. To leave. To be free. After she'd stolen a Demon's car and gone to the Emergency Room to get where he'd gouged her looked at, she went to the bank like he'd always told her to do and found an account waiting for her, almost one hundred thousand dollars in it. To her, this said, *You got out. Now, stay out. You did what we couldn't.* But now, as she colored outside the lines of the wolf she'd had staff print out, it almost sounded less like encouragement, more like a challenge.

She watched the staff and patients mill about the milieu. It was important not to make eye contact in a place like this. You'd either end up with a new best friend, or your very own worst enemy. When she turned her head, the stitches tugged at the skin on her neck. Her scar would be the true mark of Goetia.

Dad had presumably killed everyone, or just about everyone, who'd ascended to demonhood in Goetia. It wasn't unreasonable to think he'd gone back to the place. She yearned to see it, to roam its earthen corridors; to feel the soil between her toes; to touch the stones of that old fort, and feel the power vibrating inside them. Did the Giving Room still give? If she made an offering, would she receive something in return? A cure for her new cursed condition?

Mary thought of Peter's mom, dying with the silver bullet in her heart. Killing a creature such as herself felt like harnessing lightning. It got her heart racing just thinking about it. It'd been a long time since she'd felt like that, and she felt like that now. She colored harder.

2

Peter stood in the shower, scalding himself, in part, for not having thought of Katie as much as he should've. She, and everyone she had invited to the party that'd stuck around longer than twenty minutes, had been killed. Thirty people gone, just like that. Apparently, the police had to get creative when it came to identifying the remains. Show a cow ground beef, and it can't tell if you if it's looking at its brother or not. Christ, he sounded like Mary.

He pressed his forehead against the wall. His skin itched as the hot water cascaded down his back. The steam was suffocating, but he breathed it in all the same. Staring at his feet, he started staring at himself. It'd been a long time since he'd give himself a once-over. He looked like a cadaver: pale and stiff and discolored; all veins and bruises; and everywhere, cuts and gouges—diamonds of crust and well-meaning scabs jutting out of these wine-colored wounds. It could've been the temperature of the water, but where the water hit him, dead skin broke free and came away in clumps. Like he was shedding.

Why was Mom hunting him? How long had she been hunting him? Was he, like Mary, one of many on a long-list of victims? Or had she always wanted to kill him? Why now? Why not when he'd been younger? That would've made sense. It seemed as if she'd been giving it her all to kill him back then.

Then there'd been that call. The first he'd heard from her in years, and the last. *I wish you had called me, Petey,* she'd said. *Been back for a month or so,* she'd said. *I have a loose end to tie up,* she'd said, *then we'll see.* He'd asked her, *See what?* And she'd said *See about… us. Getting the pack back together.*

Peter closed his eyes and let himself cry. If she hadn't meant to kill him, then she meant to turn him. To her, that would've been the only way for them to be a family. Because he would've had to have relied on her again, being born again in her secret world.

Detective Sono had come to visit Peter. The staff had been in the middle of a code, restraining Steve the Schizophrenic (a self-appointed nickname), when Sono had come through the doors. Peter watched his reaction while staff took Steve down. A part of him seemed to want to help, and the other part, seriously considering turning around and going back the way he'd come. It wasn't something Peter expected to see from someone with a decade of law enforcement under his belt.

They were sitting in one of the cramped meeting rooms now, warming their hands with the steam of their coffees. Rain pattered against the window. It'd gone dark outside. The sky had the texture of wool. Behind the swarming nimbuses, lightning didn't strike but swell. It made him think of a police officer's flashlight passing over a crime scene, as if god, for once, had come to see what all the fuss was about. At least the wind had stopped. The only howling he heard these days was at night, right before he fell asleep.

"How're you holding up?" Sono asked.

Peter scratched the mess of hair on his face. "If nothing else, gave me a chance to grow my beard out."

"Looks good."

Silence gut-punched the both of them. Now wasn't the time for trivialities. They both had questions. They both had answers.

"I saw it."

Peter pressed his hand to his cheek, chewed on the nail of his pinky.

"The beast. The creature."

"Werewolf."

"That's what it was?"

"That's what Mom was."

Sono took a deep breath as if to protest.

"I saw her transform back after Mary shot her."

"That's what attacked you and Mary—"

"Just me. At the Melancons'." Peter took a sip of his coffee. "I lied."

Sono glanced at the door, lowered his voice. "I did, too. In my report."

"We could've been roommates here if you hadn't."

"Yeah," Sono said, laughing. "It was smart to lie. Thing is, Peter, I don't know what to do with this information."

"Me, neither."

Sono took a long drink, keeping the cup pressed to his lips, as he said, "Did you know?"

That was the thing: He didn't. Could he have? Should he have? For all his worrying, overthinking, and armchair psychology, he'd still managed to miss it. His non-professional opinion, as well as the past opinions of actual professionals, had pegged her as having Bipolar. Did lycanthropy disqualify her from having a mental illness, though? It was a disease of the body, not of the mind, right? Or had Parker told him the opposite? Why couldn't monsters be more than monsters? They weren't always evil, all the time. Sometimes, they were mothers. Sometimes, they were fathers. Sometimes, they came home. Sometimes, they did right before they did wrong.

"No," he finally said. "I didn't. I could barely believe something like that was even real."

"And Mary's killer was her own father."

"I don't think they were working together."

Lightning played off Sono's eyes.

"They were just hunting us at the same time. A mutual understanding." Peter leaned forward, driving the heel of his palm into his forehead. "I don't know what my mom had been doing these last few years."

"We're looking into her. Mary's dad, too."

Peter stared at him. "You got nothing."

"It's like they came out of the woodwork. No traces. No witnesses."

"Like they came out of hibernation." He grinned. "To kill their offspring."

Sono lowered his voice. "Do you think she meant to kill you, or turn you?"

Peter's eyes got large and heavy. Tears leaked out of them on their own accord. *Mom's gone,* he told himself, his inner thoughts just as shaky as his voice would be, if he spoke. *She's g-gone.*

"Do you have somewhere you can go when you get out? Any family?"

Peter shook his head, drinking his coffee with both hands.

"A lot of confused, devastated families in Talbot right now. You and Mary are in their sights. Quite a few have tried to get in here to talk you two."

"It's not safe for me out there?"

"Not saying that."

"It's just not over."

"Right."

"It's never going to be."

Sono started to speak, but stopped himself.

"Mary and I will figure something out."

No response from the other side of the table. Peter could feel a person's doubt. He felt Sono's now. Doubt was a like an invisible wall. You could see through it, but never eye-to-eye.

"You keep going back to her."

"We have a mutual understanding."

3

Mary sat up straight as Dr. Frank examined her neck. Hands together and on her knees, she smiled and tried not to think about how easily she could get a hold of his pen and ram it through his windpipe. She'd take him hostage, and negotiate—his release conditional upon her own. She wouldn't ask for anything unreasonable. Just a wide berth and a head-start.

"How's it looking?" she asked.

"It's healing well, and quickly," he said, somewhat distantly, as if her wound was the most interesting thing he'd seen all day. "How are you feeling today?"

"I'm not going to turn into a wolf, am I?" she joked. And then, not wanting to be accused of deflection: "I'm feeling really good." She didn't say great. Great was too much. You shouldn't feel great in a place where your new roommate treated her own ass like a buffet.

Great denoted an elevated mood. Possibly even mania. "Better than the other day, for sure."

"Any nightmares?"

"Nope."

"Thoughts of wanting to harm yourself or others?"

"Nope," she said, staring at his throat.

"Staff said you did well in group this morning."

"That's nice of them. I'm trying."

Dr. Frank checked his chart. "You were taking antipsychotics before coming in. Were those working for you?"

Mary shrugged. "They weren't making things worse."

"Did you take them consistently?"

Only in front of Peter, to lead by example. "Yep."

"You've had some significant trauma. I'd like to explore making adjustments to your regimen."

Mary tongued her canine, and then the other. "Eh."

"What's that?"

"I just… feel better. I'm just worried a medication change will throw me off."

Dr. Frank looked into her eyes. "You're doing great."

Mary smirked.

"Everything you experienced will be waiting for you, in some way, when you walk out these doors. I want to make sure you're prepared for it."

Mary swung her legs like a child. "Thanks, Doc."

Dr. Frank began to drift away.

Before he went, she added, "Hey, uh, do you think I'll be out of here before the end of the month?"

He stopped. She'd fucked up. She said something she shouldn't have said. End of the month was too specific. She should've said next year. She should've cracked a joke. Now, she just sounded cracked.

"Your father only killed on a full moon, the police shared with me. There's another coming up."

"There's always one coming up."

Mary watched Detective Sono cross the hall from the window in the unit doors. He must've just finished talking with Peter. She waited him for to visit her, but he never came.

Lying in bed, toeing her ankle where a rash had formed—the scrubs and the cheap detergent they used here were doing her increasingly sensitive skin no favors—she stared up at the half moon. The next full moon wouldn't be until November 30th. She had twenty-two days.

Mary wondered if this was more a moon half full or moon half empty kind of situation. The obviousness of her situation wasn't lost on her. If ever there was a way to fall into the flesh, becoming a werewolf was basically it. Losing complete control wasn't a notion she could stomach, but it wasn't all bad. She wouldn't have to explain herself behind the obvious. People would look at her, and they would understand, the same way you would if you caught a stage four cancer patient with a straight razor in a bubble bath. You'd disapprove, but you'd understand.

She'd done things at Goetia. Halfway things. Most people would celebrate her for stopping back then. They'd say it is what it is, but it's better this way. It wasn't, though—better, that is. Things left undone have to be done. If not by her, then by someone else, and she couldn't have that. Dad had put the knife in her hands, but she'd been the one to open up the drifter. She'd been twelve, sure, but how could she have thought running would get her anywhere but back to there? The drifter had been alive when she left him, but had she really thought leaving him with Demons would somehow save him?

When the police officer had brought her back, and after he went on his way, Dad made her walk the rest of the way to reservoir. They'd finished off the drifter. His fingers and toes had been flayed, so it looked like he had claws; and his lips had been flayed, too, so it looked like he had fangs. He was naked that time, on his haunches, staring into the sky. It'd been a full moon that night.

"Do you see?" Dad had asked her, holding her from behind. "Until you become what you are, you will make of others what you are not."

Mary put the memory to rest and, closing her eyes, she did the same.

Twenty-two days.

WEDNESDAY, NOVEMBER 11TH, 2020

1

Peter discharged from the psychiatric hospital at four-thirty in the morning. Detective Sono had convinced his doctor it was the best thing to do, because that's when it would be most likely for Peter to slip out unnoticed by the families of the victims who'd been circling the place since he'd been admitted. With crust in his eyes, he left in a fresh pair of jeans and a T-shirt, with a pre-paid cellphone and a folder full of pamphlets, resources, and treatment work, and an out-patient therapy appointment with Latonia in seven days. Sono had brought him the clothes. He'd brought him his car, too. It'd been impounded. He left it parked at the back of the lot, where the encroaching woods kept it shadowed. He was supposed to get in it and go to one of his landlord's other properties: 5166 Twilight Court, a condominium on the edge of Talbot, not all that far from Mare's Diner. Sono must've used the full force of Talbot's finest to swing such a deal with that lizard. It was a nice gesture. Sono was a decent guy. Though Sono had given him the keys to the condo, and combination to get in by the keypad (2000102 – the year of his birth, followed by the month and day) he wasn't going to 5166 Twilight Court.

The drive to the Old Country happened in a haze. Half-asleep, half-medicated, Peter ran through the events of the last two months until they started to fray, and he couldn't be sure what was real and what was remorse. He tried to imagine what it must've looked like in the apartment building after Mom… eviscerated everyone, but he couldn't. Instead, he thought of Katie, just out of arm's reach, pieces of her heart falling out of her chest, like love-me-nots.

He didn't know what came next, except for streetlights and stop signs, and soon, sunlight. He smelled like a psych ward. His skin burned, like it wanted to get off his bones. He could feel the morning in his gut, that mixture of gas and jitters, as if all the butterflies in there were being dipped in acid. Sono had warned him about the Press, so Peter found himself driving slouched in his seat, to avoid knowing eyes and feasting cameras, but as far as he could tell, he wasn't being tailed. The massacre was the worst thing to have ever happened to Talbot in a single night. Drugs and violence had, over the years, claimed far more lives, but this had happened on the Main Drag, to "decent kids" from "decent families," all in one night. It made sense for the Feds to get involved, that'd been Peter's thought when Sono broke the news. Such an investigation was beyond Talbot's scope. But where were they? In his rear-view mirror, he saw only cold pavement and darkened storefronts, and parked cars gathering condensation.

They'd patched him up and sent him on his way, a sheep amongst wolves.

"Stop it," he told himself, as he rubbed at his stitches. "Just. Stop."

Before Peter made it to the Old County, his subconscious had him take a detour. He hadn't realized where he was going until he was already there. He cut across an intersection and there, rising out of the mist, a powered-down monolith to the neon gods, the marquee for the theater Midian. Across from it, bound in caution tape and guarded by a police cruiser, the Apartment Building. It wasn't his anymore. By violence, it'd been orphaned, and only by time and ghost stories would it be taken in again. But until then, the Apartment Building would stand separate and alone, blighted and bedeviled. He'd never say something like that aloud, except maybe to Mary. But things were easier to cope with when you made them sound poetic. That'd been a good coping skill. He'd forgotten about that one.

Peter drove past the Apartment Building at a crawl. His face flushed. His heart sped up. He squeezed the steering wheel until his hands hurt. The sound of his engine gave way to a thudding bassline. He licked his lips and, for a moment, tasted Katie. She'd soured.

He'd stopped the car in the middle of the road. No one but for the officer in the police cruiser was around. Once he noticed, Peter noticed he'd noticed and quickly sped off. Only spectators and serial killers returned to the scene of the crime.

The Old Country was always early to wake. Those that lived in the neighborhood always had somewhere to be, even if that somewhere was their porch, next door, or the corner store. Everyone always had plans. You had to keep busy in a place like the Old Country. If you stayed in one place for too long, you'd start to think about your surroundings. Make excuses for them.

At least, that'd been Peter's experience, and for several years, his assumption. That was the thing about anxiety. He'd convinced himself he knew everything, and because once something was, it'd always be. It had to be. As long as he never had to confront his beliefs, he never had to doubt the truth of them.

But on this morning in the Old Country, there was no one. Everyone slept, or had decided to stay inside. The further he went, the more evident this became. It was almost 6:00 AM, and the only thing running were the buses, which passed empty stop after empty stop. He rolled down his windows as he went, the best thing he could do in putting his finger to the pulse of the place. It wasn't dead. There was life in these homes. Scattered voices. Backdoors with whining hinges. A trash can lid being worked onto a trash can, the world's most annoying puzzle piece. Cars starting. The reluctant groans of garage doors going up. A church bell chiming, the good lord's siren song.

He saw none of this, and why should that be all that surprising? Peter was on one street of many. The only ghost town around here was the one in his mind. Things will get better. His mother had told him that once. And maybe because it'd come from her, he'd swore off the sentiment entirely.

Peter floored it. He'd come here for validation. To know, as one of the Old Country's refugees, his damage was, in part, due to his upbringing. How could the entire place get better in only a few years, and yet he stayed the same? Mom was dead, and he needed his answers.

He knew these streets he kept turning down—Sherman, Mills, Courtland, Slane, Monroe—but in name only. Where were the dead yards? Where were the sewers clogged with garbage and cigarette butts? Where were the potholes large and deep enough to have all the makings of a grave? Where was the blight? Where was the foreclosure and forlorn? Where was that feeling inside him to look ahead, and to do it looking hard? Where were the Ed Jacksons with their unleashed dogs and weekly police raids? Where were the Pamela Browns lumbering around screened-in porches, trying to wrangle in their overcrowded daycares? Where were the Millers, that family whose first names you didn't know, but knew to stay away from? The ones who only came out at sundown, who all rode together in a single pickup truck, who all came back at sunrise with nothing to show for their hours gone but the mud on their boots.

Peter didn't know if he was racist, pathetic, an idiot, or as in most cases, a combination of all three. But what he did know was that he no longer knew where he was going. The Old County had become a new country, and he didn't have the figurative muscle memory to make his way around it. He took out the cell Sono gave him, punched in 1313 Stubbe Street into the GPS, and headed home.

Relief washed over Peter as he rolled up on Stubbe Street. It was worse than he remembered. Surrounded by renewal, the street remained necrotic. It was a combination of ranch-style homes and low-income housing complexes, each one identical and three-stories high. They'd gone to seed. Here were the dead yards and clogged sewers, and the scabby cement agape. Here were the foreclosures, slowly being swallowed by the weeds. Here, danger and bad decisions, and political indifference for as far as the eye could see.

Again, he rolled down his window, to hear and feel Stubbe Street's heartbeat. But there was nothing. Only the cold air that smelled of dead leaves.

Home was where he'd left it. An unassuming yellow house set further back from those beside it. They'd always had a decent backyard. It was checked by the woods that'd sprung up between the Old County and Ansbach. Now, the backyard was a field. Now, the woods were a forest.

Peter parked his car on the street and got out. His legs gave. He hadn't realized how tense he'd kept them on the way over. Instead of going forward, he fell back against the car and ran his hands through his hair. He waited for memories to overtake him. Nothing came.

Dead leaves blew across the sidewalk, scratchily, like scrabbling claws. The forest swelled in the distance, waves of decay cresting in its canopy. Peter bounced off the car and, holding himself to stave off the cold, glanced around. He searched for others, but there was no one.

Mom was the Beast of Stubbe Street. The obviousness of it made him laugh. Yet until now, he hadn't considered the possibility. *Did she do this?* He chewed the dried skin off his lip until he tasted blood. *How many people were living here before she started feeding? Or has it been like this for a while now?* His hands became fists. He slowed down his breathing. *Shut the fuck up.*

Peter went slowly up to the house. He kept to the walkway he knew was there but couldn't see beyond the weeds. How could such a small house loom? By the time he reached the front steps, it was all he could see, like it'd enveloped him. He climbed the stairs to the porch. The wood boards announced his arrival. If there was anyone inside the house, then they'd know he was here. He had his doubts, though. Mom had always been her own pack. A self-perpetuating engine of self-loathing and scrappy ingenuity. A bottom-dweller with a taste for the top.

He didn't check to see if the front had been locked. He knew it was. Mom took care of the things she destroyed. She'd called him weeks ago, to lure him into her den. She would've left a spare.

Peter crossed the porch to the furthest end, near where the window that used to be his bedroom window was. He tried to look in, but the curtains, his curtains, the ones with the moon and stars print, were drawn. He went down on one knee, pulled back the loose floorboard beneath the sill. There, on the ground, spiderwebbed against the foundation, a pouch. He took it, took the spare key out of it, and put the pouch back. You always had to put the pouch back. Mom would know if you didn't.

The key was so new that it shone, even here, on Stubbe Street, where the sunlight came in dirty and gray. He went back to the front door, slid the key into the lock. Before he let himself in, he looked over his shoulder again. This was his street. Even its current state, he knew when something was out of place.

There was someone watching him from across the street. From in between the houses. Someone who didn't live here. Someone who'd followed him.

Peter had come too far to stop now. He opened the front door. A bright orange, plastic pumpkin pail rolled out of the house, over the doorway, and stopped at his feet. There wasn't candy but dirt inside.

And a single plant he knew all too well.

Wolfsbane.

2

Mary discharged herself from the psych ward. Her seventy-two-hour hold had ended, and Dr. Frank didn't see any reason to keep her longer. She left at nine in the morning. The hospital wasn't all that far from her apartment, so wearing the scrubs they'd given her, with a garbage bag full of her belongings, she made the long trek home, through all the press and pissed parents along the way.

"Mary… Mary a moment, please!"

"What happened? The cops won't tell us anything."

"I'm watching you. Someone just doesn't go to a psych ward for nothing!"

"Hey, I'm talking to you, goddamn it!"

Tears. Pleading. Gnashing of teeth. Reaching hands not quite brave enough to grab, on account of her wild eyes and greasy exterior. It was a lot, but nothing she couldn't handle. Halfway to her apartment, a police cruiser cut through the stalking crowd and offered to give her a ride. She told the officer, "Only if you go the long way."

The officer had a name, but she didn't bother to get it. Instead, she got in the back, the hard-plastic seat digging into her bones, and started rifling through her belongings. She had her purse and everything in it, her cellphone, and…

"Oh," she whimpered.

Pink headphones. There were pink headphones. She didn't own a pair of pink headphones. But her dad had. He'd been wearing them the night he'd abducted her from Mare's Diner.

She took them out, stretched them out. *If I plug them into Goetia, will I hear the secret meaning of the world?*

"I'm sorry about that," the police officer said, his eyes darting back and forth between the road and the rear view. "Everyone wants answers."

"I do, too," Mary said, handling the headphones with care. She looked into each earbud to see if there was anything of Dad inside. Wax or hair, or a rolled-up message. There was nothing.

"Your father… That Peter kid's mom…"

"Pretty stupid twist when you say it aloud," Mary said.

He stared at her for a moment, then ducked down a few side streets until they were safe from prying eyes.

"I don't know anything," Mary said, pre-emptively.

The officer kept to himself after that.

The officer dropped Mary off at nine forty-five. Her car was still parked out front. She thought someone might've vandalized it, but apparently no one was that vindictive, or they hadn't figured out where she lived yet. She'd taken the bus to Peter's that night.

She hurried into the building, repeatedly calling Peter as she did so. By the time she got into her apartment, she'd left five messages on his voicemail. She didn't know if he was still in the hospital or not.

Mary got into the shower and kept the water ice cold. Treatment, and all the medications in her system, had dulled her senses. She turned pale, and shivered, as she washed herself raw with a rag. When she finished, she nearly tripped getting out of the shower so quickly. Pausing at the sink, she gave herself a once-over in the mirror. Her neck wound was healing, but there was something growing out of it. A single black hair. She pinched it between her finger and yanked. It came out freely. Her father... He'd had black hair.

Mary drove to Goetia wearing Dad's pink headphones. They were plugged into her ears, and nothing else.

Talbot lay behind her, like the cement piece of performance art it resembled. The founders had built the city in the middle of the area's sprawling forest, and they'd done so only to show those in Defiance, another city about three hours away, that they could. It'd been a bet amongst the rich, when, back then, wealth was measured by both flesh and coin. Talbot was, in essence, the state's longest running dick measuring contest. For Mary, it was good to get away from that syphilitic sprawl on her own accord, and return to the simplicity of dirt and stone.

She took a gulp of coffee, smashed a donut into her mouth. It was thirty-five degrees out, and still she found herself overheating. The car rocked, buffeted by the wind running westward across this empty country road. The wind, it didn't howl anymore, not like it had in October. Either it'd stopped, or she was in sync with the sound.

The last few days, Mary had only thought about two things. The first was Dad dying on Peter's rooftop. The way he lay there, poisoned. It called to mind one of those deep-sea fish, and how they die if you try to bring them out of their dark, highly pressurized depths. Dad always existed in his own world, and when he couldn't, he found Goetia. He'd always called himself a survivor. Survivors survive. They don't die. He'd told her once that if anyone was going to kill him, it'd be her, when she finally fell into her flesh and cleared his court of Demons. She hadn't killed him, though. Peter had. That didn't sit right with her. She resented him for it.

The second thing she thought about was becoming a werewolf. All signs seemed to point to the obvious: She'd been bitten; therefore, by the next full moon, she'd transform. Sharon, her therapist, would find some way to turn her nonchalance about becoming a blood-starved beast into some therapeutic moment of self-discovery. She'd say, "Mary, you look forward to becoming a blood-starved beast," and she'd be right. She'd say, "Mary, you've never felt comfortable in your own skin," and yeah, nail meet head. She'd say, "Mary, you've been looking for a reason to kill something again," and, well, that's when she'd probably storm out of the office. Probably fire her shortly thereafter.

In fact, sensing this conversation was already coming, Mary got on her phone, called Sharon's office, got her voicemail, and left a message. "I won't be needing your services anymore," she said, coldly, and ended the call.

Mary slid a finger into her mouth and pricked it on her canines.

The way to Goetia lay open to her. She turned off State Route 72 down an unnamed road still warm with tread marks. The police had been through here. A few times by the look of it. Riding her brakes, she searched the forest for signs of Detective Sono, or some Ansbach rookies looking for a big break. But as the naked trees closed in around her, their fragile limbs clipping her side mirrors, she realized, with some relief, and also, dread, that she was alone.

She wasn't overwhelmed by memories coming here, because she'd never really forgotten them. Over the years since her escape, it'd been a slow drip of recollections that'd validated her decision to leave. Things were different now, though. She had no choice but to return home, to see what it'd become, to see, without Dad's clouding presence, what it'd always been.

Mary took the dirt road for ten minutes before she came across the Welcoming Rock. She parked her car, killed the engine; getting out, she zipped up her coat, threw on her hood, and approached the boulder. Nervous jitters ran up her body like electrical currents. Taking the glove off her right hand, she pressed her palm against the Rock's smooth surface. Nothing happened, because nothing ever happened. It was manmade ritual. One rule of many meant to give Goetia an air of legitimacy. All the same, she smiled.

Leaving her car, Mary marched southward through swelling decay. She couldn't see the ground, covered as it was in dead leaves. Patches of rotting mushrooms occasionally broke up the brown and orange monotony. Though she couldn't see them, by this clear and untainted forest air, she could smell them—the carcasses, the corpses, wasting.

The Giving Room gives, so long as to the Giving Room, you give. Taking a look around, Mary wondered when was the last time it'd eaten.

Goetia wasn't far now. It was somewhere ahead, beyond the place where the trees grew out of one another. Mary, working on an empty stomach, stopped for a moment to catch her breath. She was shaking. Her neck wound, where the werewolf had bitten her, felt separate from her body. Swollen, in a way, and numb, in another. It felt sick in that way all wounds feel when they take a turn for the worse. Fall through the flesh. Goetia's mantra. She'd always struggled to understand what that meant and how to do it. Mary was never one for symbolism. Say what you mean, and mean what you say. By the end of the month, though, she'd have no choice but to fall through her flesh, as it would fall from her, and pool like a dress around her ankles; and to herself, she'd see herself, not as she was, but as what she had to be. Equations were easier to solve when you took the human out of them.

Mary kept at it. Her chest rattled when she coughed. She'd pushed herself too hard in coming here. After she was done, she had to find Peter. He'd take care of her.

Mary took a deep breath as she reached the barrier. The trees that formed it were grotesque, not unlike tumors in the way they protruded from one another. When she touched them, the hairs that grew along their barks stood upright. She didn't have to force her way in, though. The barrier gave itself to her. Like a membrane, it knew what to let in and what to keep out.

About to slip through, she stopped and glanced over her shoulder. The woods climbed to the mottled sky, hill like a hecatomb to winter's coming hunger. Gold was the death she'd walked amongst, now with the sun shining coldly on high, and out there, in the glow, a glint. She squinted. She sneered. She felt like a sniper on the fringes of a war-torn battlefield. She'd caught something in her scope. She couldn't see him, but she knew he was there: Detective Sono.

Come and see, Mary thought, turning her back and easing into her barrier. When she stumbled out onto the other side: Goetia. The old fort looked the same as when she'd left it. Overgrown, unstable; half-done, like it was merely a part of something larger that lay deeper in the earth. It was smaller than she remembered, though, and less imposing. The power was there. She could feel its currents, like electrified waves, lapping against her legs. But it did not move her. Not by its influence, nor by her own memories. It was, for now, just an old fort in the woods.

But it wouldn't be forever. There was a lot of space here. A lot of halls and rooms to get lost in on a full moon night. A lot of bones to dig up, Mom's included.

3

For all its ruin, Peter's childhood wasn't much different from what he remembered. It was just that, now, the decay was on display. It hadn't been normalized into submission. There was honesty in squalor.

"Oh, man," he said, closing the front door behind him. He locked it, and then started slipping off his shoes. Heel halfway out, he stopped and laughed at himself.

The living room was shredded. One might say a werewolf had lived here. The carpet was in ribbons. The walls were plastered with thick, coarse hairs. A couch, not their old one, but one she must've dragged in from off the street, had been chewed on; the armrests picked apart; the cushions dotted with scabby blood drops. He smelled piss, and all around the perimeter, saw it, too. He didn't bother flipping on the lights. She rarely paid the electric when he'd been a kid.

Peter cut across the living room into the kitchen. No table. Just a solitary chair at the center amongst a sea of dirty linoleum. The drawers and cabinets were open, and empty. In the sink, up to the faucet, potting soil. Everything was sticky and had a sheen, as if the room had been covered in drool.

Against his better judgment, he opened the fridge. A stench so overwhelming, like egg and ass, hit his nose before he saw what was inside. Expelling air out his nose, he recoiled, letting the door swing open fully. When he gathered himself, nose buried against his forearm, he turned around to see what Mom had been saving.

The fridge was packed with rotten meat. It hadn't been bagged or bundled, but thrown in haphazardly. Piles of gore in varying sizes, some of which had holes in them, like she'd been eating from them in passing, grabbing meals by the handful.

Did you have to eat that way even if you weren't a werewolf? Peter kicked the fridge door shut. *Or were you just trying to keep things simple?*

Peter wandered down the hall, using his cellphone as a flashlight. The deeper he went into the house, the darker it got. There wasn't much to it. He only had his old room and hers, the bathroom, laundry room, and that'd be it. Yet, with every step he took, he felt as if the floor would open up and swallow him whole, and show him the house within the house. The one he always knew was there. The one he'd carried with him ever since he'd left.

He stopped a few feet from his room. The door was shut. As far as he could tell, it was the only room in the house whose door was shut. He turned the knob, but it wouldn't budge. It was locked. His room never had a lock on it before. From what he could tell, the knob looked new.

Peter's heart started beating fast. He was sweating, trembling. His chest ached, as if it were expanding. He pressed his back against the wall and swung his cellphone like a torch, to chase away the swarming shadows. His body had figured out something, or it was betraying him. He knew anxiety attacks like the back of his hand, but this was different. It wasn't a panic attack, either.

This was fight-or-flight.

"You're alone," he told himself with total conviction.

After a few seconds, he stopped shaking. His chest felt like its normal size. He bunched up the end of his shirt and wiped down his face and neck. Letting it go, he noticed his shirt came back splotched with blood.

"Fuck," he hissed.

He touched his neck, thinking he'd torn his stitches. The thing was, he couldn't find them.

Peter put it out of his mind, tried to open his door again, and kept going. Mom's room was a little further down the hall. There was no power in the place, but still, it glowed. Her room always had its own light. She'd been radiant, like a dying star.

Mom's room wasn't a room but a garden. The floor had been torn open, and the ceiling ripped apart, to let light in on the wolfsbane that grew in that cavity where her bed used to be. The purple, hooded flowers were too numerous to count and, strangely enough, when he stared at them, his eyes burned, as if he were allergic to the sight of them.

Blinking through the pain, he knelt down beside his mother's garden. Nothing had been allowed to thrive in this house. Nothing, except for this.

Were you trying to kill yourself?

He shone his cellphone's light across the room. It caught on broken glass and a few rusty syringes.

Or cure yourself?

Peter thought of the meat in the fridge again, and then he thought of Mary. Mary, dressed in purple, a hood thrown over her head, an animal pelt for a scarf wrapped around her neck, still fresh and bleeding. She had moons for eyes and… He wasn't thinking clearly. It was the medicine. It was his empty stomach. Something was to blame.

He went to the bathroom. The sink was clogged with hair. The toilet was missing. And the cast iron clawfoot tub was filled with dirty water, and heavy chains. They weren't attached to anything, but by the wearing around the bottom of the tub and other anchor points in the bathroom, it was obvious Mom had chained herself up in here, likely more than once. Again, he thought of Mary.

The laundry room had been stripped of appliances, of everything, really. Gone was the drywall and most of the floor. There was nothing left but the innards of the house: puffy organelles of insulation, tangled masses of arterial cabling, and the moldy bones of warped studs. Out of everywhere in the home, this room was the most inhospitable; and yet, it seemed it was here that Mom spent most of her time. There was make-up and magazines and burner phones and gift cards and clothes and bowls and boxes and bags of garbage. In the dirt, a groove—in all likelihood, her favorite sitting spot. Either by sense or memory, or some combination of the two, he could smell her through the piss and shit and ripening filth. That strong, flowery smell—lavender, maybe—and also, something bitter. He couldn't place it now. He'd never been able to place it then. As a kid, he always chalked it up to her smoking, being gone for days on end without a shower, or wearing the same clothes over and over. But it hadn't been that, had it? It'd been her smell, her natural smell. The kind of smell you can't scrub away, like when you try to wash a dog.

Peter sat down in his mother's groove. It was drafty in the laundry room, given there wasn't much of it left, and he was shivering. He'd come to this place for answers. He'd gotten observations, instead.

He touched his neck. He'd killed a guy. He didn't feel badly about it, and he knew he shouldn't have to. He'd saved his, and Mary's, life. She'd killed his Mom, but after seeing all of this, and knowing what he already knew, it was obvious that'd been a mercy. That it'd been a long time coming.

I'm not a killer, though. Peter thought he might become one, with Mary's dad's blood on his hands, with his mom's genes in his. He looked around, at his mother's temple. She'd lived as much as a woman like her could live to the life of a cloistered nun. For how long she'd been a werewolf, when she'd come back, what her intentions had been in stalking him… He'd never know. But what he did know, and for some reason had been burying, was that Mary had been bitten, and by all accounts, soon, she'd be a werewolf.

I'm a caretaker. He came to his feet, the tingling of purpose at the tips of his fingers and in his forehead. He'd spent his entire life taking care of himself. He'd gotten good at it, too. The shadow of the Wolf had always been nipping at his heels. For twenty years, he'd given it the slip. Now, the Wolf was dead. That anxiety he felt back in the hall? It wasn't fight-or-flight. It was the brakes finally engaging. Things were slowing down. Paths were opening up. He was safe. He was in control. It was new and terrifying territory, but it was his to roam and mark. He was a caretaker. At last, he could say he was taken care of. Mary, on other hand, wasn't. He had to be the strong one.

"I'm going to save you," he said aloud.

On his way out the house, he stopped by the kitchen first, to have another look in the fridge.

4

Goetia had a way of exerting itself on those that roamed its crumbling corridors. As Mary went through its southern portal, a clinging warmth seeped into her skin, settling into the palms of her hands and the soles of her feet. They were no longer hers, and she would have to give to get them back. A light mist hung over her face, swaying about it like a veil. Through it, she would see things as they were meant to be seen. Her blood chilled, and all that it touched and pumped into was numbed. She was anesthetized, dead-like, and once she found a reason for which to live, her blood would boil, and the veil would part, and her hands and feet would burn with providence.

Mary took off her boots and socks and put her bare feet to the earth. It was freezing, but she told herself it wasn't, that it couldn't be, so she grinned it away. She pressed on, rock and root punishing her for not having maintained the calluses she'd honed for so many years. Outstretching her arm, she ran her fingers over the old stone, as if to decipher the meaning of the cracks and fissures that ran along them. It was easy to imagine what this place may have seen and heard during her absence, but she didn't want to imagine. She wanted to experience it, absorb it. She was a daughter of Goetia, and its heiress. Dad had discovered it, breathed life into it. And you know what? Mary might do the same. But first: answers.

She came to an intersection. It was overgrown. The walls were coming apart, separating from one another, letting outside, in. There was a lot of work to be done here. She went left.

Mary breathed in. The air tasted like November: damp soil, dead leaves, and burning wood. She peered into sleeping quarters as she passed them. Most of them had been reclaimed by plants and weeds and the small, feasting things that ran amongst them. The corners had belonged to bees and wasps, their homes hitched there, abandoned at this time to the shivering season. There was no evidence in these rooms she or the others had ever been here. It was something to be proud of, and yet, it made her sad.

The hall let out to their dining area. It was large, not as massive as she remembered, and yet, it took her breath away. A few long wooden tables had survived. She remembered one of Dad's Demons had made them in the early days. The ceiling was on the floor. Most of it had caved-in. From the breach, heavy vines tumbled down, swaying like anemones in slow-motion.

Mary stopped and gave the room a moment to impress. She'd come here for magic, yet all she'd gotten was the mundane. Even her experience at the entrance, in retrospect, was all pageantry. Disappointed, she dropped onto one of the benches and drove her elbows into the table beside it, pouting. Up close, unclouded by nostalgia, Mary saw the table in a way she hadn't before. She sat back, leaned to her side. Underneath the table, branding: not Goetia's, but His Kingdom, a local, Christian-based theme park that'd gone out of business a few years back. The Demons hadn't built this. They'd pulled it out of the garbage.

"Son of a bitch."

Mary got up, put her boots on, and went on.

Goetia twisted and turned, each stone corridor and room becoming increasingly indistinguishable from the others. She had memories to hang here, but where were the hooks? She remembered running through these halls, leading a procession of scabby children, but was that this hall? Or the one she'd just come out of? There had been that boy a few years ago. They'd made out somewhere around here. It'd been the first time she'd kissed someone her own age. She remembered doodling on the Wall of Goetia with crayons she'd stolen from school, and Solomon helping her wash it all off before Dad saw it. Or had that been Beth?

Speaking of the Wall of Goetia, here it was, rising out of the shadows and mist. This part of the old fort hadn't been part of the original blueprints. Through cave-ins, battles, and an earthquake, this part of the old fort had been reshaped. It was held fast to the rest of the place by the growths, like glue, that'd sprung up within the gaps. It was only ten or so feet in length, and at the top of a small hill that seemed so much larger when she'd been little, but there was no denying it then, just as there was no denying it now, the Wall was special. Here was her magic.

The ghosts of ghosts had been shakily scratched into the Wall. Names of contracts Dad and his Demons had taken on for the police, politicians, and the pussies who couldn't bear the sight of a little blood underneath their fingernails. They were impossible to read now. Although she didn't know much about law, something told her having a ten-foot monument to assault, robbery, and murder wouldn't look good in court. Mary could already hear Dad's excuse now: "Goetia writes the names, not us."

Mary went down on her knees. She felt at the ground until her hand closed around a sharp stone, and then brought it to the wall. She closed her eyes, waving her hand back and forth until... There. She opened her eyes. This was the spot. And this was how it was done. She pressed the tip of the stone to the Wall and closed her eyes again. Next, free association. Every movie psychiatrist's favorite technique for hard-to-reach kids. She shook her head at her cynicism. Clearing her mind of the weeds of doubt, she found faith, and then, she began to write.

She was finished before she knew it. She didn't have to search for the word. It was already there, waiting to be written. She kept her eyes shut, though, because in the dark, another: Mother. Her name hadn't been written on this wall, but a picture of her had been placed beside it, and above it: Melancon. They'd been a part of Goetia once, and Mom had run off with one of them. Mary had been too young to really remember what things had been like before then, but that must've been when everything changed. Her dad had been a right-eous, vindictive man. If someone had told her he'd been planning for years to murder everyone who'd ever been part of Goetia as a way to achieve his true goal, which was killing his wife and her lover... Mary wouldn't bat an eye. And yet, she did, blinking, but not really seeing the Wall before her. Because there'd been that woman on the slab. The woman on the slab in the Giving Room. It was the first, and last, time Mary had ever gone in there. At the time, the woman had been just another naked, bleeding woman, but over time, she'd become something more. She'd become her mother. It was the story she'd told herself through childhood to get some kind of closure. As she'd gotten older, though, she believed it less, and put more stock in the theory Mom was still out there, waiting in line somewhere for a six-pack. Now, squeezing her eyes shut, Mary was certain that woman on the slab in the Giving Room had been Mom, and all of this... all of the killing... it'd started there. It was then and there that Dad had fallen through his flesh.

Mary opened her eyes. She couldn't read what she'd written. It was gibberish. Laughing, she came to her feet and started down the hill. Halfway back to the fort proper, she stopped and glanced over her shoulder. Still gibberish. Then she thought about Peter for some reason, and kept going.

As Mary plunged deeper into Goetia's verdant depths, it became clear to her this was the place she needed to be at every full moon from here on out. The old fort was massive, serpentine, and far enough removed that, when she transformed into a werewolf, no one would hear her or come across her until daybreak. Dad had seen Goetia as a place that could exist both with and without society. "A transient experience for transient souls awaiting the invitation to the Beyond within." That's what Dad used to tell the new families who joined. The thing was, for all the "inhuman" things he and his Demons did, they were still, at the end of the day, human. They thought that, if you got dirty enough, that when you finally cleaned yourself, you'd shine brighter than before. Salvation through scouring, or some shit. But Mary? She had a real chance to see how real Goetia really was. It was like looking at god when he fucks you. The eye contact makes all the difference.

The Giving Room wasn't far. It was getting darker, too. This part of the old fort was mostly intact, and what little gaps there were had been overgrown, like the walls, floor, and ceiling, with lichen. Mary used her cellphone for light. Ahead, small shapes scattered. When they were out of sight, they hissed and growled, but the nearer she drew, the quieter they became until, passing their haunts and hideouts, they were whimpering. For years now, Goetia had been theirs. She was trespassing, but they could sense what others could not, and because they could, they knew better.

Mary's nipples went hard.

The old fort had been built against a cave system. It was here, a little past the cave's entrance, a massive steel door had been fixed; in it, at the center, a small, rectangular slide-away door for conversing. Beyond the door, the Giving Room. Mary stopped before it. She shone her harsh light on the door's rusted surface. Water ran down it, and with the rust mixed in, it looked as if it were bleeding. Why the original architects had decided to connect the fort with the cave, she couldn't say, and neither could Dad. His only explanation had been the only one anyone could ever conjure, and it was this: "They did it, because they knew."

She took a deep breath. The door was slightly open. Holding her cellphone with her teeth, so she could see what she was doing, she grabbed the edge of the door with both hands and pulled. Several days in the hospital and a psych ward showed themselves. Her body temperature sky-rocketed. Her muscles tensed and then turned to jelly. An enema of pain shot up her ass, into her lower back. She bit her cellphone so hard, the screen cracked, but still, she pulled. Screaming, grunting, and cursing incoherently - "Opnyucntfcukginwhorebisch."—the door gave just an inch. Just enough for her to slip through.

Mary limped into the Giving Room like a wounded animal. Taking her cellphone out of her mouth, she shone her light across the roiling murk. The room was small, smaller than she remembered, than she imagined, than it had any right to be. The ceiling was steepled, the walls sharp and turned inward. The floor was wet, and it writhed, for though it was November, in here, the humidity and heat held summer. There were tracks in the soil. When she turned her light on them, she saw they all ran to the same place: a ragged, glistening hole in the ground. It was from here, she knew, that Goetia's gifts were given.

If the hole was there, then the slab… Mary threw her light to the opposite side of the room. She gasped. There it was. It was there. Against the wall, at an angle. Stone slab like a gurney. On it, bones. A complete skeleton. Flesh picked clean. Long since fallen and having filled millions of tiny bellies.

Mary went to the slab. Her feet sank into the soil, up to her ankles, but the tracks were undamaged. Like wrinkles, they were deeply set and meant to stay.

"Mom…" she whispered.

The skeleton didn't respond, but she didn't need it to. She'd made up her mind on who it was, who it had to be, and why it had to be her.

"Women are the bones in all the so-called great men's hands," Mary whispered. "See them build without them."

Mary sat down against the slab and stared at the hole. Worms unlike any she'd ever seen before moved in and out of the soil.

Dad was dead, and Goetia was hers. Peter had killed him. There was no way either of them was getting out of this unchanged. She was turning into a werewolf, so what was he becoming? A killer? Maybe he'd want to kill her for killing his mom. Or maybe he'd just want to kill. He wouldn't have to worry anymore if there was nothing to worry about.

Be my Demon, Mary thought, reaching behind her, caressing her mother's bones. *Or my gift.*

The bone snapped. Mary brought it round to see. It was a piece of her mom's rib.

FRIDAY, NOVEMBER 13ᵀᴴ, 2020

1

The wasteland turned white at midnight. Snowflakes were falling, covering the craters and construction equipment. The distant highway, a black strip against the feathered sky, glowed as cautious drivers slowed on the slickening roadway. Plumes of exhaust swelled and lifted into the air, and by this, with the help of the wind, the night appeared to breathe.

Peter killed the headlights, but kept the car running. Even with the heat off, it was, somehow, too warm. He rolled down the window. The cold came in and cut through him. He shivered, and his nose started to drip, and yet after the shock wore off, it still wasn't enough. His body ran hot these days, like it was fighting off an infection.

The wasteland had started to sing. He leaned his head out the window and felt cold pricks on his neck. It was sleeting. He sat back in his seat and closed his eyes. When the ice hit the glass and metal scattered across these barrens, it chimed, ringing out a song that'd never been heard before and would never be heard again. This was Peter's favorite time of the year, and also, his favorite time of the night. There was something uniquely personal about it. Everything dialed down just enough to take it all in. He could see the appeal of a place like Goetia.

He didn't know where Mary lived. He didn't know her number by heart, either. Coming here, to the place where she'd opened up to him, made sense. He'd waited last night for her, too. She'd never shown. But now there were headlights in the corridor, drawing nearer.

Him and her, they'd never been fully in sync. One was always be-hind the other. Peter, usually. Not anymore, though. Mom was dead, and he had a death under his belt.

2

Mary crept her car into the wasteland. Someone was here. Maybe it was Peter, or maybe it was some police officer "looking the other way" as a prostitute sat next to him, jerking their way out of one sticky situation and straight into another. In either event, explana-tions would be expected.

The snow was coming down hard. She flashed her high-beams, but the light barely broke through. Hesitation wasn't something she was familiar with, yet she had the brake pedal pushed to the floor all the same. She'd been a daughter of Goetia, but now she was the Daughter of Goetia. Her life had meaning. She hoped that, soon, it would have purpose, too. Ever since her fiery, self-imposed exile, she'd burned through the world, one shallow relationship after the other, and during that time, she'd never managed to find anything to do with all the ashes. But not anymore.

Flicking her windshield wipers to spasmodic, she headed headfirst for the strange car. Was this Peter's? She knew he had a motorcycle, but she didn't remember him mentioning that he owned a car. He had to, right? If he didn't, and it wasn't him, then who was it? The aforementioned cop, scrambling to find some fast food napkins to wipe himself off with? Some random drug dealer, running a steal of a deal on cocaine on account of its similarities to the weather? Or was it Detective Sono? Maybe with one of his cronies from the bureau. There was no doubt in Mary's mind someone had been following her since her discharge from the hospital. She glanced in her rear-view mirror. Nothing. Only darkness had given chase.

Mary cringed. Her stomach was upset. She seemed to be breathing as fast as her heart was beating. What the hell was this? She pressed her fist to her chest, like some warlord about to put a bounty out on emotions. There was a time and place to feel. This wasn't one of them.

Is this how pregnant women get? she wondered, imagining the beast brewing inside her.

She went to take her foot off the brake, but the car was coming towards her. Sweat beaded down her back.

3

Peter pulled up beside Mary's car. To anyone else passing by, they'd look like two highway patrols trading stories to get each other through the long, cold night. And in a way, they were.

She looked startled, like a dog backed into a corner, whose only way out, every time, was by going through. He could only imagine what he must've looked like to her.

"Hey," Peter said, giving her a pathetic wave as she rolled her window down.

Mary's face hardened, went cold, the same way these roads would in a few hours' time.

"I didn't know your number or where you lived."

She grinned, swirled her fingers to signal to their surroundings. "Great minds think alike. Did you go home when you got out?"

"Yeah, you?"

"Yep."

Peter nodded, his lower teeth grinding against his upper lip. "I… don't know where to begin."

"Not here," Mary said. "Follow me back to my place. You can crash there as long as you need to." She pawed at her neck; the wound was itchy. "It's only fair. You go back to your apartment yet for your stuff?"

He'd driven past the building a few times at this point, but he'd never actually considered trying to go in. Everything there, be it his belongings or his memories, no longer belonged to him. They were part of the past, and now that Mom was dead, it was, too.

"Where's your bike?"

"Huh?" He fell back in his seat. "Forgot all about it."

Mary said, "Maybe we should get ourselves a minivan."

And with that, she led them out of the wasteland.

4

It took them an hour and a half to get back to Mary's apartment. A blizzard at two in the morning was nothing to be trifled with, especially in a place like Talbot, where City Hall was infamous for misallocating funds for public works into their own hungry, endless pockets. By the time they parked in the lot behind her building, the only color left in the city came from the traffic lights feebly going through the motions. The buildings and streets were completely covered in snow. The accumulation flowed effortlessly through the city, unmarred by footsteps or tread marks. To Mary, as she pulled up behind her apartment building, it looked as if a single massive white sheet had been laid across a city. It called to mind a morgue, and then, an abandoned estate, with all the antiques covered-up. Either way, tonight, Talbot belonged to Nature, and Nature alone.

Peter trudged beside her as she brought him through the building, and then up to her apartment. They melted as they went, leaving behind them a trail of water and ice. Mary considered coming back out later to clean the mess up. She didn't know want anyone to know she was here.

"Who's Laura Louise?" he asked, as they came up to her door.

Mary, getting her keys out, said, "What?"

Peter pointed to the small plaque on the wall.

"Oh, she used to live in my apartment." She tried to unlock her door, but it was already unlocked.

"You ever meet her?"

Mary opened the door to pale darkness, the light coming through the windows tinted with the eerie shade of winter. "Nope."

"Surprised you kept it up. Probably confuses people."

Mary went around Peter as he came into her apartment, said, "Yep," and turned on the lights.

5

Peter wasn't one to judge, but tonight, he couldn't help it. Mary's apartment smelled foul. Something was dead in here, and it'd been dead for a long time. She'd probably gotten used to the smell, he thought, closing the door behind him. Probably had gotten used it to a while ago, long before she moved in.

Her place was nice, though. Nice, in a snapshot of time sort of way. Mary didn't really have a style, other than maybe serrated. The décor in her apartment was, literally, too plush, too velveteen to have been picked out by her. The couch was jade, the chairs, mauve. The rug underneath the spindly coffee table was burnt sienna, and a multitude of other colors coming together in lines and circles. It looked like something you'd see hanging in a middle-eastern market, in some old Hollywood movie. She had two imposing cabinets that probably weighed as much as their cars out back. They were filled with porcelain cups and plates that'd been tinted with dust from disuse. Most of these things must've belonged to Laura Louise, Peter figured. But in the way Mary kept everything—not so much tidy as she just didn't touch anything—it was almost as if she were housesitting.

"I'm going to make some coffee," Mary said, turning on the light in the kitchen as she headed in there.

Peter went to the tall, eye-like windows that overlooked the streets outside. He said, "I'm good," and stepped into their wintry glow. "I should get some sleep."

"Come on," she said. "You and I both know we're not sleeping tonight."

Burning up, Peter pressed his forehead to the pane. The cold crept into his skull, left frost upon his brain. His thoughts slowed as he stared at the city disappearing behind the growing snowdrifts. He couldn't remember the last time it'd snowed like this in Talbot. It was nice, and it was good timing. Unlike after Mare's Diner, where he and Mary had marooned themselves to weeks of getting trashed on his couch, while at the same time trying to maintain appearances, and also, their lives… this time, with the blizzard, they could take it slow and prepare themselves for what was to come. They were fortunate in that way, he thought. Most people didn't get this kind of opportunity, except for criminals. And they didn't usually have the foresight to make the most of it. But they did.

"Here."

Peter turned around to find Mary with two cups of coffee in hand.

"I drink it black."

He took a cup, said, "Of course you do."

Mary shook her head and headed back into the kitchen, and Peter followed. He tried to get a better look at the rest of the apartment, but it was too dark beyond the living room and kitchen. It was almost as if the light refused to go further than it had to.

"Sorry about the smell," she said, dropping, with a groan, into the chair at the kitchen table.

Smiling, Peter shrugged and sat opposite her. The steam from the coffee took him by the nose like two forceful fingers and drew his mouth to the cup. She was right. They had a long night ahead of them.

"Cleaned up everywhere not too long ago—"

As Peter set his cup down, he noticed a crusty, red stain on the edge of the table.

"—but I don't know." She looked around the kitchen. "Must've missed something. You'll get used to it."

Peter grabbed his stomach as it started to growl. He stared at Mary's refrigerator, and then thought of the one back at Mom's house, the one filled with putrefying meat. His stomach growled louder.

Mary acknowledged it with a laugh, but she didn't offer him anything to eat. Instead: "Man, what the fuck?"

"Ha," Peter said, gulping down some more coffee. "My life summed up in one sentence."

"Same."

"Where do we even start?"

"Sharon would say our childhoods."

"Fucking Sharon," Peter said, his teeth buzzing with caffeine.

"Fucking. Sharon."

Mary pretended to toast him with her cup.

He did the same.

"Our parents are dead," Mary said.

"They wanted to kill us."

"You killed mine. I killed yours. That really fucked me up for a hot minute."

Peter said, "Yeah. Same. We're cool, though, right?"

Mary's eyes were glassy, and her mouth moved ahead of her words, but in the end, she said, "Yeah."

Peter pointed to his neck, signaling the wound on hers.

"Yep."

"Fuck." Peter remembered the first time Mary had seen the beast, his mom, on the roof at the Melancons'. "I guess you're going to turn into a cunting werewolf."

She snorted, made a fist, and then slouched down in her chair. "All signs point to yes."

Peter laughed. He knew he shouldn't be laughing, but it was almost three in the morning and his heart was beating a mile a minute.

"Man, what the fuck?"

"Exactly."

"Are you…?"

"Actually, yeah." Mary straightened up, leaned forward. "I can't explain it, but I'm alright. It… makes sense to me."

"I did a lot of research on lycanthropy last month. If I can get into my apartment—"

"No, I think I want to find out for myself."

Peter stared at her in disbelief. *She's full of it. There's no way she's okay with this.*

"I am," she said, as if responding to his thoughts. "I'm okay."

"What… I'm sorry. What… makes sense about turning into a werewolf?"

"I told you." She got up, brought the coffee pot over, and topped them off. "I can't explain it."

Peter didn't believe her. If anyone in this world had themselves figured out, it was Mary.

"Don't you feel different?" she asked, almost accusatorily. "Not, like, in a way that someone should. But, like, you. Specifically, you."

"I…"

She went on: "It's traumatic what we went through. It would mess anyone up, right?"

"Right."

"But they were our parents. I don't think they were working to-gether. But somehow, they decided they both wanted to kill us. Twice. Two months in a row."

"They killed a lot of people, Mary."

She got loud. "Yeah, I know that, Peter! But all of it was specifi-cally for us! This wasn't some bombing or some shithead who treats women like shit shooting up a school because he's sexually frustrat-ed…"

"Okay…"

"This was for us. I'm going to turn into something, and what I'm turning into makes sense to me. You don't feel different?"

Peter knew what she was getting at. He did feel different. She felt different, too. The air around her was different. It was like she was made of a new substance. Something reactive. Something unstable. That, or in this cold and stark, dark-light, he was really seeing her for who she really was.

"Peter," she said, bullying an answer out of him.

"I do."

"How?"

"N-Not anxious." Why was he stuttering and stalling? This was Mary. At this point, no one knew him better. But this change in him, for some reason, he wanted it to be all his own. "Not overthinking, or overanalyzing, or worrying about stupid shit like, how much the hospital bill's going to be. I don't care. I—" he stared at her, and she stared back, chewing on something, "—thought I was having anxiety attacks, but they're more like surges of adrenaline. I feel like, for the first time in my life, I'm ready to face something, you know?"

"Being one of two survivors of two mass murder crime scenes will do that."

"Yeah." He was talking too much. He'd never wanted to talk so much. "You're right. Not about that. Well, you are." He took a drink. "I mean, about… All of it being about us. These last two months, it's like there's been nothing else."

"Try my whole life, but with Dad."

Shit, he thought, *she's right.* And then he said it: "Shit, you're right. That's it." He drank some more, almost spilling it down his shirt. His hand was shaking. His mouth had gone numb, or felt larger than it ought to be. At its roots, his hair hurt. "I think that's it. Even when I'd gotten away from Mom, she was still there—"

In the mother-darkness.

"—but now she's gone. And I wish I had understood her sooner, but now she's finally gone. I don't…" He was laughing at himself. "I don't have to be that person anymore that she made me. I mean, I'm still me, but I'm more. Or, I guess, I can be more. If I do that and something comes along and punishes me for it, at least…"

6

"… at least it won't be her."

Mary put her elbows to the table, hid her face behind her hands, which were knitted together. She had a big stupid grin on her face, and she didn't want him to see it and take it the wrong way. Her first initiate into Goetia. She'd always known it would be him. She just never realized how easy it would be to get him to sign on the proverbial dotted line. She didn't need him, but she wanted him. And in her opinion, one was the same as the other. All it came down to was how honest you were with yourself, and how much you gave a shit about the opinions of others. Dad hadn't said that. She'd come up with that all on her own.

Peter was sweating. His face was shadowed. He was exhausted. He, like her, probably hadn't slept since they'd been discharged. When he'd been looking out the window, she'd slipped a concoction into his coffee. Something one of the chemist Demons used to throw together in Goetia. Nothing too strong or addictive. Just something to help people loosen up. She'd figured he'd needed it. But apparently not. There was no way it could've taken effect yet.

Nevertheless, he was waiting for her response. So, she said, "If not her, then who?"

Peter shrugged. "I don't know, and that's fine with me. But…" she felt his eyes on her wound, peeling it back with his sad curiosity, "… I feel responsible for what happened… what's going to happen to you."

And with that, the ink was dry.

7

"You, basically, are," Mary said, jokingly.

Peter let out a sigh of relief. He shifted in his seat, pulled his shirt away from his back. He'd sweated through his clothes. He'd needed to hear that from her, and to know she didn't hold it against him.

He asked her, "How do you feel different?"

At first, it seemed as if Mary was going to tell him she couldn't explain it, but instead, she dropped her attention from him to the table, and started picking at it. There was another encrusted, red stain on her side.

"I feel unlocked. Everything makes more sense. My upbringing makes more sense." She licked the finger with which she'd been picking and then rubbed the table with it, smearing the stain. "At the same time, I have this need to be restrained. Ever since I left Goetia, everything has been going by so fast. You don't have time to make sense of anything when it's a blur." She scratched at the stain, mining bloody flakes. "I have a reason to control myself. And I'm sure as hell that after that first full moon, I'll fucking regret it."

He and Mary both cracked up. Hard. They were laughing from

their bellies. Tears leapt from their eyes. Finally, they wound down on squeals and sighs.

"It's the power, isn't it?" Peter said.

Mary thought on this for a moment, and then nodded.

"You're going to try to kill people, though."

Mary didn't say anything. It was hard to tell if she was even looking at him, or at something inside herself. The stain was gone. What was left of it now stained her hands.

I know she doesn't want to hear it, but: "Something I heard about werewolves is that they protect their territory. Maybe if there's no threat, you won't need to change, or to kill."

"There's always a threat," she whispered. "Someone's been following me."

He said, "Yeah, me too, I think."

"I got an idea," Mary said, pushing her coffee cup around. "I'm still working out the details, but I think it's something we can use on the full moons to keep me safe."

You safe? What about everyone else? Peter shook his head at himself. *You know what she means.*

"Will you help me, though?"

"Yeah, of course."

They didn't say anything else after that, because there was nothing else to be said. Instead, they sat in silence, at the table, neither awake nor asleep, until the sun rose and the snow stopped.

He wasn't sure when it'd happened, but as he got up to fall asleep on her coach, he realized he could no longer smell the death in Mary's apartment.

SATURDAY, NOVEMBER 14ᵀᴴ, 2020

1

Mary still went to work when she could, because working at the butcher's shop didn't feel like work most days. She'd left Peter back in the apartment. He told her he'd help straighten up the place as payment for letting him stay there. She'd been against the idea at first, but he'd worn her down. She had to make a conscious effort to not give one, two, or three fucks.

"Why are you here?" the Bossman asked, as Mary came in through the front door, kicking the snow off her boots.

She unwrapped the scarf from her neck, wincing as it tugged at the stitches there. "What about you?" She took her knitted gloves off one finger at a time, like the mad scientist she was about to become, when she breathed life into this dead meat. "What're you doing here?"

The Bossman stood behind the front counter, white apron conforming to the swell of his bulging belly. The bags under his eyes had bags of their own. A few of his fingernails were black and dying. When he breathed, he wheezed. A big man like the Bossman couldn't afford to see a doctor. Like an old engine held together by dirt, oil, and rust, the moment he was cleaned out, they'd be playing him out—one or two people gently weeping as the crematorium warmed up.

"You holding up?" he asked.

Distractions were important. That was one thing Sharon the therapist had gotten right. You could overthink a thing. Coming to Mid-

City Meats today wasn't about finding a distraction, though. It wasn't like it was hard to find something to cut up these days. No, Mary was here because Talbot was snowbound, and if anyone was following her, she'd know it. A foot of snow had been dumped onto the streets. People didn't come out unless they had a reason to.

The Bossman carried on: "I heard."

Mary, half-listening, went to the windows that looked out onto the street. At that moment, the clouds parted and the sun came through. The snow caught the light and blinded the world with it. But she didn't look away. In pain, she peered.

"Take some time off you need to. You've been through it."

No cars. No passersby.

"I'm only open because what else will I do? Go home."

No Feds. No Detective Sono.

"Or talk to me."

Mary pulled away from the window. She blinked hard until her eyes stopped hurting and readjusted to the light inside the shop. Turning around, she found the Bossman staring at her, gloved and holding a cleaver. He looked concerned, and also, like Dad. She started to sweat. Her sweat smelled like wolfsbane.

He tilted the cleaver towards her—Dad, not the Bossman. Now, she's eighteen, and he stands before her, wearing the moon on the back of his head. He smells like the creek; his hands are dirty, and his fingers are twisted, like old roots. He tells her to leave, and now, she's ten, and he's forever, and she's telling him she's sorry. He holds her in his arms and twirls her hair into spirals and tells her that Mom's never coming back. She cries until she's fifteen, and he's getting younger all the time. He invites her to court at midnight, and with Demons, she dances until the world is a blur and she is numb. At seven, she sleeps between Mom and Dad, goddess and god respectively, as the storm rages on outside their home. A tree branch lashes their home, and she jumps. When she lands, she's sixteen, on her ass, as the school bully walks away, her blood on their knuckles. Dad, a little worse for wear, gets it back, and then some. She thanks him, and then she cusses him out, a year later. He's found ascension through descension, and he's eating a lamb alive, throat first; and with a mouthful of its suffering, he tells her that her mother thought she was better than all of this, too. Five, she gives him five kisses on the cheek, and he gives her five back, and if you combine the kisses together, he might as well have been that old in her eyes, at that time. He's her best friend, and then he's her worst nightmare, when she's fourteen and he's had that many to drink. He comes to her in the middle of the night, in the middle of summer, when Goetia's crumbling walls can't keep out the humidity; her sheets are soaked through, and the spiders won't stop biting her, and the animals won't stop screaming; and he sits down beside her, palming her knee, and he tells her that one day, she will have to kill him, and she shakes her head and says she won't, and he tells her she doesn't have a choice, and she asks him why, and he tells her he'll make her. "No one can make me do anything," she cries, twenty, as her Dad lies dying, fifty, with that many breaths left, on Peter's rooftop. "Hold out your hand," he meant to say, and so this time, she does. She takes his hand in hers. "It's heavy, but you'll get used to the weight." Now, she's holding a cleaver, and him and her mother, they are eternal, and they are staring at the old fort, unnamed as of yet. "What if I can't?" she asks, her voice shrill. "Blood begets its truth," he tells her on her sixteenth birthday, taking her into the Giving Room for her special present. "And if I don't?" she asks, eighteen, straddling the young boy bleeding out beneath her. Dad emerges from the fire, wearing fur and tracking embers, and glinting, like a reflection in steel. "You will," he promises her, when she's eleven and getting ready for school, trying not to get too much dirt from Goetia's floor on her new shoes. He gets down on his knees—they don't crack like Mom's do—and straightening out the straps on the backpack she's wearing, says, "You have nothing to be ashamed of." She smiles and stares at the cleaver in her hand. Now, she's twenty, and there's a fat man caught in its blade. "Are you ready?" he says it like he's challenging her. She nods, and goes with him into the cold, bloodied dark, and there, imagines a hole in the ground, wreathed in writhing hoofs, and asks, "Where do you get your meat?" The fat man says, "These days, anywhere I can. You know a place?" She laughs, and starts cutting, and says, "I might. I'll let you know by the end of the month." He gives her a crazy look: "What happens at the end of the month?" She doesn't answer. She just puts her pink headphones in and keeps cutting.

2

With a roll of paper towels in one hand and some diluted cleaning spray in the other, Peter stepped into Mary's room and quickly realized how little he knew about her. Mom used to say that you could tell a lot about a person by how they lived. Not in terms of cleanliness necessarily, but scents, decorations, and the overall atmosphere. Peter's house always smelled like cigarette smoke and lavender. Mary's room smelled like jeans that hadn't been washed in a while. Peter's house was always clean and filled with the nicest things from the cheapest stores. Mary's room was, essentially, the essentials: a bed, a nightstand with a lamp on it, and a dresser; one wall outlet with a laptop and a phone charger plugged into it. The atmosphere in Peter's house had always been oppressive. You could feel the tension in the air, and it only gave when Mom went away, called, he knew now, by the moon. Not only had she been struggling to make it as a woman and a mother, but also, a human. The atmosphere in Mary's room was thin by comparison. It was hard to breathe in here. It was unwelcoming. It was like a shitty motel room that'd been rented out for two months straight by someone who always went and seldom came. Laura Louise must've not left any of her belongings behind in the bedroom. Everything in here, Peter figured, was everything she owned.

Leaning against the doorway, he mumbled, "Neither of us really ran all that far, huh?"

Peter started with the dresser. He sprayed it and wiped it down. Like he'd been living here his entire life, he went through her drawers, starting with the one at the top. Underwear, a bottle of lubricant, and a dildo still in the box. The next drawer: some shirts; and the one after: pants. The last drawer wouldn't budge. He went down on his haunches, took the handles in both hands, and pulled. The drawer ground forward a quarter of the way. Red in the face, he leaned forward and looked inside.

The drawer was filled with bags of dirt and rocks, and a chunk of stone that looked like it'd broken off something. A dead, dried-out earthworm was smashed against the side of it. Peter had never been to Goetia, but like the air, now that he knew it was out there, he could recognize it anywhere. What he didn't know was how long these keepsakes had been here. It was one thing for eighteen-year-old

Mary to take mementos with her from her home, despite her reasons for leaving it. It was another thing for twenty-year-old Mary, who had just visited Goetia, to bring these things back with her. He didn't know which one was worse.

The drawer slid easily into the dresser after he knew what was in it. He came to his feet, went to the nightstand. Again, he wiped everything down, and then turned the lamp on, to make sure the bulb didn't need to be replaced. The nightstand had a drawer in the middle of it. Opening it, he found a journal inside. He took it out, sat on the edge of Mary's bed, and suddenly smelling cigarettes and lavender, flipped to the first page. It read: *If talking to myself ever stops working, there's always this.* The entry was dated for January 22nd, 2017. Peter smiled and flipped through the journal. Every page after that was empty.

He put the journal back. He eyed the laptop charger and followed its cord as it snaked up the bed and under her pillow. He reached under it and took out the laptop. It wasn't nearly as old as he thought it would be. In fact, it was a brand-new model that was worth as much as at least one of his somewhat important organs. It was in perfect condition.

He opened the laptop and turned it on. It'd been in sleep mode, and not password protected. Her desktop was empty but for a shortcut to the Internet. Clicking on it, he immediately went to her search history, which only went back a few months. The rest she must've cleared. Her first search: *Violating a social norm.* Her last search: *1717 Somerset Lane, Talbot.* And the one before that? *How to plan a party.*

Peter's hands started to shake. He clawed her keyboard. Breaking out into a cold sweat, he closed his eyes, and it was there, in the mother-darkness, that he saw it: The party, or how he'd remember it from here on out. It was now confined to a single, straight hall, the very same he'd opened his front door to every single day for the last few years. Except where it should've ended at a wall, it let out to the moon. Between him and it, puddles of pale blood and the corpses dancing in them. When they moved, their limbs ripped free from their bodies and bruised organs slipped out of their orifices. Seeing them there, in this split-second nightmare, he hated them, and hated himself for hating—

He opened his eyes, ran his hands down his face. *What the hell was that?* He took a deep breath through his nose, and then coughed. It smelled of cigarette smoke and lavender.

Peter put the laptop back, got up, and left her bedroom. Dizzy, and his senses overloaded, he ran into the kitchen, turned on the sink, and lapped the water up out of the faucet, like a dog. He'd forgotten to take his medications. They were in his glovebox. That's what this was. Nothing else.

Recovering, he made his way back to Mary's room, but instead of staying, he grabbed his cleaning supplies and headed back out, going further down the hall, where the bathroom and another bedroom—one he hadn't seen yet—waited. He didn't bother with the bathroom. Mary's bathroom was immaculate. It shone so vibrantly, that, when Peter woke up this morning, he had to close his eyes to take a piss. Instead, he went for the second bedroom, the spare bedroom. The door was closed. He had a feeling it hadn't been opened in a while. Mary never said he couldn't. Besides, he had to straighten up everywhere. He knew better than to have Mom walk in after a long day to a dirty house.

Not Mom, he said, twitching. *Mary.* He laughed at himself, screwed up his eyes, stopping just short of smacking himself in the head and crying, "Doh!" Embarrassed with himself, he opened the door to the spare bedroom.

And he screamed.

A dead wolf lay on the floor, its bedding automotive air fresheners. It was white, and its fur covered in mysterious markings, not unlike those that scarred the face of the moon. The wolf's belly had been split open, and its lips flayed away, giving it a permanent snarl. Its legs were broken, twisted around unnaturally. It had no paws: They'd been hacked off, discarded but for the nails. One, two... eighteen in all that lay before the beast, arranged in semi-circles with forking lines.

Peter went down his haunches. He pressed his hands to his mouth and was surprised to find it wet with snot and tears. He wasn't crying. He was bawling. Chewing on his thumb, trying not to throw up, he leaned in over the macabre display.

The wolf's guts were gone, but the carcass wasn't empty. It was filled with black mud that constantly poured over itself, churning in its rotting cistern. Enthralled by its horridly hypnotic movement, Peter grabbed the beast's leg and pulled upwards, widening the body-wide gash. As more light hit it, the black mud stopped moving, and then, somehow slowly and immediately, it changed, fading from solid to shadow. At first, Peter couldn't believe what'd happened. Moments later, he was certain it hadn't actually happened at all. A trick of the light. A side effect of the medications.

He stood up and took a step back. But for the autopsy before him, the room was empty. Not even Laura Louise's gaudy furniture had been allowed in here. He knew this hadn't been the first animal Mary had killed. It was subtle, but her victims were here in one form or another: the brown fur at the north corner, the curling piece of ligament along the south wall; the black stains on the hardwood floor nearly scrubbed out; the shuttered closet doors, the edges of them scratched and chewed, by the things that'd gotten away from her just long enough to leave their mark in her Killing Room. He couldn't tell how long she'd been at it, but it'd been awhile; and for all her carefulness, she'd left this one out carelessly. She'd wanted him to find it. To see if he'd be willing to clean it up.

Peter left the spare room and came back with more paper towels, some bleach, and garbage bags. It was scary how much he wanted to kill her right now. As he stepped over the wolf, he imagined tearing Mary's neck open, finishing what Mom had started. At the same time, he was afraid for her. The anxiety was back in full-force, cresting at the top of his throat in acrid belches. To anyone else, it wouldn't make sense to protect her. But to anyone else, everything that'd happened to them wouldn't make sense, anyway.

Peter lifted the wolf's head and slid the garbage bag underneath it. He worked his way down its stiff body, pulling the bag along, until it stopped midway. Peter stopped before wrapping up the rest of it. He was crying again, and imagining, for some reason, the wolf's last moments. He could see it so clearly, the beast padding through the forest, darting between the trees; eyes wide and mouth quivering, alert and aware that something was amiss; that something had come into its domain; something not like the others that'd come to kill it and its kin; not a Hunter, but a Hunger; opportunistic, driven, and unafraid. Peter tried to imagine how she killed the wolf, but he couldn't; and because he couldn't, he started to run his hands over the animal, searching for bullet holes or stab wounds. But there were none. And like the black mud he'd seen inside it, disappearing before his eyes, now, in his mind's eye, his scenario didn't seem so likely.

Mary was a survivor, but to animals and humans alike, she was about as approachable as poison ivy. So, how had she done it? Did it see her and die right then and there? Or had it been like when he'd happened upon her on that first day of class? An instant connection formed from nothing. What had Ms. Selene, his Intro to Psych professor, called it? The thing that came after extinction.

He finished bagging up the corpse. He threw the air fresheners in with it. Grabbing some tape from the kitchen, he bound the makeshift body bag as best as he could. Not wanting to be seen dragging this thing down the hall, he remembered the fire escape and opted for that route, instead. He headed to the window. It was iced over and frozen shut, but with a few good cusswords and some elbow grease he got it open. Peter threw the dead wolf onto the fire escape, and without thinking, sent it straight into the dumpster below. A cloud of snow exploded upon impact, and the air glittered around it.

Resurgence, he said to himself. *Extinction then resurgence.*

About to shut the window, he stopped and stared, instead. There was someone in the alley below. Right at the edge, where the buildings let out to the street. They were watching him. There was no snow around their feet, because they'd been standing there a while. Under that heavy coat, behind that thick scarf, they watched him for a few more seconds, as if to make sure he knew they were there.

Then they turned around and walked away.

And in their wake, a parting gift.

Wolfsbane.

THURSDAY, NOVEMBER 19ᵀᴴ, 2020

1

It was three in the morning and Mary couldn't sleep. Since Sunday, when Peter had cleared out her Killing Room with no comment, she'd found herself lying awake at night, thinking of him. Nothing sexual, of course. She'd never been attracted to him. Some days, he didn't even register as a person to her. That was generally how Mary saw people she didn't want to fuck or hurt.

She got out of bed, keeping her blanket wrapped around her like a cultist's cloak. She went to the window. The blizzard had stopped yesterday; since then, it'd been nothing but a steady shower of flurries. The roads were, more or less, cleared. Schools had started back up. Most businesses were open. The snow wasn't so much snow as it was dark, turgid regurgitations. Winter, like anything with enough time and, in this case, human interference, could decay. And with its decay would come the insects that'd been buzzing about her, eager to get a whiff of her shit. The journalists. The Feds. But especially Detective Sono. He didn't check-in by phone with her like he did Peter. The whole thing was so obvious, it made her laugh. If Sono were any more transparent, the world might come to forget he was ever here.

Mary wandered out of her room. Wrapped in her blanket, she swayed like a Victorian madwoman self-exiled to her crumbling estate. Soon, she wouldn't need Laura Louise's old life to stand in place for her not-life. Soon, this crumbling estate of the late, great feminist would be left in the hands of a better woman, and Mary would take her place in the forest and rebuild what her father had ruined. Dad had the right idea, but he'd been the wrong person to see it through. He'd tried to turn self-destruction into a self-help movement as a way by which to justify the horrible urges inside him. She wouldn't do that. She knew what she was and what she was becoming.

And I have Peter, she thought, opening the door to the Killing Room. *Peter, to clean up my messes.* He had, too, in taking care of the wolf Goetia had given to her. *Dad had Demons,* she thought. *I won't. No one's going to fall into flesh, except for me. I'll do it so they won't have to. Story of my life.*

Mary closed the door to the Killing Room and headed into the kitchen. There, in the moon-white dark, she stood, peering into the living room, where Peter snored softly on the couch. She grabbed a cleaver from the cutting block—the very same she'd used at Mid-City Meats and Deli the other day—and went to him.

2

Peter wasn't asleep. Even if he had been, he wouldn't have been for long. Having someone standing over you, watching you sleep while they held a meat cleaver would do that. Having someone standing over you, watching you sleep while they held a meat cleaver for the past two nights would also do that, and then some.

Her hot breath fell around him as she leaned over the couch. The cleaver caught on the fabric, like it might one night on his tendons and nerves, and his stomach lurched. Opening his eyes slightly, he saw her moonlit reflection in the television's screen: on her knees against the back of the couch; bent forward, each arm folded over the other, with her chin to them; head tilted, mouth slightly open. She looked like a fresh mother, staring tenderly at her newborn.

Peter closed his eyes, and then he closed his grip around the knife he kept under his pillow. He wasn't scared. He just felt sad for her. Besides, she wasn't the only one to wander the apartment in the middle of the night. He'd do the same two hours later, when the sun started to singe the bottom of the sky. He wondered if she pretended to sleep when he watched her.

What're you looking for? he wanted to ask her. Because when he watched her, he looked for signs of the werewolf within her, trying to break through the skin. *I'm not like your dad,* he thought—the similarities between Mary and Mom far from lost on him. *I'm not a killer. I'm going to get you through this.* That's generally where the internal dialogue stopped, too. He was okay with not knowing what came next, when he got her through, whatever that meant. Was there really a next, though, for lycanthropy? If Parker at Maiden, Mother, and Crone was as much of an expert on werewolves as she made herself out to be, then once Mary no longer felt threatened, she wouldn't need to protect, kill, right?

But could a woman like Mary ever not feel threatened?

Peter dozed off. Something cold touched his neck, but at that point, he was dreaming. He dreamt it'd been Mary's lips. They were sharper than he would've thought.

SATURDAY, NOVEMBER 21ˢᵗ, 2020

When the snow stopped, Mary and Peter went out as little as possible. She had food and essentials delivered to the apartment, to avoid the reporters and the angry families who were trending on social media with clever hashtags.

Peter stood at the oven, shoveling scrambled eggs onto two plates from a skillet. Then he added a few greasy strips of bacon and some toast. Grabbing the plates, two bowls with yogurt in them, and the coffee pot, Peter brought their breakfast over to the kitchen table with all the confidence of a seasoned waitress. The scene made Mary think of Rita from Mare's Diner.

"Look at you," she said, as Peter settled into his chair, handing her a plate and bowl as he did so. "Thanks."

"Years of practice," he said. "Any Goetian prayers you want to say?"

He'd been asking about Goetia more lately. It made her feel tingly inside, like she imagined most spiderlike masterminds did when something touched their web.

"Nope." She filled her cup up with coffee, and then his. "My plan's ready."

Peter's mouth was gummed up with eggs and bacon, and his ears with the sound of his chewing. He hadn't heard her. This wasn't something she was going to repeat more than once. She waited until he sensed he'd missed something.

Him: "Oh?"

Her: "Yeah. I've got it all figured out for the thirtieth."

Something dark passed behind Peter's eyes. A rare glimpse of his inner-workings. He was a boy—honestly, she didn't see him as a man—who lived his life on edge, and on the edge. It made sense for there to be darkness in there, because darkness was all he knew. To him, plans were not built with stone or brick but scaffolding: Great stretches of rickety walkways thrown together around ideas and promises, fixed to nothing but himself, so when they fell, he fell with them. This entire time, whether he realized it or not, he'd allowed her to run the show. His biggest contribution? A party that'd only come together by happenstance. That was the curse of those who lived in the Old Country. They all died, again and again, in their dreams.

I bet he thinks he's taking care of me, she thought. Then: "Yeah, man, I got it all planned out. Me and you, we're going to Goetia on the twenty-eighth. There's a room, the Giving Room. We'll use that. Huge steel door blocks it off. I'll go in there the day of, and when I transform—"

"If," he said.

"—I won't be able to get out. We'll see what we're dealing with."

Peter nodded. "Okay, yeah. That's a good idea."

"I know."

"We'll need food and water. Blankets. We got to be careful or we're going to freeze to—"

"It'll all be provided," Mary said, thinking of the hole in the Giving Room.

"There're people following us."

"I know."

He dug into his breakfast. "They're probably going to follow us out there."

"Peter, what's the alternative? Whatever happens, at least we'll be in the middle of nowhere."

"True."

Mary stared at him from behind her coffee cup. Dad always had a silver-tongue, forked as it might've been. She, on the other hand, had never been good at the brainwashing business. She lured people in with her Demon-may-care attitude, but they seldom stayed. It was one thing for Peter to be her partner-in-trauma; it was another thing for Peter to simply be her partner. She had to do this right. Because once things started to get better, he might realize how bad she was for him.

"I realized just now that all this time we've spent together, I don't really know you that well. We killed each other's parents for fuck's sake."

Peter smirked and started pushing food around on his plate. "Yeah, I've been thinking the same thing."

"You know a lot about me. More than anyone else." That was true, but not entirely. "I know where you came from. I know how much you worry. Used to worry. You said that's different now."

He smiled. "Yeah."

"What were you doing before all this?"

Peter scratched his neck, avoided eye contact. "Honestly, nothing. Going through the motions. It was like I was running in place."

Christ, she thought, *this is going to take all night.*

"Mom wasn't part of the equation. It was like I took my life and cut everything out before I turned eighteen. If anything came up, I just buried it."

Doing her best therapist impersonation, Mary said, "But it always came back up."

"Always," he said, softly.

Peter paused.

Mary leaned in, as if she were putting her ear to a safe, to hear the lock as she twisted the dial. She was close. Just a few more turns.

"Mom was fucked up, obviously." He chewed on the inside of his lip. "It wasn't just her, though. It was… everything… that happened around her."

"Did you have to do things?"

He gave her a slight nod, and then looked to the windows, where the sun and snow made them glow blindingly.

"I killed someone," she said, lying.

Peter's attention snapped to her. His eyes dilated, readjusting to the light.

"When I was a teenager, at Goetia. Dad made me do it, but I liked it, because I knew it made him happy."

His lips took the form of a question, but instead of asking something, he confessed. "I used to get drugs for my mom. Sometimes, I'd try to get her so fucked up so she wouldn't leave the house. Sometimes, she had these boyfriends and girlfriends come over, and I, uh, I'd say something or break something so they'd hurt me, or her.

Anything to get her to stay…

"This one time." Peter dug the heel of his palm into his eye. "Shit, how did I forget about this?"

Almost there. Troubled childhood. Untreated mental illness. Just need the last part of the combination.

"I was fourteen. She came home in the middle of the night, and when I woke, I found her asleep in the laundry room. She was naked. The washing machine was covered in blood. There was a big pile of bloody clothes inside. There was this woman she used to fuck around with. Sometimes in front of me, when she was really out of her mind. She didn't come around after I found Mom like that in the laundry room. I figured something happened. That woman came into my room a couple of times… Nothing happened." He emphasized this. "Nothing happened. But I was glad she was gone. Fuck, how did I forget this? Mom, she said, 'We do each other's dirty laundry. If we don't, then one of us won't make it.'"

"She was killing people to stop herself from killing you."

Peter laughed and raked his nails down the table. "I fucking guess. Jesus, how did I fucking forget that?" He wiped his forehead with his arm, got up, and got some ice water. "I feel like shit, but thanks for pulling that out of me."

Mary watched him chug the water. When he finished, he actually licked the inside of the cup, like a dog, before filling it back up again.

"After the full moon, we stay."

Peter stopped chugging, started sipping.

Mary got up from the table and went to window beside the fire escape, opened it, and went outside. The steel groaned beneath her. Her feet slipped on the ice webbed between the grating. Gripping the handrail, she then leaned over it and stared out into Talbot. The wind licked her face, sapping the heat from her cheeks with every pass, and making her eyes sting and feel as hard as marbles. But she kept her gaze fixed on the melting city and waited, because despite the cold, she had to play it cool.

And the award for best actress goes to…

"What do you mean 'stay'?" Peter asked behind her.

He came onto the fire escape with her. Bolts in the brickwork gave to his weight. In all likelihood, it wasn't mean to hold both of them at the same time. But they'd adapted. Everything else around them could, too.

Without turning around, and trying her best to hide her shivering, Mary said, "We revive Goetia. The Giving Room will give us everything we'll need. You won't understand it until you see it, but if you accept that cunting werewolves are real…"

Peter laughed and stepped up beside her; leaned over the handrail as she did.

"… then why not other things?" Still, she peered to the city, but now, she made an effort to look in the direction of the Old Country. "Wouldn't it be nice to have some control for once? Control over where you live? Control over who you let into your life? I only left Goetia because of what Dad turned it into. Before that, though? It was amazing." She pulled her arms from the handrail. Some skin had been showing, and when she did so, a layer of flesh was ripped away. "Surrounded by family. People I trusted. People I loved." She rubbed the blood into the fabric of her shirt. He didn't notice, or he didn't care. "Dad kept us afloat with crime. With what the Giving Room gives, we'll be more like a farm. I already have a connection with my job. That's just the start. We're survivors. We do this, we'll inspire other survivors. They'll come to us. People who the world just wants dead. There's more of them out there than you think. There's nothing wrong with making things smaller, simpler. There's power in that. Does that make sense?"

Peter pulled away from the handrail. His skin tore, too, but it only bled for a moment. "You want to start a cu… a commune with me?"

"I'd like you to consider it. That's all. Peter…" She placed her hand on his shoulder. "We deserve this. And I already know what to do."

Wind ripped through the alley. Loose snow fell from the roof around them, but not on them. The fire escape shook, but they held, and so it held, too. The trash in the dumpster below shifted; something was swimming in that sea of black plastic and rot, getting by, just out of sight.

"Mary, I… heh." He touched her hand. "If there's anyone else there, they'll know about you."

"And that's perfect," she said, making a fist and punching him gently in the chest.

"Is it?"

"It is. Because it won't be bullshit. We'll actually practice what we preach."

Peter smiled and asked, "What're we preaching?"

Mary shrugged. "Self-preservation."

"I…"

Mary waved her hand and headed back inside. "Just think about it. I'm going to make a list of everything we need."

She turned around, now back in the apartment, and faced Peter, alone in the cold. "Detective Sono left you a message on your phone this morning. He wants to go with you to your apartment to get your stuff. You should do it. See what he knows."

Peter didn't even bother asking her why she'd gone through his phone.

In her ears, she heard a clicking, like the sound of a lock unlocking, and smiled.

MONDAY, NOVEMBER 23RD, 2020

1

Peter waited on the first floor of his old apartment building, alone but for the death. The forensic cleaners had done their best to scrub and sterilize the crime scene. It hadn't been enough. The blood and gore had gotten into the very heart of the place. It needed to be exorcised. He could still see it, feel it, taste it everywhere around him. Massive stains were sprayed and splattered across the ceiling, floor, and walls. In the carpet, choking the fibers, stinking viscera. He breathed through his nose, because if he opened his mouth, he'd taste them—the dead, most of whom he'd never known and never met. They tasted of sweat, cheap beer, nicotine, and body spray. They tasted of where they came from, too. Stuffy dorm rooms. Moldering sublets. Mom and Dad's house, where candles always burned and dinner was always served. Peter should've been surprised by his heightened perception. He wasn't. If there was one good thing about chronic anxiety, it made you sharp, and right now, his senses cut at a molecular level.

His stomach growled. Then it contracted. The front doors rattled. The opaque glass set into them showed a shadowy figure outside, waving his arms. It was Detective Sono. He'd just been in here, and he'd gone out there to quell the growing mass of concerned citizens and starving journalists.

"Why is he here?!" someone cried.

"We want to talk to him!"

"Are you still considering him a suspect?"

"Where's the girl?"

"They were working with their parents, you fucking pig!"

"… just sweep this under the rug."

The shouting turned to screaming. Shoes and heels scraped and clipped against cement. An order was barked. Police sirens yelped. At first, it sounded as if had started to rain, then he realized the crowd were hurling rocks at the side of the building.

Better to burn it down, he thought to himself. *Salt the earth afterwards.* Saying that to himself, he thought about Maiden, Mother, and Crone. That's where Mary was at right now. Or so she said.

Detective Sono backed through the front door—

"It's a conspiracy to thin out the Old Country's…"

—and quickly shut it.

"The natives are getting restless," he said.

Peter asked, "Where'd they come from? They weren't there when we pulled up."

"This is Talbot," he said, smoothing out the wrinkles in his jacket. "Showing your ass at a public travesty is a pastime." As if he'd caught onto how jaded he sounded, Sono followed-up with: "They're scared."

Peter paced back and forth between 101 and 103, where Vanslow had lived and probably also died. His shoulders hurt. His back ached. His head throbbed, and his throat was constricted. This building, and the terrible things that'd happened in it… He was reacting to it, or it was reacting to him. An allergy to atrocity. He wouldn't be able to stay here for long, he knew. His body wouldn't let him. Another part of his life he'd have to remove. Thanks to his hospital stay and Mary's insistence on isolation, the lines were already drawn. It was up to him when he made the first cut. With a Goetian blade.

"Peter, you alright?" Sono asked.

He stopped pacing. "Yeah."

"You haven't left Mary's in days."

Peter cocked his head.

"Have you been following the news?"

He shook the burner phone Sono had given him. "Just text and call. Computer's…" He nudged his head up to the ceiling. "Still up there."

Scratching his neck, Sono said, "Sure."

"What's the news saying?"

"Worst thing to ever happen to Talbot. That the police knew and let it happen, anyway. It was gang-related. Or cult-related. They're saying everything, grasping at straws. People know about you and Mary. The hospital and the blizzard kept you two out of sight. Mary's basically off the grid."

"Not surprised," Peter said, laughing.

"But now you're out, and everybody knows it."

"They just want answers."

Sono lowered his voice. "I know yours, and no one's going to buy it."

Peter huffed.

"What's Mary's?"

"What?"

"Answer."

Getting frustrated, and wanting to get out of here as soon as possible, Peter shrugged and cried, "Man, I don't know. Just say it. You think she somehow planned all this with her dad?"

Sono shook his head. "No."

"Then what?"

"I think she's opportunistic. And I think she's dangerous."

Peter took a step forward, the carpet squelching missed blood beneath his foot. "Why don't you take her in?"

"She's long-term dangerous, like her dad," Sono said. "She's thinking about starting up Goetia again, isn't she?"

Peter jumped as more rocks pelted the outside of the building.

"I talked to her doctors. The bite mark on her neck wasn't human. She's going to turn into…"

"I don't know, Detective," Peter said, defensively.

Sono sighed and walked past him towards the stairs. "Your mom died a few weeks ago."

Peter tasted something primal in his mouth. A deep, unrefined rage ripped through him like lightning, making the hairs across his body stand on end. He faced Detective Sono and saw himself tearing him limb from limb. Seeing the wedding band on his hand, he imagined, for a split second, eviscerating his family, too.

"Katie, too. Didn't you like her?"

"Shut the fuck up!" he barked.

"I know you didn't forget, but have you thought about them as much as you would normally?"

Peter was one snide comment away from punching a crater in Sono's face, but this last one stunned him. He was right. Peter had been so quick to celebrate being cured of his anxiety that he hadn't realized what he'd lost along with it. Ever since this all started, his view on things had been so myopic, it was a miracle he could dress himself in the morning. Now, he worked in broad strokes, obliterating any finer details that stood in his way. It was becoming less about the days and more about the months, the full moons. He hadn't even reached out to Katie's family to offer his condolences, like he would've in the past. He hadn't even buried Mom, or scattered her ashes.

This is normal, he told himself. *You're normal. You almost died twice. You're fucked up. You're grieving in your own way. There's no right or wrong way. There's no manual.*

"I'm just saying she's isolating you, Peter," Sono said, starting up the stairs. "Times like these, you should be with family. People who care."

I'm not going back to the Old Country, he thought, as if he were a criminal and Sono were suggesting he had his pick of prisons to go to.

"Goetia? That 'commune' she was part of? Might be one of the best cover-ups we've ever seen in this part of the state. Creepy, little cult everybody knew about, run by a narcissistic asshole with his fingers in every pot."

Outside, the voices were starting to swell again.

"Racketeering, arson, theft, burglary, assault, kidnapping, fraud; possibly human trafficking. Murder. Mary's dad and his handpicked 'Demons' were given the run of the county, to do the dirty deeds no one else would, and because they did it, everyone turned a blind eye. Mary got out, Peter, but she didn't go far. And you can't tell me there isn't something off about her."

Peter joined him at the stairs and said, "What do you think's going to happen?"

"I don't know," Sono said. "What I do know is that the people who Mary's dad killed were his former Demons. Twice, he tried to kill Mary. I don't know what kind of logic that man was running off of, but that's telling to me. Jesus Christ, Kid, what I'm trying to say is that all of this is far from over. You're at the center of it, and I'm trying to offer you a way out."

"Why? Because your 'cop's intuition' is giving you a bad feeling?"

Sono screwed up his face. "Because when people are cornered, they go back to their old ways."

Peter leaned against the wall. The second floor hung above him like a swollen piece of meat, the ceiling raked, the walls striated with bloodstains.

Detective Sono stared at him, his hand hovering near his holster and asked, "You think she doesn't feel cornered?"

2

Mary bought another gun, on account of all the assholes following her. With Peter at his apartment building and most of the survivors' families currently outside it, like she knew they would be, she had enough time to go about Talbot, more or less, unmolested.

Pulling out of the parking lot of the park Star's Gate, Mary gave her a dealer a head nod as he quickly melted into the snow-laden woods. Dad had killed her Guy, but this guy wasn't so bad. His name was Eric. She hadn't seen him for years. That was the thing about Goetia, though. Anyone who came into contact with it were connected to one another. It was as if a spider web had formed between all of them, and when one of them was in need, another would emerge from whatever rock they were hiding under, to answer their wanting vibrations. She hadn't known Eric would be at Star's Gate with the gun she needed, but there he'd been. It felt good to rush into things again.

Mary made her way down the aisles of Canto's, the superstore that, if given a few years and an unchecked, homicidal artificial intelligence, could probably put most other small countries to shame with its sheer amount of goods, weaponry, and manpower. It was obvious they'd been prepared for the blizzard. At every endcap, snow shovels, salt, blankets, bottles of water, flashlights, knives, and canned goods. Nothing got a panicked populace more prepared and ready to fork over their paychecks than a not-so-subtle-hint that, maybe, just maybe, the end was nigh.

She went the long way to Sports and Outdoors. Like a celebrity whose mirror had lost its luster, she wanted the shoppers here to see her face, so she could gauge their reactions. She wanted to understand just how deeply the Massacre on the Main Drag had wounded the collective conscious of Talbot. By that, she could determine her and Peter's next course of action. Of course, they had to be kind and considerate and make some contribution to a fund for the victims. But how long would they have to wait until they could strike a book deal?

Her eyes met the eyes of each customer she passed, and in them, she found nothing. No recognition. No spite. No curiosity. Each of them shuffled past, wrestling with their carts as their wheels got stuck and tripped them up, their heavy layers stinking of whatever musty closet they'd been pulled from. Most were too busy looking at their phones, or their grocery lists; or the children running wild at the cart's end, like unruly sled dogs.

Only one, an old woman whose fingers were stained black with ink, likely from the newspapers she collected and flipped through obsessively, paid her any mind.

"Miss?" the old woman crowed.

Mary stopped just short of where the beauty product bazaar began.

"You're… I saw your picture on TV."

Though she'd kept Peter in the dark about the aftermath, Mary had been following the news closely. Word had already gotten out about them after Mare's Diner; once the reporters discovered they had also survived the slaughter on the Main Drag, the temptation to withhold their names and let them live out the remainder of their fucked-up lives was simply too great to ignore. Getting out of the hospital unnoticed, and the blizzard, threw the media dogs off their tracks for a bit, but that hadn't stopped the journalists from speculating in the meantime. Because very little was known about Mary, something which she was proud of, most of the focus was currently on Peter. Who was he? Where did he come from? One of the killers was his mother. Why?

"Yeah?" Mary said.

In actuality, she wanted to see if anyone would recognize her. Detective Sono clearly didn't trust her. The last thing she needed was everyone else feeling the same way. The more exposure Peter got, the more innocent she'd appear. There was a first time for everything, right?

"Awful thing what happened to you," the old woman said. "And for your own father…"

The old woman walked towards her, shakily. Mary knew what was coming, but for some reason, she couldn't bring herself to stop it. It was happening in slow motion, but it was happening: The old woman, reaching out, taking Mary's hand and holding it with both of hers.

"Thank you," Mary said, her voice as chilled as the old woman's grip.

There was one issue with her vicarious innocence approach: The killers had both been related to Peter and Mary. It could go one of two ways because of their association with them. Either Talbot would take pity on them, or Talbot would turn on them. In a world where a shockingly large swath of the sheep subscribed to the idea of there being crisis actors, pity was in short supply. Peter would try to tell her otherwise, but she knew. By Goetia, she knew.

"It's going to get better. I pray for you and your boyfriend every night."

Mary didn't bother correcting her.

"I'd like to help you two." The old woman let go of Mary's hand and started rummaging through her bright blue, bird-patterned purse in her cart. "I won't take no for an answer—" she took out her wallet; coins fell out of it, back into her purse, "—because I'm just going to spend it on something silly. The city needs help. I've been saying it for years." She pulled out three twenties and thrust them at Mary. "I pray for the deceased, too, but they've got families."

Mary took the bills, saying, "And ours tried to kill us."

"Lord, have mercy," the old woman said.

"What's your name?"

"Antonia," the old woman said. "I live at Meadowsprings behind this giant eyesore of a building. We're all thinking of you and your boyfriend."

Mary smiled, mouthed *thank you*, and thought to herself, *That's a lot of sixty-dollar bills from sixty-year-olds*. "You're so sweet. Peter and I are thinking about putting together a group. A kind of survivor's group for people this city has beat down."

Antonia's mouth became an O.

"Would you and your friends be interested?"

"Yes," Antonia said, digging through her purse for a piece of paper and pen. "Only the beat down go to a place like Meadowsprings."

Mary watched Antonia write down her phone number. She didn't know what she'd do with a bunch of rowdy nursing home rejects, but it was always good to have options. And benefactors.

By the time Mary reached Sports and Outdoors, she'd forgotten why she had gone there to begin with. Then store associate John with his silver ponytail and high cheekbones from behind the counter called to her, and she remembered.

"You look a little lost, little lady," he said, his voice rattling like a carburetor.

With a greeting like that, Mary didn't need to put her ear to the ground to know some dick-swinging misogyny would be soon be stampeding her way. She squinted at him from across the aisle and breathed him. He smelled like cigarettes, aftershave, and an energy drink. She imprisoned the scent of him deep within her mind, so that when the time came, pale, shining, swollen, she could call upon it. He wasn't an impressive first, but firsts seldom were. Nothing wrong with keeping such a tried and true human tradition.

She stepped up to the counter and laid out Antonia's tithe. "I need some silver bullets."

John stared at her, a stupid remark on the edge of his tongue. She waited for it. He swallowed it, instead. There was a glimmer of recognition in his eyes, and in his cheeks, red embarrassment. He knew her, but not in the way Antonia had known her.

"S-Silver bullets?" John scratched his forehead. "Had someone else come in here a few weeks back for the same t-thing."

"Is that so?" she said, laughing while imagining timid Peter purchasing ammunition.

It was subtle, but John lurched forward, as if he were about to tell her something. He smiled a filler kind of smile and then started rummaging underneath the counter. It wasn't a good save. There were a few—actually, more than a few—boxes of silver bullets on display, behind the glass case that wrapped around the counter.

"For, uh, self-defense?" John said, just a bald spot to Mary as he stayed low to the ground.

"You could say that." She tapped the glass. "These will do."

"Ah, yeah." John stood, palmed the counter. When he pulled away, he left behind a sweaty print. "That's right. You, uh, heard of the Beast of Stubbe Street?"

Mary scratched her neck where Peter's mom had bitten into her. "Yep. That what this is all about? Bunch of wannabe werewolf hunters in Talbot?"

"You can, uh…" He lowered his voice as a man lumbered past, a tower of twenty frozen meals swaying dangerously in his hands. "You can never be too careful." He looked her in the eyes: "You can't."

Mary laughed and licked her lips. It shouldn't have been a surprise that a guy who smelled like shit liked to bullshit. It was more than that, though, wasn't it? Was he flirting with her? Threatening her? The two registered the same.

"You want to tell me what you're getting at, John?" she asked.

He unlocked and slid back the door behind the counter, took out a box of silver bullets, and emptied from it, sixty dollars' worth. "I'm sorry, Miss."

"It's Mary."

Ringing up the bullets, he kept going. "Mary. Mary, I thought you were someone else."

"No, you didn't, and I'm exactly who you think I am."

John mumbled, "Is he?"

Mary stared at him as he cashed her out, boxed up her bullets, and threw her purchase and its receipt into a white bag with *Canto's* written in pink across it. Before he could hand it to her, she took it and she walked away.

Last words weren't only good for funerals, and they weren't always spoken.

3

For Peter, packing his belongings would be easy. All the boxes he'd used when he'd moved in were still in the apartment, in a closet. He'd saved them.

"Want any help?" Detective Sono asked from the hall outside his apartment.

Peter stood in the living room, cardboard boxes tucked neatly under his arms, and told him, "No." The police had tossed his apartment for evidence. There were footprints and traces of powder everywhere. But what really got to him was the pile of potato chips and pretzels underneath the coffee table. Hearn had spilled them, he remembered.

Liminal space. He understood the phrase now, for now, it was before and beyond him. In here, and in the hall. He could see it and touch it. This apartment was his apartment, and yet it wasn't. It was as unfamiliar as it was intimate. In between lived-in and crime scene, these six hundred square feet belonged to no one and nothing now. Not him. Not his landlord. Not even the building. It was a vestigial limb waiting to be repurposed or lopped off. He knew it like how he'd known when his mom would come back from a bad bender: He'd recognized the skin, but not the animal hiding within. Thinking along those lines, as he headed for his room, he wondered feverishly about Jungian archetypes, and if the shadow self was the self at all, or another entity altogether. He laughed at himself. Normalization. Every latchkey kid's favorite 24-hour program.

His room was how he'd left it, except the bed was a mess. Mary had told him she'd tried to have sex with Chad Bradley in it. There was a sock on his nightstand standing upright like a stalagmite. Apparently, he'd finished himself what they'd barely started.

Packing up his computer, Peter found himself calling out to Sono. "Hey, you looked into my mom, right?"

And Sono answered, "Yeah, we did."

Keeping it impersonal, because that was probably the only way he could get through this without having a breakdown, Peter carried on this way. Packing, and probing, with thirty feet between them. "What'd you find out?"

"Oh," Sono said, laughing, "you want to talk to now?"

Peter unplugged his monitor and lowered it into a box. He didn't say anything. As far as he was concerned, he'd said enough.

"You knew her."

"Apparently not."

Their voices echoed back and forth through the apartment and out into the hall, ghost-like.

"Here, I'll just come…"

"No, this is fine," Peter said.

He heard the floor outside the front door creak, but Sono didn't go any further than that.

"Your mom had a record. Wasn't the worst I've ever seen. Possession. Theft. There was an assault in there. Domestic violence, from when she was living with your grandmother." Sono paused, then: "Child neglect."

Peter laughed and aged in reverse. Back to thirteen, when mom had abandoned him for the weekend to famine and infestation. He could still smell the summer rain on the hot asphalt, and the caseworker's perfume as she settled in next to him on his porch. He'd told 911 he'd wanted to cut his throat, and for once in his life, adults had come running. Other kids would've been empowered by all that attention. Not Peter, though. It'd made things too real.

"What about…" Peter wiped his nose and headed for the dresser. "What about the last two years?"

Sono didn't say anything.

"You there?"

"Moved down south to Louisiana."

Peter, pulling out fistfuls of T-shirts, stopped. *Louisiana?*

"It'd just be easier if I…"

Peter didn't bother protesting, because Sono was already in his apartment, in the doorway, watching him in the way a cat watches something as it unravels. "Any idea what she was doing in Louisiana?"

"Feds have taken the case from us," Sono said, rocking back and forth on his heels. "Whatever they've dug up, they're not sharing. To be honest, Peter, I'm not sure how much there is."

"I left her," he said, "so she left me. Nothing to worry about but herself. Probably the way it should've been."

Sono cleared his throat. "About the only thing I do know was that she had a warrant out for her arrest. Missed a court date for trespassing."

"Trespassing…?"

"On the Melancons' property."

Peter dropped the box of clothes on his foot.

"Related to Celeste and Vernal Melancon. The same ones whose house…"

"Yeah, I fucking know." Peter ran his hand hard over his face. He threw himself into his computer chair; it spun; he stopped, when his knee slammed into the side of the desk. His head ached. His gut burned coldly hot. He tried deep breaths, but got a shallow panting, instead; so, he held his breath, and he held himself, and vomited out the words, "What. Are. You. Saying?"

"Just that," Sono whispered. "And—"

"There is a connection, then! Between me and Mary."

"—the warrant wasn't only for trespassing. Your mom had slaughtered their livestock, too, and attacked one of the sons. They found her covered in animal blood, in the barn. The morning after a full moon."

Peter shook his head "Connected."

"I don't know about that."

"How?!" he cried.

"Nothing points to anything other than coincidence."

Springing out of his chair, Peter said, "Oh, bullshit."

"I want answers, too." Sono stepped towards him. "I do. Those people out there do. All of us, including you, deserve them.

"Your mom managed to get by most of your life as a werewolf? Without ever being found out? I have a hard time believing that, especially here in the city."

Peter spun the chair around, whispering, "What are you saying?"

"Maybe your mom wasn't a werewolf this whole time. Maybe she wasn't until she went south."

Peter told him, "No," and then he told himself the same, and packed the rest of his belongings, unsettled, in silence.

4

Mary stared up at the sign for Maiden, Mother, and Crone, laughed, and let herself in.

There was no air in the store. It'd been replaced by incense. She could feel the warm scent sliding over her, seeping into her, as she stepped forward, the chimes behind her having sounded her arrival. Further on, past the glass cases and the tables filled with neatly arranged minerals, a shape took form in the lighted haze. It was woman-shaped, with short, tight dreadlocks not unlike the kind Mary used to give to her dolls when she was little, when she'd had dolls. The shape was young. The shape wore a dress and sandals. Mary, cynical as she was, had no issues with individual expression: What she wondered was if this poor woman had come here in this single digit weather dressed like this, or if she'd changed in the back on account of the dress code. Goetia didn't have a dress code.

"Hello there, my name is Andrea," she said.

Mary threw up a weak wave. "Hi."

Andrea stopped a few feet from her, beside the cash register that was covered in catchy slogans, like *Make love, not sandwiches*. "What can I help you find today?"

Before Mary could answer, a door opened at the back of the store.

Inside, fire-tinted darkness softened by the candles burning within. There were the makings of an altar, and ancient things in earthen bundles hanging from the ceiling above it. Before she could discern anything, another woman stepped through the doorway, tightening up her braids. Seeing Mary, she quickly but carefully closed the door behind her.

"Welcome!" this woman said. "My name's Parker. This is my store, and now it's yours, too, sister. What can Andrea and I help you find today?"

Mary's eyes went back and forth between these two overly-accommodating hippie-types and their inventory of rocks, roots, tinctures, toys, clothes, cards, and all things esoteric, mystical, and life-affirming, and started thinking about a partnership proposal. It never ceased to amaze her how differently someone could see the world with a slight change in mindset. She wondered how she'd see things when the wolf within finally awoke on the thirtieth. Or was she already viewing things through that blood-soaked lens? Businesswoman and beast. The line between the two was always blurred, but maybe it was never there to begin with.

At first, Mary said, "Just browsing," but it was clear to her they were chomping at the bit to call her bluff, so she gave them a half-smile and said, "Wolfsbane."

New, or naïve, Andrea nodded and said, "Oh, yeah. We've got that." Then, to Parker: "Right?"

Parker didn't confirm or deny. She walked past Andrea instead, towards Mary. "We don't usually do this—"

Mary furrowed her brow, tightened her grip on her purse. She knew she could take these two. She just didn't know why she had the feeling that she might need to.

"—but, Mary, you're in danger."

What the fuck? First, that walking cock at Canto's, and now these two dopey vegans?

Parker said, "We've been keeping an eye on you and Peter. Please, will you sit with us?"

Mary shook her head. "We?"

Andrea, who was halfway to wherever they kept the wolfsbane, was wide-eyed and slack-jawed. Something was happening that wasn't supposed to be.

Parker pointed to herself, then Andrea, and said, "Us, and others.

We know about the werewolf. The Beast of Stubbe Street. We're a group of cryptozoologists. We hunt cryptids. I mean—"

"I know what a cryptid is," Mary snapped. She thought about how she wanted to play this out. Settling on ignorance, she pulled her scarf tighter and said, "What's this got to do with me?"

"I don't think we should be…" Andrea trailed off as Parker side-eyed her into submission.

"I'm going to go," Mary said.

Parker cried, "You and Peter were attacked by a werewolf. At the diner. At his building. It was his mom."

Mary stared at her, blankly.

"We were tracking his mom for weeks before everything happened. She was terrorizing the Old Country. But when Peter came in here to buy wolfsbane, and he told us about seeing the werewolf… We get it. All of us have to be careful about what we say these days, especially us women, but Mary… We know. And we just want to help."

Mary nodded at Andrea. "She doesn't seem to think you should."

"Because—" Parker sighed and leaned against the counter, elbowing some pendulum necklaces into motion, "—we usually don't tell people. It just raises more questions, and sometimes makes things harder." She took out a vape and took a long drag off it. "But this is different."

Mary turned, thinking she'd heard someone coming into the store. But it was one of the workers from the nail salon next door passing by.

"At the end of this month, Peter's going to turn into a werewolf."

Huh, Mary thought, trying not to laugh. *He can't catch a break, can he?*

"So, yeah, we've got wolfsbane," Parker said, "but let us help you."

"I think I do need to sit down," Mary said, trying to sound overwhelmed.

Parker and Andrea converged on Mary and escorted her with kind, empowering words to the back of the store. To the door she'd seen Parker come out of earlier. They opened it to her, now that she was initiated into their secret plot, and encouraged her to head in. There wasn't much more to the room than what she'd seen earlier. Several aquamarine poufs were scattered in front of the altar. Atop it, a wolf's skull sat, stray wax from the melting candles running like blood around those bleached bones. There was a symbol on the skull, where the proverbial third eye was supposed to be. Hecate's wheel. A maze within a circle, with a star at the center. Mary only knew it because after she'd left Goetia, she'd scoured the Internet for another practice to replace it with. The walls were painted with the symbol, too, and others she didn't recognize.

Mary sat on a pouf. It was far too comfortable to have been anything less than a fortunate coincidence, which made her grin. She kept her purse on her lap and her hands on it, in case she needed to gun these girls down. It would've been a waste of silver bullets, but then again, maybe not. Maybe they were werewolves, too, and this was the equivalent of mobsters luring a mark into the back of the casino with promises of riches. *Now there's an image,* she thought, imagining werewolves in striped suits with Tommy guns, their hair slicked-back, their howls somehow Sicilian.

"It's a lot, I know," Andrea said, sitting a pouf away from her.

Parker settled in beside Mary. "Does Peter know what's going to happen to him?"

They must've got the police reports switched up, she thought, rubbing her neck with her shoulder.

"You must," she went on, "if you're here looking for wolfsbane. Did Peter put you up to it?"

Mary cocked her head: *Interesting.*

"That's what they do," Andrea said, nodding her head. "Lycanthropes. They make you part of their 'tribe' to keep close tabs on you."

Mary asked, "There a lot of werewolves out there?"

"No," Andrea and Parker said at once, almost reflexively.

"How're you going to help me?" She crossed her legs, leaned forward on her knee. "You going to kill Peter?"

Now was when they should've answered in the negative

"Not doing that," she went on. "Why's he got to die? Aren't you, like, peace-love types?"

"Lycanthropes are violently territorial," Parker said. "You ever know a dog not to piss on a perfectly good tree? When you're something as rare and feared as that, everything's a threat, even if you swear it isn't."

She talking about Peter still?

"There's no cure for lycanthropy," Andrea said. "Some have tried to cure themselves with silver and wolfsbane in small doses, right?"

Parker nodded.

"Doesn't work," she went on. "As far as I can tell. If nothing else, makes things worse."

"Throws off the cycle," Parker said.

Mary sat there a moment, breathing in the incense, burning the symbols into her irises. She gave the room a moment, but it wasn't Goetia. It wasn't bad, but she knew better. It wasn't only the atmosphere she was sampling, but the escape they may or may not have realized they were offering her. If she betrayed Peter, she'd be free to do as she pleased. None, except for these two and their fellow monster hunters, would be the wiser. Without his moral compass, she'd be free to sail the seas of fathomless debauchery. The thing was, her plans were predicated upon his own. Without him, those rickety walkways of ideas would fall, because they were built around her as his were him. You couldn't put your feet up without having something under them, now could you?

"Just give me the whole anti-werewolf package you gave Peter," Mary said, standing up.

Parker and Andrea came to their feet, too. For a moment, it looked as if they'd block her way. No matter, Mary thought. They blow the locks off doors in movies all the time.

Andrea said, "We can't just let…"

"What?" Mary said. "You can't just let me what? Walk out of here? Until I showed up today, you two were apparently content enough to wait out the month."

Parker sighed. "When he turns, you're going to be the first one he kills."

"I'm the Daughter of Goetia," Mary said, deliberately.

The two women exchanged looks with one another, their surprise coming through the swirling haze.

"You know what that is?"

"Ye-No…" Andrea said.

"Yes." Parker sat back down. "Andrea's new to *Exmoor*, our group, but… That's why you were…"

Mary cocked her head.

"I've heard of the place, but I've never been there."

"It's not easy to find if it doesn't want you to," Mary said. "My father, my almost-killer, discovered and founded Goetia."

Andrea started to say, "That's a myth..."

Mary shuffled past them to the doorway, snapping, "That's rich coming from you two."

"Andrea, stop talking," Parker said, rising again. "Mary, wait."

She shook her head. "Can't. Have too much to do. But..." She paused for dramatic effect. "Goetia's everything you've heard, and more. I'll show you sometime. How many are into all of this?" She gestured to the store. "All this stuff?"

"More than you'd think," Parker said, breathlessly. "This store's been in Talbot for forty years. It's like a secret church for many people here."

Mary nodded, chewed on her lip. "Goetia's everything you've heard, and more. I'm going to bring it back. I can do that, you know? So trust me when I say, I'm not afraid of a werewolf. You'll see and, uh—" she smiled, "—maybe your congregation can, too. I bet they'd like that. I bet that'd be good for business, wouldn't it?"

Andrea stared at Parker.

But Parker refused to meet her gaze.

Mary left the room with that last line, and like hooked fish, they followed.

5

Peter, carrying three heavy boxes in front of him, stared at the spot outside his apartment where Mary's dad had shot Katie through the heart. Unlike the rest of the building, which had been scrubbed with adolescent efficiency, this death site was unmarked. But for his memories, he wouldn't have known she'd died here. Not even his heightened senses could pick out her scent. She was just as gone as she'd always been in his life. She'd never been a person to him but a promise. He wept for a while, and then he went on.

"Come here," Detective Sono said, coming up from the rear, "give me one of those."

Peter didn't fight him as he took the top box. That one had all his clothes. Split between the other two, electronics, books, and folders that had important personal and financial information in them. He had a lot of those folders.

Grunting, Sono said, "You sure you want to leave all that other stuff behind?”

“Can’t carry it out of here. Got nowhere else to put it.”

“Your landlord gave you that condo over on Twilight Court. Hey.” Sono stopped, didn’t start speaking again until Peter stopped, too. “Everyone thinks after something like this happens, you have to scorch the earth and start all over.”

“I’m not doing that. I tried that when I left home and, obviously, it didn’t work. I just need to go back to the basics for a bit.” Sensing Sono might say something about Mary, he quickly added, “I appreciate everything you’ve done. More than any other police officer has done for me. You care.”

“I do.”

“Thank you.”

“Recidivism. Something we always keep in the back of our minds,” Sono said, starting up again, taking the lead towards the stairs. “Is a person going to commit a crime again or not? Am I going to be arresting the same asshole for the same shit next month? Every field’s got a name for it. Relapse. That kind of thing.”

Extinction, Peter thought. *Resurgence.*

“Cops, especially, get so narrow in the way we view the world.” He shifted the weight of the boxes. “I’ve been riding you all day about what you’re going to do next, but only because I’m trying not to be so narrow. I’m trying not to see you again.”

“I know,” Peter said. “I appreciate it. If you’re worried about that kind of thing, though… Shouldn’t you be talking to Mary?”

Sono smirked and said, going down the stairs, “I am, aren’t I?”

When they got to the first floor, the sounds from the crowd outside started to pick up again. They weren’t as loud as they’d been before. Either people had dispersed, or the cold had closed up their throats. Peter had already made up his mind on how he was going to handle whoever remained. He was going to face them like the victim he was, not avoid them, like the criminal some already thought him to be. He’d fall upon the sword, not only for himself, but also Mary, because if he left it to her, it’d turn into some sleight-of-hand, sideshow trick. It wasn’t her fault. Everyone had faults. His was sword-shaped and bled too much.

“Ready?” Sono asked, as they approached the front doors.

Peter told him he was, and then milliseconds later, he wasn’t. In that span of time, he had a spontaneous thought. To relieve the pressure, he had to express it, and so he asked, "Did you… find out anything about… about my dad when you looked into…?"

Sono shook his head. "Should we have?"

"Don't think so. I was just wondering."

Peter had never known his dad. Or maybe he had. There'd been a few guys in his life who Mom had said were Peter's dad. Thinking back, Peter figured it'd mostly been hopeful thinking on Mom's part. Genetic gaslighting.

"It's getting to you. What I said."

Peter mumbled, "Hmm?"

"About your mom. Maybe not having been a werewolf your whole life."

Peter threw his head back and laughed. "Fuck."

"Forget I said it."

Peter had already planned to.

Sono, grunting and cussing under his breath, went to the front door, pressed the box of clothes he held between him and it, and opened the door.

Harsh light cut through the apartment building's lobby like a scalpel. The filthy shadows split and broke around Peter. He squinted. Snowflakes like television noise danced across the doorway. Eyes adjusting, he began to make sense of the shapes. Two police officers at the threshold. Six to eight strangers crowding the steps that led down to the Main Drag. And the cadaver-gray city of Talbot, cold and uncaring, rising and falling, stretching and shifting. It made Peter think of a camouflaged hunter crawling on its belly. He'd never known another a city. As the cries of the parents fell on him, and Talbot went on, trying to go unnoticed, in that moment, he felt as if he knew them all. But not Goetia. He didn't know Goetia.

Peter stepped outside and set his boxes down. To these parents, he presented himself as a specimen to be tested, studied. He'd counted six to eight, but now, in the thick of them, there seemed to be so many more. They were staring at him, moving their mouths, making fists. He couldn't hear them, because he wasn't there. He was elsewhere, trying to find his courage. He thought he'd brought it with him. But Mary was at Maiden, Mother, and Crone.

"I'm sorry," he started, feeling sweat pool in his crevices. "I am so sorry."

From the crowd, a woman crowed, "Sorry for what?"

"Where you been?" a man said.

"Just what the hell happened?"

Peter faced them, but to him, they were faceless. Another sensory overload. Different from the one he'd experienced inside the building. His brain was short-circuiting. Sparks were flying and coming out his mouth in the form of unsatisfying answers.

"I'm sorry," he said again, blinking out the snow getting in his eyes. "They wanted to kill us—"

"Did you know?"

A man who was as skinny as a rail, and looked about as used as one, too, all scuffed and smoothed out, said, "You did it on the anniversary. One month later. My Dani's dead! Did you know?"

Peter puttered, "I-I didn't know h—"

"Listen, asshole!" the man cried. "Did you know they'd come back? Did you?"

He shook his head, mouthing to the amorphous masses *I didn't know.*

"Who are you?" another man asked, his voice breaking. "Brian never mentioned you."

Peter kept trying to tell them it'd just been a party, that people had invited other people, but the parents and people who were probably pretending to be parents went on, rattling off names like Andy, Kristen, Hunter, Skyler, Missy, and Katie. Wait. Katie?

Peter drifted from the boxes. Sono and his officers closed in on him. His sight returned to him. The finer details of this fucked-up situation expressed themselves. He'd become psychologically far-sighted. Psychosomatic myopia. But he knew Katie, had known Katie.

The crowd parted to reveal who'd said her name. An old man, with sun spots on his balding head, tufts of gray hair, like lint, lining it. His hands were shoved into his coat. His legs were shaking, those running shoes of his, eaten up by Talbot's sidewalks, doing him no favors. At the corners of his sad eyes, icicles. Her dad. Her basic dad.

"She talked about you some," Katie's dad said, his mouth quivering on account of the cold and his sorrow.

Peter didn't say anything.

"I think she liked you."

Now there were icicles in Peter's eyes, too.

"Why?"

Why did she like him? Or why did it have to happen? Or why did he and Mary survive, but the others hadn't? Entirely different questions with entirely the same answer. Peter answered, "I don't know."

But for his shaking legs and quivering face, Katie's dad didn't move. He was like a rock undergoing erosion in real-time. "I'm trying not to blame you."

Brakes. Car doors slamming shut. Down by the curb, journalists, white-knuckling microphones. They were coming.

"I know it's not your fault," Katie's dad said, loudly, as if he were presuming to speak for the others. "I know it's not. I know it's…"

"I hadn't seen my mom in two years," Peter said. "And Mary didn't even know her dad was…"

From his left: "Someone said he was in a cult."

From his right: "Yeah, wasn't she? Where's she?"

"More like a c-commune." Peter backed away from the crowd, towards the boxes. "We, uh, want to h-help."

Someone shrieked, "How the hell are you going to help?"

The journalists muscled their way up the stairs. There were bystanders in tow, too, with their cellphones out, recoding everything.

"We're going to start it up," Peter said, ever-the-people-pleaser, as he picked up his boxes. "Something for people who've lost…"

That's when Sono swooped in, taking him under his wing. As the wave of vultures, professional and amateur alike, broke over the stairs, Peter was rushed through by the police. Sono whispered in Peter's ear, "Don't say another fucking word," dropped the box he'd been helping him carry onto his load, and urged Peter towards his car.

More questions. More outrage. Flashes from cameras. All he saw were eyes, strung together like pearls, and teeth rimmed with chapped lips. He felt people grab at him. A rock cracked off his head, drawing blood, and was followed by laughter. It'd been thrown not by one of the parents, but one of the bystanders, sowing chaos. A journalist cut through the noise with the question, "Start what up? Start Goetia back up?" But the question was quickly snuffed by Sono barking, "Enough!"

The police opened the car doors, took Peter's boxes, and threw them into his backseat.

Sono wrapped an arm around him and took him around to the

driver's side.

"This isn't the time or place," Sono said, opening the door and letting him go.

Peter's hairs were standing on end. His palms bled from where he'd dug his nails into them. He got into the driver's seat and saw, in his side view mirror, his nose was covered in snot and his mouth globules of drool. Erosion, in real-time.

"That was a decent gesture, but there's more to this thing than you and Mary. Thirty people are dead because we didn't catch the bad guys fast enough. See any candles? Pictures? Wreaths? Mayor's afraid to have a vigil because this whole thing's turning into one big tinder box." Sono sighed. "I'll get you through this Peter, but don't you or her make it any more than it is."

"We're just trying to move on."

Sono took the keys from him, leaned over his lap, and started up the engine. "You don't get to move on. Not when your parents were the killers. Not when you were the sole survivors." He slammed the door, rapped the roof.

Peter stared at Detective Sono through the window, his breath fogging up the glass. He was panting, anger in place of anxiety. This was where he wanted him. In a glass cage. Be visible. Be normal. Be quiet.

Peter drove off, leaving the spectacle behind him. He decided to take the long way home. On his way there, he smelled Sono in his clothes, where the detective had thrown his arm around him. Cologne. Sharp and warm, not unlike woodchips. He'd know it anywhere from now on. He breathed it, and he held it.

6

Mary waited in the lobby of her apartment building, letting the reporters outside catch glimpses of her through the windows, behind the curtains. It was as good as showing some skin to them. They took their pictures and pointed their fingers. It was all they could do. It was all they could ever do. To her.

Armed to the teeth for threats natural and supernatural alike, Mary was feeling pretty good about things. Goetia would provide the rest. While she'd gotten in Parker's and Andrea's heads at Maiden, Mother, and Crone, they had, in their own way, gotten in hers. The constant assertion and determination that Peter, not her, was going to transform in the next few days left her feeling jealous and possessive as much as it did devious. If she were to survive the full moons to come, misinformation would be her greatest asset, and misdirection, her greatest ally.

Speaking of which, there went Peter past the front of the building, his car disappearing behind the shit-colored snowdrifts. It was smart of him, to come in through the back, but the vultures had his scent. Lacquered claws were being pointed, bearded beaks being flapped. In a matter of seconds, the news crew and four journalists were converging on the building, barreling down the alley, their fashionable winter coats and loose-fit scarves beating like wings about their bodies. She didn't think too highly of reporters, but she told herself that was for the best. She loathed the limelight as much as she loved it; and regardless of how she felt about it, if she spent too much time in it, she'd burn all the same. Those were her words, not Dad's.

Mary sprinted to the back of the building to meet Peter at the locked door that let out to the parking lot. She watched him through the peephole in the door. Halfway into a parking spot, he slammed on the brakes and fumbled to put the car in park. Getting out, his feet slipped on a sheet of ice and his arms went opposite directions, as if they'd suddenly become self-aware and ill-intentioned. He got to the backseat, started pulling out boxes. Before he could get them loaded, the vultures were upon him, shrieking for scoop.

I should save him, she thought. She wasn't going to, but there was something to be said for still having the sentiment. She couldn't, anyway. If they were going to open Goetia's borders again, they would each have to stick to their roles. Mary, the mysterious leader. Peter, the personable prophet. Two opposites, magnetized and magnetizing. Sure, it was a bit much to assume things would go that far, get that grand. It'd taken Dad years to build Goetia. She wasn't building, though. She was rebranding.

Peter was all hands and gaping mouth as he spun through the carrion birds. He'd be in the building in a minute. But a minute was a long time under a microscope.

Mary thought back to the beginning of the semester when she'd first met Peter. How they'd entered class at the same time, sat down next to each other at the same time. All the while completely unacknowledging each other. Mary didn't believe in fate, but it was hard not to entertain the idea. They were like two tectonic plates torn apart, one shock after the other, until they were up against an edge that'd turned out to be a corner. And in that corner, they came together. It was romantic, in a two graverobbers meeting on a corpse-strewn battlefield kind of way.

The full moon wasn't long off now, she thought, as Peter hurried towards the door, seeming to literally dodge the questions being hurled at him. Mary refused to look up lore on lycanthropy, but she couldn't help but speculate what the transformation would be like. Would her body twist and stretch? Would her nails grow long and her teeth longer? Would hair push through her pores? Or would her flesh fall from her frame? Would she emerge like a butterfly from its cocoon? It would hurt. Of course, it would. If it didn't, would it even count?

Mary laughed at herself for sounding like an edgy teenager and unlocked the door. Peter came through, both of his feet nearly coming off the ground at the same time, as if Winter had given him a kick in the ass to clear the final stretch.

"Oh, hey," he said, his face bright red.

She slipped past him, asking, "What's the verdict?"

"Sono doesn't trust us. He definitely doesn't trust you."

Mary nodded, said, "Neither do the hippies. They think you're a werewolf."

She went to shut the door, but before she did, she made sure to let the journalists see her face. She smiled at them. It wasn't a wide smile, or a small smile, or a sardonic smile, or a sadistic smile. Just a smile. Harmless. Infinitely interpretable.

TUESDAY, NOVEMBER 24TH, 2020

1

Peter had never been to a crematorium before. For him, the word called to mind smokestacks. Burning a body didn't seem like something that should be done in a small, white building with red trim and a sign out front that read in fat, non-offensive font, *Mungo Society.* Nor did it seem appropriate to box up ashes inside a place where the carpet was corporate-gray and the furniture was brightly colored, soft, and rounded. With the terminals packed with pamphlets, denominational and non-denominational alike, walls covered in calming imagery, like flowers, vistas, and smiling, racially blended families, the whole place came across like a chimeric combination of church, daycare, and a doctor's office. It was this decade's form of sterilization.

"Huh," he said aloud.

Mary, beside him at the front desk, shifted her weight to one leg. "I know, right?"

He'd never been to a funeral before. Plenty of people had died around him growing up, but Mom seldom associated herself with anyone who "had enough scratch to get six feet deep in dirt." There'd been services, one or two for the men she'd tried to pass off as his dad, but she never let him go to them. She always told him he was too young. That he wasn't ready. That she didn't want him getting that close to death. "Your mom's going to be here forever," she'd told him. "Things like that make death look too good, anyway. All those people crying. All those beautiful flowers. All that money. Some people get a better turn out when they're dead than when they're alive. Life's hard. That's all there is to it. Last thing I want you to think is the grass is greener on the literal other side."

Mary hit the bell on the front desk. "Surprised they kept our parents' bodies as long as they did." Her voice dropped to a whisper. "You think they found anything inside your mom?"

He laughed. "Like what? A human hand? Chew toys?"

"A little from column A, a little from column..." Side-eying him, she said, "Are we cracking jokes again?"

Peter sighed and held his stomach. "Feel like I'm going to puke."

"Maybe things are getting back to the way were."

"I hope not..."

The office door behind the front desk opened. A worker in khakis and a pastel shirt came through, his hands clasped. He smiled like he was being held at gunpoint. He knew their parents were the killers, and here, the killers' kids.

"Peter. Mary." The worker—his nametag read in thick letters: Andrew—came around the desk and planted himself before them. "At Mungo's, we are here with and for you."

"Alright," Mary said.

Mom was back there, he realized. He hadn't seen her since that night she tried to kill him. And before that... Man, he hadn't thought about "before that" in years. He'd always recalled her being two states away, pleading for him to stay until she returned, which he hadn't. But there was a span of time leading up to his pivotal decision to cut the proverbial cord that he'd redacted. The reason why she'd been two states away, and probably the reason why she went further south afterwards, too.

"We're it," Mary said, as another worker, Kimmy, emerged from the back, hands clasped in front of her swishing, pastel skirt. "No one else's coming."

Two years ago, Mom had crossed state-lines to get away from Peter. She'd come home at sunrise, obliterated. Wherever she went, so, too, did the guy attached to her hip, or rather her ass, as his hand had been perpetually down the back of her pants. They woke Peter, while they were fucking around and falling over furniture. When he found them drifting between the kitchen and the living room, something overtook him. Maybe it was because he was half-asleep. Maybe it was the hot sun burning his eyes, the lavender and cigarette smoke burning his nose. Maybe it was the way his mother was staring at him, challenging and child-like. Mom had crossed state-lines to get away from Peter, because he'd hit her. Twice, in the mouth. Her lipped popped like a blood-filled balloon. He'd cut his knuckle on her canine. The scar was still there, on his right hand, faint but there, if you knew where to look, if you knew what you were looking at.

Andrew said, "If you'd like, you can have a seat before we begin."

"We have a de-stimulation room," Kimmy droned, in need of a little stimulation herself.

"We ordered the basic package," Mary said.

Andrew and Kimmy nodded in sync with one another and said, at the same time, "Of course. It's free-of-charge."

Mary asked Peter if he needed a moment. He didn't, because he was having one all to himself. There was Mom, in his mind's eye, still and cold as a stone, looking up at him, gushing a fountain of blood from her busted mouth. He'd hit her just like someone else once had. It'd triggered something, and to it, she'd surrendered, defeated and in disbelief. *Not you,* she'd seemed to say, as her mouth leaked. *Not you.*

They were following Andrew and Kimmy through *Mungo's.* Peter was self-aware enough to follow them, but everything else was lost on him. Words were being said. Calming gestures being made. Mary kept laughing in a these-fucking-guys kind of way. He'd let her handle today, just like she'd handled setting up today altogether. Apparently, she'd made these arrangements a week or so ago.

The guy Mom had been with was the equivalent of some mid-tier fast-food restaurant manager for a bunch of drug peddlers in the tri-state area. Him and her had spent the entire tonight getting fucked up on a package that was meant for, per Mom, "a bunch of niggers richer than God." They'd gotten fucked up grandly, too, in plain view; and the guy had gotten into a fight a few hours before with an off-duty police officer at the *Sticky Hole,* a tiny bar like a canker sore on the mouth of the Old Country. They were wanted, but too far gone to realize it. Until Peter had punched her.

"We have placed your mother and father in the boxes you specified," Kimmy said. "You—"

"Pine," Mary whispered to him. "Nothing fancy for these fuckers."

"—will have time to say your last words, if you wish."

Last words. What had been Mom's before she stumbled out, a roll of toilet paper pressed to her face. He couldn't remember, probably because he didn't want to. All he could remember was the dew on the grass and the bottom of his feet from him following the two of them outside; the smell of exhaust coughing out of the drug peddler's tail-pipe; and his rear lights, red as an exit sign, fading, as they drove away into the morning fog.

"This way," Andrew said, opening a large door with two hefty bolt-locks at its top and bottom.

Alright, Peter told himself, breakfast sailing the shores of his esophagus. *Don't…*

He thought he'd have more time. Another door, or another hallway. Or something like a metal detector. He didn't know. He'd never done this before. But his time was up. There was no ceremony, because they hadn't bought one.

On the other side of the door, a massive room, tiled white and red, and at the center, in two pine, open-faced boxes, Them.

Peter gravitated towards Mom, like waves to the moon. Sound stopped. Vision narrowed. For all he knew, Andrew and Kimmy were the people who'd been following him and Mary, and they'd tricked them into walking into an oversized oven. If that were the case, and if the room were burning, and he was turning to ash before their very eyes, he wouldn't know it. He wasn't here. He was there. There, in the mother-darkness. And for the first time in two years, so was Mom, not just as a voice or a figment or fragment, but spoiled body and tarnished soul. He recognized her as much as he didn't. They'd dressed her in wool-white. She'd been washed and manicured, and done-up in make-up that didn't quite match her death-tone. Her flesh had been manipulated. Her eyes and mouth glued opened, wired shut. Mary had told him they sewed cavities shut, too, to stop them from leaking. When it came down to it, there wasn't much of a difference between a funeral visitation and a sadist's torture chamber other than the ceremony surrounding it. That made Peter laugh. Then, laughing, he started crying. He gripped the side of the pine box until he was sure he'd break it and stared into Mom's lifeless eyes. She wasn't a corpse. She was taxidermy. A stuffed wolf. Maybe it would be better if she were hung on a wall rather than buried in the ground. Not to serve as a trophy, but a warning, the warning she'd always been, to him and for him. "Don't be like me," she'd say, and, "I want you to have what I didn't," she'd claim. And that was it, wasn't it? Her. Who she was, and what she did, and the impetus behind it all. That thing Sono said about her not having been a were-wolf until after she'd gone south had really fucked with him. Because if she'd been completely human up until that point, then any clarity he'd gotten from the last two months on who she was and what she did was for nothing. It'd be back to the drawing board with all his favorite explanations: mental illness, alcohol and drug use, poverty, and a traumatic childhood. Cold, hard facts that fit well together, yet were always hard to swallow. But lycanthropy? Confirmed lycanthro-py? He imagined what'd it been like for scientists and scholars of yore to stumble onto new knowledge to solve old problems, and for him, Mom being a werewolf was just that. No one was to blame. Not him. Not her. Just the monster within. But if Sono was right—he was real-ly gripping the box now, and Kimmy was asking if he was okay—then Peter was the cause of her turning into a werewolf, wasn't he? Because he'd hit her, and he'd abandoned her, and without him, the one person who, according to her, had saved her from a life of dying in some gutter, doped up and choked out with her own panties… Without him, the beast had found her. And if that were the case… Peter noticed Mary had her back to him, as she looked down on her dad (she'd comfort him, if she could.)… And if that was the case, then Mom hadn't come back to Talbot to turn him. She really had come back to kill him. Because he was a threat. Because he'd wronged her. Because he'd forced her out of her territory. Because he was her territory, down to each individual atom, and his being alive was defiance. His existence, trespass.

No, Sono wasn't right, Peter thought, taking a step back, the tears he wept dotting the tiles before him. *Don't be like me,* he said to him-self, staring at Mary. *I want you to have what I didn't.*

2

At first, hearing him huffing and puffing and sucking up snot so hard, it probably ricocheted off his brain, Mary thought Peter was hamming up the grieving act. He'd been so calm and collected since getting out of the hospital that she'd forgotten how emotional he could be. It was genuine, though, the scenery chewing. Frustrating, too. Because of it, she couldn't have her moment with Dad. She was like that. If someone else was losing it in the room, she couldn't. She wouldn't. She was a like a boat in a lock on a river waiting for the water to rise. She stayed shallow, while everyone else flooded. It didn't get her anywhere, but she never lost sight of what was coming, did she?

So, she stood over Dad's box, her back as stiff as his own, and considered climbing in there with him. If she wrapped her arms around him, would they meet in the middle? Just how far had he fallen into the flesh? His cheap suit, which looked like something you might rent from a costume shop, and sterile smell set her nerves on edge. This was a man who always smelled like dirt and sweat and oils, who bathed in creeks and basked by fires. If she were a wolf sniffing her pack—and she was—he'd stand amongst them a fake and a fraud. She didn't recognize this man, not as her father, nor as her killer. This was simulacra. Something meant for grieving widows and whimpering children, and opportunistic relatives just as wooden in their mourning as the woodwork out of which they'd climbed. If they'd invited strangers, or even kind-hearted acquaintances, who knew nothing about Dad, they'd say their nice words and speculate on his great deeds, and presume to speak on how difficult it must be for Mary to have lost him. It wasn't difficult. She didn't miss him. She didn't feel anything but curiosity towards him. Here lay, in the eyes of many, herself included, a great man with nothing to his name but the names of those whom he'd murdered in pursuit of her. Soon, the flames would find him and his flesh would melt from his bones, and then she'd see, yes then she'd see, how deeply he'd fallen. Only a black hole inside him would do. Anything else would be anything else, and then she'd know, yes then she'd know, she had her work ahead of her.

Mary went to touch his cheek, but her hand stopped short of his stubble. It started to shake. Her throat constricted. Something was wrong with her heart. It throbbed, and it was too large, like it was expanding, like a sponge. She itched all over. Fever broke across her brow. She rained sweat. As impossible as it seemed, she couldn't help but believe that there was still wolfsbane clogging his pores. If she touched him, he'd kill her, now that she was a werewolf. She laughed, snorted, wagged her finger at his corpse. He'd almost got her. Just another centimeter of sentimentality, and he would've got her.

Stepping away from him, Mary thought of her mother. There wasn't much to think about. She was all bones, in her mind and in the ground. Time had flayed her. Goetia had, too. She'd become part of its mythology. A story within a story. She felt nothing at this. Goddamn, Dad had been a hell of a cult leader.

Sniffling, Peter stepped up beside her and said, "You doing okay?"

"Let's burn these fuckers." She caught herself and looked at him, as if to apologize. She didn't.

Peter nodded, whispered, "I hope… werewolves… aren't some kind of hive-mind kind of thing."

Mary, staring at Andrew and Kimmy to see if they'd overheard him: "What?"

"Like if we burn my mom, hopefully that doesn't hurt you." He grinned. "Sorry, I'm just…"

Mary laughed at him like he was an idiot, but she was the idiot. He had a point. What the hell was she thinking? This supernatural bullshit always had some kind of rules or stipulations. She might not immolate as soon as his mom did, but what if she was somehow cured by her destruction? She couldn't have that. This was her chance to kill unconditionally.

3

Andrew and Kimmy closed in on Peter and Mary and told them in a quiet, measured tone, "It's time." That made Peter's blood boil. Who were these two to make that decision? *You get what you pay for,* a voice, not unlike his mother's, told him. This was true. Another thing was true, as well: Mary looked bad. He'd never seen her look this bad before. He never knew what Mary was truly capable of, but right now, he had an idea. In the end, the moon was always full, wasn't it?

Exasperated, Mary blurted, "I'll go first."

Mungo Society had two cremators installed into the far wall. They were massive, large enough to call into question if the building were bigger on the inside than on the out. The apertures for each of them were stainless steel. Now that he was aware of the cremators, they became aware of him. One of the apertures spiraled open, feeding into itself with a sound not unlike snipping scissors. Heat rolled out, filled the room. Beyond, arching brickwork, blackened, with no visible back-end, like an infinite crypt, or an endless underpass. A tangible sense of history seemed to spill from the aperture. It was the smell. Texture of the air. The chamber might've been newer, but it'd consumed centuries.

"Uh," Andrew said, in a whisper, "I believe the arrangement, Ms. Mary, was to cremate both the bodies at once."

Peter stared at Mary, who looked simultaneously caught and trapped. He didn't know that, that she'd requested the bodies be burned together. It seemed illegal, and if it wasn't, it seemed like something he'd have to consent to. She knew how to get things done. He just didn't always know how she got them done.

4

Mary had chosen *Mungo Society* because they had a cremator large enough to burn two bodies at once. Also, they accepted bribes.

Andrew and Kimmy loaded the bodies onto the track that fed into the cremator. Everything was digital, automatic. Dad was first, her Maker second. They hadn't turned on the flames yet, and already Mary felt as if it were two thousand degrees in here. What if Peter was right about burning his mother? For once, he could be right.

The track started up. The pine boxes shook and then slowly went forward, like two flimsy carts on a one-way rollercoaster. Everything is symbolic when you've belonged to a cult. The idea of burning their killers together made sense. They'd be inseparable, just like her and Peter would be.

Dad's body passed into the cremator. The track paused. Mary sucked up air, relieved, and violently coughed it out. Peter tried to touch her arm, but she pulled away.

The track started up again. His mom was on her way in.

"I…" she started, then stopped herself. She feigned sadness, squeezed her eyes shut, opened them, and waved off everyone's concern. She didn't say anything else. If she said anything else, about Peter's mom, about the lycanthropy… They'd know. Actually, they already knew, didn't they? They did. She could tell by the looks in Andrew's and Kimmy's eyes. They knew what she was, what was at stake. This was a test of her resolve. They wanted to see if she'd expose herself, expose her weakness. She wouldn't give them that. She wouldn't give anyone that. She'd rather lose what she had and try again than give someone that. Only Peter could know.

Mary stared at Andrew and Kimmy with fire in her eyes. The cremator hadn't even started yet.

5

With Mom's corpse in the cremation chamber, the aperture sealed shut.

"This will take about two hours," Kimmy said.

It took twenty years, Peter thought.

The cremator had been pre-heated, but now, it was coming to life. Something shuddered within it. The eerie silence of *Mungo's* was replaced by the whine of machinery. Whether he imagined it or not, he heard it: fire building, billowing, and whipping into an incinerating frenzy. He closed his eyes, and it was there, in the mother-darkness, that he saw the flames. He saw them as Mom would be seeing them now, if she were still alive. They framed her dead-vision and licked at her feet, and as they climbed her, they consumed her. Her woolen dress gave way to flesh, that gave way to fur, that gave way to muscles and bones. With every part of her that was reduced, another part of him was restored. He felt a weight well within him. When he breathed, he breathed her in, wholly, and her remains fell through him, like sand in an hourglass.

When he was full, he opened his eyes, and found himself standing on the surface of the moon.

6

Mary waited for a change, but it never came for her. Her curse was beyond immolation. She put her Maker out of her thoughts, to think of Dad, her other Maker, instead.

She had a moment between them that she'd kept locked up all these years. If she didn't get it out, it'd go up in flames with him. She closed her eyes. It came to her.

Mary sat in a field outside Goetia, leaning back on her hands with her legs sprawled. She was wearing a dress. The back of her calves itched. She wore a line of ants like jewelry on her ankle. Her hair was longer then; sitting this way, she could feel the grass tickling her knuckles. She didn't know how old she was. She tried to tell by the length of her limbs, the size of her breasts; the hair and its thickness under her arms, between her legs; even the things she thought, the feelings she felt. None of it helped. In Goetia, she measured time by her age, rather than individual days and months. She never felt her age, anyway, so she'd always figured she'd find another use for it.

The grass was taller than her, standing. Taller, still, was Dad, who came to her now. His beard was so big, it often got snagged when they went on walks through the forest together. He was wearing shorts that'd been mended more times than should've been possible and no shirt. His fingernails were dirty. Black mud wriggled beneath them, like the leeches in the creek bed when the water dried up. He must have been in the Giving Room, if he had the black mud.

Dad stared at her for a while. Every part of her. Not in an uncomfortable way. More in a this-is-what-I've-created kind of way. Finally, he spoke: "I see myself in you."

She smiled, thinking this was something she should be proud of, but his sullen face said otherwise.

"But you don't," he said.

Mary knew better than when to contradict him.

Dad sighed and his eyes left her for the sky. He stood there awhile longer and walked away; and everything he touched turned to ash.

Mary stayed sitting in the field a little while longer, wondering if any of this had ever happened.

WEDNESDAY, NOVEMBER 25TH, 2020

Peter lay on Mary's couch at midnight, jerking off to the darkness. He estimated he'd been at it for fifteen minutes. He wasn't thinking about anything, nor did he really want to be doing this to begin with. He was sore from it. These past few days, he'd felt so… agitated. Aroused might've been the better way to describe it, but that's not what it felt like to him. All his senses were heightened, more so than before, and all his nerve endings, raw. He had to do this, in the way you feel the need to scratch a spider bite. He'd been eating more, too. Sleeping less. And if he had any intention of sleeping at all, then he had to have the fire escape window open; otherwise—

Mary appeared, standing over him in her pajamas. He gasped, jerked in another way entirely. She looked at him, not his dick in his hand, and then walked away.

He lay there, panting.

The floor creaked. A white object sailed over him, bouncing off the coffee table.

"You should come prepared," she said, her voice softened as she returned to her room.

Peter leaned over on his side. She'd thrown a roll of paper towels at him. He lay back, listened for the sound of her mattress giving as she got in bed, and then finished thirty seconds later.

THURSDAY, NOVEMBER 26TH, 2020

Mary sat with her legs crossed in front of the closet in her Killing Room, admiring her trophies. There were three shelves. Her collection ran from oldest to newest, left to right, top to bottom.

The first shelf: four canopic jars she'd stolen from Goetia and had yet to open; a piece of the Wall of Goetia, which she'd also stolen, the name *Sheena Fulci* carved upon it; five black rocks she'd found the night she'd lost her virginity; a piece of heart-shaped pottery that still held some of the Giving Room's ever-shy mud; a platter of fingernails, also from the night she'd lost her virginity; Dad's lighter; a box of animal bones she sometimes liked to run her hands through; and half of a human skull—the other half at the bottom of the Ansbach reservoir.

The second shelf: a paw, from the dog she found and killed in the alley a few days after moving into the apartment; rat tails and cat tails bound together by pony-tail ties; an old knife; bird feathers; a stack of movie ticket stubs from Midian; a plastic container with mouse parts; a polaroid of herself at the back of a bar, her lip bleeding; a bundle of sticks, perpetually bound together by the small spider perpetually binding them with its wispy webs; a dead squirrel turned inside-out; petri dishes; a human skull she'd stolen from her anatomy class, riddled with tiny cuts she'd put on it on bad days.

The third shelf: several vials of blood, animal, man, and Mary alike; her dog's leash, frayed around the edges; a pile of scales; a page from a coloring book some little boy had randomly given her—a written decree that, to her, meant she'd assimilated; a black candle; pink headphones; her *Introduction to Psychology* textbook; the wolf's reproductive system; and now, in a rugged, moon-white vase, atop a bed of moss and dried skin she'd picked off her lips this last month: her dad's and Peter's mother's ashes.

It was Thanksgiving, and she was thankful.

1

"This is it," Peter said, as he and Mary cleared the outskirts of Talbot in her car. "We're doing this."

It started snowing again. Icy flakes tapped at the windshield before dying there. Peter, with the window down, leaned out to meet the frigid air head-on. He closed his eyes and opened his mouth and let it douse the nervous fire building in his belly. He always heard people talk about detoxing their bodies. This right here, being buffed and buffeted by nature? This was it for him.

Mary said, "Look at you. If I throw a stick, you'll probably fetch it."

Peter came back into the car, hair wet, face stinging as he forced out a frozen smile.

"You're going to love Goetia."

"I'm ready."

"I know you are."

The clock in her dash turned over to noon. She hit the wipers to clear the crystalline sludge away. A flyer that'd been jammed down in the gap at the top of her hood caught on the wiper and flew off into the roadside murk. They'd hit the tail-end of a protest as they'd skipped town. One organized by the loved ones of those that'd died in The Massacre on Main and concerned citizens who felt as if the city's response to the murders had not only been inappropriate, but in some ways, intentional.

"Pretty convenient," Peter said, remarking on all that.

"Goetia Gives," she said, as if he should know this; and he should: It was to become their slogan. "The perfect cover for out getaway. I mean, you can't deny it, Peter. Everything's worked out in our favor."

"Aside from our parents trying to brutally kill us."

"Sure, but... Even that." She slowed to a stop at a red light, hit the defogger like it'd wronged her in a past life. "Look where it got us."

Peter laughed. "We're not there yet."

"Yeah, Goetia... But not just that."

"You're going to turn into a werewolf," he said, staring at her.

"Do I look the least bit concerned about that?"

"Not. At. All." He laughed. "Nope."

"You're different, too." The car lurched as she left off the brake and drove on. "Can't tell me you don't feel better."

The jury was still out on that one, but she had a point. "I don't think the end justifies the means."

"Well, yeah, but it's not like we had a choice. Right?"

He said nothing.

"Right?"

"Right."

"Also: We're not at the end yet. Are we?"

He smiled, said, "We sure aren't," and stuck his head back out the window. He watched the trees whip by until his eyes got screwed up and he felt as if he were going to puke. He'd always tried to keep his eyes on everything all at once, all the time, and it'd always made him sick. It was a miracle he ever had anything in his stomach.

Mary hit the button for the passenger's side window on her armrest. The window came up quick, a reverse guillotine. He gave it the slip just in time. He stared at her, mock-pissed. She howled with laughter.

"Glad we burned them," she said, getting off the road and onto the bi-way.

"Me too," he said, and that was true.

"I don't think it would've been the same if we'd buried them."

Peter smiled, nodded his head. She was right. Werewolves existed. Self-aware swathes of lands were apparently out there. Who's to say a body couldn't come back from the grave? That'd be just like Mom, too. A knock on the door in the dead of night, lit cigarette pressed between her moldering lips, as she rasped, *Because I'm your mother*—the grammatical key to all childhood kingdoms.

The snowfall fell harder. Mary turned the wipers up a notch. She should've slowed down on the icing roads, but the speedometer kept climbing. She asked, "Nervous?"

"A little."

"You won't believe until you see it. But you will."

He smiled some more. About forty-percent of him believed Goetia was actually what Mary made it out to be. The rest of him was just glad to be out of the city. Yet, that wasn't entirely true, either. Because he'd burned his temple. It'd be a lie to say he wasn't hoping to find a new God in the wilderness.

"Is Goetia going to 'give' us some things to hold us over for the next few nights?"

She snorted. "Yes."

"How about something for frostbite?"

Mary ignored that one.

"Don't we have to give to get?"

"Uh, huh."

"What're we giving?"

She pointed her finger back and forth between him and her. "We'll get what we need to get by."

Peter cocked an eyebrow. "And then what?"

"We'll have more people by then. Goetia's not some demonic place. It just wants to be useful."

Peter's belief in the whole thing went down about five percent. "Okay."

"Hey," Mary said, getting over to get off at the upcoming exit.

"Hmm?"

"These last two months, we've gone through own personal fucking hell. We got out, with nobody's help but our own. We can do whatever the fuck we want, wherever the fuck we want to do it. Your mom? My dad? The city? Everyone wants to make something out of all this. Fuck. That. Fuck that, man. We're going to Goetia as we are and we're going to get ours."

Peter caught himself nodding to her rallying cry. "Hey," he started.

"What?"

"You're going to make a great cult leader."

She grabbed a quarter from a cupholder and lobbed at him. "Shut the fuck up."

The quarter hit his hand hard enough to draw blood. He told himself she hadn't meant it.

Mary must've been going the long way, because there was no way they were just now rolling past the Welcome to Ansbach sign three hours later. The town was an hour and a half away at best. There was going the long way, and then there was going the paranoid way. Mary had looked into and readjusted her rear-view mirror so many times on the way here, it was a miracle she hadn't twisted it off. They weren't being followed, as far as Peter could tell. He'd had his fair share of the air. It didn't smell like Pig.

Everywhere: forest. Black Oaks, as far as he could see, stripped bare but for the few decaying holdouts tucked within knotted branches. In between them, Sycamores, towering, sprawling; their sun-bleached limbs fat and knotted. Everything had the faded, creased quality of an old photograph. The sun sat low. All colors, dull. Even the snow, still a few feet high in the forest itself, didn't spark. The road they were on wasn't any better. Grass and weeds had drawn-and-quartered it. He'd never been to Ansbach, but by its surroundings, he had some idea of what it might look like. A few streets, squat, mismatched buildings with mismatched offerings running the length of them—the jaw of a slow to snap tourist trap. Everyone else, he imagined, lived in the dug-out hills he'd spotted through the breaks in the foliage. Blood cells, he imagined morbidly, coming in occasionally to keep the town's heart beating.

He was getting poetic again, he thought, which meant he was getting anxious. He shifted in his seat, pulling the seatbelt out of the crook of his neck. Why shouldn't he be anxious? Mary's father ran a cult in this forest for over a decade. In a time where everyone knew everything about everything, how had no one else heard of the place?

"So, uh…" He bent over, digging around his feet for a water bottle he'd lost there earlier. "Goetia did some pretty messed up things. How'd they keep it such a secret?"

"They didn't," she said, turning down a road that ran deeper into the forest. "I went to Ansbach for school when I was younger. Everyone knew. It just went on for so long, so quietly, that it just became normal. It wasn't really until those few years ago that shit really ramped up. By that point, no one cared enough to realize what we were doing."

"Did people leave around that time?"

"Yeah, actually. Dad pushed a lot of them away."

Peter shifted in his seat; his ass was falling asleep. "And we're going to do it differently?"

"Yep."

In that moment, Peter remembered he and Mary were twenty-years-old. Everything they had planned with Goetia suddenly made sense.

"We're just going to 'be'," she said, "and people can 'be' with us."

"And that's good for us?"

"It's great," she said. "You can see everything when you're at the center."

Peter nodded. He felt better.

Fifteen minutes after turning them down a dirt road, Mary stopped the car, killed the engine, and got out. Peter followed, his feet plunging into shin-deep accumulation. Ahead, a boulder, ice and snow clogging its pitted face. It wasn't until Mary went up to it, took off her glove, and pressed her right hand against it that Peter felt something. A stirring, not unlike reverence. A simple rock transformed into something more by her touch and her words. She called it the Welcoming Rock, and she told him he had to touch it, too, before they went to Goetia.

He didn't question this. He realized some part of him had expected Goetia to not exist, or at least to be nothing like what'd been described to him. For there to be something like this, it was proof of some forethought. It grounded the myth.

Peter went to the Welcoming Rock. He didn't need to take off his gloves, because his hands were already exposed, to try and cool down. Drawing a sharp breath, he touched the boulder.

And the boulder touched back.

Not coldly, but warmly. Slight, but not subtle. Like scaled liquid grazing the meat of his palm. Startled, he pulled away. There was nothing there.

"Heh," he said to Mary, rubbing his hands.

She looked more surprised than he did.

They hiked through the forest in silence, each of them wearing a backpack packed with food, water, fire starters, blankets, a first aid kit, and the remnants of their medications, in the event they got attacked by a wild animal, or needed something to help them fall asleep at night. With the sounds of them trudging through the snow, crushing what lay beneath it unseen underfoot, it was still, in some ways, too quiet for Peter. It wasn't like when he'd go camping with Mom. Even when she wasn't talking or playing her tunes from two decades ago, when there was nothing to hear but the wind passing through the trees, or the bright notes of birdsong, it was still serene. This quiet was different, though. It was heavy, almost suffocating, like when someone holds a pillow over your face.

Peter put on his gloves, zipped up his jacket. His breath contorted out in front of him, like ghostly shadow play. His teeth were chattering. Since when did his teeth start chattering? He looked to the sky in search of the sun, but it wasn't there. His stomach growled. Fatigue, like a wet rag, slapped the inside of his skull. He dug into the side pocket of the backpack, took out a protein bar, and wolfed it down. When there was nothing but crumbs on his fingers and the wrapper left, Mary glanced back at him. He stowed the wrapper in the side pocket. She looked away.

He was about to eat another protein bar when myth took shape before them. The forest pulled apart, like set pieces changing out on a stage, and there, at the end of this frigid corridor, a wall of grotesque, conjoined trees. They'd grown out of one another at every place and angle, creating a cancerous wooded mass so densely packed no light could escape it. Peter didn't need to ask what it was or if that's where they were headed. Some things you just know.

Mary led him to the wall, making the slightest corrections to her course along the way, until when they reached the barrier, they reached it at the exact spot they needed to be. Peter climbed over the snaking roots after her, careful not to damage or disturb anything. Everything glistened, as if the wall were warm enough to melt the snow that'd fallen on it. But when his hand slipped, and he clipped his exposed wrist against a branch, it didn't feel wet. It felt viscous.

Slipping her body through a break in the trees, Mary nodded at something beside him. He turned, faced the wall. Thin, long, erect hairs reached out from the bark. All of the trees were covered in these hairs, and all of them were interested in him. He looked back at her, and again, she nodded. He pushed his face against the hairs. Tiny pricking sensations erupted across his face. When they stopped, he pulled away. Mary was gone, and so marked, he followed.

The forest went black. Darkness overtook him. He pushed forward, but it was like walking through sand. He felt branches at his ankles, in the crook of his elbows, tugging at him, trying to drag him. Panic welled inside him. He opened his mouth to scream for Mary's help…

… and a second later, light returned to him. Sight returned to him. And then there it was, waiting for them. Waiting for him. Goetia.

The old fort lay upon the land, decayed and ruined; collapsing upon itself in places, and rebuilding upon itself, with itself, in others; but altogether, sinking. It looked like an animal caught in a snake's mouth, desperately clinging to the dirt as it was slowly forced, one century at a time, into its cavernous gullet. Or maybe it was the opposite. Maybe the old fort was wrenching itself from the bowers of the earth, the heat of Hell escaping from this old vent the reason for which no snow had fallen here. He didn't know. It wasn't his place to know. It wasn't a place for anxious minds. It was a place for acceptance and complete devotion. He knew this, because again, there are some things you just know; and because, right now, he could feel a current running through his body. He stood before power.

Mary was already by the front door when he was finished taking everything in. "Come and see!" she shouted, her words finding him intimately, like a lover's whisper.

Peter tried to absorb what he could of Goetia, but Mary was quick to move him along. It was going to take him some time to get his bearings: Every hall and room, small or large, had a similar look to them: collapsed, overgrown, rooted, ruined. He tried to make a mental map as she led him deeper into the fort, but found his mind wasn't willing. He'd have to get it down by instinct alone.

"Where are we going?" he asked, as they entered a massive room with several long, wooden tables. They both took out and clicked on their flashlights.

"The Giving Room," she said.

He tugged on the straps of his backpack. "I'm not trying to be an ass, but I thought you said we'd have everything we'd need."

"We will, once we get to the Giving Room." She went silent as they left the large room and re-entered the crumbling corridors, then followed with: "What we need and what we want are two different things out here. Takes time to adjust your appetite."

They plunged deeper into Goetia's sweating depths. There was a massive room along the way, one with something Mary called The Wall of Goetia holding the whole thing up like a load-bearing structure. She told him they'd have time to look at it later. Instead, they kept on until stone gave way to dirt, and the old fort's gunpowder-kissed hallways let out to the chiseled maw of a cave that was blocked by a massive, rusted steel door.

Peter stood before the oddity, wondered why the original architects had connected the two places. Which one had been built out of the other? Which one had come first? Thinking that, he thought about him and Mary. They were both the same age, but which one had come first? He didn't know her birthday, but that wasn't the point. The point was…

"This," Mary said, stopping them. "This is it."

He cocked his head.

"The Giving Room."

Mary went to the door, threw her weight into it, but it hardly budged. Peter took her agitation as an invitation and he joined her. With the two of them pushing, the door gave right away. They stumbled forward, laughing and son-of-a-bitching, into the space beyond.

The Giving Room. Given the size of the door and all this talk of caves, Peter couldn't believe how small it was. His flashlight made several passes over the room. The ceiling was steepled, like a church's; the walls severe, turned inward, calling to mind the surface of an uncharted planet. The floor squelched beneath their feet, as if the soil inside were melting from the impossible humidity trapped within the hollow. He trained his flashlight on the ground, following the odd marks that raked it, until they ended, each one of them, at a ribbed and gleaming hole in the ground.

Peter had so many questions, but neither the words nor the courage to ask them. His stomach fluttered, as if it were walking on a tightrope: on one side, brazen stupidity, the other, pants-shitting cowardice—which way it fell, not entirely up to him. Mary went on. She took off her backpack, considered laying it on a stone slab opposite the hole, before placing it on the floor, instead. The gesture meant something. In a place like Goetia, everything meant something. Or rather, it could. It was up to them to assign the meaning.

Peter quickly realized why his backpack was so stuffed, when Mary opened hers and took out a vase. The same rough, moon-white vase that held Mom's and her father's ashes. She'd plugged the top of it up with cork.

"Why'd you bring that?" he asked.

Her answer was in what came next. Without thought or consideration, she crossed the Giving Room to the hole in the ground, pulled out the cork, tipped over the vase, and poured their parents' ashes into the roiling deep.

"What the fuck are you doing?!" he cried.

Peter ran over to her, ripping off his backpack and dropping it in the soil. He slipped on the grooves in the ground. It only took him a few seconds to get to her, but by the time he did, They were gone.

At the hole's uneven precipice, blood boiling and images of Mary's mutilation playing across his mind, Peter watched the last few grains of Mom disappear into the darkness.

As he turned towards her, Mary said, "Think of all the things closure Gives."

He made fists and a promise to himself he'd only hit her once, when a soundwave shot through them; when the Giving Room shook, and then went still; when the humidity cleared and left in its wake, a more temperate climate; when their flashlights weakened, as light, but not sunlight, filled the room and the fort outside it; when the hole spoke, and out of the dark came a lamb to lay down beside them.

Goetia was awake, and alive, and for the first time since Peter had known her, Mary was crying.

2

There were some things about being a kid that just didn't translate well into adulthood. Hope, and trusting in your fellow woman, for example. But what Mary hadn't expected, especially after an already lackluster reunion with Goetia a few weeks back, was for the place to inspire in her the same childlike wonderment she'd felt so many years ago. Goetia was everything she had remembered, and in some ways, more. Fueled by the ashes of their parents, the place seemed to be going out of its way to accommodate them. Every room and hall was lit, heated. Pools of water, so pure they sparkled, like in the commercials, formed in the floor for them to drink from, and circulated spirally. The tree roots that'd ravaged the old fort took on the shape and sharpness of spears and daggers. Along each wall, a glistening, black port, that, when you plugged an electronic in, would power it with electricity, or something of the like. In the Feasting Place, where the long tables sat and where they and their future followers would eat, they found two pairs of shirts, pants, underwear, and robes; basic, but fitted. Even the lamb that'd crawled out of the hole in the Giving Room came with two sharp, stone knives tied with rope to its leg, in the event they didn't have something to slaughter it with. Mary had done the slaughtering, of course. She could tell Peter wanted to, but he still had one foot firmly planted on the moral high ground. Not her. And she knew better than to refuse Goetia's gifts.

It was morning, that much Mary knew, as she lay in soft soil, blankets from her bed around her legs. Five-and-a-half feet deeper and this rut, perfectly configured to the contours of her body, might as well have been a grave. It was comfortable, though. Better than the one she used to have, when she used to live here. Funny thing, nostalgia. Trauma of a different sort.

She turned over. The room was dim, but as she woke, it did, too, the lights coming up dreamily, like at the end of a matinee. Peter was in here, a few feet away, in his own little customized dirt-coffin. He was still asleep, hands crossed over his chest. He looked like a vampire. In his own way, he was, wasn't he? Kept others fed so he could feed off them. She wondered about who he'd tried to save after he'd run out on his mother. A girl, probably. Someone like Katie. Something sweet and doe-eyed. Someone, but certainly not himself. She laughed, spit rich with spite. A lot of sharp roots in this room. Looked a lot like stakes.

This room. She rolled onto her back, stared through the brick-and-weed-knitted ceiling. Mary had told him this room was just a room like any other room, but that'd been a lie. This was Mom's room. Her and Dad had slept separately towards the end. She never questioned this as a child, and as an adolescent, figured it had to do with their failing marriage. Recently, she'd wondered if she'd slept separately to get away from Dad, on account of him being a megalomaniacal, homicidal psychopath. That explanation didn't sit well with her, though. Mary knew more about herself, so by extension, she knew more about Mom. What if Dad had quarantined her here to this part of the old fort for his own sake? Because, like Mary, she could undo him. Consecrate him and his works. Maybe that's why he'd killed her, not because she may or may not have slept around with one of the Melancons. That's where Mary and Dad were different, though: She'd stared into the flesh for so long, she knew how far she'd have to sink before she came out on the other side. But she wouldn't descend alone. With tooth and claw, she'd cling to Peter, and her feet would never touch the bottom, because he would always be there. To break her fall.

He started snoring. She thought about killing him.

They ate lamb for breakfast in the Feasting Place. The fire over which they'd cooked it blazed in a Goetia-made fireplace. Hot blood had baked into the stones around it.

"How'd you sleep?" Mary asked. She was deeply interested in his every thought, feeling, and action. This was her project. He was her experiment.

"Good," he said, laughing. "Really fucking good." He slipped some mutton into his mouth "I had my doubts about all of this, but…"

"Werewolves," she said matter-of-factly.

"Yeah, I know." He smiled. He smiled at everything since last night. "I think it's easier to imagine the fucked-up shit than the good things." He drummed his fingers on the table. "No catch?"

"We're the catch, man. Power corrupts. All that crap."

"You sure?"

"Who lived here for eighteen years of their life?"

His mouth hung open. "You did."

"Yes, I did. Finish your food. I need to give you a proper tour."

Going through Goetia was like going back in time. As Mary marched the halls, Peter in tow, she caught herself conjuring ghosts. Ghosts of people. Ghosts of events and exchanges. Faint glimpses of faceless figures coming and going; carrying things here, rebuilding things there. Goetia had always been so busy, with everyone, thanks to Dad, having a daily job to do. To explore it now, empty as it was, unsettled her. They would have to fill it quickly, she realized, or it would die. Goetia had never been immaculate, but it had never looked this bad, either. The more it gave to them, the less it would have for itself. She had to keep it alive. Peter alone was not enough.

Mary brought Peter to the Wall of Goetia and let him gander awhile. She stayed in the back, in the shadows, to watch him.

"What is this?" he asked, his hand hovering around the moss-like growths pushing through some of the names that'd been carved into the wall.

"I don't know," she said, which was true. "Never knew. Wouldn't touch them."

He jerked his hand back.

"Dad used to say Goetia wrote the names on the Wall."

He went down on his haunches before the great memorial, right near the place where she'd broken off a piece of the wall as a keepsake years ago. She thought it was funny, and strange, for him to be drawn to her vandalism.

"Awfully convenient that the names that showed up there were the same names that ended up on the news a few nights or weeks later."

"Pretty moronic to write your victims' names where everyone can see them," he said.

"Sure is."

Peter stood, knees cracking all the way up. "But why?"

"Pageantry."

He laughed and shook his head.

"If we're going to get this place up and running again, we have to do the same thing."

Peter looked over his shoulder, in shock.

"Not... that." She waved her hands at the names of the wall. "Everything has to mean something. Everything has to have a story, and a little bit of mystery. People need something to cling to. Question a little."

"Have faith in."

"Yep."

He cocked his head back, said, "Oh, man."

"We're going to recruit people to build our own little world out there. Our world has to give them something theirs can't, or won't, if we want them to stay."

"Sounds like we're starting a religion."

Mary pinched the bridge of her nose, groaned.

"I know we're not." He turned back to the Wall. "I'm just surprised you want to share…"

"Have people around?" she said, correcting him.

"Ha, yeah."

"I like people," she said, and to some extent that was true. She'd grown up in a commune. It'd been rare for her to ever truly be alone. People taught her things, whether they realized it or not. About themselves, about herself. People were the puzzle pieces she manipulated into place to get a clearer picture of the world. People entertained her. People pleasured her. People hid her. She liked people plenty, as long as they belonged to her.

"I thought I did," Peter said, arriving at the end of the Wall. "Don't think I do anymore."

Intrigued, Mary drifted towards him and asked, "How come?"

"I mean, Mom tried to kill—"

"No," Mary said, grinning, "why'd you like people in the first place?"

Peter's mouth hung open. He squinted his eyes. Tongued the back of his teeth.

"I mean, you had a shit life."

Peter didn't know what to say.

So, she said it for him: "You could've gone anywhere, but you came here. With me."

Mary could've sworn she heard the proverbial click inside his head.

"You, uh, think that door's going to hold when you turn tonight?"

"With you, it will."

The Feasting Place. The Giving Room. The Wall of Goetia. These were the main sights to be seen on their short-lived tour. There were others, but their meaning died with those who'd given it, so Mary made up shit as they went. It didn't take long for Peter catch on and join in.

A room with the ceiling completely missing and a pond in the middle became the Cleansing Spot. In the East Wing, they found a room with animal pens fashioned from rock and tree, and so it became the Barn.

The South Wing hardly existed. It fed into the sinkhole that'd been forming around the old fort, so that when they reached the Wing's end, they were greeted by a sheer cavity flanked by ancient pillars and filled with slow moving streams of black mud. Much to her surprise, Peter suggested the sinkhole could be the cemetery. He laughed as if he were joking. She laughed, too, but only because staring into the sinkhole made her uncomfortable. There was something about the black mud, the way it folded over itself, and the hint of darker depths within it, that disturbed her. It was the rawness of the sinkhole. It looked tender to the touch, ready to lash out at any moment. A wellspring of destruction. The seat of Goetia's power. Death's brooding womb.

They doubled-back through the old fort. Peter was taking Mary's suggestion about assigning meaning to everything to heart.

"We could hold weekly meetings in here," he said, as they passed a small room whose walls were completely covered in ivy.

"Monthly meetings in here," he said, finding an even larger room further down the hall, not far off from the Barn. This room had an eight-foot-tall, diamond-shaped orifice at the back of it. "Fill it with candles," he said. "That'd set the mood."

They headed outside. Snow fell continuously from the cloud-bleached sky, but the flakes melted before landing on the old fort. The forest was closer, too. Or was it Goetia that had moved? All the same, things were out of place. Shifted, or displaced. Something had happened last night, after their offering of ashes. Either the world was moving in on them, interested like the media vultures had been in the stink of bloody guilt that drenched Peter, or Goetia was moving in on the world. To impose itself.

Or maybe she was just imagining things. And this old fort was the same as it had always been; and the only change she was seeing in it was the change she saw in herself. *Huh,* she thought, watching Peter go about the snow-dusted grounds. *Ain't that something.*

"How about this?" Peter cried out.

Mary met him at a collection of small stones that looked as if someone had piled them up by hand. It was very Zen. She wanted to knock it down.

"The Great Rock Altar!" he said, voice booming.

She stared at him, unimpressed.

"All knowledge springs forth from these simple and unassuming—"

"Alright, asshole, I get it," she said.

Peter shoved his hands into his pocket and surveyed their surroundings. "Ever do anything fun here?"

"Huh?"

"It's not all ritual and mystery, is it?"

She scoffed. "What? No. What exactly do you imagine when you think about Goetia?"

Peter thought about this for a moment, even though it was clear he didn't need to, then: "Monks."

"I'm confused. Shouldn't that be right up your alley, Mr. Nervous Pervous?"

"I…"

"Goetia was a bunch of rednecks, wannabe intellectuals, and shit-kickers whose masculinity was about as fragile as—" She knocked over the stone pile. "Trust me, it was anything but boring."

"But we're going to stay here, right?"

"As much as we can. Peter, what're you thinking?"

He shrugged. "I'm in. I am. I'm just being me. I'm thinking ahead."

"Overthinking."

"It's a big…"

"Dude, if you don't like it, then you can leave at any time." That came out harsh, but not as harsh as she thought it should've. "I'm not going to hold you against your will." Before he could answer, she went on. "Is that what you think I'm going to do? I brought you to this place because we are in this together. But I'm not going to make you go through with this. Is that how you see me? I'm trying to help us move forward in the way that makes most sense to me. To me. Might not make sense to you, but it does to me." She caught her breath, caught him looking at her in that you-poor-thing kind of way. "The fuck is this? Is this just one big joke to you?"

Mary stopped. She'd been in this situation before. With men and women alike. It'd taken longer to get here with Peter than it did with the others, but here she was, her old stomping grounds, where all relationships were stomped out, until nothing remained, not even the embers of second chances. It wasn't a reaction. It was instinct. Dad had been the same way. But once he'd shielded himself with Goetia, he'd gotten better. Soon, she'd have Goetia, and once a month, whatever she wanted.

She didn't apologize, but she did screw-up her face to let him know she'd shown her ass.

"I'm in," he said quietly, likely from all that bait he'd just taken. "I'm not going anywhere. After everything I've experienced in my life, this place is a breath of fresh fucking air." He ran his hand through his hair, held it there against the back of his head. "I just think we could create something pretty special, and for me, that's a lot of pressure. A lot of people to take care of."

"If we're taking care of each other," she said, "then they'll be taken care of, too. You know what I mean?"

He nodded.

"I'm going to turn into a werewolf tonight," she said, plainly.

Peter didn't say anything. Instead, he bent down and started stacking up the stones she'd kicked over.

They ate rabbit for dinner. Peter had sniffed out two of them. He'd chased them down and killed them, too. At first, Mary took it as a pledge of his loyalty to their cause. But after he broke the second one's neck, he almost seemed surprised to see her standing there.

When the light started to leave the sky, Mary and Peter made their way to the Giving Room. She didn't know when exactly the change would happen. She figured it had to do with the moon being at a certain point in the sky, but not wanting to risk it, she had them pack up their weapons and head to her cell. Imprisonment, like most things, went down smoother when it was your own idea.

They pulled open the massive door to the Giving Room, just enough for Mary to slip through. Peter stowed the pistol in the front of his pants like an asshole. It had twelve silver bullets in the magazine. One for each hour until sunrise, if it came to that.

"I don't know how you're not shitting your pants," he said, setting out the rest of the rabbit and a thermos full of water he'd brought. He had also brought a pillow and a blanket, but mostly out of formality. They both knew no one was getting any sleep tonight.

Mary shrugged and, with his help, pulled the door shut. He slid the small, rectangular door in the center of it open so they could see and talk to each other.

"Warden's going to call," she said.

"Huh?"

She chuckled. "Nothing."

"How do I lock this?"

"Bolts around the door," she said.

Peter said, "Oh," then ducked down, disappearing out of sight. While he went to work on the bolts attached to the door that could be driven into the cave and walls, she wandered into the Giving Room towards the slab where the skeleton of her mother lay. She sat beside it and ran her fingers against her bones, playing them like an instrument. The notes came out dull, the song uninspired, like the life this woman had led. It wouldn't be the same for Mary. When people played her bones, their fingers would ache and their ears would bleed; and while they might not like what they heard, they'd hear it all the same. Mom had died because of Goetia. Mary would die in spite of Goetia.

"Got it," Peter said. The door thundered as he threw himself against it. "Yep, got it. Hey… where… Oh."

Mary got up and approached the door.

"I don't think I saw that skeleton there before…" He furrowed his brow. "Was that there before?"

Mary said through the small door, "No."

"Hmm." His attention lingered on the bones for a bit. "Alright."

They didn't say anything else after that. There was nothing else to say after that. Nothing was as important as what was to come. Peter stayed by the door, the ever-vigilant warden, while she retreated into the Giving Room, pacing back and forth between the hole and the stone slab. A million thoughts raced through her mind. They came and went so quickly, she found herself unable to grab a hold of any one of them, choking, instead, on their fumes. Unable to track time, she found herself drifting through it. Her body ached. Her stomach burned. She was sweating and seeing indescribable shapes out the corners of her eyes. When she moved her limbs, they seemed to move twice as fast. Not once but thrice, she almost lost her footing in the soil and nearly tumbled into the hole.

Thirty minutes to three hours later, Mary started imagining what she might look like as a werewolf. Her fur wouldn't be white like Peter's mother's. It'd be darker, tinged with red. She'd have claws, too. Sharp as knives. They'd tear through flesh like paper. And her mouth. She touched her mouth. It'd expand into a snout. Her teeth might be as sharp as her claws, maybe even sharper. Altogether, her body would be bigger, more imposing. She'd be all muscle. Words and weapons would bounce off her hide. Nothing but silver and wolfsbane could take her down. For the first few months, she'd stay in here, learn the ins and outs of her bestial nature; but after that, when she was settled, she'd sabotage her cage; she'd get out. She'd run these woods, and then the streets, and she'd kill. Anything. Everything. Animal. Human. It wouldn't matter. She'd violate every social norm and sleep soundly afterwards on a fully belly. And when she woke, naked and wild-eyed, she'd do so safely within the confines of Goetia, a congregation of strays at her side. They'd find out eventually, she knew, but they'd know better than anyone else to not say anything. Strays keep their heads down. Strays keep their mouths shut. Strays are content to eat scraps as long as they know there's scraps to eat. Strays look up to those who've endured only what they could survive, but that's all they would do. All of them, except for Peter. He'd endured. When his likeness took form in her guttering brain, he was wearing pink headphones.

Dripping sweat, Mary stopped. She'd heard something. And then, contorted and listening closely, she heard it again.

Peter screaming.

She ran to the door, thinking feverishly, *They've found us.*

"Peter," she rasped, pressing her body against the door, her eye to the slot in it. She couldn't find him, but he was still screaming. It wasn't fear. It was pain. He was in pain. "Peter! Where… Where are you?"

Someone ran past the door, too fast for her to make them out. She smashed her face against the slot until her eyeball was nearly bulging from its socket. The screaming cut out to violent coughs. She heard something heavy slap against the floor. *There were others,* she thought. *Other werewolves. Of course there were! Why wouldn't there—*

Peter lumbered into view, bent over, holding himself, as if he'd been disemboweled. She didn't see it at first, so focused she was on trying to find the blood, but when she did, she nearly fainted.

His limbs. They were growing. Stretching beyond their limits. The sleeves of his shirt ripped. Followed by his skin itself. He reared up. His belly split open like a tent flap. In place of what should've been a tide of gore, thick tufts of moon-white fur. His screaming grew louder, more piercing. Behind the agony, cracking. Bones cracking and grinding as they slid around through the jelly of his musculature.

More hair. Patches of it. He spun around, like a harlequin in mongrel motley. His legs grew, arched. His shoes split, shredded by the claws and his paws that'd broken through them.

Mary whispered a barely audible, "Peter…"

He turned towards her, heavy sheets of skin hanging off his body. Face buried in his paws, he staggered to the door until he stopped short of it. He dropped his paws to reveal for but a moment his face. It was puffy, swollen. One eye larger than the other. His jaw was dislocated, tongue lolling out the side of it. Fluids were leaking from his pores. His scalp swelled into two prominent bumps. He looked like a piece of rotten fruit filled with flies and about to burst.

She started to say his name again when the flesh on his face twisted up and fell off, like wood shavings. His teeth shot out of his gums. In their place, growing fangs. His mouth jutted forward, elongating, as his nose sank into his skull, to be reused, as it quickly reformed into two dark and sniffling holes at the end of his muzzle. His head expanded, became severe. Two ears wound through his pate. His eyes, those bloodshot and fearful orbs, sank into his sockets; the veins in them burst, and filled, until they were a deep red, their coloration broken only by small the pinprick of a pupil.

In less than a minute, Peter was gone. All that was left of him was all that was left on the floor: a curtain of flesh, shredded and steaming.

Still shaking from growing pains, Peter steadied himself as he stood, his height now well past seven feet. Mary had to crouch behind the door to see his face. He stared at her, his blood-red eyes not unlike dying stars. Spikes of drool hung from his mouth. He flexed his claws, went down on his haunches. The hairs on his back stood upright. He started panting, his black tongue licking his black lips. He was going to lunge. He was going to rip through this door and…

Peter's head twitched. He sniffed the air. Every time he tried to refocus his attention on Mary, he caught the scent again. It overpowered him. He wanted it more than he wanted her. But it was faint. Whatever it was, there wasn't much of it left. His head snapped back to her. Their eyes met. And then he bounded into the dark.

Mary stood there, dumbstruck. She didn't bother breathing. She didn't want to breathe. She didn't want anything. Anything but what he had. What he'd stolen from her.

"What the fuck?!" Mary screeched, dropping to her knees. She made fists and punched the ground until they were bloodied. Rearing back, she fell on her ass, grabbed her knees, and squeezed them against her chest. "No!" She started to rock. "No! This is bullshit!" She ground her knuckles into the floor, getting dirt and rock into her seething wounds. "Fuck, fuck, fuck! Why?!" She sank her teeth into her lower lip and ripped a hunk of skin away. "It's mine. It doesn't make any fucking... sense!" Now she was breathing hard, nearly hyperventilating. "I'm going to kill. I have to kill him." She laughed. Her eyes fluttered, as if she was on the verge of having a seizure. She tore at her clothes, ripping her shirt off. "Where...?" She scoured her skin with her fingers, poking and prodding and pulling at the skin until it was speckled. "It has to..." But no matter where she looked, or hard she dug into herself, there was nothing there. Nothing but human.

Mary shot to her feet, her shirt around her right wrist, her pants around her ankles. She beseeched Goetia for one more gift.

"Mary?"

She went stiff. That'd been a woman's voice.

Again: "Oh my god. Mary?"

In the viewing slot there were now faces. Four faces. Three she recognized—Parker and Andrea from *Maiden, Mother, and Crone,* John, the gun clerk from Canto's—and a fourth, a woman whose face was ninety-percent grandma glasses, she didn't.

"I'm so sorry we're late," Parker said. "Did he lock you in here?"

The fourth woman added, "Why would he...?"

"Doesn't matter," John said, his words followed by what sounded like the cocking of a gun. "Young lady, we're going to get you out of here."

Mary nodded, smiled for all the wrong reasons. "There's latches," she murmured, "all around the door."

"We got you," Andrea said, disappearing as she went to work on the latches at the bottom of the door.

Parker went to work on the latches on the left side. "We've been following you two for weeks. Mostly him. Tracking him. To be sure. We didn't want to..." she yanked back a latch with a groan, "... intervene until we had to. That's our Order's way."

With every latch that was undone, Mary took a step back. This was not what she'd asked Goetia for, but it was exactly what she needed, wasn't it? This was her night. This was supposed to be her hunt.

"Almost there," the fourth woman said.

Mary took another step back, stopped. She'd hit something. She glanced over her shoulder. She was at the edge of the hole. But it was what lay beside it, what hadn't been there before, that had her attention.

A knife.

As the last of the latches gave, Mary bent over, grabbed the knife, and held it behind her back, ready to open her gifts.

PART IV

1

Detective Sono had locked himself in the laundry room to wrap some of his daughter Elise's Christmas presents. He did this for two reasons. One, she was on the prowl, her senses, like every child's, precisely attuned to pick up the sounds of crinkling paper, doors being opened that were usually kept shut, and exchanged whispers between parents who sounded like plotting crooks. The second reason he was wrapping Elise's Christmas presents was this: He needed a distraction from the guilt gnawing through his gut every time he caught a glimpse of the moon, full and foreboding, in the night sky.

I should've stayed with them, he told himself, unrolling the tube of wrapping paper over the top of the dryer. He'd told himself this multiple times already. But he'd been afraid to—stay with Peter and Mary, that is. He'd been following them, Mary, mostly. They were at Goetia now. Been there since yesterday. He'd tracked them and found their car parked in the forest not too far from the old fort. Twice, he'd passed through the barrier of trees that surrounded Goetia. Twice, he never went much farther than that.

"Dad!" Elise cried, outside the laundry room. "I need my clothes for tomorrow!"

That was a lie. He'd made sure to clear out the washer and dryer for that very reason. She was trying to use every trick in the book to get in here. Being a cop's daughter, it was probably only a matter of time until she kicked down the door, or picked the lock with that lockpicking kit he'd bought her last Christmas. She was ten, yes, but only when it served her.

"Nice try," he quipped.

She rattled the doorknob and pretended to stomp away, but he knew she was still there, biding her time.

Sono had given Peter his classic speech about recidivism back at the apartment building. It was the same speech he had prepared for all the pivotal moments coming up in Elise's life, like working, dating, or getting a tattoo. He was proud of that speech. He could repurpose it for anything. And he did truly believe in the power of being proactive, being an advocate. Not tonight, though. Tonight, he'd let things run their course. Tomorrow, he'd bag and tag what remained. And the day after, he'd regret his decision for the rest of his life.

Elise had asked for a new sketchbook and colored pencils amongst the tens of other presents she'd written down in order of importance on her Christmas list. He combined the two gifts together and drew the cheap, anime-themed wrapping paper over them. Carefully, blocking the sound with his body, he pulled out a few strips of tape.

"I hear you," she said, voice lilting.

Sono coughed dramatically and kept at it.

Peter and Mary… Mary and Peter. There was something archetypal about their names. He'd lost a lot of sleep these last two months because of those names. They were more than victims. They were more than possible perpetrators. They were pioneers lost in the wilds of the evil and unexplainable. They were dealing with things his years of training had in no way prepared him for. Sono had seen how Goetia came alive last night. He had put away a lot of terrible, sadistic, and vengeful men and women over the years, and yet he feared what Peter and Mary may do to him and his family far more than them. He thought he could reach Peter, lead him back to reason, because he was so obviously the lynchpin in Mary's self-serving designs. But after having learned what he did about Peter and his mother from Old World lifers that'd finally come forward a few days ago, Sono knew the kid was a lost cause. Mary's lost cause. It couldn't have been more perfect. For either of them.

Finished taping the present, Sono held it out for inspection. No extra paper. No peepholes for prying eyes. It was aesthetically, texturally, and even geometrically sound, as his wife, Nancy, liked to say. He set it on top of the dryer, then went to work on the young adult novel she'd asked for. *Your Body is a Cruel Mistress*. That was the title. By Jamie/Jamie. Him and his wife had thought Elise had asked for porn. When they confronted her, she went red in the face, laughed at them for being so "conservative," and told them it was about the intersexed community. Nancy, who leaned so far Left she walked with a limp, bought the book to spite the child.

From what he'd heard, Peter, like Elise, was a clever kid, too. Sounded like he had to be. His mom was a mess, and he was the mop that cleaned up her messes. The Old World lifers said Peter used to steal and sell drugs for her, to keep the lights on. Not all the time, but when you're twelve or thirteen, once was more than enough.

He used to fight a lot, too. "Like a wild animal," one of the lifers with the dead tooth had said. "He'd go hard, man. Sent a few kids twice his age to the ER. Then he'd go and blackout. Bunch of shit. That mom of his would use that for an excuse."

It was all hearsay in a court of law, but these people had no reason to lie. They'd come to him on their own. And when he'd asked them why, they looked away, like they were harboring a secret. The Beast of Stubbe Street. You didn't need to be a detective to know that's what it was. It was strange, though, the way they handled this information they'd brought to him. It was as if they felt... responsible.

There was a stack of sealed juvenile records on Peter. One of the Feds had tipped him off on them before they blew the city a day after Thanksgiving. Sono had already put in a request to have them released to him. The case was closed, but it was only a matter of time—hours, maybe—until it opened again.

The floor outside the laundry room creaked. Half-smiling, he finished wrapping the book, hid the rest of the unwrapped gifts in the dryer—*Tell Nancy about that*—and stomped towards the door. He wrenched the laundry room door open with such force the knob almost came off.

Elise jumped, eyes wide, mouth open. Her hands were at her hips, palms out. Her body was half-cocked, ready to take off at a moment's notice.

"What time is it?" Sono boomed.

"Uh…"

He crossed his arms.

"Midnight," she said, cringing.

"And how old are you?"

"... Ten."

"That math doesn't add up," Sono said. That was one of his go-to phrases, when she was up past her bedtime. It didn't make much sense. But it didn't have to. Dad logic.

Elise nodded slowly, her eyes shifting to the side of him. He blocked her field of view. It wasn't as if she could see anything from here, anyway, but also, he wouldn't be surprised if she could somehow see around corners.

"Okay..." she said.

He braced himself.

Elise bolted forward, shoulder-first. She slammed into his stomach, unyielding from her plan to go straight through him, crying, "You're... Obstructing... Justice."

Sono gave a little to give her the impression she was making progress, then he picked her up, threw her over her shoulder, and hauled her away from the laundry room.

"This isn't proper police procedure," she said, trying to wiggle free.

"It is when you're my daughter."

Elise started blowing on his ear, which he hated.

Sono started massaging her shoulders, which she loved. Elise had so much energy, physically and intellectually, she ended up winding herself up tight by the end of most days. She was like a tetherball, going around and around the same subjects until she got so wrapped up by the end of the night, she needed undoing. This right here? This little massage he'd been doing with her since the age of two? This was her undoing. And his.

He carried through the house like this. Through the kitchen, which smelled faintly of cleaning products—Nancy always gave it one last wipe-down before turning in. Through the living room, where snacks and Elise's art supplies were scattered, and her music player left on the couch buzzed out pop-punk beats. Up the stairs, onto the second floor, and down the hall, past his and Nancy's room, where she sat awake in bed, propped up against a quarter of her absurd number of pillows, reading a book by lamplight. To, finally, Elise's room; also lit by lamplight; also filled with an absurd number of pillows. He'd joked once that there were enough pillows in here that, if they glued them to the walls, they could have their very own padded room. He'd made that joke after having visited Peter in the psych ward. He wished he hadn't. He didn't like taking his work home.

Elise's breathing was steady, and her heartbeat, the same. If she were a cat, she might as well have been purring. In one movement, he pulled back her covers, laid her down, and tucked her in. Elise drew the blankets to her chin as she wiggled her feet.

Sono sat down beside her. Whether it was bedtime, midnight as it was now, or the final moments before a nuclear holocaust, Elise expected her late-night talks with Dad. Nancy got to see her throughout the day, more than he did on account of Talbot killing off its citizens at odd hours, so the two of them were always with one another. And while these late-night talks weren't the only moments they spent together, they were the only moments that were theirs and theirs alone. Neither he nor her could sleep without them.

"What'd you get me for Christmas?" she asked, dreamily.

He laughed, had a look around her room, as if to say she had enough. From her white vanity, the mirror on it swallowed by cat stickers, to her desk, which had a tablet, laptop, and a small TV on it, to even her bookshelf, which probably held half of Maiden, Mother, and Crone's inventory on it—crystals, baubles, tarot decks, stones, coins, and fairy statues—and also, half the public library's stock— tens of young adult books she'd "forgotten" to return—and finally her closet, which was so densely packed with clothes on hangers you'd need a crowbar to get them apart... Despite all of this, she, in his opinion, still did not have enough. A quarter of this wasn't here last year. He hoped there'd be even more next year. He wanted her to keep growing as a person, not to stagnate, like so many do in Talbot. It was all "stuff," but all this stuff spoke to Elise's interests, her personality. He couldn't have her stagnate. That's how you got people like Peter, like Mary, who mistook propagation for progress.

"Dad."

Sono snapped out of it.

"Everyone's freaking out."

She was talking about the demonstration that happened after Thanksgiving about the Massacre on Main. Things had calmed down since then, but the local news were doing their best to stoke the flames.

"No one freaked out like that when those people got killed at that one place," she said.

"Mare's Diner?"

"Yeah."

"That was fewer people," he said.

Elise looked at him as if to say *Seriously?*

"I know." Sono thought for a moment on how much he wanted to tell her. "It's a mess, Ellie. Politics. That kind of thing."

"What's politics got to do—" she turned over, away from him, "—with dead people?" A second later, she rolled back onto her back. "That's stupid."

He pressed his hand against her face, ran his thumb down her cheek. "It is. It's all stupid."

She didn't laugh like he thought she might. She couldn't have appeared more serious.

"What?"

"Are they mad at the police?" she asked.

"They're always mad at…" He caught himself, catching her meaning. "Do you mean are they mad at me?"

She nodded, pushing her lower lip out.

"A lot of people died, and I was assigned to the case. Some people blame me for that."

"But you did everything you could, right?"

"Yeah, I think so. My job's one of those jobs, Ellie, where it's easy to tell yourself you could have done more. We're only human, though, and we're dealing with humans. There really is only so much…"

"I know you did all you could," Elise interrupted.

Sono put his hand down on the opposite side of her, leaned in. "Ellie, did someone say something to you?"

A single tear slipped down her cheek. It could've been there all week, but he hadn't noticed it until now.

"At school? What did they say?"

She turned away, so she could say this without looking at him: "That it was your fault. That you didn't do your job. That you…" Her voice broke. "That you wanted them to die!"

Sono lay down beside her and held her in his arms. She was shaking, but she wasn't crying. She was still wound up too tightly to cry. He buried his face in her hair, kissed the back of her head. He pretended to spit out her hair, as if it'd gotten in her mouth, and she laughed a little.

"Kids know so much more nowadays than when me and your mom were your age. They know a lot, Ellie, but they don't know what the hell they're saying. It's just stuff they've picked up from their parents. It's scary for them, like it's scary for you, right?"

She mumbled, "Yeah."

"It's nobody's fault except the killers. They're the ones who decided to kill all those people."

Her shaking started to lessen. "I can't believe you were there." She grabbed his wrists and held them in her clammy hands. "Weren't you scared to go in?"

Sono remembered seeing the werewolf scaling the side of the apartment building, taking the girl's head off with one swipe of its claws. "Yes," he said.

"But you called back-up. You did save some people, right?"

"I think so…"

"You did. The same people from the diner place."

Sono didn't answer.

Elise didn't ask any more questions.

Instead, they lay there for a moment in silence until their breathing was in sync with one another's. Sono didn't think of much, except for how the cowlicks on the back of Elise's head reminded him how hurricanes look on those weather channel maps. To rectify, you had to simplify. Nancy's words.

"Bedtime story," Elise said, turning over, her snotty nose to his chest.

Sono bunched up his shirt and wiped it off. "A quick one since it's so late."

She nuzzled him.

To call them bedtime stories was a bit of a stretch. They were less bedtime stories, more summaries of the talk they'd just had. The only difference being that, unlike most things they talked about, there was an ending. Some closure. Something the overactive and too-smart-for-her-own-good mind of this ten-year-old right here could sleep on.

"There were once two people, a boy and a girl, who grew up very differently, but both had really hard lives. The boy had a mommy who treated him badly. Sometimes, she let people hurt him, or she'd forget to feed him. The girl had a daddy who was very mean and very strange. He did things to her so she'd be just as mean and strange as him. One day, they—"

Elise started snoring. She was already asleep.

2

Waiting for Parker, Andrea, John, and the fourth woman she'd heard called Charlotte, Mary, careful not to reveal the knife behind her back, slipped off her shirt and pants, so that she was down to nothing but her underwear. Four against one, and John had a shotgun. The odds weren't great, but she had to play all the same. The moon willed it.

Charlotte hung back while Parker and Andrea fanned about the room. John cut down the middle, his hands wrapped around his gun, his eyes locked on her tits. He had to be the first to her, she figured, so he could be the one to carry her out. Ass first, if he had it his way.

"I knew he was a werewolf," Mary said, making her voice tremble. "I think…"

John was about fifteen footsteps from her. Ten, if he got hard and had to lunge, on account of his dick getting in the way.

"I think…"

Eight steps away. John was lunging.

"I think he was trying to protect me…"

Five steps, and Parker and Andrea were right there, too, on opposites sides of John. They were probably chomping at the bit to get her back to the store, to get her sick on tea and cakes until she vomited up everything they wanted to know.

"I think he was trying to protect me—"

Two steps.

"—from myself."

Mary screamed, drove the knife into John's neck, and ripped it out. Blood shot out of his neck into Andrea's eyes. He dropped his shotgun to hold the gash shut. Mary fell forward, grabbing the gun mid-air. Hitting the ground, the soil sucking in her shoulder, she turned her sights on Parker, who stood there, stunned. Mary squeezed the trigger. An obliterating wave of silver shells exploded from the barrel and blew Parker's stomach open. Her gut was shredded. A curtain of ragged intestines spilled out and hung over her waist. The smell of shit and piss and burnt blood broke over Mary. She got up, as Parker collapsed, dead, and fired across the room, at Charlotte, who was halfway out the door. The shells clipped her side and sent her reeling and wailing into the cave. She'd get her when she was finished—

Everything went black. Everything went silent. She lost her footing and stumbled sideways until she caught herself against what must've been the stone slab. Then she felt something wet pouring down her face. She touched it, tasted it. Blood.

"You fucking bitch!"

She heard that.

And then she saw who'd said it. Andrea, albeit blurry, but it'd been her. She was a few feet away, the rock she'd smashed into Mary's head sitting blood-and-flesh-flecked in her hand. Between them, the shotgun. She must have dropped it.

Andrea dove for it.

Mary didn't bother. The Canto's store clerk who probably jerked off to guns and ammo magazines had only loaded it with two shells. She'd been able to tell by the weight, thanks to Dad.

Andrea, getting to one knee, pointed the shotgun at her and pulled the trigger. It clicked, and she cried. She dropped the gun, tried to get to her feet, but she was too slow. Mary ran at her, fell on top of her, and hacked at her arms as she threw them up to protect her face.

At the same time, John finally fell to the ground, also dead.

Andrea, unable to take the pain anymore, dropped her arms. They were torn apart, cut to the bone. Mary wrenched the rock out of her pathetic hand and cracked it against her skull. Andrea's eyes went sideways. Blood shot out of her nose. She was too dazed to fight back, so Mary readjusted herself atop of her, held her in place by her neck, and bashed her face in. Over and over. Flesh and blood flew into Mary's gaping mouth. When Andrea's skull finally gave, her entire hand sank into the woman's head.

Charlotte moaned somewhere outside the Giving Room. Mary, still bleeding and not far from losing consciousness, got up and hurried towards the massive steel door. On her way out, she dropped her weapons, found one of the holes with the black mud growing in it— the same they plugged their electronics into—and rubbed it all over the side of her face. It seemed like the right thing to do.

Mary didn't have to go far to see that Charlotte hadn't gotten far. She was near where the old fort had been annexed to the cave. She was standing, only barely. The side of her leg was bleeding, but from the way she was walking, she must have broken something. Fragile thing.

"Don't!' Charlotte pleaded, craning her neck as Mary walked towards her. "I don't... I don't..."

Mary didn't realize how wet she was between her legs until Charlotte's begging caused her to orgasm. She stopped, braced herself against the wall, and squeezed a hand between her thighs. She didn't like this, she thought, gritting her teeth as her vagina contracted. It was a liability, a weakness. Predictable. Cheap. Cliché.

Charlotte kept crying. Kept crying as Mary caught up with her and pushed her to the ground. Grinding herself against Charlotte's oozing bullet wound, she punched her in the throat until she couldn't breathe. Giving herself some time and, but for Charlotte's scrabbling hands and feet, quiet, she thought about what Peter had taken from her and did her best to take it back.

Mary sank her teeth and fingernails into Charlotte's throat, and for the next few agonizing minutes, she was allowed to breathe again.

3

Sono slipped outside without Nancy knowing. She must have been in the bathroom when he passed by. If she'd caught him, she would have told him to get in bed, get some sleep. She was right to say it, but he wouldn't have gotten any sleep. Elise had gotten the closure she'd needed. His wouldn't come till daybreak.

He stood on their back deck, staring out at what little he could see by way of the moon and stars, their backyard. It wasn't much. The forest saw to that. His backyard, like the backyards of the houses beside him in this small, set aside sub-division, all let out to the forest. The Ansbach Forest. The very same forest that harbored Goetia. Granted, the old fort was about an hour away from here, but still, it was strange how near it felt to Sono now that he knew it was there. It'd always been there, and yet, he could sense it now; feel the spark of its power running through the branches, like electric through wiring.

Sono had heard of an officer who'd gotten shot by a drug dealer over in the off-campus parking lot for the community college. In the heat of the moment, the officer hadn't realized it until later, when the ordeal was over, the perp was belly-up, and a paramedic was checking him over. He'd been shot in the chest and lost more blood than should've been possible for him to keep on the way he did. As soon as he realized this, he died. In all likelihood, it was a stupid cop story, but all the same, it got him thinking. Now that he knew Goetia was out there, how long would it take for Goetia to realize he was out here, too?

He dug into his pocket for a lighter, and into his other for a lone cigarette, and lit up. He took a drag and blew smoke at the night. It couldn't have been more than twenty degrees out here. He welcomed it, even as he shivered himself into a hunchback.

"Give me that."

Sono jumped. He sucked in air, sucking on the cigarette. He coughed as he spun around, and blew a cloud into Nancy's grinning face.

She plucked the cigarette out of his mouth, put it in hers—"Elise okay?"—and then offered it back to him.

"Yeah, she's okay." He took it. "Kids have been saying things to her about the murders and the riots. Blaming me."

"Little fuckers," Nancy said, taking the cigarette back from him.

His wife was the smartest person he'd ever met, but she was fiercely protective of him and Elise, and anyone else she loved. Before she became an English teacher, and before they started dating, Sono used to run into her from time to time, at the jail, for getting into brawls with her younger sister's various and consistently abusive ex-boyfriends. She'd always tell him, "Put another one in the hospital for you," as if she'd done the police department a public service, which, in a way, she had. Most of her sister's ex-boyfriends were drug pushers with warrants out for their arrests.

"The faculty at school aren't much better," she went on. "They've been keeping their distance. Unless they want to know something." She gave him the cigarette. "It's gotten ridiculous. Respectable staff, men and women whom I used to look up to, keep regurgitating that Old Country myth about the Beast of Stubbe Street as if it were a credible piece of evidence."

Sono finished off the cigarette, crushed it underfoot. He hadn't told her about the werewolf. He wanted to. God, how he wanted to be able to talk about it with someone other than Peter. But he knew his wife: For all her devotion to science, she'd just as quickly cut all ties to it if he, her husband, told her the myth was real. Nancy was more like her younger sister than she realized.

"The Feds pulled out," she said.

He threw his arm around her, pressed the side of his head to hers. Nancy was Grammar, through and through. She lived by structure and self-appointed rules. Case in point: "The Feds pulled out." A classic Nancy-ism. Bringing something up as if they'd been talking about it the entire time. She wanted his response, so she could say what she'd been meaning to say this entire time.

"The case was basically closed by the time they got involved. The two killers were identified, and dead. There was the riot, but it was by a bunch of white people, so it wasn't exactly their highest priority. Whatever they found out, if anything, they kept it close to their chests."

Nancy looked at him as if he were being naïve. And he was, purposefully. That's how you keep the wolf from catching your scent.

"I found out a few things about Goetia," she said.

The wind kicked up. The forest, blacker than the night, swayed, and the sky seemed to twist, as if its fringes were caught in the canopy. Somewhere in the neighborhood, a car passed by, hot tires crunching on cold pavement. The wind died down.

"Basically, scraps."

Sono had only just told her about Goetia a few days ago. On impulse, really. But out of preservation, in retrospect. For their family.

New heat radiated from her body, into his, as she explained: "Carol? The librarian at school? I had her help me. Don't worry. She's not going to tell anyone. Librarians are like priests. None of this I'm about to tell you was on the Internet. She had to dig deep in the interlibrary system between Talbot, Ansbach, Defiance, and Ose. Like I said, scraps. Vague references to articles and dates. I didn't write any of it down. I know you said not—"

"Good." Sono held her closer, his eyes never leaving the black smear of trees before them.

"That's endemic to the problem, though." She brought her other arm around the front of him and pressed her hand to his chest. "Goetia wasn't always named Goetia, as far as I can tell. Sometime in the late 1700s, that old fort was built. It was a garrison. It was to keep watch over the northwestern territories of the country. Essentially, to protect the settlers by slaughtering Native Americans, the British, and the French. At that time, the old fort was going by Grant Rock. Only other piece of information we found on it referenced the place about twenty years later, when it was no longer in use. It read like a ghost story, and talked about how the soldiers at Grant Rock would take women and children in the night, then return them weeks later. They'd come back pregnant and estranged from their families.

"We went through year after year, the best that we could, but Grant Rock wasn't mentioned again until 1849, shortly after Defiance was founded, and it wasn't called Grant Rock this time but Graywatch, and it wasn't a garrison, either, but a small farming community. A year later, the Catholics got a hold of the fort and turned it into a seminary. They renamed it to God's Gift, because they found the land in that part of the forest particularly fertile. We found a newspaper article that'd been written five years later mentioning an investigation into a series of missing persons. All the farmers from that small farming community? Gone. Thankfully, Carol has the eyes of a hawk, because she found a piece of another article that'd been written two years after at the back of the binder, stuck to another page. The writer of the first article? Benjamin Thomason? Missing. And God's Gift? Shut down over night. No one ever saw the original staff or their students after that, either. A year later, a hunter was in the forest and found, about ten miles from the old fort, a half-buried infant in the snow.

"Until the Prohibition hit, we really couldn't find any references to the old fort. Either it wasn't in use, or…" She stared at him. "No one was writing anything down."

Sono swallowed hard and ground the skin of his lips with his teeth. His eyes met the moon. It was so bright, it made him light-headed.

"Prohibition came around. It was 1925, and people started calling the old fort Goodman's. Bootleggers used it as a kind of cooperative. Imagine that. Talbot was founded about six years prior. A lot of booze poured out of that place, from what we could tell. But the full story? We didn't find any reference to anyone talking about that until 1940, a year after World War II started. Angela Lipman wrote a piece about the degradation of the Northwest and how there was a rotting heart at the center of the counties. She referenced organized crime, and specifically, an "oft-spoke of vice in our backwoods" funded by "gangsters and corrupt politicians." She made references to Goodman's becoming a brothel and even alluded to some occult elements. Her husband was drafted a year later. I know that, because there was an article about Angela's apparent suicide after she found out." Nancy's eyebrows couldn't have gone any higher than they were already. "The last reference to the old fort as Goodman's came in 1945, shortly after the War ended. An earthquake struck the area, and half of the old fort was swallowed by the land."

Sono was shivering so hard, it hurt. He needed another cigarette.

"Remember Harold Goldman?"

Finally, he looked away from the moon. "Of course? Talbot's first serial killer."

"The Mourning Murderer?"

He pulled slightly away from her. "Uh, yeah. We all have to study the case in… Wait. What're you…?"

"He was a necrophiliac. He killed five women and three men, and he left their bodies in graveyards and cemeteries."

Sono knew all this. But he also knew Nancy had to get it out, line by line, to get where she was headed.

"That was back in '80s."

"1982," he said.

"I know you know he was raised by his aunt. They lived in a trailer park over on West Bend."

"Yeah, there's a gym there, now."

"They didn't always live there."

Sono didn't say anything. The Mourning Murderer was an extremely well-known case. It'd been dissected down to its smallest, most inconsequential pieces. Also, he didn't want her to think he was invalidating her efforts. For her to discover something now after all these—

"Aunt Debbie Goldman used to live with her extended family out in the Ansbach Forest. The location wasn't named at the time, but wherever they were staying, it was raided by the police. She had a little boy with her at the time. Harold. He went to another family member for about six months, and then, when Debbie got out, he went back into her custody."

"Shit," Sono said. "You're right. I forgot about…"

"Remember why they raided the place?"

"They'd kidnapped…"

"The chief of police's daughter, Cheyenne. She was thirteen. We found an article from 1987 from the Talbot Gazette that talked about Goldman, the chief of police, who'd died about three months prior to the article's release, and Cheyenne. She said, 'I didn't know I was missing until they picked me up from the Getting Place. There were a lot of people there with funny accents.' The writer interviewed Cheyenne from her room at the Hurst Psychiatric Hospital a few states over. She was thirty years old. She'd been there since she was twenty-three."

"Why?" Sono asked quietly.

"Danger to herself or others. Not fit to be in society. Or… she knew too much." Nancy looked at Sono, but she wasn't looking at him. She was listening for something. Something she'd heard that he hadn't.

"What….?"

She shook her head. "You got out of the academy in 1996."

He nodded half-heartedly. He was trying to hear what she'd heard. But there was only wind, and the trees, and the hum of what sounded like powerlines.

"Goldman was executed in 1990. A guard in 1998 searched his cell and, by chance, found a piece of paper rolled up and jammed into the wall. It was a note written by Goldman, they theorized. It said, "I Gave what I could Give, and now the Getting Place will Get me.""

"I didn't hear about that."

"You were out of the academy. It was a footnote at that point. Talbot didn't want to talk about Goldman anymore. It wasn't bringing the tourists in, but pushing them away. I remember that."

"Me too."

"Did you know there was a spike in homeless people for about three years in Talbot after they raided Aunt Debbie?"

He shook his head.

"An increase in Eastern European people, too. A lot of them? Homeless. It was like they came out of the woods."

She paused.

Then continued: "The only reference I found to Goetia through all of this was fourteen years ago," Nancy said, resting her head on his shoulder as she hugged his arm against her body. "It was a story in a defunct publication out of Ansbach. The Woods Recollect. It was a hippie-type, cryptozoological-slanted newspaper. It only ran for about a year. They have a website, though. They're still running. That, uh, store Elise likes—"

"Maiden, Mother, and Crone," Sono said, already anticipating her.

"Yes. They're endorsed by The Woods Recollect. Anyway, they ran a story about a commune in Ansbach Forest. It read like an advertisement.

"And I promise you, in another year or so, people will write about something terrible related to Goetia, and then the place will go dormant again. Until it has a new name." Nancy snapped her fingers. "Oh, I forgot the devil-worshippers. That was part of the raid on Goldman's aunt. Honestly, I think that's the only reason it happened in the first place.

"So," Nancy said, letting him go and heading towards the door that led into the kitchen, "the Feds pulled out. You don't have to be police to see a pattern, Sono."

No, you don't, he thought. *And here Peter and Mary are, waking Goetia back up. Everything's repeating, like it has before. Corruption, cover-ups. Repeating, like everything always does.*

"The killers were part of Goetia, weren't they?" Nancy asked, hand on the doorknob.

He hadn't told her that part. She was half-right, but that didn't matter. She was still half-right.

"Over thirty people have died in the last two months." She opened the door. The heat from the kitchen spilled out, washed over him. "No one's going to get the full story for years, if the trend continues."

Sono shoved his hands into his pockets and walked towards her.

"I love you, and I know you know more than you're telling me, but that Thing is in our backyard. If we can do something to break the cycle, we should. Doing nothing at all has clearly not worked. Peter and Mary? Those're the survivors' names, right? Is someone watching them?"

He didn't answer her.

"Someone should be watching them." She said this with conviction. She said this as if it were, and as if, and it was, an order. And she was right. Someone should be watching them.

Nancy led Sono back into the house, told him he owed her some "candy" for all her efforts (their codeword for sex). He laughed, pretended to be into the idea, and told her she had a sweet-tooth. They didn't get much further than the kitchen before she was already stepping out of her pajama pants. He did what he could, she told him not to worry, and when she moaned, he thought he heard howling.

4

Mary dragged Charlotte's body back to the Giving Room. She left her and knelt down beside the corpse of Andrea. She took the woman's cracked-open skull in one hand and, with the other, jammed her fingers into her exposed brain. It was softer than movies or television would have her believe. Her fingers broke through the frontal lobe. Soft wasn't the right word, actually. Squishy, almost like custard. Mary dug around in the soupy remains of Andrea's memory, removed her fingers, and with but a fraction of a second of hesitation, held them to her lips. A hunk of brain matter had gotten caught under her nail. If someone had told her it was raw meat, she would've been none the wiser. Context was everything, this place and moment not-withstanding. *When in Rome,* she thought, and then tongued the piece of brain into her mouth and down her throat. It was bitter, but it wasn't bad.

Mary fell back on her ass and gave herself a once over. She was naked. She didn't remember getting naked, but she was definitely naked. Granted, on first glance, someone might think otherwise, on account of how she was almost completely covered in dirt from the Giving Room's floor. Pasted to it and her: twigs, pebbles, insect carcasses, hair, and pockets of blood. Her body was the palette by which she'd repaint this world.

She touched side of her face where Andrea had clocked her with the rock. The black mud she'd applied from the walls was sticky and seemed to be dulling the pain. It'd staunched her bleeding, too. She should've passed out.

Four people dead. She'd gone her whole life without killing anyone (literally, at least), and in under five minutes, she'd claimed four. *Look at me,* she thought as she stared at herself. *Like a pig in shit.* Ever since she first left Goetia, and to an extent, even while she'd lived here, Mary had maintained a carefully controlled existence. She'd always viewed her wants, needs, and desires as three separate pressures in three separate pipes, and she was the one, moving from valve to valve, that held them in check. It'd been the only way to keep the machine that was her mind running efficiently. Dad had tried to get her to kill and engage in all kinds of Goetia-sanctioned debauchery at a younger age, but she'd known better than to indulge. On her own, she'd had plenty of opportunities, too. And because she'd been on her own, she'd forced herself to be even more disciplined.

Not anymore, though; or rather, not right now, at least. The promise of lycanthropy had been enough to convince her to let the pipes burst. Her belief had been that the disease would've reinforced her mind with enough justifications to prevent it from being completely destroyed by her orgiastic release of violence, sex, and cannibalism. But she wasn't a werewolf. Not in the literal sense, at least. And yet, her mind had survived. She… had survived. And the pressures? She could hardly tell they were there. It wasn't like before, either, where she pretended not to feel them. It was, in a sense, her first true orgasm.

Knife between her teeth, Mary crawled on all-fours towards Cantos' store clerk, John. She sat on his shins, unbutton his jeans, and pulled them down, underwear, too, past his knees. A patch of scraggly pubes shrouded his crotch. She flicked his cock a couple of times with her finger, watching it flop this way and that. Then she took the knife out of her mouth and impaled his scrotum, pinning it to the ground. She jerked the blade towards her. His sack split open and his testicles oozed out. Turning the knife around, she rammed it between his legs. She fucked him like this for a while, but felt nothing. His perineum looked like a carved-up turkey when she was finished with him.

Leaving the knife buried in his guts, Mary got up and went for a walk.

5

Sono and Nancy sat at the kitchen table, both wearing only their shirts and their underwear, sharing a bowl of ice cream. Chocolate chip. Separate spoons. Carton close by. Lid nowhere to be found.

"Feel better?" she asked, the metal spoon clinking as it hit her teeth.

He let out a satisfied sigh, said, "I do," and he did. While he hadn't been fully there in the moment, when they finished having sex, his body had finally blacked-out his brain, and ever since, he'd been slouching in this chair, shoveling ice cream in his mouth, thinking about nothing but his wife and how beautiful she was to him.

"Me too. Thanks for asking."

He gestured with his spoon-hand—"Oh, come..."—and accidentally flicked a sizable chunk of chocolate chip at her chin.

She laughed, swiped it off, and held it before her.

"Hey, that's mine," he said, smiling.

She ate it off her finger slowly. He couldn't tell if she was trying to be seductive, or a little shit. Probably a bit of both.

It was dark in the kitchen, the dimmer lights one click away from being off. The bulbs cast across the room a coppery haze. It was hard to make out anything that wasn't ice cream, or one another. That was fine with Sono, though. There was nothing else he needed or wanted to see. He just needed to hear.

So, he listened to the house: to the warm air blowing through the registers; to the refrigerator humming contentedly to itself; to the dishwasher burning the midnight oil for one more cycle; to the heavy footsteps upstairs—Elise was a stomper; to the toilet flushing thirty seconds later; to more heavy stomping; to Nancy's phone chiming out a notification upstairs; and finally, to Elise's door shutting.

No out of place movements. No ragged breathing. No strange smells. No howling.

Not much was happening.

Other than what should be happening.

Sono slouched down further in his chair. He folded his hands across the small bulge that was his stomach. He felt like a watchman winding down for the end of shift. All doors and windows were locked. Everything was accounted for. Everyone where they ought to be. Most days, for a man like himself, that was enough. He knew the statistics. He knew the bad parts of town. He knew what to look for, what to ignore. He knew when to go off his gut, or when to defer to Nancy's. He had a gun in the safe. He had a brotherhood of boys in blue at his beck and call. And yet...

"You're good a man." Nancy leaned forward, chin to her palm. "You are a good man."

He gave her a half-smile instead of grief.

"You are."

"Yeah."

Chin still in palm, she cupped the side of her face: "You are."

No one ever told women they were good, Sono thought to himself. At least, not in the way women told men they were. He didn't understand that. Why did men have to be reminded of their decency?

And why was it when they (he) heard it, did it feel so essential? He wanted to tell Nancy she was a good woman. A good wife. A good mother. If he did it now, it wouldn't be genuine, would it? She'd smile and thank him, but the impact wouldn't be the same. He wondered about the last time he had complimented her on something other than her looks. Nothing came to mind.

She continued to stare at him, while stirring the melted ice cream in her bowl. Nancy was Grammar, through and through. Subject and predicate. She'd started the sentence. It was his turn to finish it. He couldn't tell her she was good, but he could tell her why he wasn't. In general, she accepted his weaknesses more than his compliments. To share them was to compliment her. At least, that's what he told himself. She deserved better, and more, he thought. Problem was, he'd forget this come morning. When the world was awake, and the air was heavy with blood and the sounds of gunshots, and those he met were just as alive as they were dead; and all the good he was grateful for, he kept locked up, behind bars, so no one could get at it, not even him, sometimes; not until it was late, at least, when no one was around, except for Nancy; and when he'd think to let it out, all that good, his hand would shake, and she would see; so she'd unlock him, instead; and by the time the tears and the self-loathing stopped, she'd be asleep, and Elise would be asleep, and the sun would be rising.

"I am a good man," he said, "but I have to tell you why I'm not."

Nancy straightened up, blinked her eyes rapidly to keep sleep at bay.

"The survivors. Peter and Mary. They're directly connected to the killers."

"I know."

"Mary's father was the founding member of Goetia."

She drew a sharp breath. Her arm jerked, elbowing her bowl away.

"Peter's mother…" He shrugged. "Peter's mother was a werewolf."

Nancy choked out a laugh. He could see the linguistic gymnastics she was running through in her head to make sense of what he'd told her. Thinking she got it, she said, "She was a serial killer. Is that what they've been…?"

"No, she was a werewolf," he said, plainly.

Nancy's head bobbed forward, as if his statement had slapped it.

"I saw her. That night on Main. Right before I went into the building. A giant wolf, crawling down the side of the building. Forensics found both crime scenes, the diner and the apartment building, covered in wolf hair. Most of the victims at the building were covered in bite marks from a wolf. The evidence was all there. They just never found the wolf, because they didn't know where to look."

Nancy stammered, "I…"

"Peter and Mary lied to people about it, so they wouldn't think they were crazy. But I saw it, and Peter confirmed it. The Beast of Stubbe Street? All that bullshit? It's real. His mother had been back in town for about a year, hiding out, killing people every month in the Old Country."

Chewing on her lip, Nancy kept quiet.

"I swear to God, I saw it."

She nodded.

"I did."

"I know, I believe you," she said, and it sounded like she did.

"Mary got bit by Peter's mother before they killed her with a silver bullet. She and Peter went to Goetia yesterday to prepare for tonight."

"She's going to… to turn?"

"They seem to think so."

"I don't…" Nancy fumbled for her words. "I don't… Whatever the case, none of this makes you a bad…"

"It does," he said. "She's going to turn. She and Peter have become so enmeshed, so dependent upon one another, that she's brainwashed him to be her caretaker, just like how he was with his mother. Neither of them are clean, you know? They seemed normal at first, but like anyone, when you dig deep enough, you find bodies. She was born in a cult, and I'm pretty sure when she was younger, she either killed or tortured people. And Peter… I can't get a read on what exactly he did in service to his mother, but I'm guessing nothing was off the table.

"So, I am a bad man, Nance, because she's going to turn into a werewolf and kill somebody, and he's going to cover it up, or help her do it, and it's going to go on and on. And you know what else?"

She didn't.

"Goetia's not just a place. I went there yesterday. It's… alive. They did something to it and woke it up. There's no electric there. No machines or appliances. Lights came on inside it. Heat poured out of it. This shit is so far outside of human jurisdiction." He shook his head and laughed to himself. "Mary's going to start Goetia all over again. Or at least, she's going to try.

"I've got two suspects who might have done terrible things in the past, and who will likely do terrible things tonight, and keep on doing them, and instead of doing something about it, I'm here, letting it happen, because I've already judged them. I can't help them. I don't want to."

Nancy scooted her chair closer to his until their knees touched. She put her hands on his thighs and told him, "Arrest them?"

"On what charges? I don't know what they are capable of. I don't know what anything's capable of anymore." He shivered. "She could hunt us. Even if I'm prepared, I don't know if I can stop something like that. I can't tell someone something like that without getting hauled off to Hurst. There's no cure for her, except for a silver bullet to the head. Do I just kill her?"

"No… No."

"Like you said, that thing, Goetia, it's in our backyard. If you don't believe me about the werewolf…"

"I do."

"… then you have to admit there's some black magic fuckery going on with that place. With its history? Yeah, the Feds did pull out. Who actually gave that command, you know? What the fuck's it's influence?" Sono stopped to stop himself from crying. "I've never been so scared to do something. But I'm almost just as terrified at the idea of doing nothing, either. Fuck." A tear ran down his cheek. "What did you put in that ice cream?"

Nancy smiled and wiped his cheek. "You're not a bad man, Sono."

"But what do I do?" he asked, kissing the side of her hand. "What do we do? Do I quit? Do we move?"

"Are you serious?"

"Yeah."

"I've never… I never thought you'd…" She stared at the floor, in thought. "You've always kept us safe. Are we in danger, now?"

"No," he said, "I don't think so."

6

Detective Sono has to die, Mary thought, as she roamed the dimly-lit halls of Goetia, rattling her car keys. *He knows too much. Got to kill him.*

She wandered into the Feasting Place and found the old fort had anticipated her. On the nearest table, a thick, hooded, sheepskin robe. She threw it on, tied it tight with the fleshy sash that looped around on it. Glancing at the ground, beneath the bench before her: boots. She recognized them. They were Parker's. She hadn't thrown any of the four bodies into the hole in the Giving Room, and yet Goetia had taken Parker's boots and placed them here before her. She'd never seen this place do that before. It was more alive than she realized. She wondered what else it might regurgitate to satisfy her needs.

Mary slipped her feet into the boots. They were warm, and wet. Given how she looked, she couldn't complain. She patted herself down, stopped at the large pockets on both sides of the robe. Inside each, a butcher knife. Replicas of the Bossman's from Mid-City Meats. Cocking her head, she stared at the buckling stone walls of the Feasting Place, as if to ask Goetia, "How did you know?"

It didn't matter. Whether it took bodies, or images from her mind, Goetia had been good to her, and so, she had to be good to Goetia.

There were large paw prints in the ground, and sometimes, across the tops of the tables. Peter's prints. Wide-eyed, she tracked them, out of the Feasting Place, back into the halls, where otherworldly light poured through the brickwork. He hadn't just run out of here, she thought. In his rebirth, he'd ripped through Goetia, leaving gouges in the dirt and gashes in the stones. But the more she looked at the damages, she couldn't help but wonder if he'd been eager to leave, or desperate to stay.

Mary made it outside. She was drenched in sweat. The sheepskin robe had done its job and then some. She opened it up. A wintry wind blew in from the surrounding dark. She let it wrack her naked body awhile. Cooling off, covering up, Mary felt the black mud she'd applied to the side of her head dripping down her face. Without thinking, she wiped it away. She expected pain, but got only a dull sensation. Taking out a butcher knife, she angled it, catching the moonlight in its frosted steel, and looked at her reflection.

Like Peter, she was an abomination herself. Her bloodshot eyes were huge, and the skin around them, puffy. Her lips were split, flaking. Her hair wasn't so much hair, but a massive bezoar of dirt and sticks that'd stylized it into something not unlike a crown. The veins in her face were throbbing, tented to their fullest extent. Dried snot encrusted her nose and her upper lip in a yellow film not unlike phlegm. None of this surprised her, though. No, what surprised her was the scar on the side of her head. The scar that shouldn't have been a scar, but a swollen, spewing gash. What should've killed her, or at least should've taken two months at best to fully heal, instead looked like a wound she'd received years ago.

The black mud, she thought. *That's convenient.*

Mary stowed the butcher knife in her pocket and broke out into a sprint, quickly clearing the clearing between here and the barrier. Reaching it, she forced herself through the trees, yanking her robe loose when it got caught on the branches.

Coming out on the other side, where Peter's prints started again, she ran even harder, murder having revitalized her. Snow started to fall. She had to squint to keep it from getting in her eyes. It was dark in Ansbach Forest, but not dark enough that she couldn't see where she was going. There was already snow on the ground, and it held in it the moon's guiding light. Soon, she'd be back at the Welcoming Rock. Soon, she'd be back at the car, opening the glove box. Inside it, there was a scrap of paper with Sono's address. It'd been easy enough to get. His wife had posted a picture on social media of their daughter on the front lawn of their house two years ago. The house number (1717) had been in the foreground, the street sign (Somerset), semi-blurred in the background. She'd left the address in the glove box for Peter, though she still hadn't figured out how to incorporate him into her plan of killing the detective.

"Doesn't matter," she said, starting to shiver. "If you want something done…"

Mary stopped. The forest rattled like a sick person's throat. All these thoughts of killing Sono, and yet she wasn't headed back to the car. She was going the wrong way. She'd been following Peter's tracks this entire time. When she thought of Sono, she felt anger, yes, and disdain, but not hunger. Not the hunger, the yearning, she felt when she stared at the snow and imagined Peter bounding through it.

She spun in the dark, trying to find her way.

7

Sono stood at the sink, his back to it, while Nancy cleaned out their ice cream bowls. The clock on the oven said it was almost two in the morning. It seemed much later.

"Snowing," Nancy said, steam from the hot water building around her.

He turned around to face the window above the sink. It was snowing, but slowly; so slowly, that the flakes, at times, seemed to be suspended in the air. They fell only when others hit them, and then they fell together, as one.

Nancy racked the bowls, turned off the sink, wiped her hands down with a dishcloth, and asked him, "Do you have any silver bullets?"

"Uh," he said, caught off-guard, "could get some."

"You should." She threw the dishcloth over her shoulder. "I'll do more research with Carol at the library. I'll see what else we can get to protect ourselves. Wolfsbane?"

"Yeah."

"We've got a whole month to figure out what we're going to do."

Sono nodded. He could feel all the tension in his body leave through his toes. "Right. Right."

She threw her arms around his shoulders, held him in the way she might've had they gone to Prom together. She pursued his lips, until he got the hint and planted one on them.

"I'm being fucking ridiculous," he said.

"The whole thing is fucking ridiculous. The situation calls for it." She started to sway back and forth. "What did it look like?"

"The werewolf?"

"Yeah."

"Like a werewolf. Huge. Strong. It ripped through those kids like they were wet paper."

Nancy's eyes lost their sleep-starved luster.

"What's wrong?"

"Scares the shit out of me." Nancy leaned in, pressing her forehead to his mouth. "It's worse coming from you."

Sono kissed her head. "Like you said, after tonight, we'll have a month." He ran his fingers through her soft yellow curls. "If those two don't kill each other tonight, I'll try to get to Peter through Mary.

She might use me, if she thinks that'll somehow hide what she's do-ing at Goetia."

Nancy took a step back. She ran her hands down his arms, until they met his. "I want to see it. I can do without the werewolf. I'll take your word on that one. But I want to see the place."

"I…"

"How about this: Elise's winter break is coming up. Mine, too. Let's skip town early. We'll put some distance between us and all this, and then we can figure out what we want to do long-term."

Sono nodded, a stupid grin on his face. But the longer he thought about her suggestion, the more it turned his stomach.

"What?"

"Someone should be watching them. You said it."

Nancy rolled her eyes. "You don't know what you want, do you?"

"I just wanted to be able to tell someone about this without sounding like a lunatic."

"You're just…" she drummed his chest, "… going to do what you have…" She scrunched up her face. "No, you just told me were-wolves and self-aware buildings exist. No, Sono. No. You have a wife and a daughter who love you. You can't just vent this out and ex-pect—"

"Nancy…"

"No," she said. "I'm supporting you by not supporting you."

Sono didn't want to fight, but if they kept at it, that's exactly what would happen. So, he told her, "You're a good woman," raised her hand to kiss it, and—

Glass exploded somewhere inside the house.

Nancy screamed and fell backwards into the counter.

Sono reached for his holster, which was upstairs with his pistol, in the safe.

A second passed, excruciatingly, like a knife through their ribs.

Nancy, trembling: "W-Where was that…?"

One of the window sensors let out a blood-curdling chirp. The alarm system started counting down.

"Sono…"

He grabbed her hand, squeezed so hard that, in another situation, the bones might've broken. But they were both, now, reinforced with fear. "Guest room," he whispered.

The guest room was connected to the living room. To get to Elise, they'd have to go through there. In thirty seconds, the alarm would go off, waking up the entire neighborhood. In three minutes, the police would be here. But their daughter was alone. They didn't have thirty seconds, let alone three minutes.

A draft whipped past them. Cold air, trespassing.

Sono and Nancy, hand-in-hand, skulked towards the living room. The light from the kitchen crept across it. He could just barely make out the outline of the guest room's door. Still shut, but someone, or something, was definitely in there. He could hear shattered glass crunching beneath their feet, and heavy breathing.

The tiny, terrified voice of Elise warbled from the staircase: "Dad?"

The guest room door burst open.

Sono and Nancy ran into the living room, screaming, "Go upstairs! Go upstairs!"

Elise, blubbering, cried, "What's…?"

In the doorway, the werewolf appeared. Nancy screamed until her voice broke. Sono's stomach sank, and like looking into the face of God, he felt powerless before the beast. The stench of death and dirt poured off the hulking mass of muscle and fur. Its claws gripped the sides of the doorway as it ducked and heaved itself through. Seven feet tall. Maybe eight. Bone-white but for its red eyes and bloody drool that dripped constantly from its quivering mouth. Darkness gathered at its hind, eating away everything that it touched, forcing Sono to acknowledge one thing and one thing alone: This was how he was going to die.

Elise hadn't spoken, but he'd heard her all the same. In a fraction of a second, everything she'd ever said to him came back to him. Her voice rang through his mind like chimes, but as they went on, they were getting quieter and quieter, for there was no wind ahead to move them.

Nancy hadn't touched him, but he felt her all the same. In a fraction of a second, a lifetime. She moved him, outside and in. Warmth and indescribable, irreplaceable contentedness washed over him where she'd left her small and changing marks. But it was growing colder in here, and the places where she'd touched him, or would touch, numbed to her effect.

This house was a grave.

He wouldn't be buried alive.

Sono, wrenching Nancy along with him, bolted for the staircase. The house alarm went off, piercing his ears. The werewolf cleared the living room in one leap. It slammed into Nancy, smashing her against the wall. Her body cracked. Her head bounced off the wall. Bone fragments protruded from her broken nose. She held onto Sono's hand until she couldn't. When the werewolf ripped her arm off at her shoulder, leaving him with nothing but a face full of blood and a spurting limb. Nancy crumpled to the ground, shaking on her side, gasping for air, but choking on her blood, as arterial spray rained down on her, filling her pleading mouth.

Sono dropped his wife's arm and bounded up the stairs towards Elise. He made it up four before his feet went out from under him. The werewolf had him by his ankles. He landed teeth first on the steps. The top row of his teeth broke, and those that didn't shot through his gums, into his skull. A gout of blood exploded out of his mouth. He tried to tell Elise that he loved her, but no words came out. So, he stared at her, and hoped that she could see it in his eyes, instead.

The werewolf climbed up him, sinking claw after claw into the meat of Sono's thighs and back as it moved past. He yelped in pain. Huge chunks of flesh and muscle were torn from his body with every step the beast took. When it passed over his head, Sono tried to cover it with his arms, so his daughter wouldn't have to see it be ripped open. Instead, the werewolf took his neck in its jaws and shook him, like a pup, until his spine broke. Now, he couldn't scream or distract or fight back, or put a bullet in his head. He could only watch.

Elise, who hadn't moved this entire time, did just that: She spun around and ran as hard as she could up the stairs.

But she didn't get far.

Not before the werewolf knocked her down and mounted her from behind.

8

Mary returned to Goetia, teeth chattering and skin frostbitten. In two days' time, she'd gotten too used to its comforts. There was no need to rush out in the middle of the freezing night to murder the detective. She told herself she could just as easily kill him tomorrow. Besides, she had work to do. There were four bodies that needed to be disposed of.

She entered the Giving Room, let loose her robe so she could breathe a little, and gazed upon her Work. Parker, on her back, intestines like a ball of mating snakes sitting heavily over her gut. Andrea, on her side, head split in two, the remnants of her eyeballs smeared into the remnants of her brain. John, face down, hole in his neck whistling when the air went through it, the shredded gash between his balls and his ass still leaking. Charlotte, the fourth and final hunter; she'd dropped her off near the hole; her hands, outstretched over it, had already been chewed off by the forces inside. They didn't look any different than her neck, or her tits, which Mary had feasted on, too, spur of the moment. She'd forgotten she'd done that, but now that she was reminded she had, she felt like that might've been a bit much.

Taking off her boots, she stomped across the Giving Room, the rich soil squelching between her toes. She drove her heel into Charlotte's side and forced her corpse into the hole. Mary listened to hear her hit the bottom. She never heard anything.

Mary grabbed Parker by her foot, started dragging her towards the hole. The more she looked at it, the hole, the more she felt one of her own growing inside her. Out in the forest, she'd though it was a kind of hunger, a need to kill again. But it wasn't that, not entirely. It was the stinging pangs of gluttony telling her that, despite her best and bloody efforts, she was not satisfied.

She went down on her haunches, rolled Parker into the feasting abyss. Her intestines shot out of her mid-descent like a failed a parachute.

Catching her breath, Mary then went to Andrea. She dragged her to the hole and kicked her in it. In the grooves her body had left in the soil, pieces of skull and brain: fat red worms threaded out of the dirt and clung to them like leeches.

Mary stared at John awhile, not thinking, only feeling. Feeling the hole growing inside her, not wanting to be fed, but to be acknowledged. She had to be honest with herself; otherwise, she'd be back where she started. If she were going to continue to kill, and she would continue to kill, it had to be under the right circumstances

Mary grabbed John by both his hands, spun around, brought him to the hole, and gave him away. Half his body hit the side of the hole as he fell. When flipped around from the impact, the skin there was flayed and charred, as if he'd gotten dragged by a car down a mile of bad road.

She wandered for a bit before finally collecting her sheepskin robe. Making her way to one of the rooms with a pool of water, she set the robe down beside it and climbed in. The water, which smelled faintly of iron and fish, came up to her hips. She washed herself. Her hands, coarse from all the killing, like sandpaper on her flesh.

Goetia started to shake in appreciation of her offering. Then it began to brighten. Otherworldly light poured through the gaps in the stones and bricks. It rose up from the floors, from the cracks and fissures at the bottom of the pool. Just when she thought it would stop, it kept going. Brighter and brighter. Until it was blinding. Until every one of her senses was completely enveloped, and she was certain the light was shooting through her pores, refracting off her cells.

9

Elise couldn't breathe beneath the werewolf's girth. The beast thrust itself against her backside. She beat her fists against the stairs, until she couldn't.

In his mind, Sono was screaming. In his mind, Sono was tearing the werewolf apart with his bare hands, emptying clip after clip of silver bullets into its monstrous skull. In his mind, Nancy was bleeding out, but still alive, and Elise… she was so traumatized, her mind would wipe this night from her memory forever.

He thought the werewolf was going to rape his daughter, but it wasn't. It was lying on top of her, suffocating her with its weight. She was deflating, the last of her life escaping with a strained rattle from her scream-scarred throat. It didn't take long for his daughter to die. He didn't know if that'd been the beast's intention or not. And if it had been, why did it disable him? So he'd know?

He didn't have a chance to figure it out, though.

The werewolf rose off Elise's small, lifeless corpse, turned around on all fours, took Sono's sweaty head in its jaws, and bit through half his face, turning him into an anatomy doll.

By the time the police were kicking in the front door, Peter was already gone.

10

Depraved thoughts swam through the purifying light inhabiting Mary, and as if told by God Itself, an epiphany formed.

I can't kill anyone else.

Until I kill Peter.

And it was then that she knew what this light was, where it was from: The moon. And it was then, right then and there, she knew when she had to do it.

Thirty days to go, she thought. *We'll both be transformed this time.*

11

Peter shot up in the dead field, screaming. He was naked. His skin, hot and raw. He hurried to his feet, only to be knocked off them by the sight before him. A solitary tree, bare and brittle, and slung over its boughs, sheets of fur and flesh; and in its roots, piles of partially digested organs, melting through the snow still gathered there. He scooted away, the flattened grain scratching his ass and back. His head snapped to every direction, but a thick fog had broken over the field, so he couldn't see but a few feet in front of him. He looked to the sky and found the moon there, faint behind the velveteen atmosphere. It was leaving him, and the thought of it doing so hurt in a way he didn't understand.

He didn't get up. He wasn't sure he wanted to, or if he could. The weight of what he'd done was too great. He remembered everything.

It had to have been in the single digits. Shivering, he tried to hold himself, but his slowed circulation left his limbs tight and rigid. He dozed off, quickly woke back up. If he wanted to die, here was his chance. Hypothermia had come for him, its dogs of frostbite teething his numbing appendages. There were worse ways to die.

He heard a noise in the fog. It sounded like a car door shutting, but then it also sounded like how Detective Sono's wife's body had sounded when Peter had rammed her into the wall. He thought he heard an engine starting, but the rumbling sound of ignition combusted into screaming. It wasn't Sono's, or his wife's, or his daughter's, but all of them, all at once, building inside his head, until their screams were so loud, Peter vomited. Blood and sticky flaps of skin spewed out of his mouth, down his chest. Seeing this, tasting this, he fell over and kept going. What he'd easily gulped down as the beast was coming back up, far larger than his throat could handle. He hacked and coughed. He shoved his hand inside his mouth and fished out globs of human meat. Disgusted, he puked all over his fist, and kept going until everything that was left in his stomach was now before him, steaming. For a split second, he thought about eating them, to cover his tracks. Instead, he stood up, his bones cracking, sharp splinters of pain radiating outwards from his joints, turned around, and kicked snow onto it.

Peter picked a direction and started walking. The remnants of the field's crops crunched like bones beneath his feet. *I should die,* he thought, the fog parting before him, and yet he kept going.

Vomit dripped from his chin. Curdled regurgitation ran like sludge down his chest. Every step he took nearly took everything out of him. When the wind blew, the pressure on his body reminded him of the small body of Sono's daughter. He hadn't wanted to mutilate her, but to give her a decent death, he'd made her suffer more.

He could see the sun sitting feebly against the firmament. He'd always liked that word "firmament." Mom used to say it. They'd laugh about how snobby it sounded.

Peter knew why he had murdered Sono and, to a lesser extent, his family. When he'd transformed, the first thing he smelled on the air was the detective's scent. The detective, who'd trespassed on their land and plot. He wanted to kill Mary, but he had to protect her first, so that he could. He'd tracked Sono's scent back to his house. His wife and daughter had to die, because they were there. Because they might know, or want revenge. On him, or more importantly, Mary.

Fading fast, Peter's heart gave a mighty thump when the fog was teased apart. He wasn't in Ansbach Forest, or on some farm. He was behind a bunch of condominiums. It was still too early for most people to be awake. He hurried to the back of the nearest building, keeping low and clear of windows. Edging along the building, he reached the edge, glanced over, and laughed.

A street sign.

It read: Twilight Court

His landlord's condos. The very same Sono had convinced her to rent out to him, on account of his building having turned into a crime scene.

Teeth chattering, he wiped off his mouth and his chest and covered his crotch, and moved around the side of the building. His eyes darted back and forth, on alert for early-risers. He heard people, but couldn't see them. He wondered if he'd ever see people again. And if he did, what he'd see them as.

Peter's toe caught on the upturned pavement. He flew forward. He skidded across the ground on his elbows, splitting them open. Afraid someone heard him, he panicked and ran to the nearest condo. On the front of it, four numbers of providence: 5166.

His condominium. The one that'd been waiting for him. The beast had known. But what he didn't know was why it had chosen this place over Mary's.

Peter threw himself against the front door. He didn't have the key, but there was a keypad lock. He pounded numbers into it to no avail. Sweating, with residual vomit streaming from the sides of his mouth, he racked his brain trying to remember the combination.

Not far from where he stood, he heard voices.

A light came on in the condo next to him.

Then he remembered something: There had been presents at Sono's house. For Christmas, or his daughter's birthday.

Peter punched in 2000102, ran into the dark, and slammed the door behind him, just as the neighbors beside him were coming out to investigate the noise.

He stumbled in the dark until he found the bathroom. He got in the shower, turned it on and the hot water all the way up, and screamed into his hands.

Because he should've never made it this far.

Because there was still so much farther to go.

Mary arrived at 5166 Twilight Court at eight in the morning. She had the key to get in. Peter had left it at her place. She knew he would be here, because he hadn't been there, or at his old house on Stubbe Street. She'd brought a box of his belongings. Things he'd need. Clean clothes. His wallet. Cellphone. Canned food and water. She rolled up in front of his condo, in his car. She'd leave him the keys, call for a ride back. He needed to be kept on a short leash, but not that short of a leash. She didn't want to be the one coming to him. It wouldn't work like that.

In case she needed to defend herself, she left the box in the car. She got out, quietly closed the door, and walked up to the condo as if she'd lived there for years. There was a large group of Hispanic parents at the corner with their kids, waiting for the school bus coming up from the main road. Mary glared at them, for the simple fact that she used to have to get up at five in the morning to go to school; and she got up that early because she hadn't wanted to share the baths at Goetia with Mr. Peep. The name conjured the smell of cooking oil. Ignoring it, she looked around the sprawl and imagined the flyers she'd made posted like declarations to each of these doors.

Mary slipped the key into 5166 and let herself in. The door squeaked, so she stopped a quarter of the way and squeezed herself through. The lights were out. The shades and curtains were drawn. There were no furnishings, not that there should be. It had all the makings of a space that'd recently been purged and sterilized, and yet, it already felt lived-in. A caged, wild animal would do that, she thought, her nose catching the acrid stench of piss. Like mother, like son.

She snuck through the condo, his car keys in her hand, ready to strike. It was hard for her to get her bearings when there was nothing to go off but her own assumptions about what each room should be used for. *Liminal space,* she thought, until she found him. In the furthest bedroom. Butt-ass naked. Curled up in the fetal position. Snoring.

Mary knelt down beside him. He wasn't sleeping, so much as he was hibernating. He'd crashed. His body had been unmade and then made again. He was recuperating, regaining his strength. She could do anything to him right now. He wouldn't know.

She lay down beside him, her face to his. His breath smelled like shit. She reached into her pocket and removed a pocket knife she'd found in Goetia before she'd left the other day. She took out the blade and drove it at his stomach, just stopping short of his skin. She wanted to kill him, but she couldn't bring herself to do it. Not right now.

Her cellphone vibrated in her other pocket. She traded it for the knife. On the home screen, from her local news app: "Police Officer and Family Slain in Vicious Copycat Killing." Mary brought up the article, scanned it until she saw the name Sono, and then put her phone away.

"Good boy," she whispered, cringing at herself as she said it.

Seeing Peter like this, vulnerable and depleted, Mary found herself feeling less resentment towards him for having taken what'd been rightfully hers. She touched her neck where Peter's mother's mouth had bitten her. Maybe she hadn't sunk her teeth in deep enough, or they could've had it all wrong. Maybe lycanthropy wasn't a virus but a genetic disease. Or maybe there could only be one werewolf per bloodline. She didn't know, and it didn't matter. The last thing she wanted was to be lying naked on the floor, curled up into a ball, while someone else watched her sleep with a knife to her chest. She might've gotten the short-end of the stick, but at least the beatings weren't as bad.

Mary got up, left the condo, went to the car, grabbed the box of Peter's belongings, and brought it inside. She placed it on the bar in the kitchen. She took out his wallet and a brown paper bag, closed up the box, and put it on top of it. It was practically bursting with bills. She'd put two-thousand dollars-worth of her own money in it.

She opened the brown paper bag and shook its contents out onto her hand. Two small security cameras she'd already connected to his neighbor's wireless network when she came by yesterday, to scope the scene. Her network didn't have a password on it. In all likelihood, half the complex was leeching off that woman's stupidity, so she didn't know how clear the footage would be with them sucking down the bandwidth. All the same, it was better than trying to hide her phone in here with the hotspot on.

Mary went back to Peter's bedroom. He hadn't moved this entire time. She fixed the camera in the corner, above the door. It was small, an inch or two in width. It'd take him awhile to realize it was there. She was sure he had more things on his mind than the fear of surveillance. Though he'd killed, he wasn't a killer like she was.

She put the other camera in the kitchen on top of the fridge. From there, she'd see most of the kitchen and living room.

Mary left the key to the condo on the bar. She'd already made five copies. She put the directions to Sono's house she'd originally had in her glovebox in one of the drawers under the sink that Peter was likely never to open. Just in case.

FRIDAY, DECEMBER 4TH, 2020

Peter sat on the living room floor, opening packages he'd ordered off the Internet. He'd taken eight hundred of the two thousand Mary had left for him, went to a nearby store at two in the morning, and loaded it onto a gift card. That was the first and last time he'd left the condo. It was better this way. He couldn't be around other human beings right now. There was something about them that made him irrationally angry. That, and he could never be sure some of the beast wasn't showing. Some telltale sign, like a mismatched pupil, claw, or tuft of fur, that might give his parasite away. At first, he thought it was his anxiety returning in force-full, but it wasn't that. It was survival instinct.

He'd ordered a two-hundred-dollar mattress that came rolled up, a cheap bedframe; blanket, sheets, and pillows. Also, a week's worth of microwavable meals. He'd get delivery, otherwise. On Wednesday, he had his utilities transferred to the condo. With what was left of Mary's money, and the thousand or so dollars left in his bank account, he could make it here for about a month or so until he had to find a job, or kill himself.

Unrolling the mattress, he watched, with some satisfaction, as it slowly inflated. He'd come to terms with what he was. It made sense in a way he couldn't explain. Like whatever he'd been running from all these years had finally caught up with him and told him it was fine to catch his breath awhile. A part of him was glad he'd turned and Mary hadn't. She would've probably done something awful. He could control himself. Now that he knew what was coming, he could plan, and he could control himself. He didn't expect her to take care of him in the way he'd intended to take care of her. She did have Goetia, though. Next time, he'd be on the right side of the door.

What the hell was he saying? He'd slaughtered an entire family for her. She'd hadn't even asked him to. What the hell did that woman at that hippie store tell him? *Werewolves, like wolves, have their dens, their territories,* she'd said, or something like that. *It's not about geography anymore for them. The territory is within.* But that didn't make any sense, he thought. Because even now, he wanted to kill Mary. And yet, he needed her. *Oedipus must be rolling in his fucking grave.*

Peter got up. Carrying the microwavable meals to the fridge, he stopped in the kitchen, realizing he was missing a package. He yanked open the freezer, dropped them in. *Shit,* he thought, doubling back to his sad pile of loot. *It should be here.*

Peter jumped before it happened: Two loud knocks at his front door. Making fists, huffing the air, he crept towards it. He put his eye to the peephole. On the other end, not Mary, but a woman holding a package. She was short, five-four or five-five, and pudgy, carrying what she drank in her cheeks and the sides of her stomach. Her dyed black hair was pulled back in a ponytail. She wore a long-sleeve shirt with the name of a local bar on it—*Bruno's*—and slate-gray leggings; and from the numerous tears and stains across the both of them, it seemed like she didn't wear much else most days. She had an Old Country kind of face: pale, and severe out of necessity, to keep people at a distance, until she was sure they were safe to be around. Peter never managed to make it work for him. He'd certainly tried. It just made him look wounded. It just made him look weak.

He made fists and punched them against one another, deliberating, and then opened the door.

"H-Hey," he said, the sunlight nearly blinding him.

The woman seemed surprised. At a loss for words, she thrust the package at him, instead. "I think this is yours? Ha, it's… heavy."

It was his, but he pretended to read the shipping label, anyway.

"People's stuff always ends up over here." She nodded to the condo beside his. "I'm Kennedy, by the way. If someone didn't already tell you." Now, she was glaring at the condo on the other side of his. "But, uh, yeah. You're new to the place, right?"

It was less a question, more a statement. She was getting at something.

"You ever meet the couple who used to live here?" she went on.

"Nope, they were gone when I got—"

"Pretty cool. Kept to themselves. I think they moved up to Ose for the wife's job. They came over a few times to smoke with me. You like to smoke?"

He shrugged one shoulder. "Uh, I don't know. Been awhile—"

"That's Alejandro's place," she said, whispering. "He… Never mind." She laughed, rolled her eyes at herself. "I'm sorry. I talk a lot. Way too much. Want to know my life's story? Ha, ha." Kennedy caught her breath. "Yeah. Uh, yeah. Just wanted to give you that."

Peter smiled, started to shiver. "Thanks," he said, about to turn away, as Kenney had turned away, when—

"I—" She faced him, faced screwed-up. "I saw… I saw you."

A cold sweat oozed from his pores. He knew better than to ask her what she meant.

"No judgment." She put her hand to her heart. "Swear to God."

His insides screamed violation. Her swagger said interloper.

"The, uh… The, uh, other morning." She bit the back of her lower lip. "I work third-shift sometimes. Got out a little early and… I'm sorry. It's none of my business. Shut up, Kennedy." She huffed, shook her head, then kept going. "You looked…" She laughed and said through her grin, "You looked fucked up."

Peter clicked out a chuckle from deep in his throat.

Kennedy took that as an invitation. She drifted closer to him, having mistaken this secret as their bond. "I was going to call the cops. I thought you were hurt. But I'm not a busybody…"

"Uh, huh."

"… and I don't do that. I don't call the police. What people do… Not up to me. No judgment."

"Sure," Peter said through his teeth, scoping the scene, thinking he could pull her into his condo by the neck before anyone noticed. He didn't want to, but if he had to, he could.

"I like to, um, get fucked up, too." Kennedy pressed her lips together, her blue eyes taking on an oceanic sheen. "That's all I'm getting at. Mouth diarrhea. Talk too much." She ran her hands through her hair, undoing and redoing her ponytail. "I wasn't sure if you saw me that morning, but we're straight. It's cool."

Peter told Kennedy he appreciated that, shook the package as if to tell her thank you for bringing it over, and then, without thinking, winked at her, said, "Talk to you later," and slipped back inside the condo. He shut the door, locked it, and smashed his face against the peephole, to see what she might do next. She stood there a moment on his stoop, moving her jaw back and forth like a snake, probably replaying everything she'd said. She went in to knock again, stopped herself, and walked away, cheeks flushed.

He stepped into the kitchen and dropped the package by the sink with a thump. He didn't know what to make of what'd just happened, because he felt just as threatened by Kennedy as he was intrigued. She seemed easy, and not easy in the she'll-blow-you-for-blow kind of way as Mary would probably put it. A palate cleanser. That's what she was. A palate cleanser. A reminder not all women in the world were Mary.

Peter didn't have any cutlery, so he disemboweled the package with his long nails. He hadn't given up on Mary, or Goetia. She'd visited him while he'd been asleep and left all this stuff here, so, to him, it stood to reason that it might be best to give her some space. He'd go to her soon, though. When the urge to kill her wasn't as strong. Why he was experiencing it to begin with, he didn't fully understand. Maybe it was like when animals imprint: She just happened to have been the first person he saw when he transformed. Or maybe it was because she had seen him transform. Either way, he wouldn't let either stand in his way. They'd managed to get this far together. He'd make it work. It had to. Without Goetia, there was only this:

The package. The smelting kit and hunk of pure silver inside. An ass-backwards, backup plan brewed in the dead of night, in the depths of despair. He could make a killing cocktail and overdose on it. Or he could steadily poison himself over the course of the month with silver-infused tinctures to delay, or stop entirely, his transformation. When he visited Mom's house, it seemed as if she had tried to do the same by exposing herself to wolfsbane. That seemed too risky. That'd kill a human, werewolf or not. Too much silver ingestion would just give you argyria, which would turn his skin blue-gray. Not ideal, but better than nothing. Especially if Goetia failed.

He plugged in the smelter and waited for it to heat up. A trial run; he'd melt just enough silver to do half a shot of it. He wanted to see what it would feel like. If he'd be in pain, or have an allergic reaction. If that alone would be enough to dull the images in his mind of him standing over Mary, chewing her smirking face off.

SATURDAY, DECEMBER 5TH, 2020

Mary spent most of the week in her apartment, on her laptop, in bed, tracking the news stories on Sono's family, as well as the disappearances of Parker, Andrea, John, and Charlotte. The protests over the Massacre on Main had fizzled out, then reignited with the detective's death, only to die down again when all signs conclusively pointed to him and his family having been killed by a wild animal. Sono lived on the edge of Ansbach, not Talbot, and so the investigation fell under their jurisdiction; all the same, since he worked for Talbot's Police Department, there was a memorial planned for tomorrow. Several streets would be blocked off for the procession of police officers who would walk in his honor. The families of the victims of the Massacre on Main and Mare's Diner agreed to join them, perhaps as a symbol of solidarity, or because the mayor had begged or bribed them to, as some conspiracy theorists on social media postulated. People were looking for unity, and they were looking away, with even a large group of local hunters pushing for legislature to let them hunt the Ansbach Forest ahead of season, citing restrictions as the reason for which there had been an increase of animal attacks. In this disarray, now couldn't have been a more perfect time to move forward. Peter had been the Face. She'd be the Word.

It was getting harder to conjure her victims. Like a high, she chased their bloody countenances, but only got counterfeits. She could feel the pressure building inside her, and yet release wouldn't be so easy this time. This time, she could work the valves as she worked over her prey, but she knew, at the back of her mind, it was only ever Peter she was truly after. If she killed him, this throbbing feeling inside her might go away, and she could go on, as she hoped to now, unabated. But what if she did kill him and it didn't go away? The thought turned her stomach.

She checked her security cameras. Peter was on his new bed, in his new bedroom, sitting up against the wall, watching something on his phone. The feed came through at a delay. The microphones on the cameras were shit, so even when that woman came over last night, Mary could barely make out anything they were saying. She did catch her name—Kennedy—and that she was his neighbor. They got high on the living room floor and streamed a movie on her tablet. She'd kissed him on the neck. He sent her home not long after that. He spent the rest of the night puking his guts out. That much she could pick up from the microphones. Served him right, for trying to poison himself.

Mary closed out of the cameras and returned to her laptop. Starting tomorrow, her pre-scheduled posts and advertisements would be sent out across various social media platforms, each one tailored to the audience she was trying to attract. Though she'd carefully chosen her wording and images, the message was, essentially, the same: This part of the state had suffered significant losses and was in great turmoil; and those that'd managed to survive not one but two of the defining incidents wanted to finally come out of the shadows and give back to the community that'd had so much taken from it. It was beautiful, and also, so fucking stupid. Mary loved it.

The exact address of Goetia hadn't been given, but she had acknowledged Goetia in her posts. If people wanted to find it, they'd have to find it on their own. She had no doubt they would try, though; and if they didn't, they certainly would once the local and out-of-state newspapers caught wind of this. Once everyone who'd been around long enough came to terms with the county's history, they'd remember Goetia; they might even remember the terrible things they'd heard about it. But that wouldn't stop them. That wouldn't turn them away. Because people liked a fixer-upper. People liked to think that something that was bad could be made better. Everyone liked a good abusive relationship here and there, whether they realized it or not.

Everyone liked to save, and to be saved, too; that's why, tomorrow, she'd make her rounds around the Old Country, some nursing homes, and Peter's condos. She'd hand out her flyers, rub elbows. Enough time had passed that people could start looking at her in a less resentful light. They'd see her efforts, rather than see through them. *This must be what it feels like to run for Office,* she thought. In a way, she was.

Her nose twitched. Some smells you just didn't get used to. This one was potent. Ripe. It was coming from the Killing Room. She needed Peter to get his shit together and come back to her. The place needed to be cleaned up.

She could've gone back to Goetia, but the old fort was a lonely place when there was no one else around. That, and she'd literally felt its growing pains, like nails, digging in her skin. By the time Peter returned, public interest would probably be at its peak, and they'd go back together, a ragtag of curious and wayward misfits in their wake.

Mary had it all figured out. Except for one thing: His reaction to her murders. He wouldn't take them well. She'd have to guilt him hard. Get inside his head. Enough to convince him he was, in some way, responsible for them. But she couldn't turn him against her. She still needed him. How can you empower a person, while simultaneously dismembering them? She typed the question into a search engine. Nothing.

A timer went off on her phone. "Shit," she said, digging it out of the blankets. It was a reminder to message Dominic on the dating site, *Bumper*. He wanted to "hang out" tomorrow night. She'd spent almost an entire day on *Bumper* looking for someone like him. Five-seven. One-hundred-and-seventy-five pounds. Dark hair. Trash haircut. Business major. Had a sweatshirt of an Old Country high school on in his profile picture. Quickly took the bait when she told him she didn't have a mom and he told her he didn't have a dad. Said he'd deleted his account at least five times before this one because he'd get anxious about the whole thing.

A perfect recreation of Peter before he'd spoiled. It'd been a lot harder than she thought to think of his defining qualities. She'd never paid much attention to them before.

See you at seven, she said, in a message, including her address and phone number.

She got up, to start cleaning up, and then sat back down on the bed, instead. If he were truly Perfect in everything but name only, then the mess shouldn't bother him. Everyone liked to save, and to be saved.

Mary closed her laptop, got up. Her legs were asleep, but she shambled on, anyway, into the Killing Room. She needed to prepare for tomorrow night. She needed to get in the mood.

1

"Will you be back later?" Kennedy asked, as he got up from her couch, dodging her hand as it pawed for his ass.

Peter gave a her a non-committal grunt and swiped his phone off the coffee table. Heading for the door, he put his shoes on one at a time as he went. He could feel her, so he faced her. Elbow to the armrest, eyes TV-colored, she stared promises into him. Kennedy wasn't bad. Her place wasn't either. In design, it was an exact replica of his own. In decoration, they couldn't have been more different. You could tell a lot about a person from the way they set up their house, Mom had told him once. There wasn't a wall in her condo that wasn't covered in at least four to five cheaply framed photographs of landscapes or family members; her electronics—phone, tablet, laptop, television, and the tiny robotic vacuum she lovingly called Spaz—were all a few generations old, but in perfect condition; her cushions and pillows, ragged and faded, breathed lavender when you sat against them; the cracked tiles in her kitchen and bathroom sparkled like snow and smelled like bleach; all across the carpet— marks from where furniture used to be, or where it might return to, when she needed to reset the vibe; he'd seen her room, too, albeit for not as long as she might've liked, and if she would've told him she were a professional book thief, he wouldn't have doubted her for a second, so vast and diverse was her chewed-up collection spread across eight buckling bookcases. She was a second-hand kind of person; a scavenger and scrounger. She picked up used up things and people and tried, with her own personal concoction of weed, flirtation, and a carefree attitude, to bring them back into the fold. At least, that's how Peter saw it. Not that he'd seen it that way two days ago. He'd pegged her for something not unlike himself: An Old Country refugee hiding out in hostile territory, hoping to carve out an uneventful life. He'd expected low expectations. He'd sensed emptiness. He'd assumed farce. Or maybe he'd hoped for these things, thinking that one void could somehow fill another. If he were being honest with himself, he'd admit he hated the poor and all his failings they reminded him of, but he wasn't, so he didn't.

"I'll be back in a few hours, I think," he said, at the door.

Kennedy nodded, unconvinced. "Sure. It's eight o'clock on a Sunday night."

Peter shrugged.

"Alright." She shooed him off. "Tell her I said 'Hi'."

She didn't know about Mary, let alone that he was headed to her place now to see her. About an hour ago, when they were on the couch watching one of Kennedy's favorite movies—a thriller about two predatory lawyers stalking one another—the hairs on Peter's body stood on end and blood rushed to his head so fast, he nearly passed out. Kennedy plied him with water and a blanket, and he told her he was okay, but that was a lie—one of many he'd already graced her with about himself. He hadn't been okay. He wasn't okay now. And he wouldn't be until he drove to Mary's and saw her for himself. He imagined the feeling wasn't all that different from that feeling parents seem to get out of nowhere, when they sense something is wrong with their child. It was that, and also, withdrawal.

Peter flew through Talbot, as if he meant to make his speedometer measure the beating of his heart. He ran stop signs and red lights, went wide around turns into the empty streets. Caution wasn't so much thrown to the wind as it was drawn and quartered and scattered to the four corners of the Earth. Eyes that might've otherwise been probing shadows and cars for signs of the prowling police were intensely focused on the road ahead of him, and at the end of it, still ten miles away, Mary, tall as a building, besieged by some indescribable threat. It was his condition, he knew, because this wasn't like him, or so he told himself. He didn't know what he was anymore.

He hadn't come to terms with his lycanthropy, unless contemplating suicide counted. Mary was the only person he could talk to about all of this. She'd told him she'd killed, too, when she was younger, likely at the direction of her father. She'd understand. She'd help him add excuses to the proverbial scales until things came out balanced. Because right now, despite his best efforts, nothing weighed heavier than that little girl's body.

Anticipating Press or prying eyes, Peter parked a block down from Mary's building and hoofed it the rest of the way. The city was quiet. No one was out. Cars seldom passed by. The snow was mostly gone, but everything looked wet, almost amphibian. The street smelled like an open sewer, as if all the filth that'd flooded those subterranean tunnels was coming back up to be put on display. He could relate, his gut churning as Mary's place pushed through the background, an antique splinter stubbornly stuck in the surrounding modern sensibilities. She had a way about her when it came to getting him thinking and talking about things he didn't otherwise want to. Mary was like a priest in a confessional with a gun instead of God to his head. All the same, there were sins worse than murder he dared not share; and it was these sins he was most worried he'd share. Two-in-the-morning kind of sins. Alcohol-and-ecstasy-kind of sins. Dreams-that-smelled-like-lavender-and-smoke-kind of sins.

Peter swallowed old sewage and veered into the alleyway that ran adjacent to Mary's. No Press, but no reason to risk exposure, either. He ran up on the dumpster where'd they dumped all the animals and mounted it. She'd let the fire escape down some. He jumped, grabbed the lowest rung, and, grunting, hoisted himself up onto it. Old paint flaked off and pricked his palms, but he paid it no mind. His heart was beating so hard, he thought he might lose his grip. Not because he was afraid someone might see him, but because he could hear someone inside Mary's apartment. He scaled the ladder in a blur. His teeth hurt from gritting them so hard. He heard laughter, and then he tasted it; and it wasn't all that different from Sono.

2

Dominic leaned back in his chair at the kitchen table and laughed. Mary hadn't said anything particularly funny, but he was smitten, so everything she did say was met with shiny eyes and a toothy grin. He liked her. In all her painstaking research to find the perfect stand-in for Peter, that was the one thing she hadn't accounted for her. It made her wonder, then, as she watched Dominic chew with his mouth open the pasta she'd made, if Peter had ever truly liked her. Probably not. They'd never had time to make the mistake of lusting after one another. Instead, they were like an old married couple who slept in separate beds and talked solely about business as opposed to pleasure. It was better this way, she thought. It'd do. It'd get her through. Peter would drink silver to stave off his curse, and she'd kill his lookalikes to stave off his slaughter; and with all that, they and Goetia would thrive; and none but the moon would be the wiser.

"I think I saw you on campus once or twice," Dominic said.

Sure, she thought.

"What're you majoring in?"

"Psychology." That was true, but she'd only picked it because she had to on admission. "You're Business, right?"

Guiltily, he said, "Yeah. It's not the most exciting Major…"

"It's safe," Mary said, stirring the noodles in her bowl.

"Yes, it is, and that's exactly what I'm looking for."

"I think you might be in the wrong apartment, then."

Dominic blushed and rubbed the back of his neck. "Ah, I, uh, I… I mean it's because of how I was brought up."

Mary licked her lips, took a bite, and stole a glance at the clock on the oven. She was getting bored. She helped herself to some more wine, filled his cup up, too. He moved his mouth as if to protest, but no words came out. Her damning gaze kept them locked up in his five-o'clock-shadowed mouth. Mary wanted two things in life: to dominate, and to be desired. Excuses were not conducive to either.

Dominic kept on. "This is a nice place."

She caught the implication like the flu. Temperature rising as her temper flared, Mary ignored his last comment. He was equating their upbringing to soften the soil so that he could dig into her for more details about herself. She'd already exhumed her past. There was nothing left to be learned from it. So, anticipating his follow-up ("How'd you manage to get it together? 'Cause I'm still figuring it out."), she said, "Ever hear of the Beast of Stubbe Street?"

He didn't answer at first.

She'd given him five seconds to decide if he wanted to lie to her not. There was no way he wouldn't have heard of the Beast. He lived two streets over from its hunting grounds.

"Oh, yeah. Damn." He drummed the edge of the table. "You

know about that?"

"A little bit," she said, measuring her knowledge with her fingertips. "With you being from the Old Country, I thought maybe…"

"Yeah." Dominic straightened up. He drank his wine, like a good boy. "Yeah. I'm pretty far removed from all that these days—"

He wasn't. He was in the Old Country a week ago for a party. Two weeks ago, a family reunion. She had the pictures to prove it.

"—but it was this urban legend. People said there was a werewolf…" He stopped, gauging her reaction to see how stupid he sounded. "There's a lot of weird deaths in the Old Country. Maybe someone with an animal they trained, or something. But that's—"

Mary rolled her eyes. She looked out the window, and the quarter moon looked back, sickle-shaped and insincere. She had a compulsion now, to kill by the full moon. Gutting the basic bitch right here, while arousing, also left Mary feeling that, if she were to do so, the curse inside her would germinate, and its corrupting spores would sprout and spread until she was dead, a halo of smoke and police lights above her leaking head.

But she had to do something, she thought. Something to tide her over. The question was how much would Dominic let her get away with and for how long? She couldn't and wouldn't prowl the Internet like a some greasy-fisted Jane Doe looking to get stuffed by the lowest common denominator. Not with what was coming next. Even now, her phone was blowing up in her pocket, tiny explosions of interest in Goetia from Talbot citizens and news outlets going off every other minute. The best serial killers were the ones you didn't expect. The normal ones. The disciplined ones. The ones at the head of the table, their shit so together it was a wonder they weren't constipated more often. Admittedly, a cult leader was already a suspect position, but she wouldn't be a cult leader. She'd offer an alternative lifestyle. Not as a former victim but as a survivor. The meaning of the words were essentially the same, but there was a subtle difference. Victims went on daytime talk shows to talk about what they'd been through. Survivors owned the talk shows.

"You know Mare's Diner and the Massacre on Main?" she finally said.

"Yeah, I…"

"I survived them."

Dominic's mouth dropped open. "Wait." He got out his phone,

searched something. "That is…" He stared at the screen, then flipped the phone around for her to see. It was a picture of herself, and Peter, beside an article with a headline that read *Still Not Safe Enough: Survivors of the 'Talbot Terrible Two' Go Unseen. Why This Should Concern You.*

Mary laughed at the headline. "Haven't read that one yet."

"It's…" His eyes darted back and forth between the screen and her face. "It's, uh, about how the city has failed you and, uh—"

"Peter."

"Yeah. About how the city has failed you and him, how it's still too dangerous, even though the killers are dead."

"When did that come out?"

"Yesterday?"

"Guess they're not blaming us anymore."

"For what?"

Mary ignored the question. Everything was falling into place. The public often oscillated between scorn and sympathy, and now the fulcrum rested in their favor. She got up, took her wine and her chair with her, and planted herself next to Dominic.

He said, "I don't even know what…"

She put her hand on his thigh, not far from his crotch. His hard-on hit her pinky a few seconds later. She squeezed, sinking her nails into his skin until she was sure he could feel them. He didn't say anything. He just stared at her, a little bit of spit on his wine-colored lips, star-struck and stupid with lust. She told him to get on the couch, and as he staggered to his feet, she grabbed a sharp knife off the table and followed him to it.

He sat. She pushed him down and laid on top of him. He tried to kiss her, but his mouth kept missing hers, so he looked like a fish gasping for air. Her hair fell in his face. He smelled it. With her free hand, she took him by the neck, pressed her thumb gently against his windpipe.

"I've been through a lot, and some of it, I kind of liked," she purred.

At that moment, with that statement, something changed within Dominic. She could see it happening beneath his flesh, like the shadow of water running over rocks in a creek bed. It was his manners, she realized as he grabbed her breasts, melting away. They'd both been playing each other.

"I bet you fucking did," he said.

Mary clenched her teeth. This close to Dominic, she could smell him. He smelled like coal. She needed to break him down into something beautiful. Something worthy to wear. She showed him the knife. He flinched, and her heart fluttered. "Cut me," she said, but before he could register her request, she jabbed the tip of it into his side, where his T-shirt had ridden up on him.

"Ah!" Dominic bucked her off him. "What the fuck?"

Holding his shirt, wincing, he dabbed the lightly bleeding hole. She sensed protest in his posture. He showed her the wound like a child would to their mother. His eyes demanded an explanation. She spread her legs and held the knife between them, so that it caught the light.

"Only one person's getting fucked tonight," she said, almost laughing at herself.

To stare at her crotch, he had to stare at the knife she had erect there. And he did, briefly, before shaking his head, crying, "Fuck this," and turning around to stand—

Mary sat up and slashed the back of his calf. She split his jeans. A superficial cut wept through the fabric. Dominic, surprised, hobbled backwards, clipping his knee against her coffee table. "What the fuck?!" he yelled.

But he wasn't yelling at her.

She heard pounding feet before she saw him, but then saw him: Peter. Coming through the fire escape window. Into her home. A singular purpose etched into his ink-black irises: to knock Dominic's dick in the dirt.

Mary got up, got out of his way. Peter shouldered past her.

Dominic, backing up towards the front door, fumbled for his cellphone. "I don't know what… You can fucking have her. I'm fucking…"

Peter closed the gap between them and, in a blur, punched Dominic three times in the face. Dominic fell against the front door, huffing blood from his broken nose. Peter, standing over him, stomped his gut, then punched him again. His head hit the door, cracked off it, and he slumped over, unconscious.

Mary ran out of the living room, into her bathroom. She grabbed the Rohypnol she kept next to the pack of condoms, both of which she'd bought for tonight. On her way back, she grabbed a glass of wine. Dropping to one knee, she forced two pills into Dominic's slack mouth, tipped his head back, and, holding his nose, made him wash them down with some Red.

"That works, too," she said, coming to her feet.

Peter didn't speak, just stared. For the first time since she'd met him, Mary actually felt intimidated by him. He reminded her of something rabid. Something to give space until death or sleep put him down.

"Let's get him out to his car," she said, quietly. "He'll think he got robbed on his way over or—"

Peter punched Mary in the mouth. Her lip popped like a balloon. Her teeth felt huge and numb from where his knuckle had almost knocked them loose. She didn't stagger. She stood there, chest puffed out, chin held high. Like she was ready, and she was, to go toe-to-toe with a nuclear holocaust.

They said nothing. Instead, Peter grabbed Dominic by his ankles and started dragging him towards the window he'd emerged from. All the while, he avoided eye contact with Mary. His hard exterior contrasted starkly against his softening eyes. The cut on his knuckles from her tooth sucked up the blood, as if his entire body were working in perfect coordination to escape this situation as guilt-free as possible. She wondered if this was what would've happened had his mother not stormed out of the house with her fuck-for-the-night. Mary wasn't going anywhere, though. In fact—she pressed her hands to her mouth and smeared the blood there across her face and hair, like warpaint—she felt closer to him than ever. This was so much easier. This made so much more sense.

"I'm sorry I did that," Peter said, his voice warbling like a warped record. "I'll leave him in the alley, and then I'll go."

Mary still had her knife. She approached him with it. "Why'd you come?"

He looked at Dominic.

"You could sense he was here?"

He didn't say anything.

"Possessive much?"

He still didn't say anything.

"Why'd you hit me?"

He swung one leg over the sill and braced himself on the fire escape as he took Dominic by his armpits.

"You feel it, too." Mary grabbed Dominic's legs and helped Peter get him outside. "You want to hurt me, don't you?"

Peter's breath fogged around him.

"It's all I've been able to think about. Thought I'd get someone like you to take my mind off it…"

"Me, too," he said.

"You did?" Mary laid the knife on the sill. He was talking about Kennedy, wasn't he? "I knew it wasn't going to work five minutes into talking to this moron. Is it working for you?"

He shook his head. "I'm here."

"Something went wrong that night," she said, pacing back and forth. "We were already tied together." She knotted her fingers. "But now we're really twisted. Maybe it was Goetia. We have to go back there. Before the next full moon. For you. And me. Us." She realized how excited she sounded, and why shouldn't she be? Aside from the camera feed, she hadn't seen him in a while. "I was racking my brain trying to figure out how to tide myself over until the twenty-ninth, but—"

Grunting, she grabbed the knife and threw herself over the windowsill. She slashed the air so hard, she smelled burning. Peter didn't move, and he wasn't bleeding, either. She'd missed him. Barely. Not intentionally.

"Next time," she said, pushing off the sill, going back into the apartment. She closed the window and waved him off as he struggled down the fire escape, Dominic's body like a sack going slackly down the stairs.

Woman's Best Friend, she said to herself, settling in on the couch. She grabbed her wine and her cellphone and propped herself with a pillow against the armrest. Wiggling her feet, and satisfied, she ignored the tens of messages and e-mails from people and places asking more about Goetia, enquiring if she were open to interview. Instead, she made her way to the Internet and searched for ways to torture someone without killing them.

THURSDAY, DECEMBER 10ᵀᴴ, 2020

Peter had started doubling-down on his silver tinctures. One in the morning, one in the evening. His body must've been getting used to it, or the parasite inside him must've been getting weaker from it, as he found himself vomiting less and less because of it. After what'd happened at Mary's, he'd decided he couldn't lose control again. It was one thing if it were a full moon—Nature begets nature—but it hadn't been a full moon. Despite his urges to kill Mary, he hadn't actually killed her, either. He'd hit her. In the same way, in the same general situation, he had Mom years back. The moon was a sphere, and a circle. The beating begged the question: How much was beast? And how long had it really been in there, in him?

He hadn't seen or spoken with Mary since, and yet, every day, in some way, she found him. It began with the flyers he noticed on some of the windshields and doors in his complex. A black and white picture of trees, and behind them, faintly, an old fort. The picture was slightly out-of-focus, not due to user error, but almost as if the scene had been reluctant to have its photo taken. Below it:

A New Year, a New You. The Survivors of Mare's Diner and the Massacre on Main Invite You to Their Gathering and Retreat.

In place of an address: Ansbach Forest, December 30ᵗʰ, 2020. Peter found himself crumpling up the flyer over the pretentiousness of it all, but as he slowly unraveled it, he understood Mary's intentions. She knew people would want to hear them talk, but it was a fine line they'd be toeing between enlightenment and exploitation. By turning it into a literal scavenger hunt, it would guarantee that only those who truly wanted to know would show up… At least, until the puzzle was solved and they texted the answer to all their friends. The ink from the flyer had stained his fingers. He couldn't get it off for the next few days.

Peter rarely used social media before his life went to shit. He had all the necessary accounts to connect with friends and acquaintances, but he seldom put anything about himself out there. He'd stayed off it throughout everything, but today, after having been at a store and run into Jackie Dee, a local reporter for Channel 3, who'd grilled him so hard he left the place with emotions charged and charred, he decided to feed into his anxiety, which had been starved for information ever since getting out of the hospital.

Leaning over the kitchen counter, he went one by one through each platform, trying to remember his password, inevitably resetting it each time. He hadn't loaded his e-mail on this phone, either. Sono had given him this phone.

"There you are," Jackie Dee, standing at the end of the aisle, had said to him as he'd searched for the cheapest paper towels the store had to offer. "Peter."

He'd acknowledged her upon hearing her name. That was his mistake. It was like she'd been serving him his summons, or asking for his papers. Once she knew, she knew.

"How are you doing, Peter?" Approaching him, she pulled a pad of paper and a pen out of her purse. "Peter, I am so sorry about Detective Sono."

He wasn't sure how he'd reacted to that.

Which might've explained this: "Well, I figured you two must've been close. He kept you and Mary out of all of this craziness that's been happening in Talbot. Until you showed up at your apartment last month, we thought the Feds might have put you in Witness Protection. He was one of the best, Detective Sono."

Peter got choked up at that. Because his daughter might've been one of the best, too, if he hadn't crushed her to death.

"You two have been through so much," she'd said. "But it sounds like you and Mary are ready to tell your stories."

Peter must've hit the notification limit on his various social media platforms, because all of them read 99+ in regards to unread messages. His e-mail wasn't any different. Except it went up to 250+.

"Your parents were the killers," Jackie Dee had said. "We've had several of Mary's classmates and teachers confirm we she was part of her dad's cult. Goetia. Is that where the gathering is being held before New Year's Eve?"

Peter, holding a pack of paper towels to his chest, craned his neck in search of a way out of the aisle.

"What do you know about the cult? Are there more members out there? You two have been through so much, but if there are others like her dad out there, then people need to know." Jackie Dee had gotten close enough to grab him by his proverbial scruff. "Was your mom a part of the cult? How did she play into all of this? I am so sorry for your loss, but this city and its people have been through so much these last two months, and the only people who might be able to give it some closure have been kept from them. Which I get, I do, Peter. I get it. But if you two are coming out, and it sounds like you are, then let me help you. This is a sensitive thing we have on our hands, okay? Look at your hands, they're shaking."

They hadn't been, but that didn't matter: Jackie Dee spent so much of her life in front of a camera, she naturally assumed one was always on her.

"It's hard to stay quiet for so long. To keep it in. Trust me, I know. I've been through…" She'd caught herself. "I've worked closely with so many like you and Mary. Let me get you through this. Tell me about the gathering. Tell me about Goetia. Is that where it's taking place?"

Peter nodded, said, "Yes."

"Oh, no, no." Jackie Dee touched his arm, squeezed his bicep; her fingers were like cold forceps. "Why?"

"Closure," he said.

Jackie Dee got what he was saying, but hadn't got what she wanted, so she'd stayed the course. "Where is it? Where are you staying? Let's set up a time. You two have to be smart about this. No one's going to hide you anymore."

Peter scrolled through his e-mails until he got to one from Katie's dad. He kept scrolling.

Thanks to Mary, the word was out. The clock had been started. It was only a matter of time until their self-induced isolation was ended. They'd both moved through life with their heads down, under the radar; and they'd tried to maintain that, even as the body count continued to mount. But Peter, like Mary, wasn't rich enough to buy an out, wasn't important enough to become someone else, somewhere else. They had to face what they'd done, what they'd become. He wasn't sure what was going on with Mary. But what he did know was this: The more they hid, they sooner they'd be found. No one looks for you if they already know where to find you.

Peter went outside. The school bus rumbled in the parking lot, disgorging children to parents nowhere to be found. Rubbing his hand against his pant leg—it'd been itching ever since Mary nearly cut it—he decided to call Maiden, Mother, and Crone. To see if Parker was there, to see if she had any other ideas about how to control lycanthropy.

Nobody answered. He decided to check their site to see what hours they were open. In place of their homepage, a stark proposal from the e-zine outlet *The Woods Recollect*. It was simple, to the point, and not all that different from Mary's flyer. Below a black and white photo of the Ansbach Forest, it read:

Parker Wits, Andrea Rice, Charlotte Truce, and John Hammersmith—longtime members and contributors to The Woods Recollect and Cryptozoologists—went missing on November 29th in the Ansbach Forest. If you have any information on their whereabouts, please contact us immediately.

Peter felt as if someone had punched him in the gut. He remembered Mary telling him about how Parker and Andrea had been watching them, tracking him, thinking that he'd turn into the werewolf. She'd known about the Beast of Stubbe Street. Probably knew the Beast was his mom, too. *Fuck*, he thought, smashing the phone into the side of his head. *That night, when I ran out of there to Sono's... There had been another smell. His had been the only one I recognized, though.*

He read the proposal again. They went missing on November 29th. In Ansbach Forest.

They were there. What did she do to them? Better yet... Why?

He stared out at the complex. Eyes darting back and forth, he was certain he was being watched.

Protecting me, he'd decided. *Like I was her.*

A crumpled-up flyer bounced over the cracked parking lot pavement. It came to a stop at the side of a fourteen-year-old's scuffed up sneakers. She'd been the last to get off the bus. About to kick it, she bent over and picked it up, instead; and read it as she made her way home.

"Stop it," Kennedy said, scraping at the bottom of her takeout box with her chopsticks. "This was me like a year ago."

They were in Peter's condo, in his bedroom, sitting against the wall on his bed, popping benzos and eating Chinese while they watched a horror movie on her laptop with the lights on. He hadn't done much redecorating since he'd moved in. He'd bought a few totes to separate the clean clothes from the dirty clothes. Kennedy had insisted on coming over tonight, despite his embarrassing accommodations. He knew she'd try to stay the night, and right now, he wasn't sure how to stop that from happening, or if he even wanted to altogether. She wasn't Mary, but then again, she wasn't Mary.

"Okay, okay," Peter said. He shoveled some Lo Mein into his mouth. "A year ago?"

Kennedy traded her chopsticks for some crab Rangoon. "Yeah. Yeah…"

"You don't—"

"That's when I moved in over here. With Alejandro." She banged the back of her head against the wall; the wall Peter and Alejandro, his neighbor, shared. "Didn't work out." She chewed on the Rangoon, took a sip of her soda before swallowing it all together. "Mother fucker has a mean right hook." She punched the air, just like he probably would've. "So, what do I do? I stay with him for nine months, then I work up the nerve to leave him. Then I move two fucking doors down." She closed her eyes, appeared to nod off for a moment. "Why do I do these things to myself?"

The benzos were kicking in. Peter folded his hands across his lap. The wall felt spongy against his back. It was a little harder to see the movie: The image looked fuzzy, almost like a detuned signal. It was about werewolves, the movie was. He'd chosen it. Werewolves who had their own society under the guise of a commune. He'd seen it once a few years back with some high school buddies. To Kennedy, it was cheesy. For him, it was a confession.

"I don't know if I stayed close by hoping things would get better, or if I stayed close by because I thought things might be worse somewhere else. I don't… I don't fucking know." She scratched her scalp hard. "I'm doing alright, though. All things considered."

"Yeah, no, yeah." He was having a hard time keeping his eyes open. "I get it. I had a messed-up childhood. Swore I'd get away from my mom. What do I do? Move twenty minutes away."

Kennedy rested her head on his shoulder. "Why do we do that?"

"Well…" He smiled, feeling the warmth radiating from her. "I was taking this Intro to Psych class and…"

Kennedy started snoring.

He wasn't sure how he was planning on answering her, or if there was even an answer to give her. His professor, Ms. Selene, had told them about abusive relationships and how difficult they were to leave because people in them often told themselves they didn't deserve anything better. He didn't think that was it, though. That was too simple an explanation. In his opinion, most people knew they deserved better. It was just a matter of finding "better," and most of the time, better was just a less-is-more, beggars-can't-be-choosers kind of situation. Fuck, he sounded like Mary.

Peter woke up to Kennedy's lips on his neck. He hadn't remembered falling asleep, or having her hand down his pants, either, but there it was. High and horny, he buried his face in the top of her head, slipped his hand underneath Kennedy's shirt, and grabbed her breast through her bra.

Ten minutes later, they both came as the credits rolled. She asked him if he liked to film himself having sex. He didn't know what she meant. She nodded towards the door, then went to sleep.

Peter snapped awake. His mouth was dry. His nose felt as if it'd been stuffed with gauze. The smell of the leftover Chinese seemed to be egging on his headache into a full-blown migraine. He moved his eyes around, and it took his room a moment to catch up with them. Kennedy was lying next to him, facing away from him and on her side, on top of the covers, completely naked. A stripe of sweat ran down the center of her back. The lights were off, so the only thing he had to go off was the harsh glow of the laptop, which should've gone to sleep by now. It hadn't. He didn't remember turning off the lights in here, either.

He sniffled his nose, rubbed his eyes; leaned over the edge of the bed for his cup. It wasn't there. Outside the cone of light coming from the laptop screen, he couldn't see anything. Right now, the light switch felt a million miles away, but he had to pee, and he needed some water, so carefully, quietly, he got out of bed and headed for the bathroom, and realized along the way he was naked, too.

He pissed into the toilet with one-hundred percent accuracy. The first few days had been rough, pissing in the dark, but he'd since gotten his bearings. He didn't flush, on account of not wanting to wake Kennedy up. Remembering there was a cup next to the sink, he clumsily moved his hands around the counter, as if he were shifting chess pieces, until he found it. He flipped on the faucet, filled it, downed it, and repeated the process three more times until his drinking left him breathless.

Peter staggered into the kitchen and checked the fridge for nothing in particular. He stood there a moment, the door open, letting the cool air blow past him. Like being out in the frigid air of Ansbach Forest the day before he and Mary went to Goetia, it was just what he needed right now to cleanse his senses. He soaked for another thirty seconds and, feeling a little more sober, staggered back to his bedroom.

Kennedy hadn't moved. Seeing her there, naked, pale skin made paler by the LCD light, asleep in his bed and seemingly comfortable, Peter felt a contentedness he wasn't sure he'd ever felt before. Maybe it was the drugs. Or because he knew Kennedy would still be lying there come sunrise. Or maybe it was because, when he looked at her, she almost seemed to float above the covers. She might've been held back, but she wasn't weighed down. Him, on the other hand, it was a miracle he didn't leave craters in his wake.

It could work, he thought to himself, getting back into bed. *She's the kind of girl who won't ask too many questions. She might even like Goetia.*

Settling in, trying not to wake her, Peter stared at her awhile longer. For a second, he thought he saw roots growing out of her, and was about to wake her then and there and tell her she had to go, but it was only shadows.

As soon as he lay down and closed his eyes, he opened them. He smelled something. Something familiar. Something out of place. He sat up, heart racing.

A small light shone from beside the door. Light from a cellphone screen. Then the figure holding the phone stood. The light flashed across their face—Mary—and then she turned it off. She'd been sitting there the entire time.

Without saying a word, she walked out of the room and left the condo.

Peter's first instinct was to follow her.

He ignored it for his second, which was to check on Kennedy. He leaned over her, tried to wake her. But she wasn't moving. Fuck, she wasn't breathing. He grabbed her shoulders and shook her. "Kennedy? Kennedy!" he screamed in her ear. Peter rolled her onto her back, pressed his head to her heart. "Kennedy! Jesus Christ, please…"

"Fuck, what the fuck?"

Peter fell backwards off her.

Bunched up like a dying bug, she scooted away.

"Oh, god. Oh, thank god." Crazed, Peter tried to take her ankles in his hands, but she quickly pulled away. "I'm sorry. I'm sorry."

Kennedy didn't just stare at him. She stared into him. With wide and doubting eyes, determining, for the mind behind them, if he was a threat. It was the Old World stare he'd first seen on her face the first day they'd met. She'd inherited it from men like Alejandro and women like Peter's mother.

"What the hell, man?" She took deep breath. "You scared the shit out of me. What the hell did you think happened?"

Peter didn't have to think about the answer to her question. Mary had been here, and so the answer would always be the same: "Anything."

Mary had stolen Kennedy's keys to her condo from her purse while she'd been passed out on Peter's bed. Now, she was lying underneath Kennedy's own bed, waiting for her to fall asleep. The best way to hurt Peter, Mary realized, was to hurt the people closest to him. He'd probably like it too much if she came after him directly. He'd say he deserved it. Besides, if she were to have him become the martyr, and that was part of the ten-year plan from now, then it didn't make any sense for him to tap into and waste that energy now. Once it all dried up, he'd stop being Peter and just be Dad.

Kennedy started snoring. She had sleep apnea. A pill problem, too. Mary had spiked her water bottle she kept on her bedside table with the last of the Rohypnol she'd bought. So, when she washed down her nightly regimen, she did so with a dissolving dose of Forget Me. Mary wasn't sure how all the drugs would interact with one another in her system. The last thing she wanted was for her to overdose.

Mary gave her another five minutes, then came out from under the bed, to check her pulse with the edge of a knife.

SATURDAY, DECEMBER 19TH, 2020

Peter hadn't heard from Kennedy all day. It was four in the after-noon, and she hadn't answered any of his texts or calls. He did a lot of thinking and had come to the conclusion he wanted to take her to Ansbach Forest this weekend and, if they could find it on their own, Goetia. If she were a part of this thing, he thought, then Mary might spare her.

Yet, even after having come this conclusion, he paced his living room for the better half of an hour, worried about what Mary might say, or how Goetia may react. Because, in the end, Kennedy didn't belong there, did she? She was an outsider, a trespasser. She was bet-ter, because she was less. He was the "more" who'd…

"Fuck!" Peter tried to call her one more time, gave up the indif-ferent fuck-buddy act, and stormed out of the condo.

He went over to her place. The first knock he laid on the door pushed it open. Gooseflesh. Cold sweats. Vision occluded. Heart eclipsed. He backed up. Kennedy's name was stuck like a rock in his throat. It was the middle of the day, but all the lights were on. He could hear the fan in the bathroom, whirring. A cold draft rushed up behind him. Bracing himself, he sniffed the air for foreign smells, but all he sampled were the usual suspects: lavender, the fruity smell from her vape, and the faint hint of old person lotion. What he couldn't sense was life. A throbbing pulse. If he'd welcomed any gift from the parasite, it'd been that. He could usually tell when someone was close. Unless they were Mary. She was neither alive or dead, but liminal. She wasn't here. Neither was Kennedy. But that didn't mean she wasn't here. That didn't mean she wasn't…

Peter shed a single tear. He knew he should've turned around, called the police, but he was cliché, through and through, and so he pressed on. Into the condo. Into the revealing light, where false hope had burned before it could bloom. He didn't move so much as glide through her place, a ghost haunting someone else's grave. He hadn't felt this weightless in a while. He didn't know why.

Her door was open. He was right outside it. All the lights were on. He couldn't see much else from where he stood. Just her foot in a white sock at the foot of her bed. He waited for it to move, or for her to make a sound altogether. He waited so long, his memories recalled her in reverse, until after their days and nights together, in his mind, he found himself standing outside, Kennedy before him, handing over his package that'd been mistakenly delivered to her. In return, he'd mistakenly delivered himself to her. And when she was finally able to start opening him…

Peter forced himself into her room. Kennedy was dead. She was in bed, in her pajamas. Her shirt was unbuttoned, her breasts underneath speckled with blood. Her mouth was white and crusty; eyes wide and hard and mascara-smeared. Her hair hung off the side of the bed, heavy and wet, like seaweed. When he got closer, he noticed a vertical cut on the underside of her forearm. It started from a deep gouge, then tapered off in depth the further it went, until by the time it reached the crook of her elbow, it was no more than a superficial scratch. A suicide attempt, or something made to look like a suicide attempt. He couldn't believe she would kill herself. He didn't know her well, but still: She wouldn't kill herself.

His thoughts turned to Mary, and so he saw Mary everywhere, in everything. Her form played out before his eyes, five of them in all, moving about the room separately from one another, carrying out small and mundane terrors. There she was in the closet, standing behind the clothes rack; there, in the corner, a knife to her chest like a communion candle; there, on Kennedy's headboard, perched like a nightmare; there, Mary's feet, disappearing, as she pulled herself under the bed; there, in the doorway, half-turned, disappointed as she looked on her work unfinished. She did this. But not all of this. Something had gone wrong.

The urge to kill Mary overcame him. It ripped through him like a hurricane. He could feel his insides being teased apart, his bones being heaved against his flesh. He fell to his haunches, pressed his fists to his head, and squeezed. He screamed wet, guttural noises. Despite his mouth being wide open, his teeth met. He snapped his neck to the nearest mirror. In it, him: transforming. His rage had raised the parasite. Fear sobered him, slumbered it. His teeth shortened and took on their original shape.

I can't do it, he told himself. If he did, then she would truly be bringing out the worst in him. But he still wanted to hurt her. God, he wanted to hurt her. He'd killed Sono and his family to protect her. Maybe this was another form of protecting her. Because it could be a lot worse for her. Because if… if he fucked her up enough, she might not be able to fuck up anyone else…

Peter rose, laughing. He sounded like an abusive piece of shit. Like all the abusive pieces of shit his mother had brought into his life. He wouldn't become them. He knew now that it wasn't only the moon he had to fear. It was Mary. The pull she had over him. The tides she'd cause and send to try and take him.

He had this moment of clarity, and then his mind clouded over. He wanted to touch Kennedy's hand, to let her know, wherever she was, she wasn't alone. But he didn't want to leave any more evidence than he had already of his having been here, of his having known her. It would bring scrutiny to him and Mary, and now, to Goetia. A wolf couldn't hide with pigs at its door.

SUNDAY, DECEMBER 20TH, 2020

It was one in the morning, and Mary was at the Melancons' fore-closed farmhouse, sitting on the front porch in a rocking chair, watching the snow fall from the vaulted sky, waiting for Peter to arrive. She pulled a blanket she'd found inside tight around her. It smelled like tobacco. *This is nice,* she thought. *It's not Goetia, but it's close.* From where she sat, she had a clear view of most of the property. Twenty acres of snow-dusted fields whose only noteworthy yield were four dead bodies that'd been carted out of here nearly three months back. This place had been a nexus for her, for Peter, for their murderous parents. Twenty years of trauma and terror had converged on the same night, at the same time, and formed the alchemical abomination that was now her and Peter's life. The reaction from mixing had been deadly: nearly all those who'd come into contact with them had died. But now they were nearly fully formed, and in a few days, under a full moon, if all went according to plan, they'd be as one.

Mary had spent a lot of time lately waxing poetically. It was an important exercise, given all the cryptic messages she'd been casting across the Internet. People were definitely interested. Her only mistake may have been getting people too interested too quickly. Ansbach Forest was massive, but Talbot was filled with twenty-and-thirty-somethings with too much time on their hands and too much skin in the outrage game. She wasn't too worried, though. Goetia understood her true intentions. It'd keep itself hidden until after the

29th. It could wait. It'd told her so.

Coming to the Melancons', though? That'd been a gamble. This place was a ghost story waiting to happen. But violence, like anything else, got dull the more you were exposed to it. The slain family couldn't compare to Mare's Diner or Peter's apartment building. The corpses just didn't stack up.

Mary kicked her heels off the porch, setting the chair into motion. The creaking rockers cut through the winter quiet. Something stirred in the distant forest. She thought it was Peter, but after a few seconds, a fox darted out, weaving through the snow towards the lone tree that stood near the old pumpkin patch. She remembered Peter telling her that, when he'd run past it, there'd been something like skin hanging from the branches. His mother's skin. She'd chosen this location for her transformation. In all likelihood, she'd been on the land at the same time Dad had been inside the house, torturing the Melancons. It was hard to believe in coincidence given what she'd read on the Wall of Goetia. Disregarding that, Mary couldn't help but wonder what would've happened had Dad and Peter's mother killed them. Would they have come together like she and Peter had? Would they have retreated to Goetia? Brought it back to life? Or would they have gone their separate ways, a mutual understanding of selective mutism between them? Mary couldn't imagine separating from Peter, unless she were separating Peter limb from limb. She wasn't obsessed. She was resourceful.

Dim headlights burned at the end of the long driveway. Peter had sniffed her out. They grew as he drew near, until he hit the high-beams and flooded the porch. Mary lit up, pale, and rocked madly. Beneath the blanket, she held a knife and a gun—which one he'd be on the receiving end of being entirely up to him. She wouldn't make the same mistake she'd made with Kennedy.

Peter parked his car where the Melancons' van used to sit. He got out, slowly; his face, half of which was hidden behind his scarf, the only thing she recognized. He was wearing a black peacoat. Black gloves. Black jeans. Black boots. Things so new she could smell the dye from here. The scarf was pink, though. Pink like Dad's head-phones. Mary laughed and muttered, "Mother fucker."

He stood there a moment, snow twinkling in the creases of his scarf. Likely considering, or reconsidering, things. His face was hard to read. Neutral but for his eyes: They were feral, deep-set. She couldn't help but wonder if his new, all-encompassing get-up was to hide the fact that he'd somehow transformed early. That was one thing she hadn't considered. What the lycanthropy would do to him when it wasn't his time of the month. How long would it take, she wondered, until his humanity became an inconvenience? If she could track it by calendar, that'd save her a lot of headaches.

"I was wondering when we'd come back here," he said.

She stopped rocking; leaned forward as far as gravity would let her. "A little on the nose?"

He stared at her for a while. Then: "Did you kill those missing people?"

"Did you kill Sono and his wife and kid?"

He stammered, "I d-did it—"

"You and I both know there's no real way to justify killing someone," Mary said, "short of self-defense."

"That's what it was!"

She laughed. "Peter, come on. I think you have the size advantage…"

"To protect you."

Mary squinted in disbelief. "Same." She thought that was a lie, but a second later, she wasn't so sure.

"I didn't want them to suffer…"

"You killed him in front of his family. Fast or slow, they suffered." Mary stood up, pulling the blanket tighter around her body. "Let's go inside. We need to get caught up."

As she turned, he cried, "Why'd you kill her?"

"I switched her pills. She must've had a bad reaction and overdosed from something else she took that day. I didn't realize it until I started cutting on her. I stopped shortly thereafter. I mean, really, you killed her."

Peter took a step back.

"Doesn't matter," Mary said, pleased with herself. "What if I told you Dominic died from you beating the shit out of him?"

"Yeah, but I didn't…"

"You sure?" She headed for the front door. "If nothing else, you gave him a traumatic brain injury, and then left his ass to freeze in an alley on a cold December night. You can call the kettle black all you like but…" She twirled her finger at him. "You dressed yourself."

It was cold inside the farmhouse, and the color had faded from it. Relatives must've run a raid at some point, removing anything that related back to those that'd been here before. And yet, to Mary, it didn't possess that uncomfortable emptiness she'd come to expect from the places she passed through. To Mary, it felt as if this space had been waiting for them. It wasn't liminal, but inevitable. Where they would break bread, or each other.

She lit a candle she'd purposefully placed by the staircase near the foyer and led Peter through the house. They eyed each other along the way. Some trust had been lost. All they could expect from one another at this moment was a burst of violence, so they each went with a hand hidden, ready to draw their weapon of choice.

"Where are we going?" he asked.

Mary reached the door to the basement, opened it, and pressed the candle into the musty dark beyond.

"Why?"

"It's simpler than up here, and less room to run." She turned in the doorway. "We have to go down together."

Side by side, they descended. The stairs threatened to snap under their combined weight. The temperature plummeted ten to fifteen degrees; their breath played out before them. Reaching the bottom of the stairs, Mary broke rank to light the other candles she'd pre-emptively set-up on the various shelves and chewed-up desks. Two rickety, wooden chairs occupied the middle, where they could face each other. She gestured for him to sit. To sit in the chair she'd sat in months back, when Dad had bound her with belts and prepped her for Death.

Peter took a seat, slowly; as if to be sure the chair wouldn't collapse, or that it wasn't rigged to explode.

Keeping the blanket around her—the smell of tobacco was really bringing out some old Goetian memories—she sat, too. Without realizing it, she scooted her chair slightly back. And once she did, she realized why: Peter intimidated her. He was too quiet, too composed. Too unlike the Peter she knew. His body looked so tight that the littlest change in atmospheric pressure alone might cause him to snap. Her lip still stung from where he'd popped it. Whether he'd figured it out or not, he was, for the first time in their relationship, more powerful than her. She didn't like that. It was hers to have, that power. He was hers to have.

"Nothing's going anywhere," he said, breathing heavily.

"That's because we've been apart."

He considered this.

"It's true. We're stronger when we're together. We were supposed to be together on the full moon. Look what happened when we weren't."

"Things didn't exactly go according to plan."

"No, they didn't, but everything's still the same."

Peter's eyes went black. "I want to kill you so fucking bad."

"Me too!" she said. "Me fucking too. We can't, though, can we? The time's not right. Something like that, I think."

"But I also want to protect you."

Mary laughed and thought, *Dumb fucking men.*

"Was that part of your plan?"

"What?"

"Killing Kennedy?"

"Well, when you scrambled Dominic's brains, I started thinking about my predicament… our predicament. See, I invited him over to hurt him so I wouldn't have to hurt you. Isn't that what you were doing with Kennedy?"

Peter shrugged.

"It was," she said, definitively. "Didn't work, though, did it?"

"I don't know. You killed her."

Mary waited to respond; watched his arm spasm, instead. Then: "I think there's value in taking out our urges on others. Quick fixes to tide us over. But at the end of the month, me and you? We're going to have to do battle."

Showing his teeth, Peter said, "Ha, it'll be a short-lived fight."

"Maybe," Mary said. "Maybe not. But don't you see how fortunate we are?"

"I really don't."

She sighed. That was one thing she hated about Peter, sometimes. How fucking stupid he was.

"I'm waiting," he added.

"Heh. We're fortunate, because we have Goetia. People will come to us and let us do whatever we want to them for the promise of something different. And if not them, then the sacks of shit on the Internet begging to be debased. We've been through it. Everything we do, someone else will qualify by our trauma. We know what's wrong with us. We figured it out faster than most. And every full moon, we can measure precisely it by how much we tear each other's asses up. Then we patch ourselves up and go about our business. People get hurt, but not necessarily killed. Not unless we want them to. And we've got Goetia. We create the narrative. We establish the institution. You take your curse and turn it into a condition. A blessing. When the time is right. Listen, you're not going to find anywhere else aside from the coroner's slab where you can live like this. Your mother tried. Look at her. Bet you she's got a lot of bodies under her belt. You want to be like that? I don't think you do. I do. I really do, Peter. But I don't want to get caught. Locked up. Killed. Do you want to die? I know you don't. All the silver you've been sucking down, and really, all you had to do was turn it into a bullet and put it between your eyes, instead. We're not going to kill ourselves. We're both too fucking selfish and self-sure to do something like that. People like us don't do that. Why the hell would we spend all that time fighting just to kill ourselves? I don't believe in God. I know you do. If there's a Hell, we're both going there. But I'd rather go to Goetia, instead. It's all there. It's all waiting. I've been working my ass off on that. I know you still doubt it. Is it really going to be that big? No. I don't know. It doesn't matter. Whether fifty people come, or five… It doesn't matter. One alone gives us legitimacy. One alone is an entire family ripe for the reaping. That's how Dad did it. Some things just work. But we're not going to be making Demons. We can't surround ourselves with other people like us. Fuck those people. They're not like us. They're sick. We're different. Our people, like we talked about… They're going to be the lost, the desperate. The forgotten. The traumatized. I see the look on your face. You think it's exploitive. You didn't think it was exploitive last month? You know just as well as I do everyone exploits everyone. We're not going to torture them. We're not going to rape them. We're going to clothe and shelter them and move them like chess pieces. We're going to wear them, so no one sees us. And Goetia will grow. You've seen what it can do. There's this thing I've found out about it that you don't even… We have an opportunity here. To carve out, sometimes literally, our place in the world. I see that look on your face. But what's the alternative, huh? I'm waiting. Never mind. I'll tell you. It's this: cold basements and secret meetings with your conscience, and waking up every day with so much pressure inside you, you might as well be a suicide bomber. A liability. That's what I'm getting at. And I know you. And I know me. We keep our distance. We don't make friends, but acquaintances. That's alright for me. I know you want more, though. You want more, like you did with Katie. Remember her? I'm sure you do. There's going to be more of her. Your lycanthropy? That's what you're protecting. It's not me. Not entirely. I just get a free pass because, deep down, you know you can exploit me. You know I'll keep your borders safe. You going to let anyone else get that close to you? It's not a matter of being a monster. People fall in love with monsters all the time. But when it's your time of the month, it's not up to you whether someone loves you or not. You killed a child. I know you wouldn't have done that, otherwise. Kind of sets the tone, doesn't it? Kind of speaks to the need to get this shit squared away. I'm trying to help us. Me and you and Goetia... that's the only option. That's the only way anything goes anywhere. I need it, too. I'm not above admitting it. You should've seen what I did to those people. Yeah, maybe you should've. Then you'd get it. Trust me when I say that now that I've killed, goddamn, do I want to do it some more. But I can't. Not with you in my sights. So, I could kill you, but then what next? A hundred more? Nothing? I don't know. But it's perfect. I could easily kill you as you are. But it wouldn't be the same. Timing's not right. Only time I can do it is when you're damn near unkillable. You know, you're responsible for this... for me... to some extent. But if you're going to let me out, then you have to keep an eye on me, too. And if you really want to get all humanitarian about it: Again, you've seen what Goetia can do. We could help a lot of people, if we wanted to; if we "fall" far enough to see what's on the other side.

"So, what do you think?"

Peter lunged out of his chair at Mary. His hands wrapped like shackles around her neck. She kicked both feet into his stomach, sent him flying back into his chair. It tipped over on one leg; the wood snapped, and he fell on his ass. She dropped the blanket, her gun bundled up inside it. Brandishing the knife, she charged. Peter, on the ground, grabbed the chair leg, nail still sticking out of it, and swung. The nail sunk into her calf. She screamed, turning away before winding around and driving the knife straight down at Peter's face. He jerked back just in time. The tip of the knife caught on his cheek, tore a piece of it away. Screaming, he rose up and tackled Mary into a shelf. The knife flew across the room, as mason jars rained down around them, shattering when they hit the blood-spattered cement. She rolled over a blanket of glass, screaming as they sank sharply into her back. Peter reached for her, missed; handplanted a shard. He got to his feet, crying out, one eye closed shut from blood, as he eased the glass of out of his palm. Mary licked her chops, got to her feet, and ran at him, full speed. He ripped the shard out of his hand, drove it straight into her breast. She wrenched his wrist, kicked him in the balls. His knees buckled. He gasped. In one motion, Mary pulled the shard out, dropped it, and with the same hand, punched him in the jaw. He staggered, but he didn't go far. As she went in for another blow, he faced her, fangs protruding from his mouth, claws growing from his fingers before her eyes, and swiped at her stomach. Her shirt turned to ribbons; her belly bled blackly. Gasping, she ducked, dodging his next swing; grabbed a lit candle and flung it at him. The flame caught instantly on whatever fluid was left in the jars. Peter screamed, punching and patting his arm as the fire snaked up his sleeve. Grabbing the bulk of the fabric, he tore it off at the shoulder and hurled the ball of burning material at Mary. She dodged that, too, and looked on with throbbing arousal at Peter's engorged, mutating arm. It was larger than the other and covered in coarse fur. He was transforming. For her. To her. And so, to push him further, she kicked a pile of the shattered glass at his face. It sailed sharply over his skin, making new cuts on his cheeks and lips. His eyes were larger now; the pupils mismatched. His back bubbled beneath the remains of his coat as new musculature tried to express itself. Mary, panting and laughing, circled around the blanket to grab the gun, thinking that, if she put a bullet in him, he'd fully fall into the flesh. But Peter anticipated her. He howled and hurtled towards her, drool oozing from his maw. He grabbed her by her armpits, lifted her as if she weighed nothing at all, and, spinning around, threw her into the stairs. Two broke on impact. Something else broke inside her. She wheezed, tried to get up, but couldn't. Peter, going down on all fours, padded towards her. She kicked at him; hit his collarbone, his hand. He deflected with indifference and got on top of her. His fangs were receding. His claws, merely nails. The fur thinned out and uprooted into the air. He'd gotten his pound of flesh, but the scales weren't balanced, not with her on her back. So, she reached into his panting mouth, grabbed his tongue, and with her free hand, fumbled in the shadows until she found something hard and smashed it—a brick—into his head. He whined, spinning off her, cutting his tongue on his teeth as he went, and crumpled at her feet. Nerves overloaded with so much pain she felt nothing but stomach-churning numbness, she walked over to the blanket, shook the gun out of it, picked it up, and shot Peter in the arm. The bullet went straight through, into the cement floor. He rolled over, wailed. She tossed the gun to him, told him, "I'll see you on the twenty-ninth," and, stepping over him, headed up the stairs. He cocked the pistol, fired a bullet into her shoulder. She stumbled forward, grasping the stairs, and kept going as he softly whispered, "Okay."

MONDAY, DECEMBER 21ST, 2020

1

Mary lay in the black mud of Goetia, watching as it filled the bullet wound in her shoulder and forced out the slug festering there. She closed her eyes, steadied her breathing. She smelled herself. She smelled like a newborn.

2

Peter lay in an emergency room bed, arm bandaged and stitched, still groggy from the anesthesia. He pissed himself, because he didn't want to move and alert the medical staff he was awake. They had questions he couldn't answer. One recognized him and wanted his autograph.

THURSDAY, DECEMBER 24ᵀᴴ, 2020

The Giving Room wouldn't give her a shovel, so she dug out its floor, instead. The black mud was there, beneath the soil, where the fat, feasting, red worms writhed. She needed more. It was the only way they'd see the sun again.

Peter didn't go back to the condo. He knew the cops would be waiting for him. He didn't go back to his apartment or Mary's, either. Instead, he drove, a couple hundred dollars in his wallet, between Talbot, Ansbach, and Defiance, never staying in one place longer than
twelve hours. He ate and slept in his car, and frequented rest stops
and fast food restrooms frequently. Either it was the cocktail of pain-
killers and antibiotics the doctor had given him that was making him
sick, or it was the cheap food itself; not because it was cheap, but because the full moon was two days away, and he wanted nothing more
than cold, raw, stinking meat.

When he took a shit in the woods, his thoughts often turned to
Mary.

MONDAY, DECEMBER 28ᵀᴴ, 2020

1

Mary had taken too much, too quickly. She had to Give if she were to get out alive.

She waited all day by the side of the road, hazards on, hoping for a good Samaritan to happen by and offer her a lift.

She got two: An old man in a pick-up truck with a white beard and a beer belly, and his granddaughter. She was six. Wore a ribbon in her hair.

In the end, she only needed the one.

2

An inferno raged on Stubbe Street. Peter watched it from afar. His childhood home, collapsing before his eyes; swallowed up by the dark, billowing flames. The fire department hit it with everything they had, but it wasn't enough. The water only seemed to feed the blaze. Out of the outskirts of the Ansbach Forest, a howling wind blew, and the conflagration spread, leaping from roof to roof. Soon, the entire street was burning. There was no one to evacuate, though. They'd already died some time ago.

Peter considered walking into the flames, but he'd lived so long in Hell, he wasn't sure he'd actually burn. So, instead, he put the matches in his pocket and drove away.

TUESDAY, DECEMBER 29TH, 2020

1

Mary, naked, paced the halls of Goetia, her cellphone having been a permanent fixture in her hand for the last eight hours. It was getting late—almost 7:00 PM—and Peter wasn't here. It was that, and it was them: the people in the forest, a party of ten, with beer and flashlights, trying to find the old fort. She could hear them, sometimes see them. Peter had to get here before he transformed; otherwise, he'd kill them; otherwise, they'd be fucked.

This was it. The culmination of all things. If any part of her plan failed, it'd be the end of them. They'd be discovered, or they'd be divided. Forced to fight for their right to a fair trial, or left to fend for themselves with their own defective devices. Mary already knew she'd kill him. She had to. He'd be no use to her after this. He knew too much. About her. About everything. Without him, she'd become what she feared: a serial killer, a sociopath. The objection of others' obsessions, twenty-five to fifty years from now, when she was dead or incarcerated, and the bones of her urges were unearthed. She reveled in her violence as much as she reviled it. It made her weak as much as it made her strong. Murder invited too much scrutiny. But mutilation? Mutilation could be mundane if you got your hands on the right kind of mind. The broken kind. The wanting kind.

And if this failed, her plan, then what would Goetia do? She'd taken so much already. She'd escaped it once. She wouldn't again. A debt was owed.

Chewing on fresh lamb's leg, Mary, holding a torch in her free hand, made her way to the South Wing. She hadn't visited it since she and Peter came upon it last month. There was something about it that seemed forbidden. It was the sheer cavity, and the freestanding ancient pillars and the thick, slow moving streams of black mud that filled it. It was the depths, spread wide like an inflamed gullet, and the heights, exposed through the brickwork, unreflecting of the actual world outside. It was all of it. All of it, and more—the kind of more she couldn't touch or taste or see, but feel; in her flesh, in her bones, buzzing and vibrating; pulling on the fabric of her person; stretching and constricting her, trying to mold her innards into something by which it could attune. It was here, she thought, fantastically, that all the violence in the world had been born. The façade that'd been built over this place contained Goetia's powers and influence, but eventually, the sinkhole would swallow it, and the savage elements would be set free.

Mary knelt down beside the sinkhole, in the black mud, and fixed her torch to the closest pillar. Feeling the pull of the depths, she resisted, as she had for so many years before. Instead, she scooped up the black mud and began to paint her body with it. The Giving Room's floor was filled with the substance, but tonight, they'd need all they could get.

For a moment, she wondered if two people were enough to make a case for mass hysteria. She wondered, but only for a moment.

2

Peter stumbled through the forest, full moon taunting him from black heavens. He still didn't know what exactly triggered his transformation, but it was obvious he didn't have long. The parasite was restless. Like an animal coming out of hibernation, it knew it was time to wake and stretch its limbs and feast. He buried his mouth in his arm, to stop his uncontrollable growling from giving away his position. Clambering up rock-strewn hills, he gripped frozen roots like ropes, only to rip them free from the soil with his increasing strength. Branches whipped his face. Trunks clipped his sides. But as seconds passed, he found himself navigating the forest with increased ease. His senses were sharpening; this curse of his, a whetstone. The night became less abyssal, more grayscale. The interlopers were no longer soundwaves, but scheming shapes, laughing drunkenly as they tram-

pled his dreary domain. He could smell them, and on them, the places they'd come from (a hemp shop, a pet store; an art gallery; the
riverfront). They were right outside the barrier. Either they couldn't
get in, or Goetia hadn't shown itself to them yet.

He pushed through the trees, now a few feet from the barrier of
ingrown trees. The interlopers had scattered in groups of two. They
were speaking, and yet he couldn't decipher the language. All that
made sense to him were their beating hearts and the blood pumping
through their veins. He went down on his haunches, cupped his head
with claws. His back started to stretch. His shirt grew tighter in the
shoulders until it tore. He slipped off his boots so his feet could
swell. Legs extending, he lost his balance. Excruciating pain coruscat-
ed through his body. His muscles liquefied, and from their boiling
sludge, instantly reformed into something harder, stronger. Old
bones dislocated and broke apart. New bones, from the infinite
growth vat within, sprung forth. They fused to and reinforced his
skeletal system. Together, the cancerous rods distended his pliant
flesh until it, too, split. Howling through his clenched fangs, he
grabbed handfuls of skin off his neck and chest and tore them free,
revealing the patches of sticky fur beneath.

Peter reared up, skin sloughing from his body, and bounded for
the barrier. His thoughts disintegrated. Moving like a crippled
hunchback, he pushed through the trees, and to him, they gave; almost stepping aside to let him through. He tripped over himself as he
cleared it. Falling on his hands and knees, he looked up to find the
old fort waiting, warm, granular light pouring through gaps in the
ancient brickwork. He nodded off, let loose lunacy to take the wheel.
Disassociating, he gagged on his own voracious hunger. It was
enough to wake him up, bring him back. He reached out to the flesh
and feebly clung to it.

Who was that?

Who was that standing at the entrance?

It wasn't human. His senses didn't register it as human.

And while it might not have been human, it was Mary.

Mary, blackened. Her skin looked wet and charred. Her counte-
nance, demonic. With bestial eyes, he saw the beast she'd become.
She'd fallen through the flesh; and so, too, had he.

Peter shook off the last of his husk and settled into his curse. As
he drifted from his mind, he remembered why he'd arrived tonight

when he did.

He didn't want to wait out the night in the Giving Room behind the locked steel door.

He wanted to face Mary, to see if he'd truly kill her.

3

The hairs stood up on the back of Mary's neck. The werewolf was here, fifty feet from where she stood. *This isn't right,* she said to herself, making micro-movements. *This isn't going—*

The werewolf sprung, earth exploding around it. Mary booked it back into Goetia. The black mud she'd covered herself with cracked and dropped from her joints. *Fuck,* she thought. *My armor.*

Snarling swept through the old fort's halls. In the space of seconds, the beast had cleared the gap between them. Mary, having left her silver-bullet loaded pistol and silver-coated machete in the Feasting Place, frantically grabbed what she could as she went. A rock here. A branch covered in thorns there. The sound of scrambling claws played off the bricks. She turned down hallway after hallway. Some she remembered, others she'd never seen before. He was close. Too close. Hot shit trickled down her leg. She pressed the rock to her chest, to keep her beating heart from bursting through her chest. *I'm going to die.*

Mary, panicked, threw herself in no particular direction, beseeching Goetia for guidance as she went. A piercing howl drilled its way through her skull. Blood bubbled out of her ear canal. She dropped the rock and branch; held her skull to drown out the sound. Weeping, sweating; still shitting, now pissing; Mary glanced over her shoulder. The werewolf stood at the opposite end of the hall, a crown of roots floating over its menacing head. It outstretched its arm, its claws on each massive paw reaching each wall along its side. It was an invitation. Peter's invitation. To end the hunt. To meet the inevitable. He said he wanted to protect her, but that might not have been what the beast wanted.

"Save me from myself, huh?" Mary said, shakily. She spat black mud and blood. "Try it."

The werewolf went down on all fours and bounded towards her. Her leg went out. She cried and hobbled forward around the upcoming bend. The hall broke away. Broke away to the Feasting Place.

And there, on the nearest table, her gear.

Mary leapt onto the table as the werewolf burst into the room. Losing her balance, she rolled over the top of the table, hitting the pistol, pushing it of reach. The werewolf snapped towards her, leapt. As it crashed down on her, she grasped the sweat-slick handle of the machete. She swung, caught the blade in its meaty side. The werewolf wailed, dragged its claws across her thighs as it jerked mid-air and fell beside the table. Mary screamed. Scorching pain shot through her pelvis, stirred her stomach until she almost got sick. Scooting backwards, away from the werewolf, she grabbed her pistol. By the time she climbed down, the black mud over her thighs was gone; it'd filled in the gashes and healed her fully.

Backpedaling, grinding her teeth at the taste of bitter triumph, she watched the werewolf rise, to see the extent of her damage. Its side was bleeding. Fur was missing. The skin beneath was purple, almost necrotic. The beast stood half-cocked, as if to protect itself from another attack on the area. In those black hole-like eyes, there was, for a fleeting moment, a glimmer of agony; the last bit of human light yet to be taken by their event horizon. She'd wounded the werewolf, but she'd hurt Peter. Her body tingled at the thought. She had to pace herself. For his sake.

Mary hauled ass out of the Feasting Place. The werewolf gave ragged chase into the old fort's depths. Cocky, and cocking the pistol, Mary spun around, machete out. A paw punched the side of her face, the werewolf having caught up quicker than she realized. Gasping, Mary fired the pistol blindly. The werewolf yelped and scrambled away, knowing better.

Her nose was broken. Her head was swelling. And then it wasn't. As the black mud seeped into flesh and bones and repaired the damage. By the time she reached where the old fort ended and the cave began, it was as if nothing had happened at all.

The werewolf howled and took off after her. Passing the Wall of Goetia, Mary fired off two more precious bullets. She didn't hit it. She didn't want to hit it. But maybe she should've. Because it didn't care anymore. It wasn't stopping. And there was no way she was going to get to the Giving Room without it—

The beast raked its claws along her back, exposing a part of her spine. Mary dropped to the ground. Everything went black.

4

Gone. Dead.

The werewolf lowered itself over the Bad Mother's body and nuzzled her side.

Empty.

Whimpering, it rocked the corpse with its snout. It was awash in relief and remorse. It moved her harder, faster, desperate. To make sure she wasn't sleeping.

Smells wrong,

The werewolf licked her spinal cord and the tender flesh swollen around it.

Tastes wrong.

It lowered its head beside hers, so that they were eye to lifeless eye. The werewolf realized what it had done. The werewolf realized it was lost.

It heard something. A sound it couldn't place. Almost like stitching. Almost like wet meat. It glanced back at Mary's back: The black mud around the wound was gone, and so, too, was the wound.

And when it looked back, thunder and lightning. Mary, on her side, firing a bullet straight into its hip.

5

Mary shot the werewolf and dragged herself along the ground, away from it. The beast crumpled. Watching it, she saw the silver bullet going to work, rotting the creature from the inside out. Skin shriveled and fur went brittle and dropped free. Pale patches of Peter, bruised and bleeding, reformed. She heard sounds from inside the werewolf: bones breaking, organs sloshing; the parasite recoiling, removing itself and its curse from that part of Peter's body, forcing him to regress. He didn't have long, she thought, coming to her feet, taking off. She had to get the bullet out.

"I didn't just kill those four hippie fucks," she cried. "I fucking gutted them. And I'll keep doing it!"

The werewolf followed. Not as fast as it had before. It lumbered behind her, holding its hip, as it drooled and wheezed. With its free hand, it swiped, but it was nowhere near close enough to catch her. The beast was poisoned. Delirious. Not much better than a dumb, rabies-riddled dog.

"What the fuck are you going to do, Momma's Boy?" she goaded, the Giving Room up ahead. "Nothing. Like always. You can't even kill me. You fucking need me!"

Mary's momentum slammed her into the massive steel door of the Giving Room. Half-open, she slipped past it, into the room. The black mud squelched beneath her feet. Red worms by the thousands threaded through the stinking, staunching muck. She pressed herself against the back of the door. Once he was in, she'd slip out. The door would shut. Goetia had promised that much. And the black mud would heal him. And she'd taunt and shoot at him through the window in the door all night long, until dehydration did her in from being so wet from it all. He wouldn't kill her. She wouldn't kill him. Win-win.

The werewolf stumbled into the room, breath labored. Mary slid along the door, not yet noticed. Dropping to the ground, the beast rolled in the mud, covering itself. Mary smiled, proud, almost, that it'd learned a new trick, and was about to leave the room when…

The steel door slammed shut. The locks outside were engaged. Mary, panicking, dropped the machete and the pistol and pulled the handle with all her strength. The door didn't budge. Goetia had locked her in.

They'd Taken.

Now, They'd Give.

She could feel the werewolf behind her. It was silent but for the hot, acrid breaths spewing like flames from its mouth. She heard a sucking sound, and then saw an impacted silver bullet fly past her head and plink off the door. In its recovery, it'd also developed a sense of humor.

The beast grabbed her by the arm and flung her towards the hole in the floor. Arm dislocated, she flew through air like a greasy rag doll. She hit the ground a few feet from the hole. By the time she was up, her arm was back in its socket.

The werewolf cleared the room in one leap. It landed on top of her, breaking ribs. She gasped, drove two thumbs into its watering eyes. They exploded like olives; fluid oozed down her hands. The werewolf reared back, buried its face in the black mud. Dragging herself like a snake along the ground, she felt her ribs reform as she reached the machete and pistol and took them up once more.

Mary fired the last two silver bullets into the werewolf's back. It bucked and fell over, head coming free of the ground with a new set of eyes. She plodded over to it, nipples cutting through the mud caked on her breasts, and hacked at the creature. The machete chewed through its fur and flesh, leaving deep, seething gashes in its arms and sides. But the harder she swung, the faster the wounds healed.

The two bullets popped out of the werewolf's back. Going in to cleave its head, it sank four claws into her calf, wrenched her down to the ground, and wrapped its snarling mouth around her throat. It bit through, shredding her esophagus, and then twisted, snapping tendons. Gasping for air, she took the machete in both hands and ran it straight into the werewolf's heart. It let go. She let go. They both fell to the ground, and both, like junkies, started shoveling the black mud into their mouths, consuming it.

As quickly as they were healed, they were dying just as fast. Mary cut off three of the werewolf's fingers, only to have the black mud use itself to stitch them back onto the beast. The werewolf did the same, except it ripped off her entire arm. Instead of swallowing it, or throwing it down the hole, or holding it out of reach to taunt her, it let her have the limb and waited until it was reattached before it pounced on her and put a dent in her skull. They traded blows as equally as they could manage until the mutilation developed a rhythm; and they stopped being victims and victimizers, but dancers dancing to choreographed carnage. It became a game of escalation, to see how badly they could maim without flat-out killing. It didn't take long for Mary to stop experiencing pain altogether; it was through the beast's blood-choked cries that she felt anything at all. It wasn't pain, nor was it guilt. But something else. Something communal, almost charitable. Fulfilling in a sad kind of way, like feeding the homeless in a soup kitchen. The werewolf felt it, too, she knew; especially when it unspooled her guts from her gaping belly and ran with them in its teeth around the room. *Therapy and surgery*, she had thought, packing the spurting cavity in her gut with the black mud. *Therapy and surgery. And you can only get it here. From us.*

6

Captive to the Giving Room, Peter had no way by which to measure time until, chewing on Mary's foot, he started to seize up and transform back to his human self. He let go and limped away, wracked with the pain of forced rebirth. His bones broke and reset, and his musculature went flabby and then thickened, and all the excess blood and fluids wept from his orifices, until the pressure in his body was such that he no longer felt as if he were going to explode. Fur fell from his body like ash. His claws were pushed from his fingers and toes, new nails beneath them already in place. Grasping the bed-like stone slab in here, he had to bend over so that his fangs, which were dropping from his softening gums, didn't fall down his throat and choke him to death. Voice hoarse from screaming, he turned around and sat naked on the slab.

Mary was watching him as she piled the black mud onto her foot to restore it. She was naked, too. He'd never seen her naked before, and after acknowledging this, never noticed her nudity again. This was her natural state: stripped-down, beat-up, and batshit. The surprise, for him, was that he hadn't seen it sooner. He might've known, but that didn't mean he knew. And like her appearance, he found her state slipping from his concerns, settling into the background noise of his fevered mind; only to be noticed when it was relevant to him.

"One month down," she said, pulling her knees to her chest, resting her arms there, her head atop them. "I'm exhausted."

Peter thought about crossing his legs, but didn't. "Was that the plan?"

"Yeah," she said. She was lying. "What about you? Did you know? That why you came late?"

"Yep," he lied. "I knew it'd work out."

Mary stared at him, twisting her mouth. She was either about to laugh, or tear his head off. Instead, she didn't say anything, and neither did he. "I feel indifferent towards you. I mean, I don't want to hurt or kill you right now."

Peter searched inside himself and found he felt the same.

"This stuff." She pushed the black mud together beside her. "I found it after one of the Maiden, Mother, and Crone workers bashed my head open. I don't know why, but I rubbed it in. Instinctual, I guess."

Fighting to stay awake, he lowered himself off the slab, onto the ground. "What is it?"

Mary shrugged. "No idea. It doesn't work on everything, though."

"Huh?"

"Yeah, it doesn't. After it took care of my head, I tried to test it. I cut my wrist—" she rubbed off the mud dried on her forearm to show a horizontal slash that looked puffy from infection, "—and I put the mud on it, thinking it'd heal it, but it didn't. I used it on my lip, after you punched me at my place, and it cleared that up, no problem."

Peter said, "That's weird."

"I think it only works on violence. Like a chemical reaction. Self-harm doesn't count. Has to be something done to you by someone else."

"That's really specific."

Mary bit her lip. "Does it smell? Can you smell it?"

Until she'd suggested it had a scent, Peter hadn't noticed it. But now, he could, and it smelled like lavender and cigarettes.

"Smells like tobacco to me, and leather," she said. "I had to dig pretty deep to find all this."

"Do you think there's only so much?"

"I think there's enough, between the both of us."

"So, we're going to keep doing this every month?" he asked.

"We're going to keep doing this forever," she said. "We're never going to reach the bottom."

At that moment, the steel door that'd been locked all night shuddered and crept open. Goetia had undone the locks. It'd had its fill. They were free to go.

Peter cocked an eyebrow, laughed. He stood and helped Mary up. About to leave the Giving Room, she murmured something and pointed behind him. Glancing over his shoulder, he saw two freshly pressed woolen robes laying on the edge of the hole in the floor. They donned their gifts and went on their way.

Nearing the Wall of Goetia, Mary stopped him and said, "Hang on. Do you hear that?"

Peter didn't. His ears were clogged with mud and dried blood, and he wasn't exactly paying attention. His thoughts were elsewhere, back at Mare's Diner, when he and Mary had sat down together to violate a social norm, and how indifferent those around them had been to their little charade. They were horrible people, he thought, who had done horrible things and had horrible things done to them. Yet, here they stood, brutalized and, at the same time, unscathed and unjudged; with the world spinning on.

"Yeah, shut up."

He wasn't talking.

"There's someone…"

An older woman's voice echoed from Goetia proper: "Hello?"

Peter snapped out of it. Mary stood in front of him, his abusive protector. Together, they marched forward, each scanning the rocky stretch around the Wall of Goetia for something to defend themselves with.

"I'm here…" the older women went on. "I'm here."

Ahead, where the cave twisted and connected with the old fort, the hunched shape of a tottering woman emerged. She wore a puffy winter coat with a fur-lined hood thrown over her head. A single gray curl hung down, spiraling over her left eye. Her breathing was ragged. Coming here hadn't been easier for her, but she didn't look like a woman to be put off by adversity.

"Miss Mary, is that you?" she stopped, bracing herself against the cave wall. "It's me, Antonia. We met at Canto's."

Mary laughed in disbelief.

Peter had no idea who this woman was.

"I saw your flyers at Meadowsprings. Me and the others got on the Internet and met up with some others." Antonia caught her breath. "I brought them. They're back there. Some others, too. They've come, Miss Mary, to hear you."

Mary stared at Peter; her eyes wet but not watering. She looked as if she'd realized just how hungry she'd been this entire time.

"You must be Peter." Antonia approached and took his hand. Her hand was soft, almost paper-thin, and yet it was burning hot. He was afraid she'd catch fire. "It's so good to meet you."

He nodded.

"The others?" Mary asked.

"Oh, I told them to stay back. I wanted to make sure you were ready for us. It's so early in the morning. We slept in tents overnight." Antonia touched her back. "Lord knows I'll be paying for it today."

Mary, whispering, asked, "How many are there?"

"Don't you know? We saw all the lovely food back there on the tables. How'd you all make so much?"

Peter and Mary exchanged looks with one another.

"About thirty or so of us," Antonia said. "Mm, that food smells good. Apologies if they got to it, already. It's…"

"Take us to them," Mary said. "You've done well." She pressed her knuckle to Antonia's wrinkled cheek. "The world won't take care of us. So, we'll take care of each other, instead."

Antonia said, "That's very good," and headed with them to the Feasting Place. "We're all so blessed to be here in Geharra."

Peter said, "Geharra?"

Mary leaned into him, whispered, "It's tradition to change the name under new ownership." Even more quietly: "Crazy thing is… I didn't come up with the name. That's just what people knew to call it."

7

They were about to leave the Wall of Geharra when Mary noticed Peter had made a detour up the hill. "One moment, Antonia." She made the climb and came up behind him. There was no reason to ask him what he was doing. She already knew. Somehow, he'd found it: a piece of the Wall she'd stolen when she'd first left Geharra. Why she'd taken it, why she'd kept it all these years, even Mary didn't know. She'd never told him about it. What was there to tell? The answer had died with the name of the person written on it.

"Sheena Fulci," he said, trembling. "My mom's name."

"Yeah."

He fell to his knees before his mother's name and traced each letter with his finger, going over them again and again in a trance-like loop. "This part was missing before."

Mary didn't say anything.

8

Peter came to his feet; the grit from his mother's name staining his fingertip. Some stones did bleed, but not this one. Not anymore.

More voices entered the cave. Their visitors were getting curious, restless. Peter saw what seemed like their shadows on the walls, drawing nearer. He smelled the air, but for the life of him couldn't place the food Antonia had mentioned. He reached out to Mary and took her hand. She squeezed it, as if the gesture were a confirmation from him that he was in, that this was it: that they were moving forward. But that wasn't it. He did so just to make sure she was still real. That all of this was still real.

Together, in sheep's skin, they walked hand-in-hand down the hill to meet their new flock.

"We don't have to be better," Mary whispered in his ear, "when nobody knows better."

Peter smiled. When he squeezed her hand again, they Fell right through each other.

YOU HAVE BEEN READING

"IN SHEEP'S SKIN."

ABOUT THE AUTHOR

SCOTT HALE is the author of *The Bones of the Earth* series and screenwriter of *Entropy, Free to a Bad Home, and Effigies*. He is the co-owner of Halehouse Productions. He is a graduate from Northern Kentucky University with a Bachelors in Psychology and Masters in Social Work. He has completed *The Bones of the Earth* series and his standalone horror novel, *In Sheep's Skin*. Scott Hale currently resides in Norwood, Ohio with his wife and frequent collaborator, Hannah Graff, and their three cats, Oona, Bashik, and Bellatrix.

www.ingramcontent.com/pod-product-compliance
Lightning Source LLC
Chambersburg PA
CBHW051608100726
47898CB00001B/270